W9-BFH-510

THE SHADOW BOXER

THE SHADOW BOXER

A Novel

Steven Heighton

Alfred A. Knopf Canada

The Shadow Boxer is a work of fiction. Any resemblance between its characters and real persons, whether living or dead, is a coincidence.

PUBLISHED BY ALFRED A. KNOPF CANADA

An earlier version of pages 84–89 appeared under the title "Finals" in the anthology *Turn of the Story: Canadian Short Fiction on the Eve of the Millennium*, edited by Joan Thomas and Heidi Harms (House of Anansi, 1999). The author is thankful to both editors.

Canadian Cataloguing in Publication Data

Heighton, Steven
The shadow boxer

ISBN 0-676-97193-8

I. Title.

PS8565.E41S52 2000   C813'.54   C99-932759-3
PR9199.3.H4443S52 2000

First Edition

Printed and bound in the United States of America

2 4 6 8 9 7 5 3 1

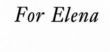

For Elena

It was a huge ship, hewn out of solid gold,
whose masts grazed the skies over unknown seas;
its figurehead, with hair blown back, breasts bold,
arched high at the bow through the blaze of the days.

But one night it ran aground on a massive reef
in the dissembling ocean, sirened with wind,
and the terrible foundering that brought it to grief
filled the sea's coffers, where it lies now, coffined,

still. It was a gold ship whose diaphanous hull
was a window on troves of loathing, sickness, lust,
and on the crewmen competing to hoard all that

in their drowning. What's left of it, in the lull
after the beating storm? And my heart—what has become
of that ghost ship? Gone—sunk in the gulfs of a dream.

EMILE NELLIGAN, "The Ship of Gold,"
translated from the French by Steven Heighton

Innocence is like a dumb leper, who has lost his bell,
wandering the world, meaning no harm.

GRAHAM GREENE, *The Quiet American*

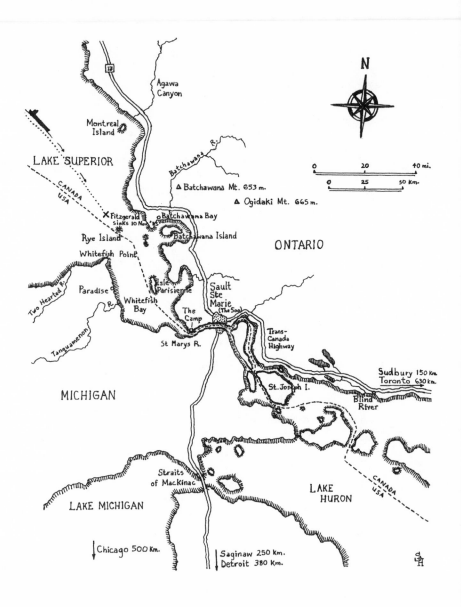

N

Agawa
Canyon

Montreal
Island

LAKE SUPERIOR

CANADA
USA

Batchawana R.

△ Batchawana Mt. 653 m.

△ Ogidaki Mt. 665 m.

0   20   40 mi.

0   25   50 Km.

ONTARIO

✕Fitzgerald   o Batchawana Bay
  sinks 10 Nov.'75

Rye Island   Batchawana Island

Whitefish Point

Isle
Parisienne

Sault
Ste
Marie
(The Soo)

Paradise

Two Hearted R.

Whitefish
Bay   R.

The
Camp

St Marys R.

Trans-
Canada
Highway

Tanquamenon

Sudbury 150 Km.
Toronto 630 Km.

St. Joseph I.

Blind
River

MICHIGAN

CANADA
USA

Straits
of Mackinac

LAKE
HURON

LAKE MICHIGAN

⬇Chicago 500 Km.

⬇Saginaw 250 Km.
⬇Detroit 380 Km.

SH

CONTENTS

- - - - - - - - - - - -

I

Road
of
Souls

I

The lake is not a lake but a landlocked sea . . .

A T TWENTY-FOUR, soon after his father's death, Sevigne Torrins went down from the Soo to the city to make it, to make himself a writer, swagger, shine and recite on the ivory stages, find love—all the old dreams. He took a tiny bachelor flat with a view of the CN Tower a half-hour's walk to the south. World's tallest freestanding structure, according to all signs and brochures. But no real match for his old man's lake. In the depths of Superior the massive glass-rimmed disc of the observation deck would still be a hundred feet under water, like the wheelhouse of a sunken freighter—the giant ore barge *Edmund Fitzgerald*, whose turbid image, retrieved by bathyspheric divers and reproduced in many magazines and TV documentaries, had haunted Sevigne more and more the farther he travelled from the site of the wreck. The staved-in windows of that wheelhouse agape and tracking him like the eyes of a staring portrait, or the sockets of some *memento mori*. Those are caves that were his eyes. But not his father's. His father had been safe, and soused, aboard another ship that night, 10 November 1975, while the *Fitzgerald* with radar down, off course and running for Whitefish Bay before hurricane winds and steep, following seas of up to thirty-five feet, had gashed her hull on Six Fathom Shoal and foundered a few miles off Rye Island.

If Sevigne had been on the island that night he would have seen the ship bearing straight for him, twenty minutes northwest when she finally dived, her siren screaming and the light buoy just off-shore stammering red like a squad-car beacon as if in answer to the scream. But the island was deserted that night, as it had been for years.

Sevigne's father had told him about the place. A small wooded island on the wild threshold where Whitefish Bay met open lake, it served also as a rough marker of the U.S.–Canada border that split lake and bay in two. It lay on the Canadian side, barely, with the dark Precambrian cliffs and scarps of the Algoma Highlands jutting up ten miles to the north, and the American shoreline, rolling and blue with distance, a dozen miles south.

Sam Torrins remembered passing the island in the late fifties, just after the lighthouse was abandoned. The main shipping lane lay a few miles to the south-west, but sometimes in daylight the freighter on which Torrins served as second cook would pass within a mile or so, and he would try to get up on deck with binoculars. Yet even in late fall when the birches, maples and scrub oaks were bare and only the spruce and runty pines gave any cover, Torrins could see nothing of the "still-house" where his own father, Noel, had lived and worked for a few years back in the twenties. If you could call it work. The old man had claimed it was the hardest, coldest work he'd ever done in his life and ever hoped to do again. Coldest and hottest, what with the stillhouse like a sauna and thirty god-damn below outside. With the help of the lighthouse-keeper— an old acquaintance happy for the company and the extra income—Noel and his associates had built her into a dip in the forest floor, harder for the Coast Guard to spot, so could be it was still there. More likely she'd caved, though. Weight of the snows would do that—thirty-five winters, forty. Some day, Noel said, maybe Sam would get a chance to land there, have a look around, let him know what was left of the place. Wasn't a bad place when the weather was fine, summers, early fall—

and come winter coming back in the Chevy after a run over the ice she looked home enough, and glad as hell you were to get there.

Sam Torrins had had to explain to his increasingly senile father that lakers bound down for Cleveland or Hamilton stowing 20,000 tons of taconite could hardly break to see the sights. But then for a few years in the early sixties he'd held a job as cook on the *Alexander Henry*, a light-tender out of Ottawa, which laid in buoys at the season's start in late March, removed them at freeze-up in December, and otherwise ranged the Great Lakes checking, repairing, replacing. So he got a closer look at the island his first season aboard, and next summer, when the Rye Island buoy needed work, he and a few others motored round into the cliff-rimmed cove under the lighthouse and beached the dinghy.

"Alone would have been the ticket," Sam Torrins told his son, pouring himself more Stock Ale from a bottle dewed, dripping gorgeously in the soft mocking warmth of Indian summer. Sevigne held out his glass. Delicious breezes soughed in through a thicket of quivering birch leaves and the torn porch screen.

"Don't want to end up like your grandfather," Torrins said, splashing a stingy dram into his son's glass as if measuring out something stronger. "Goddamn awfullest malady you could ever bequeath."

"I know, Dad."

"A bane and a bitch of one." He began humming softly— "Corn Whiskey," a folk song off one of his old Limelighters LPS. *Corn whiskey, corn whiskey, I like you pretty well—you've killed all my kinfolk and sent them to hell.*

"Be a fine and private place to do your scribbling."

"Dad?"

"The island. You're set on Toronto but good luck getting any privacy there. If that's what you want. And who wouldn't."

Torrins swigged grimly. "All your time eaten up by the fawners and the phonies, you'll get a one-room flat, pay with the skin off your ass and you'll still have their faces stuck in yours from sun-up to curfew."

You could set your watch to Sam Torrins. To one version of him or another. Sevigne glanced at the fogged old waterproof on his father's grizzled, hawser-thick wrist: 1:50 p.m., sure enough, the metamorphosis dead on schedule. By four o'clock the daily embittering would be complete, Torrins's creased, craggy face glaring speechlessly at the river, devolving as the day wore on, growing prognathous and stubbly and brute-dumb.

Five p.m. and the sun was sliding earthward over the flat drab forests a mile off across the river—upstate Michigan. Torrins's cabin, or camp, as such are known in the Soo, sat above the St Marys River at the bend where its channel, funnelling down out of pristine Superior, narrowed and braced itself for an influx of unspellable toxins from the great steel and paper mills of Sault Ste Marie. The Soo. A place that now figured in Sevigne's mind as the static, void centre from which the real world compassed outward: westward the oceanic expanse of the inland sea, then the Great Plains and Prairies fanning out beyond as far as the Rocky Mountains and the Raincoast; to the south, beyond evergreen forests and the Two Hearted River, the dark fields and thoroughfares of America unreeling onward to the borders of Mexico and the Gulf; to the north the mute, brooding weight of Shield country taiga tapering off into muskeg, tundra, frozen sea; to the east the lower Great Lakes and the smouldering port cities of the lowlands: Detroit, Buffalo, Toronto, Montréal.

Time to follow the flow of the river east southeast into the smaller lakes and the bigger cities. Real cities. Yet his father still needed him, nursemaid, here.

Sunlight sloping in through the birch leaves and the screen had laid a lap rug of amber light over Sam Torrins's still powerful legs. This was a benison. But Torrins's moods were increasingly impervious to those changes of light, weather and season that had once moved him so profoundly and still affected his son like a drug. Torrins was caving in on himself, sinking inward to a place where the once-loved world could no longer reach and stir him. . . . A half-mile off, mid-river, a huge grain ship was sliding east towards the Soo. The birch leaves blotted out its green hull so that the whitewashed bridge seemed to float there alone, silent as an iceberg; Sevigne pointed it out to distract his father from the black beetle scuttering over the floorboards at their feet. If Torrins saw the bug, he would crush it without scruple. Yet just a few hours hence, after the crash into unconsciousness that he called his "kip," and after their supper (when the frowning Torrins would only prod at his fried egg on toast like a petulant child), the faint guillotine-thunk of a mousetrap (hidden by Torrins so Sevigne would not find and disarm it) could trigger actual sobs, fierce tears of contrition. *Jesus, when I think what all I've killed. Poor Dog.* Which would mark the start of the day's final stage, calling for tumblers of rye neat or rock-bottom Scotch and a soundtrack of maudlin nocturnes, arias, the martial anthems of the doomed Highlanders, Delta blues and Celtic laments that Torrins would play over and over on the eight-track system he'd purchased just before the technology was scrapped. So that he—and now Sevigne— was stuck with a dwindling supply of battered tapes that the old machine was feeding on, one by one.

Sevigne would try to shut out the sound of it. Or flee. Prone on the rag rug by the woodstove, hands over his ears, he would be sipping rye or gin as he lip-synched his way through the *Inferno*, through Dickens, Dickinson, Dylan Thomas, Pound's Sappho, Emile Nelligan, Lawrence and Berryman and the Beats and F. Scott Fitzgerald of the green light and the orgiastic future; or rushing out through the screen door for a night paddle on the river—past where Meeka's camp had been, where he and his older brother Bryon had once pounded each other bloody—where he would let the canoe drift and throw his head back and, because of the night, belt out Patti Smith or Leonard Cohen songs at the stars, then paddle on up the snye of the Alagash to where he and Meeka, amid sighing reeds and wild rice, really had made love in a canoe. Sevigne would burst back inside sad and passionate, the door slapping shut behind him with a rifleshot crash. Lone hunter in the hills. That would rouse Torrins, a little. Who on seeing the boy so nostalgic and susceptible must draw him into the lamp-circle of his own nostalgia:

The rich humid smells of nutmeg and frangipani the sailors caught wafts of hours before they first saw the coast of Oahu, this in '53 when Torrins was a cook in the Canadian navy bound for Korea on the destroyer *Nanaimo*. Or that time in the fall of '67 just after Sevigne was born, with Torrins's new ship the *Algonordic* on Superior downbound for Cleveland with a cargo of taconite, mid-afternoon, Torrins alone in the galley when the Texan steward rushed down and urged him to get hisself up top and have a look, he'd take care of matters at the stove. When Torrins reached the deck there were sailors strung out along the fence-rails and Captain Sykes and Cole Proudfoot and one of the wheelsman on the balcony of the wheelhouse, all peering upward, shielding their eyes. And Torrins had seen high above the ship a quivering ribbon of orange like a long swath of cirrus at sunset, but flowing slowly, a vein or a river, over the face of the sky. Monarch butterflies, migrating in their millions from the Arctic to the Gulf of Mexico; so that at night the Milky Way, stars tremulous like fine wings, seemed *the ghostly sequel of their flight*.

Sevigne's translation.

Then the flies they called water blisters. Old-time lake sailors believed Superior spawned them, in summer, if it was calm and hot, so that suddenly they would be layered on the surface around the ship as deep as hay bales. Then all over the ship. One time Torrins recalled they had actually eclipsed the sun, streaming down like wind-driven sleet or snow to collect a foot deep on the decks and knee-deep between the coamings. The single ones that lighted on rails and clung there would die right before your eyes. At first they were sea-green with delicate yellow wings and black tail hairs fluttering out behind, pretty enough, but then as you watched they would lose colour, go dun brown and greyish, till finally they were like wisps of cigarette ash. For a while they would hold their shape, then disintegrate completely. Except where they were piled deep. There they wouldn't vanish on their own and it might take the crewmen hours to hose and shovel the decks clean.

Then the island, always the island—how it had seemed a kind of paradise that day in July when he and the men off the light-tender had explored it. The lighthouse and the keeper's house they had found locked up, undamaged; the roof of the stillhouse, after forty years, was sagging but intact. Torrins had wandered off while the others lounged on the house stoop by the padlocked door, rolling smokes and eating blackberries plucked from bushes gone wild. He'd walked along a rough path through mixed pines and emerged in a clearing ringed by poplar and birch, their delicate small leaves spangling in the breeze. In the clearing was a pond, spring-fed, banked with granite and drained by a creek flowing down through a meadow of devil's paintbrush, goldenrod, purple vetch and sumac, and on the rocky edges of the meadow a heath of blueberries, countless berries ripening from pink to deep blue in that vivid sun. And then, lower down near the shore, three weathered crosses. One illegible, one for a sailor washed up after the Great Storm of '13, the other for a light-keeper who had hanged himself in the forties.

"Poor son of a bitch. It was the winter did it." Torrins's voice was suddenly hoarse, half broken, as if he'd known the man personally. Or was he just warming to his grand finale, which he performed at least once a week towards the end of the night? It was a story Sevigne had long loved but now dreaded because of the way Torrins would always scuttle himself in the telling, his words at first mending but then cracking his heart's brittle hull along ancient lines of stress. How he and Martine Sévigné Chambaz had met in April '65, the *Algonordic* docked in Montréal, Torrins at large in the cobbled streets of the Old City, when out of a doorway steps a small, fine-boned woman with black eyes and tight black curls and no overcoat despite the rain. The sign over the door said something about palms read, fortunes told, and there was an abysmal painting of that tarot character, you know, the one hanged upside down by one foot. Apt when you think of it. Martine had been in to consult the fortune-teller, she and a pal from the dance school were out on the town and did it for a lark. And the woman told her the first man she set eyes on as she came out the door would be the man she married, and Martine being herself she wastes no time, orders her friend to have her palm read and she'll return in a few minutes, she'll just step outside and look her future in the face. So she runs downstairs and comes out the door with her eyes peeled, laughing at herself, and there's Torrins—thirty-three years old and dressed in the best stuff he has, steel-grey turtle-neck and blue blazer, fresh-cropped and shaved from the bar-ber's, feeling like a million bucks. Still with a boxer's body then, heavyweight, and fit from the swimming too. She looks him up and down with a sparkle in her eyes and says something lively in French, and when Torrins shrugs and grins she switches to English: "The gypsy has told me that the first man I encounter once I go out her door, I will marry. I believe it's you."

By the end of this retelling Torrins would seem almost himself—his old self, his morning self, full of spunk and flushed with the furnace heat that came off him in waves, chuffing out bullish breaths through that great dented nose, the whiskery bores of his nostrils, bantering, reciting: "Go, stranger, to Sudbury, and tell / How, here, we did as required, and fell." But all too soon he would slip back and fall silent, test-patterns filling his eyes; pour himself another sloppy VO; pass out in his armchair after skimming a few pages of London or Conrad, or talking back to the TV weatherman.

Enough, Sevigne wanted to tell his father, times like that— enough looking back, enough with the tears, enough drinking. And he did tell him so, often. Not often enough. And the word *enough* never really was enough, was it? *Just shut the fuck up*— maybe that would have been sufficient. Or had it reached the point where nothing would be?

Mornings, though. Mornings still counted for something.

The manic first stages of Torrins's day usually went unwitnessed because the boy, as Torrins still called him, slept "late." Six a.m.: as Torrins erupted from his bedroom for another business meeting with the dawn, his son in the bunkroom would just be entering the deepest, sweetest phase of sleep. Not for long, by God. But first a stay of execution while Torrins barged near-naked out the screen door, left it clapping behind him like the steely hands of a drill sergeant and double-timed it down the slate trail to the dock. Sevigne knew the drill because now and then he stayed up until dawn writing or reading in the cabin's main room, and at six—his chilled hand cramping round the pen and his whole body an exposed nerve—his father's door would burst open and he would spin in alarm: Torrins framed in the doorway in Speedo and open bathrobe, beaming, shadow-boxing, goggles set high on his crew-cut head like horn-stumps on a polled steer.

"Come for a swim? You look a bit pale. You let the fire go out again, I see."

That old note of affable triumph. Sevigne lacked his father's pelt and padding and would have to decline—as Torrins knew full well. It was mid-September. In the heat of summer

Sevigne loved a brief hard swim but his father swam long and at times even now crossed the freighter lane and the floating border to Michigan and home. Two miles and change. In fifteen-degree water.

Torrins grunted impatiently, scratching his hairy back by rubbing up against the vertical-log wall beside his bookshelves and the RCN flag that dominated the room. "Didn't think so," he said, grinning. "Go get some sleep, boy. We'll go a few rounds when you get up."

"We'll see, Dad."

"You could use a few rounds with a barber too."

"Right."

"Maybe the full fifteen."

And Torrins would be gone, his gruff beerhall baritone fading as he jogged downhill to the river:

"Oh, the cook she was a grand old gal,
She wore a raggedy dress,
We hoisted her upon the mast
As a signal of distress.
Oh, the E-ri-e was a'risin'
And the gin was a'gettin' low
And I scarcely think we'll get a drink
Till we get to Buffalo
Till we get to Buf-fa-lo. . . ."

Sometimes instead of heading for the tiny bunkroom Sevigne, coffee mug in hand, would follow his father down the slate riprap to the river, where young birches leaned over the shallows as if to study their own flawless reflections, and scrub oaks hunched like willows along the white-lilied shore. Sevigne loved to watch his father swim. Torrins had been Soo regional champion in high school before dropping out to join the navy—lying about his age, and at six-one and 190 he'd looked man enough—and in the navy he'd swum too. And boxed. Somehow despite the years of hard drinking and the softened flesh he could still swim beautifully. He couldn't box— in the ring they made each summer in a red-needled clearing, stringing a tow-rope around four jack pines, he was lumbersome and wheezy and Sevigne could dance circles around him, landing jabs at will—but the old boy could still swim. Churning up the motionless river he would push straight off for the Michigan shore, his wake widening and dying on the black water behind him while his reaching arms flashed, vanished, flashed in the sun's inaugural rays. At times like that Sevigne could imagine him in the late morning of his life, winning a race, or one time on a cash dare swan-diving overboard when the *Nanaimo* was anchored in Pearl Harbor, circumnavigating the ship, clambering back up the anchor chain and through the hawse-hole before any of the officers knew a thing. So the stories went. And now Sevigne, weak but elated after a night of reading, or of writing his own stories, letters, poems, would feel that special rapture of the dawn known only to those who are rarely awake to see it. As he sat on the listing, sway-backed dock and lights blinked off on the American shore, the sound of his father's deep-fathomed breathing was borne back to him by the day's first breeze, with the tremolo calling of a loon, while miles eastward the sun shuddered up in a fireball over the flame-breathing stacks and flues of the oxygen plant at Algoma Steel. Satanic Mills: in high school Sevigne had been wolfing down Blake and the Romantics while working part-time at the plant, as a "runner." But that was long behind him now and at dawn, jacked up on coffee and exhaustion and watching a freighter pass downbound with a bellyful of grain for some waking metropolis—Chicago, Toronto, Montréal—he could believe in himself, in his writing, believe the energy and inspiration and the orgiastic promise of his deferred but impending life were inexhaustible. Though he had crashed before. Sunk into the silt and shit of the bottom. Took pills for it once. To think his father plunged that way daily. . . . While the freighter, which had somewhere to get to, sailed calmly on.

Heaving himself onto the groaning dock scarlet as a lobster, in a nimbus of steam, ankles weedy and grizzled chest glinting with pearly drops, his father lacked only a trident. But no mythic being would wear those goggles. For a while they would brand him with blue, cadaverous eye-circles, as if while swimming in the waters of Eldorado, to keep that body young, he had aged his face two decades, into a death-mask. Yet behind the mask such roistering energies, such high relish, the eyes themselves in their grave-pits spirited and fierce.

He was, to translate Martine's favourite term, farting fire.

"Breakfast!"

At this point Torrins usually routed his son up with the navy cry of *Drop your cocks and grab your socks*. "The coffee's on, boy. Rise and shine." Torrins in the tiny kitchen off the main room in black terry bathrobe, hood over his steel-grey crew cut, moving boxer-like foot to foot as he whistled and sang, flipping flapjacks, grinding coffee; keeping up the patter of an intellectual pugilist. *Keep 'em on their toes*. Like any autodidact, Torrins was proud of his learning and touchy about its gaps and combatively verbose in argument, loud, as if to drown out his own doubts; Sevigne, soft college boy and at low ebb in the dawn, was no match for him.

"You mean to partake today, Sev? You hardly touched your rashers yesterday. Rations, more like it. Right, I keep forgetting, you're a Buddhist now. Peacenik. Gandhi with a great left jab."

He slapped two quivering eggs onto Sevigne's plate.

"Sunny side up, boy, it's a new day."

It was. The twin yolks seemed to ogle Sevigne with wide-eyed perkiness—the dawn sun seen double by a man slouching out of a boozecan after an all-nighter.

"In the cream-gilded cabin of his steam yacht," Torrins called from the kitchen.

"Pound," Sevigne said.

"One for one. Better start than yesterday." Fussing at the stove he began to whistle a Stan Rogers song, "Barrett's Privateers," then burst out with the words, "God damn them all, I was told we'd cruise the seas for American gold"—then switched back into Ezra Pound, then back into the song, then another song like a chain smoker of lyric tags, lighting each line or thought off the last. His patter seemed—at first—as random as the jabbering of some ancient rubby downtown on Queen, the Soo's main drag, staggering east towards detox. Pale, leaky-eyed skeletons broken by the mills, old lake sailors, shuffling Indians—Sevigne saw his father in every one of them.

"Aboard for the next round? Buckwheat flapjacks."

"Sure, Dad. Thanks."

There was an odour of smoke.

"Someone had blundered!"

"Tennyson," Sevigne said automatically. Framed in the kitchen doorway, Torrins was frowning as he dumped a full carton of baking soda into the flaming skillet.

"Dad, you need a hand?"

"Not to worry," Torrins said heartily. "Where there's smoke, there's breakfast." Then, softer, "These days anyway. You get a half-point for Tennyson. It was also Ginny Woolf. In *To the Lighthouse*."

Ginny Woolf, Joe Conrad, Gus Herodotus—Torrins was on a nickname basis with them all, like a man who'd never expected to be let in to some elite coterie and now must constantly remind you of how fully, and by his own bootstraps, he's arrived.

"Had a call yesterday." Torrins on his stool across the table, appearing there in a draught of ashes and aftershave, bay rum. His bull neck was nicked and bloody in a dozen spots.

Buckshot. He'd brought the surviving flapjacks. Over the
trembling lip of his cup his grey eyes blazed out of the dark
sockets left by his goggles. "From your mother. In Cairo."

"I know where she is, Dad."

"Nobody ever knows where she is!" Torrins brought his cup
down on the table, slopping coffee over the butter. "She could
pack up her kit bag and leave him tomorrow, next we'd hear
she'd be living with some diamond baron in the Transvaal."

She's been with him thirteen years, Sevigne wanted to say.
She's not going anywhere.

"Meant to tell you she called but I wasn't . . . must have
been in one of my moods. They're giving serious considera-
tion to jetting in for Christmas, all four of them, your brother
and his girl too."

"Fiancée."

"Rose, isn't it?"

"Tralee."

"Your mother misses you, of course. In her flighty way.
Says she'll be mailing you a letter. Says you should go over
there to write your books, but in the meantime there's Christmas to think about. Just like Sears does and The Bay." He
frowned. "So little cause for carollings . . ."

"You got me on that one," Sevigne said wearily, as if sad-
dened by the lost point.

"Hardy. Thomas Hardy. Your mother and Mr Prig will
stay somewhere in town. Honorary consul, stuck in the sticks.
Won't he get a kick out of the Soo. When it's forty goddamn
below and he saunters out for his *Times* and his Turkish
coffee."

Sevigne—even in his punch-drunk morning state, even as
Torrins's bonspiel of morning energy wound down—could
still appreciate the man's ship-galley breakfasts. Even on active days when Sevigne waited tables at the Ancient Mariner
or pumped gas at the marina, those breakfasts stayed with him

till late afternoon. There would be stacks of flapjacks or sour-dough waffles stained crimson around berry-filled niches (cranberries from the freezer, blue- or rasp- or cloudberries from the roadside or the dockside in season) with a yolk of melted butter and maple syrup gleaming atop the stack and drooling over the sides to pond with rich drippings from the back bacon, the beef sausages sizzling and babbling in the skillet, where he would next scramble eggs with wild chives and chopped onion, green pepper and tomato, and there'd be spoonbread blended of cornmeal and butter and blackstrap molasses, then beans, then buttered toast, then home fries fringed and crowned with the rusty crackling Torrins knew his son loved. All these wonders alchemically conjured out of the seeming barrens of cupboards and fridge—or out of the river on days when Torrins took his rod down to the shore before dawn and caught a brace of trout or menamani, then pan-fried them in butter and cheap rosé.

Driving back from the diner in a rotting Pontiac sedan with prolapsed muffler, Sevigne would stop for provisions: second-hand paperbacks, groceries, liquor, beer. "Just use the pension money for the works," Torrins would urge him with a regal sweep of the hand—"no use scrimping, there's no pockets in a shroud." *No pockets in a shroud*—he was always imparting that wisdom to his son as if Sevigne were the stingy one—Sevigne, whose skimpy tips and paycheques made up the shortfall when the pension money wasn't enough for all the booze, which it never was. Underwriting your old man's dissolution—now there was a pretty odd kind of Samaritan-ship, Mr Great Soul. And yes, he did keep threatening to pull the plug, to let the keg sputter dry, but if he did that Torrins would just tap into savings—whatever was left of the money he had banked in '85 when Amy bought him out of the Ancient Mariner. And when the savings were gone? Borrow from Amy. And then? Into the hypothermic streets with those slumped, wobbling derelicts who swilled Listermint or Sterno or Aqua Velva, slathered themselves in liniment to produce bogus heat under threadbare coats and passed out in snowbanks or over coffee in the Mariner (where Sevigne and good old Amy would never kick them out) or in the pews of the Cathedral of the Precious Blood (where sweet, obese Father Moroni—"Father Moron" to the rednecks—would turn a blind eye). Yes. It would happen that way unless Sevigne came dutifully back from wherever he'd escaped to. Banner high, bugle blowing. *Cavalry. Calvary.* As a child at occasional masses with his mother and brother he'd confused the words, and now it seemed natural that he would have, the confusion seemed to sum him up. Both ways drew him. Be the lone man on the cross on Calvary, naked and saintly, your power a serene turning of the cheek, in a spirit of divine apathy, in an ecstasy of compassion; be the man among men, on a warhorse with the Roman cavalry under the cross, on crowd detail—robust and masterly, your power the power of the world, all whetted steel and will. Nowadays when he sparred with his father he would sometimes feel an urge to open up on him, knock him down— make him pay cash, as Coach Hogeboom used to say—and at the same time an aching desire to cradle that great, sad, battered head in his hands, to heal, detox him body and soul. *Gandhi with a great left jab.* He'd been both—the playground pariah, bookworm, altruist, swarmed and ground into the schoolyard cinders, and years later the teenaged boxer looming over a fallen opponent, arms still thin but wiry and raised high.

"You're making headway with the grub this morning, paleface." Torrins chucked Sevigne under the chin. "Care to avail yourself of my razor? Your publishers wouldn't approve, I know, but. . . ." And he was off again, improvising rave reviews of his son's nonexistent books.

Finally interrupting himself, he frowned down into his

empty mug. "I seem to recall saying something to you a few days ago about not going to Toronto on account of the crowds. *Les foules.* Hell of a word for crowds, eh?"

"It was yesterday," Sevigne said, half expecting Torrins to croon back that line from the Beatles song, about faraway troubles.

"Whenever the hell it was. My point is, going to reside on some far-flung island is a commendably romantic notion and in some moods I might prefer it myself, but on the whole I think you would be better going down to Toronto. Didn't seem such a bad place when we all lived there, did it? Christ, imagine that, all four of us." With no warning his voice cracked and he lowered his face to his cup, brimming his brow with one shaky hand; after a few seconds he looked up again, squinting hard, and drew a bead on his son. "See, Sev, if you're going to write a novel, people are your stock in trade, your quarry, by which I mean ore and I mean prey. In Toronto you've got a few million of them. Headaches down every cul-de-sac and expensive as hell, but still. You can find a day job. As for the island, I'll take you out there some time but that is no country for young men. Freeze your eggs off anyway." He swiped his plate clean with a wedge of toast and stood up. "Maybe next summer we'll go."

He bustled into the kitchen. For as long as Sevigne could remember he'd been promising to take them all out to the island, and now only Sevigne was left to take, and still there would be no journey. They'd had to sell the motorboat. And it would be a full day's trip—impossible—only nine a.m. now and already Torrins was showing marks of weakness, marks of woe. Yet such was the force and promise of his daily leap out of the tomb that Sevigne always found himself in doubt of the coming decline, hoping and somehow faithful that *today* the man had enough of a jump that his momentum would not fail. Or maybe he would give in to Sevigne's gentle prodding and go back into detox. . . . There was always that moment in late morning when things hung in the balance. Dad, you want to take the canoe out? Can I fix you a coffee? Sevigne would even spar a few rounds if his father preferred, though as an aspiring Bodhisattva he felt he should not, any longer.

By eleven the new leaf that Torrins had turned over would be starting to wilt. His face would be losing colour and his pale eyes taking on a raw, stalked look, as if the mind behind them, sobered from its manic high, saw itself clearly once more. Bewildered, betrayed. The first beer of the day could not be far off; and the first whisky soon after.

Sun's getting up there, Sev, it gives a man a thirst.

Sev, I feel myself called to the bar.

It's cocktail hour in Cairo, Sev, think I'd be none the worse for a beer.

Sevigne said little, little enough, having learned years before—as had his mother, though the learning changed nothing, saved nothing—that objections in the bitter phase would only make him more defiant, while pleadings in the evening when he was woozy and pouting would only drive him outside, down to the dock in self-pity, singing, "Carrickfergus," "St James Infirmary," " 'Tain't Nobody's Bizness If I Do." Still drinking. "Wreck of the *Edmund Fitzgerald*." Too late by then anyway, the evening doomed.

"Half o'er, half o'er, to Aberdour, 'tis fifty fathoms *deep*." Torrins's low voice, on poetry now, echoing up from the dock where the river's slow current flowed indiscernibly in the dusk. The sound of a bottle smashing on *deep*.

" 'Twas on the *marge* of Lake LaBarge we cremated whatshisname."

So it always went: Torrins starting his days in the bracing river but by noon requiring a change of element, so from then on he must thrash and crawl and finally founder in the brook-clear waters of vodka or gin, the muddy, brackish snyes of dark

ale and porter and stout, or in brandies and ryes the colour of
ocean made molten by a drowning sun. Torrins forging upstream as if aimed for a fresher, far earlier sea, before the rivers
of liquor flooded in, caustic as foundry sewage; as if bound
back in time for the piers and wheat-pool silos of Thunder Bay
and Duluth and the vast, cold savannahs of grain and fallow
beyond. Racing the sun's arc, as if in moving swiftly enough he
could keep it from ever sinking.

2

Sevigne, Sevigne, where have you been?
Up in the forest with sweet Meeka Greene.

IN THE SEVENTIES the family had lived in a beige-brick townhouse on the western fringe of Toronto—in Malton, among the freeways, the dreary service strips, the industrial parks around the airport—and they had gone "up to camp" in the Soo only in summer. The camp was Papère Noel's home in those days, before he died and before his son's family broke up and scattered to all quarters of the compass. Should have seen it coming, Sevigne thought later, should have seen it in the skies—whether during the school year when passenger jets like airborne freighters, huge and slow, lumbered down in thundering succession a few hundred feet overhead, or in summer when the float-planes and antiquated DC-3s buzzed up out of the Soo strip like stunted simulacra of those southern giants, the air was always a vapoury grid of arrivals and departures, a lesson in loss, in transience.

The message was not just skywritten, it was there on water too. When Bryon and Sevigne were boys they used to clamber up the wild grape trellis on the forest side of the cabin to hunker on the roof and watch the freighters pass. In mid-July the tarpaper was blazing hot, a stovetop smeared with blackstrap molasses, though there was always a patch of it dappled with shade. Often their "girlfriend" Meeka, two years younger than Bryon, a year younger than Sevigne, would follow, ignoring their warnings about the steepness of the roof and its deadly

heat, climbing nimbly, cheeks squirrelled full of the tiny as-
tringent grapes ripening on the trellis vine. On the roof they
would dare her to chew the little tags of tarpaper that came
loose and she would do it while the boys hooted and nudged
each other and agreed it was the grossest thing they'd ever
seen. Liquorice-lipped she would leer back at them, extruding
her terrible black tongue, grinning with black rotted teeth, and
her fingers would blacken and her face would grow smeared
and dirty as a chimney sweep's. Her hair was black anyway.
Her eyes evergreen. Both boys claimed her and then agreed
they could both marry her, this was done in certain countries, it
was known as polygamy and they decided this made the three
of them Polygamites. They lived in a muggy and breathless
equatorial land where the rooftops were the only places cool
enough to breathe, though even there it was insufferably hot
and only the shade of the trembling acacia (the common white
birch) made existence possible. Polygamia lay on the shores of a
tremendous ocean that the three would scan with an ancestral
spyglass for barbarous pirates or spice-barges, or tugboats tow-
ing icebergs down from the Arctic—bergs from which pieces
would be cut and rationed to the sweltering populace (the boys
sucking ice cubes while spare rations thawed in their pockets
and trickled down their thighs, and Meeka chawed and spat
out tar and tried to kiss them).

Papère Noel's "spyglasses," Martine had told the boys with
evident pleasure, had been used by the men on Rye Island to
watch for the Mounties and the American Coast Guard. In
daylight one of the moonshiners had always been up in the
lighthouse with the keeper, scanning the lake. The boys were
not to touch the small binoculars, they were an antique, and
precious, but when Noel and Martine and Meeka's parents
were gathered on the screened porch, they would whisk it off
the mantel and sneak outside and scale the trellis, mutineers
scrambling up a ship's rigging.

To scan the river for ships. For Sam Torrins. He was on the lakes each year from late March till mid-December and in summer they saw him only when the *Algonordic* docked in the Soo. As for the months when he was home, in Toronto, they were Martine's busiest, teaching French in a nearby Catholic grade school and modern dance at a small academy downtown. When would they ever be home, both fully home? They were a tag team, not a common front; forever arriving and departing.

Adult chatter and laughter rose from the servants' quarters (the screened porch) beneath the Polygamites' tarpaper eyrie. If the domestics were sounding so cheerful despite the heat (and Martine always sounded cheerful, vibrant, hardly the pining sea-wife) it was because they were treated with such indulgence.

"You up there again? Sévi? Bryon? *Attention à vous, hein?*"

Sucking ice cubes in breezy shadow in the canopy of the acacias, the Polygamites would let such impertinence go. Often they were preoccupied fighting for the spyglass, and especially when the big freighters ploughed into view, Bryon and Sevigne pretending it might be their father's ship and he up from the galley at the fence-rail to wave. They'd learned to recognize the chimney insignia and the flags of other countries and to focus on the bow till the names leapt to clarity and they could try pronouncing them—*Arkhangel'sk, Espirito de Oporto, Star of Monrovia, Algohuron*—the last being one of the *Algonordic*'s sister ships, the first syllables of its name tantalizing the boys with momentary hope.

In fact whenever their father's ship was due to pass the camp, they all knew days in advance and were ready, Noel standing at the end of the dock with binoculars levelled as if back on Rye Island, Martine behind him with her chin propped coyly on the epaulette of his greatcoat, in ruby lipstick and Jackie-O shades, her cropped curls and Campari-coloured summer dress tousled by the wind. When the spyglass was

passed back to Meeka and the boys they would grapple for it—
"Yous be careful now," Noel saying in his high, croaky voice,
"that's no toy"—then try to focus on the deck and vie for a
glimpse, their small heads scrummed together, Sevigne's and
Meeka's dark-haired, Bryon's blond. "There he is!" somebody
would cry out, "I see him, he's waving!" And at times they
really did, and he was.

Once the *Algonordic* was out of sight, the children would
rush back up to the cabin and onto the roof and pretend to be
bootleggers watching for the Mounties, or Gilligan's Islanders,
or lake sailors high up in a pilot-house. Meeka, who had once
planned on becoming a dinosaur, was now set on the life of
a Great Lakes sailor. As was Sevigne. Bryon meant to be a
Mountie.

If the *Algonordic* docked in the Soo for a few days, festive
chaos prevailed. The Tar-Eaters squatting on the pumice slope
of their volcano (the roof in its latest guise) would hear and feel
a mighty ferment below: the steady rumble of adult conversation punctuated by geysers of laughter, explosive toasts, erup-
tions of off-key song. Then from the new eight-track stereo, a
sinuous bolero, jazz, snatches of Jacques Brel, Torrins's tap-
room troubadours Johnny Cash and Stompin' Tom Connors
and then back to the antic jazz—"Ain't Misbehavin'." A stac-
cato rapping of pumps on pine as Martine Chambaz, cigarette
slanting from the side of her mouth, did a Lola Montez mock
flamenco, the ice in her upraised tumbler rattling like cas-
tanets. *Olé!* Torrins yelling—or maybe he would be down on
the dock with Meeka's father driving a pail's worth of golf balls
out into the river with the Greenes' clubs, the two competing
to see who would be first to sink a freighter and one time by
chance almost torpedoing Dr Pacini, out in his rowboat.

After Torrins and Greene had emptied the pail—the coast-
guard cutter a half-mile out still afloat and not deigning to
return fire—their children would dive into the river off the

dock's end and try to retrieve the balls. They were allowed to go only to where the flashing shallows sheared away into the depths of the main channel: black as a flooded cellar. Since Torrins couldn't golf—disdained the game, though after a few drinks he would always rise to Greene's challenge—there were plenty of duffed shots to find, the balls glowing under water, and they would race to pluck them from tiny silt craters sometimes right on the lip of the drop. They were the lone eggs of sea turtles, the eyeballs of great sturgeon or sperm whales.

One time while they were still in the river collecting balls, Papère Noel came down to the shore. Perhaps the merry ruckus and repartee of the screened porch had overwhelmed him. The children—waist-deep in the shallows, unmoving—watched as he shuffled onto the dock in his slippers and ancient greatcoat the colour of overcooked peas. His trembly, freckled hand was carefully planting the foot of his cane on each separate slat. The dock made no creak or motion as he edged along.

At the end of the dock he straightened up. With a testy frown he tapped his cane hard three times on the final slat.

"Is your daddy out there swimming?" Meeka whispered.

Bryon shook his head. "He swims in the morning."

"Maybe it's some code." Meeka's voice was hushed yet excited. "Morse code. Maybe he's signalling somebody!"

"Or calling a ship," Sevigne said. But there were no ships on the river. Nor any small craft. Papère rapped with his cane again, his fierce eyes sounding the waters, scanning the far shore.

"Starter's gun," Bryon said, "is what I hear."

"First one to shore," cried Meeka, and Papère was forgotten in the frenzy of the race. Caught off guard and still small for his age, Sevigne surfaced to the sight of triumphant grins.

At bedtime, when he asked his parents why Papère was acting so strange, they'd answered at the same time but said different things. Love, was what his mother thought—he must be missing Mamère. (Who'd died twenty years before. Who, claimed Noel, had been so aghast at all things French, she'd never have stood for being called Mamère had she lived to become one.) The island, his father believed, his voice rich with a generous, gin-soaked melancholy—that's what Grandpa had been thinking of. The close friends he'd made there under the pressure of common dangers. All of them back from that asinine war and no thanks for it but a few one-eyed jacks a day in the steel mill, or the pulp mill where Noel's father had bought it, and what a goddamn awful farm to buy. No chance the company store would get his soul too. And after a few years he found a way out, he and his chums, they did so. . . . (Torrins when speaking of his father would always slip into the old man's North Ontario accents.)

And more power to them too.

Most of them dead now and kissing clay.

And within a few months, just before he was to come down to Toronto for Christmas, Noel Torrins had rejoined his friends.

And walked the plank of the dock. Of the pier. Over moonshine rivers. Over rivers of rye. Sevigne, baulked by the elegy he was trying to write for his grandfather, set down his pen. He remembered too little of the man, dead now sixteen years. And his effort to politicize Papère's flight from the strike-breaking satanic mills seemed Tinker-Toy simplistic, like some of the sincere but obvious stuff he'd seen in the library in recent issues of *Strophe* and *Re/sound*. Time to try those magazines again; a litzine in Toronto, *splodge*, had just taken a poem, which made four acceptances since his first one a year back.

Torrins, in a heavy flannel plaid shirt of the type known

locally as a Sudbury dinner jacket, lay dormant on the scruffy couch, his mouth open, reading glasses slumped on his swollen nostrils and the grey square of the Panasonic reflected in either lens. The weather report: cooler tomorrow, a first autumn front moving down out of the northwest bringing Arctic air in a high-pressure ridge over Manitoba and as far south as the Soo. Bringing with it the ash and haze of huge forest fires along the eastern shores of Lake Winnipeg. . . .

Another inland sea. Where pelicans swooped over lime-coloured shallows, and children of the Icelandic diaspora fished among skerries humped and bare as grave-barrows.

Sevigne closed his notebook and coughed sharply, hoping his father would wake. Nothing doing. He got up and cranked open the woodstove and rammed in another log. Slammed shut the iron door. Stomped over to the TV, turned it off, stood pondering his father—the slab of him sprawled unbudgeably on the couch. Back in the navy he'd lost a couple of close fights but he never had been knocked down, not once, just like good old George Chuvalo. One of his evening refrains. He'd need a hand tonight, though. Almost every night now. Yet only a few weeks back Sevigne had been ripped awake at dawn by one of Torrins's most rampant benders of energy. Surging free of a dream where mosquitoes the size of float-planes barnstormed the cabin, he'd focused eyes on a snarling drillbit boring through the wall in a froth of sawdust, inches above his blanketed knees.

"For Jesus' sake, Dad!"

The drillbit whirred to a stop and pulled back through its hole. His father's face, grinning hugely, filled the small window above the bunk. "Ha!" Sevigne heard, "wasn't thinking. Washroom's a few feet over, eh. Well, that's what you get for sleeping through the best part of the dawn."

Bootsteps briskly receded.

"Torrins' latest work called 'riveting' . . ."

And by the time Sevigne was up and dressed, his father had

dropped whatever project he'd been embarked on and was attacking the dock with a buzzsaw.

Now Sevigne, grunting, stooped and hefted his father's hulk, and with Torrins helping slightly though snoring on his feet, he braced him through the bedroom door. Dumped him on the bed and stripped him of his shirt and khakis with the same jerky sliding movements he guessed you'd use to skin a bear. Got him under the sheets. Turned off the light. Sevigne was not sure if his father knew this had ever happened.

He folded Torrins's reading glasses and set them on the night stand. Then pulled the cover to his chin. From the open mouth ringed with white stubble came a clogged, phlegmy wheeze. The bedroom was cold, and faint grey plumes of breath were ascending with the sound and diffusing. He took a Hudson's Bay blanket down from the top of the closet and nestled it over the cover, then bent to his father's slack face—the cave of the mouth with its sluggish rale, its sickly breath—as if summoned to hear some last word.

Through the outside wall, a sound of wind shrilling in the trellis. He straightened up, left the room, went into the kitchen for the Scotch. He had an impulse to smash the bottle in the sink or lob it into the river, but it was no use, tomorrow he would just have to replace it, and with money they could hardly spare.

3

Retirement

I N 1976, a year after Papère Noel's death, Sam Torrins had
"retired" from the lake boats. He was forty-four years old.
The firm had decided he was "too ill" to continue and
they'd asked him to "take some time off." If it was morning
when Torrins said the word "ill," he would spit it out, snort in
hearty disdain, let rip with a big laugh, his eyes all asparkle, as
fit as a butcher's dog. If it was afternoon, he would ration out
a few barbed remarks about the "boarding-house pension"
he'd been offered—*offered*, as if he'd had any choice in the
fiasco! And if it was evening when his retirement came up, he
would protest to Martine in a cracked, wavery voice that the
pension was more than he deserved, that she and the boys
were more than he deserved, and would she just forgive him,
please, just be his sweet one and let it go? The boys overheard
more than one such monologue. Monologue, just that, because Martine, by nature voluble and responsive, would make
little response, or none.

Bryon grew daily more hard-mouthed, squinty and secre-
tive. Sevigne was either quietly holed up in books or manically
active at the dinner table—babbling, buffoonish, a rodeo-
clown setting up comic distractions while the bull begins to
chuff and bristle. Our little Kissinger, Torrins would call him;
but the mission was failing. The brothers themselves began to
fist-fight, the larger Bryon always winning but Sevigne, even
pinned and bloodied, unwilling to submit.

In the years before the firm had mothballed Torrins, his long absences on the ship had lent him a kind of mythic stature in his sons' eyes—a myth Martine had sometimes called on to keep the boys in check. Her warning that He would be home not in an hour but in three months' time somehow carried more weight, as if the boys, though punishable now, were being remanded in custody pending arrival of the hanging judge. They did see him briefly now and then during the season, when the *Algonordic* docked in Hamilton, and on occasion Martine would go off on her own, leaving the boys with the boring Barneses next door while she went to see him in Collingwood, Windsor, or Montréal. Once she took them along for an overnight visit to Buffalo where their behaviour in the motel room was so outrageous they surprised even themselves. And never got to go again. At some point in the night Sevigne had found himself awake and realized Bryon was too: the boys lying on their backs hearing their parents whisper and chuckle, rustling sheets, their mother seeming to sob and then murmuring a string of strange words, French words they'd never heard, and the boys, with one will, without a word exchanged, had slid out of bed and crossed the room and climbed atop that blanketed mass as if it were a rakepile of autumn leaves with playmates squirming underneath. But all in silence, in full knowledge of the eruption to come, the monster suddenly rearing from the whirling, scattering leaves. *Beast with two backs.* Their parents going to a Christmas party as wolves, wearing the big skins that Papère and Torrins had taken off two timber wolves they had shot on Batchawana Island in the late forties. Martine had rigged the skins so the stiff cartilaginous faces with eye-slits would wrap tight to the wearer's face, while the body and tail draped down the spine like a cape. Martine beaming as Rabe Barnes moves in for a close-up and the flash-cube flares: laughing she tosses back her head so that her ivory throat shows lean, sinewy and human under the wolf-face, her eyes at an oblique angle gleaming red through the slits.

Before the "retirement," Torrins had been home for three months a year, and the arc of his mood over that time was a drawn-out replay of the pattern of his most manic days. When he was first back, in the weeks before Christmas, the family enjoyed a kind of honeymoon, a familial spree of high spirits and sportive ritual, so that years later when Sevigne and Bryon could agree on little else they could still come together round the memory of those weeks: Martine laying a picnic blanket on the den floor beside the festooned spruce they'd gone out and cut together, then the family (save for Papère seated vaguely in the wingback) crowding onto the blanket for their Christmas ham, Torrins with his arm round Martine's small waist, she with her legs tucked up beside her, all of them toasting the reunion with flutes of hot cranberry punch, spiked or not, depending. After dinner, with Torrins campily chording his ukulele and Sevigne warbling on the Hohner Marine Band harmonica he'd just pulled from his stocking, they would sing carols, Bryon loudly amending "the feast of Stephen" to "the feast of Sevigne"—Sevigne being notorious under his own roof for an appetite that did nothing to pad his skinny frame, so after big dinners he looked, Torrins laughed, like the snake who swallowed the hat in *Le Petit Prince*. And at the rasp of Torrins's execrable accent Martine would begin singing a French carol, allegro—*De bon matin j'ai rencontré le train . . . de trois grands rois dessus le grand chemin*—then maybe fling some Brel or Beatles on the record player and pull Torrins to his feet, *Viens, dansons!* The dancing bear would be only too glad.

The mood of those first weeks staled by slow, mysterious degrees. How can something be there one day, in however spectral a form, and then gone, gone utterly, the next? Like love. Like a human pulse. Years later Sevigne would hear, with ears he wished temporarily deaf, his father recalling something from the time when Martine had absconded, yes, and dragged his boys along with her into the bargain. To goddamn *Cairo*. Torrins reminiscing in the cabin, late evening, his bleary mind on the verge of station sign-off, as was the CBC, but the stupor didn't take him soon enough and Sevigne had to hear how his father had smelled his mother's pillow for the scent of her hair and skin every night after she left; and soon enough there came a night when the scent was difficult to find, and the next night it was the faintest trace, and the next night. . . . Well. Next morning there was nothing there to smell. Sayonara.

At this point Torrins had stopped his story dead and gaped at the TV with an incredulous, appalled expression, as if seeing himself there on the screen—an anchorman who'd snapped, flung his script away and was spewing out confessions or delusions of the most pitiful kind. He'd looked down at his inert hands and tried to chuckle, make a joke of it—tried to feign the mode of the morning, bantering and buddyish: "So that's the secret when you're bacheloring, boy, to keep your expenses in reason. Don't wash anything. Just let it all air. Before long nothing smells of anything."

And the last trace of homecoming levity faded as the raw, slushy Toronto winter deepened, the white stucco jags of the den ceiling like tiny icicles and stalactites in a cave where his father sat insulated back of the sports pages or fat nautical potboilers, smoking a pipe and drinking mugs of cheap brandy warmed with coffee. More often now Martine would go out at night with her friends from the dance school or the Alliance Française, while over the dinner table—*tawdry* table, she burst out one time, *tawdry* suburban townhouse—the talk was monosyllabic and lifeless, as if Torrins, cooking less as he drank more (on his first days back he would insist on cooking nightly), was shocked into silence by Martine's perfunctory fare.

By late February, when Toronto was at its bleakest and across the country the suicide and general death rates soared, an unseasonal warmth would begin breathing through the cramped rooms of the house and the grim grotto of the den, the stalactites and icicles of the ceiling turning back into stucco nubs, a Chinook gust of fresh fragrant air billowing from the mouth of the oven as Torrins yanked it open to reveal a pork tourtière, or perch and Swiss-cheese casserole, with apple-raisin dumplings to follow. The whole family was becoming pre-emptively nostalgic, sentimental, as the days till Torrins's departure ticked down. Martine drank sociably more, Torrins sensibly less, and he confined himself to Martine's good Bordeaux. Now both of them were big on theme dinners and the boys might come in from shovelling driveways for spare cash to find Torrins cracking a cherry-checked tablecloth in the air over the table: "Italian night!" he'd roar. "Midway through this life's journey I woke hungry as a bear. Hope you little paisanos brought your appetites." And he would put on one of Martine's records, Verdi's *Aïda*, or Sinatra, or Mancini. Or it might be Mexican night, or Indian, or Greek. "No throwing your plates into the fireplace, boys!"

"As if we have one," Martine might say, though now with gentle, rueful humour, no ashes in the throat.

No one could say exactly when the season would start, so the boys kept a weather eye on the brightening, jet-crammed flight paths above the suburb, and while the rest of the city prayed for spring they were summoning fresh cold fronts down from the pole, freak masses of Arctic air that might settle over the upper lakes and delay spring breakup for weeks, for months—possibly till the onset of the new ice age the boys were also trying to arrange.

"Be gentle to your father," Martine would tell the boys, stooped and strategizing over their milk and shortbread after school (if Dad woke from his nap soon, would there be time for a game of ball hockey before he started supper?). "Let him relax while he's able still."

Years later Sevigne would see how addicted Martine had

become—and Torrins too—to the seasonal rhythms of arrival
and departure, the romance and mythic reverberations of his
annual leave-taking for the inland seas, then his festive return.
Most of all, he thought, she had loved the freedom of his absences balanced by fleeting rendezvous in anonymous cities.
She had been having a long affair with her husband. Then he
came home for good and became . . . a husband, and that *ban-
lieue* of duplicate, sexless streets and drab decent neighbours
with their lawn-trim souls and prefabricated aspirations became undeniably her reality, her true home. Till death do you
part. Much less money now, so less hope of escape, from Malton and her hated parsing of French verbs; and in Sam's drinking—downing her wages by the shot, by the magnum—less
romance. Then none at all. Sam was never violent with her or
the boys, but there was a moment—the one, she said, that decided her—when she found herself wishing, *Only one night let
him hit me instead of asking for my pity, we would leave this house
with no glance back.* Hearing the Barneses' television muttering
through the wall ten hours a day now filled her with an almost
murderous rage, the thunderstorm of jets overhead seemed at
once unbearable and inviting, bitterly she recalled her vow
somehow to build a life of elegance and grace in this place,
until such time as they should find one better. Because the better life was merely being postponed. Other things had been
merely postponed—such as her dancing, and the dream of her
own dance school, postponed when Bryon arrived not a year
after the sudden wedding—but that was what love could do,
make you happy to postpone what had been closest to your
heart, or to renounce it altogether; and then when the love
died, it was too late to return.

So life became but a sequence of irreversible postpone-
ments.

Sevigne came to know her side of the story because, years
later when they grew close again, she would talk to him about

anything: sex, money, her vexations, her dreams. Martine had come out of a gypsy's garret into a cobbled street of Old Montréal and met a sailor *en congé*, smartly dressed, with a swagger and a spark in his eyes, his small ears made red by the sun of who knew what seas, on his breath a warm suspicion of brandy. Romance had mounted the perfect ambush. Others talked about living on impulse; Martine really did it, every time. An accident was what she had been, born a decade after her parents' "last child." The neighbours all said she was *du sang de Lord Byron*—something they had been saying for well over a century about anyone who seemed at all unconventional, ever since the clubfoot satyr, *en route* to Italy, had stayed a night in their drowsy townlet outside of Lausanne. Supposedly he had seduced a scullery maid and thus left in the town an undercurrent of rogue blood that periodically welled up to test the serenity of the burghers. Martine as a child had embraced the idea of her kinship with Byron, and for a time had seen it as direct and undeniable. In the town park, facing east towards the Alps, stood a small noseless statue of the poet, which she had loved and whose inscription she had read over and over. She would name her own son Byron. Though when the time came, Torrins, finding Byron too, well, Byronic, had countered with Brian—Brian!—before agreeing to split the difference.

Sevigne had seen photos of his mother in her youth. Tiny photos. Sometimes he would find them in the cabin, forgotten among empty glasses, after hauling his father off to bed—off the couch in front of the gibbering TV where Torrins would have been shuffling through wallet-mementoes. *Memento mori*, he should say. Game of bloody solitaire with a foregone upshot. Every one a joker. Several times now he had complained to his son that the photos seemed to be shrinking—it was the strangest thing. At least he'd never suggested they review them together, this surely seeming even to a man tippled past reason a faintly shameful act, a kind of Oedipal pimpery.

It had taken just half a year for Martine's feelings about Torrins's constant presence to become plain to the boys. After another year of mounting strife and despite his shambling efforts to ease off on the drink and hold down some kind of job—short-order cook, salesman, cabbie—she was gone to join Everson Milne, Canadian cultural attaché in Egypt, and the boys with her. As they flew in over a tract of great dunes a half-hour west of Cairo, Sevigne, curled fetal in the window seat, thought of the ribbed sand bed of the river in the shallows by the camp dock and of his father, beloved predator, cruising towards them spouting water like a Kraken. The boys had not yet met Milne. Something dreadful had been haunting the townhouse over the past year, and towards the end of it, as things got worse, they had overheard enough to figure out that it was a man. He lived far away but was sometimes over on business. Years would pass before Sevigne could forgive his mother for trying to convince him that Torrins would be coming too, in good time, to visit them, but for now he was ill, *malade, il avait besoin d'un médecin.*

But weren't there doctors in Egypt?

Si, mais ils ne sont pas aussi bons.

That's racist. Dad hates racist remarks!

Ah, chéri, assez! Her small quick hands spanking the air— *Ne m'énerve pas!*

Speak English! he had cried, wondering how she could think him stupid enough for her lies.

4

Everson Milne

THE TASTE FOR GARLIC is acquired, like the taste for dark ale, which to a tempered tongue like Sam Torrins's is smooth as oil and sweet as treacle, while to a neophyte it's bitter as the coaldust dregs of black coffee, days old. Garlic was the smell of Everson Milne. Not of his person—conscientiously soaped and cologned—but of his house, and especially of the room he gave Sevigne, so in the boy's mind garlic came to seem the very odour of the man's soul.

Everson Milne's antique house was in the old city of Cairo, a few minutes' walk south of the Bab-al-Futuh, one of the old city's main gates. Close around the massive gate, the pavements were crowded with the slaphammer carts and stalls of Cairo's main garlic market, so whenever a north breeze blew it brought to the house not only a cool promise of the distant Mediterranean but also a reek of garlic—heaps and hillocks and barrows of bulbs, fresh garlic, dried garlic, garlic fried or roasted or squeezed into oil or paste, the stale or spoiled bulbs sulphurously composting—as when a rare east wind in the Soo would bring upriver to the camp the smelter-stink and the stench of the pulp mill.

Here Bryon and Sevigne for the first time were to have rooms of their own, and Sevigne, winner of the coin toss, had chosen a room on the west side looking down on a small fountained bower of mimosa, aloe, and rose of Sahara. High above it, over the neighbouring house and the roofline, the fretted ramparts of the Citadel and the blue domes and minarets of the Muhammad Ali Mosque shimmered through rippling heat, bus smog and dust blown in off the desert. Sevigne could see in three directions because the window, or *mashrabiyah*, projected like a bay—though instead of glass it was of finely latticed, filigreed oak, like the grille through which Father Moroni's wistful moon of a face had appeared to him in the confessional.

But the *mashrabiyah* not only gave a poetic and surprisingly clear panorama of Cairo, it also seemed to act as a suction vent for the city's sounds and airs, drawing into Sevigne's room—along with leaded exhaust fumes and the muezzin's heart-breaking plaint—an odour of garlic from dawn until the market closed soon after dusk. Martine, unlike Torrins, had used garlic in her cooking back home, but there the smell had always been married to other smells—French loaves warming in foil, sautéing mushrooms, spaghetti steaming in the colander—the odours of home.

Here the fountain, repaired for the boys' arrival, soon broke down and in days became a stagnant muddy pool, starting to reek. And in the small hours while Sevigne lay sleepless there were gusts of drunken laughter or song from tourists headed back to their hotels, the sound echoing up from the walled bower and sucked in through the *mashrabiyah* so it seemed the scoffers were there in the room beside him—Sevigne, who since grade school had seldom overheard laughter without thinking it must be aimed at him.

Bryon couldn't hear or smell anything bad and told Sevigne to shut up. Always were Dad's pet anyway. And the truth was, in any other circumstances Sevigne would have adored Cairo's shrillest sounds, sights and stinks. The diamond laser of the desert sun on molten domes and towers and portals, the slap-stick, stampeding herds of tiny cars, growled r's and melodic arabesques of sung Arabic from countless café radios, Cairene hawkers with their affable badgering, even the shock of leprous poverty and haughty wealth tripping over each other in the streets—all would have dizzied, disturbed and intrigued him.

Instead, his grief numbed and then politicized him and at dinners he would bait Everson for the comforts of his home, for his hired help, for the bounty of his table. Everson treated his attacks with an infuriating thoughtfulness and diplomacy, while Bryon backed the man and chastised Sevigne for eating less and less and donating the fat allowance Everson gave them to phony orphans and amputees.

Sevigne was only too glad to purge himself of tainted money. But more than the allowance, he hated how Everson played down to him with regular gifts and promises and badly told stories and other maladroit little diplomacies. *Hey, none of that "Mr Milne" stuff, Sev, just call me Ev.* Maybe Sevigne would have come to like him if he hadn't tried so hard. Bryon came to like him. Bryon came to be like him. But then Sevigne had hated Everson far more at first, so the man had worked harder to win him over—Martine even coming in at bedtime once to plead his case.

He treats you so well, Sévi. He treats us all as we deserve.

His slaves do anyway.

But *mon petit*, with the *domestiques il est toujours*—he's always a gentleman! You would prefer that I was still—

But what about Dad? You said he was coming soon!

—like a maid? A slave to all of you? Now I can finally start, I can have my dream and you only—

But why did you lie?

—*ma petite académie.* It's little enough, God knows!

Answer me, Maman!

They'd betrayed him, that much was plain. Fresh in Sevigne's mind was the sinking of the *Edmund Fitzgerald* with all hands near the end of the '75 season, a year before his father was let go. Although Martine urged him to believe that his father would not be going back on the boats, that he no longer did well in bad weather, that none of the companies would send a sick man to sea (sick! as if Sevigne, almost twelve, didn't know what was wrong)—in spite of these assurances Sevigne, in his room or at the American school where he was failing everything but English and Art, was haunted by the idea of his father back on the *Algonordic*, down in the rattletrap galley fighting to keep skillets and cookpots on the stove while the ship bucked and yawed in a Beaufort ten gale, his father roaring orders at the panicked stewards, flames and steam everywhere, spillage, vomit. When the ship nosedived to the bottom and flooded with freezing lake water, the iron stove would explode and cremate the galley crew. Though when a ship went down that fast, pockets of pressurized air were said to form in cabins or at the end of manways and maybe some of the *Fitzgerald* men had slipped into those pockets and lasted a few hours, or nights, a hundred fathoms down.

Maybe his own father would survive that way.

Trapped there he would be calling out their names.

In early autumn Sevigne and Bryon climbed with a file of huffing tourists to the top of the Great Pyramid at Giza, Martine and Everson sipping highballs below at a canvas-covered bar among scores of parked Mercedes buses. From the summit the boys scanned the flat-roofed metropolis that spread over the Nile's ancient floodplain like a vast span of toppled masonry and dusty blocks, the ruins of a desert city, minarets still standing—though downtown there was a clump of corporate obelisks and a needle-like tower that recalled the skyline of Toronto. Shading their eyes the boys tried to decide where home was. Bryon, Sevigne noticed with a sinking heart, was calling it home. To Sevigne it was still Everson's house. They wrangled about that, and about the exact location of the place; the Citadel and the Muhammad Ali Mosque were easy enough to pick out, and the Zuwaylah Gate to the north of it. Sevigne grew more interested in a heavily freighted barge plying north in the river, seeming to ride so low that a boy's merest game of gunwale-jumping would bring the water flooding in.

Lately Martine had grown tired of assuring him that his father would not be going back on the boats. Perhaps she sensed the truth: that the boy, who talked to the surprisingly sober Torrins long distance every week, now believed it himself, and was just trying to punish her. How can you be sure? Sevigne would repeat, and she would turn from him and light a cigarette and squint with lessening patience at the door— or sometimes erupt and start squalling at him in her Swiss French. That was more like it. Yes. And Sevigne would yell back in English or slap at her until she pinned him down with her tiny, steel hands, or stormed out slamming the door behind her, or they embraced.

How she had wept at the airport when he had left to go back to his father, now living, stone dry, in the Soo. Bryon and Everson had pulled off to a tactful distance and stood together, Bryon refusing to meet Sevigne's eyes with his own, which were Torrins's eyes, while Everson with his golf-pro tan and sleek silver hair looked fresh and unruffled as ever: a crisp nod, the old thumbs-up, a Win-one-for-the-Gipper smile. Martine spoke softly to Sevigne in English, her breath hot and wet on his temple and ear while her tears made mascara rills down her cheeks. For the first time ever he clearly perceived his own features in her face, and when she clutched his forearm he felt, and then saw, how her painted nails were again chewed ragged. Years later those flamboyant, flamingo-pink nails bitten to the quick would recur to him as poignant epiphany, a miniature of his mother's soul.

"My big boy. You'll call if he gets sick again? We'll have you again at Christmas, *hein*? Every Christmas. Or I'll come back to Canada for it. You're both my loves."

"Me and Everson?" Sevigne had hissed, horrified.

"You and Bryon, who else? My sons."

5

Passage Island

S AM TORRINS had been born and raised in the Soo, and he had some good memories of the place, but at first the returning was bitter. He knew it for what it was—the shameful retreat after a bad beating. Nothing strategic about it. Like a grown man going home to mother, only his mother was years dead, and now the old man buried beside her in that cramped Presbyterian churchyard—a hoard of boxed bones for the Holy Miser, his mother's God. A time comes when more of the people you care about are under the earth than walking on it. Under, or on the other side. He had to get out of Toronto. Anyway the Soo was cheap and he had the camp there and a few old high school and shipping friends, the last time he'd looked.

So Torrins sold the house and left Toronto a few months after his family's departure. Abduction, he should say. Strangely enough, that calamity had jarred him into a brief dry spell, a time of utter and dizzying sobriety in which the roar of the jetliners overhead, usually no more irksome than the fridge's fitful whirring, had become a constant provocation. B-39s on a bombing run—the sound of an echelon of those monsters scudding through low-lying cloud over the ship, bearing for the Korean coast. Why so low overhead? Could be his mem-ory—his powerful memory, breaking down. The ship's rail is palpitant as if the sea itself is quaking with the roar. . . . Christ Jesus, a lifetime back and irredeemably lost, the lucid eyes that saw those things, his youth.

Martine had taken none of the furniture, yet his steps seemed to echo as if the rooms were empty. Drink must have deadened his hearing for years. And now without drink to keep everything blurred and slurred and inconsequential, Torrins was in a place where all things repercussed terribly, past actions, his lightest step, the shuddering overhead and in his temples, even his thoughts seeming to echo through the tomb-like house. Not *seeming*. And one morning as the first cold, tremulous sweat of the day seized him, he heard the sound of his pores prickling open and the sweat seeping out, a faint hissing and sizzling as of droplets on a red-hot stove. He could end the sound, the sweats, with one good drink. One bottle.

Other times when he had tried to quit, the first drink back had tasted wonderful, peace and absolution easing through him with every sip. Now it all tasted of bile and stank of stale draft and ashes like the carpet at the Soo Legion, and just the thought of a drink could make him retch, or nearly. Sleep was the thing and he did a lot of it. All the instant coffee he drank and still he could sleep all day. Sometimes the booming of the jet planes would drag him up from dreamless deeps like those cannons they used to fire over the surface of the river in his grandpa's day, to raise the drowned. Corpse-cannons. The boys were poking their toqued heads out of a hole in a snow-bank they'd burrowed into and he was looking down at them, his big shadow across them, and he could hear his own hearty laughter, years gone; a refinery was burning on the coast, with intermittent explosions, air-raid sirens carrying over the Yellow Sea like screams while flurries of snow tickered down on the grey swell.

He became obsessed with weather systems, the daily reports and data in the newspaper that still clunked through the slot every morning as if nobody knew the bill was unpaid and everything in the house dead as stone. TV reports. Reports on radio. With that goddamn ballad playing every hour, Gordie

Lightfoot having read his mind, *That good ship and true was a bone to be chewed.*

Came the wreck of the Edmund Fitzgerald.

Beer had a sumpy, septic flavour, as if he'd been dozing on the chesterfield for years and it had rotted in the fridge. But then one afternoon he came to and it was dark, seasonless, the rain falling as forecast, no lamps on, only the TV where the puppet stars of some after-school show were screeching and socking each other and as he tried to bring the stucco ceiling into focus his eyes filled, the weight in his chest and gut was like an anvil and his cock was hard, one of those sleep erections he seldom got when he was drinking, or was it just the getting older? He'd been dreaming of Mart. Like a fever dream, senses scrambled—making love to her voice, no body. *You must never see me old.* He tried the beer again and it tasted better. By suppertime he'd promoted himself to CC.

So now he found the steadiness of mind and hand to carry through on the sale, the move north, since it was clear to him that the break was final—he never had known Martine to change her mind—and the house was an unbearable memento of their lost life. A real estate agent had been phoning for days, tipped off, it seemed, by Everson Milne, who would have heard from Martine that Torrins meant to sell and thought of the tip as a gallant favour—as if Torrins in his present state could not manage on his own! The agent had had to be put off several times, then told off, then graphically threatened. And at last Torrins had managed on his own, stolidly giving the grand tour to retiring couples and dewy-eyed newlyweds while Lightfoot's quavery voice echoed up from the radio in the kitchen.

Does anyone know where the love of God goes
When the waves turn the minutes to hours?

Torrins could not tender any educated surmise about God's love and where it got to. He hadn't believed anyway since boyhood. Though on the night of the *Big Fitz*'s sinking, he had slurred out a few prayers. The *Algonordic* had been up-bound for Thunder Bay to pick up 17,000 tons of wheat, and though her ballast tanks were full she was still riding high, hold empty, so that Captain Sykes, having trouble with the rising cross-seas, had brought her north within a few miles of the Canadian shore, into the lee of the Algoma Highlands. At some point on their new course, probably around suppertime, the *Big Fitz* would have passed them a dozen miles south through the sleety darkness, downbound for the Soo at full throttle, already gouged and shipping water.

With winds gusting to hurricane force two points off the starboard bow, and the bow fighting to rise to the breaking, close-ranked seas, the *Algonordic* was making poor time. According to Jazy, the Haitian steward, Sykes had already wired Thunder Bay that they would be hours late and proba-bly would not clear Passage Island before dawn. Torrins and Jazy were closing up the galley—usually open twenty-four hours a day, coffee and rolls always there for the men—and Torrins tried to take in what Jazy was telling him. Worst storm in twenty years, the man said with a pained smile. *L'ouragan le plus terrible.* She would be better riding with iron in her hold. Was Torrins all right getting back to his cabin? Torrins had grinned and given the man a mock punch on the shoulder, shooing him away.

Torrins was very drunk. The pitching of the freighter—and it was rolling now too—reminded him of being punch-drunk in the ring, or on a bad spree when he was younger. He no longer got the reels and the carpet-pulls. Though he was drinking more than ever. He found himself at the aft end of the six-hundred-foot-long access tunnel linking stern to bow, where his own quarters were. A cavernous booming and groaning came from the massive, empty hold invisible under his feet and through the walls of the manway. Jazy was right, they'd be better with a load. Over the bass thrum of the straining engine came a high-pitched chugging, one of the bilge pumps kicking in. The storm must have loosened a coaming.

Torrins stood braced in the doorway of the access tunnel, transfixed by what seemed an optical illusion, or the hallucination of a drunk, though he never got hallucinations, not back then. Lit by a long file of hanging, swaying bulbs, the tunnel was dazzlingly bright, as if the generator were surging, so he could see how the tiny steel door at the tunnel's far end kept disappearing and reappearing—rising into the ceiling, settling back down. This in time with the waves. The tunnel, the whole goddamned hull was bending in the waves. The *Morrell* had bought it that way in '66—split in two like a party favour. Torrins froze in rapt fascination a few seconds more, then the vertigo hit him, and a stab of fear. The far hatch opened and somebody stood framed there, a puny silhouette. The figure was borne up out of sight as if on an elevator. When the hatch came back down it was closed, the tunnel empty.

Torrins stumped back to the galley and locked himself in, took down his thumbed copy of *The Stories of Conrad* and spiked a coffee with the unmarked rye he stored with the frying oils—another shade of gold—in slots above the range.

At dawn the stark, lonely tableland of Mt. McKay appeared to the west, the cloudline running along its sheared top like a lid of stone braced on a squat column. Sunrise over the calming lake eastward flushed the ship's wake pink as if the seas to aft were roiling with salmon, while above the wake blushing gulls plunged and fussed, Torrins there to greet them as usual, belting out snatches of song as he shadow-boxed at the taffrail, snapping jabs and overhand rights at the darting, jeering birds.

When they docked around eight, in pool 2B—Torrins

making corny jokes about Hamlet and eggs as he served a late breakfast—a longshoreman told Tex Harmer the *Fitzgerald* was missing, and the news moved, electric, among the crew.

One morning about a year after the *Fitz* went down, Torrins was sitting in the galley, feet up, sipping coffee, pure coffee, trying again to read Proust, who bored him, while Harmer and Jazy finished their breakfast; and Captain Sykes had come in to say the company agent wanted a word with him ashore. They were docked and unloading wheat in Buffalo. Old Sykes, speaking softly as always, had not been able to meet Torrins's bright jocular morning eyes. But then Torrins knew his barging energy could be cowing to men of the quieter persuasion, on a level where rank and class figured for nought. He'd never believed in those things anyway. Fuck rank, fuck class. Fuck the company agent and the company. And fuck Ed Sykes into the bargain—their star witness.

Now a red plastic strip bearing the word SOLD was stuck at a jaunty angle over the FOR SALE sign on the sallowed lawn. Down the river, old man river. Bitter, vindictive fantasies were his daytime fare, though he had not and never would have hit Martine, a man might hit other men but never, drunk as Detroit or stone sober, a woman, Noel had drilled that much into him, for all the good it had done. Maudlin songs again, come evening. Sittler and the Leafs had surprised the Islanders and were into the semis. Toronto, in a May heat wave, was hotter than Cairo. The boys were missing it all. The boys, goddamn it, were *missing*. And yet—come evening—he could hardly blame her for leaving, or even for that divorce in the works; but for leaving with that? Culture was a good thing and he had worked fist and folly to get it, but he was still a North Ontario boy, a man's man—someone who could turn a blind eye to homosexuality in Left Bank poets and painters long dead, but not in the fellow next door. Milne wasn't that, but he was effete, oily, like the film that warmed cognac leaves on the sides of a crystal snifter. Not that Torrins had any objection to warmed cognac. But he did object to the men who could afford it, the ones with the fidgety vowels and prissy enunciation, who figured culture was a good suit and an address in Yorkville, the right accent with the wine list and the odd Swedish film. Big-city types, he thought of them. And despised them as his father had. He had more bona fide culture than an opera house full of them. He'd had to fight for every ounce of it too, a labour of love and hunger, while doing the world's real work into the bargain. Men like Milne figured on breathing it in like the smoke of a good cigar just by poking their heads through the door at cultural shindigs. Maybe Martine herself was more that type than he had cared to see. A slide show, wasn't it? Or was it just a lecture? Something about Byron in Italy. Martine and a girlfriend had gone to see it at some hall at the university. Milne was an old friend of the speaker's and back in Canada on holiday and he'd been there.

With his share of the money from selling the townhouse Torrins found a wartime bungalow in the Soo, not far from the larger, older house he had grown up in. And although each dawn he still woke with that anvil of sadness weighing on his chest, the clear crisp thrilling air of a north country spring and summer was restorative. The air down south had been— what? Cluttered. Jammed with traffic sounds and jetstreams, squatting clouds of smog, a constant oppressive humidity. He got in touch with a few old friends who were delighted to see him back, who said they wondered where he'd got to, and there were times—especially after breakfast when he would head out in his best stuff and feel the sun on his brow and the lake wind on his aftershave, cool as pine—when he was surprised by a sense of reprieve, a stab of pleasure at the new clarity of his life. Which seemed not to be over after all. His old friends were going to fix things for him. Jobs would be coming

up. And after years of spotty exercise he could swim again in
the icy, reviving waters of the St Marys River, off the dock at
the camp that had been his since his father's death.

By Christmas the Soo locks were frozen shut and all tugs
and Coast Guard cutters iced into their berths, but the good
ship Torrins was caulked and seamed and cruising with a following wind in whatever seas were still unfrozen at the heart of
the big lake. The drinking was under control, Sev was home
not just for Christmas but to stay, and he had brought an appetite for his old man's food and his old man's chatter. Christ,
how he looked like Mart. Big coffee-coloured eyes, those black
curls, and sometimes he was hammy and effusive like Mart, or
wilful and fierce like Mart, though a minute later—shy and
timid as a deer. As Mart had never been. Now where the hell
had that come from? Just a stage, you had to think. He was
bound to start filling out soon. Sometimes Torrins would take
him up on the ridge with the .30-06 and a bagful of empty cans.

Torrins had a girlfriend now, Amy Carson, a cheerful chain-
smoking redhead, forty-five, big-bosomed and sturdy of hip,
quick to laugh and to tease poor Sevigne in a way that made his
face flame up, first pimples showing. "Feel here, Sam, he's still
smooth as a baby's bottom. My boy Blair was shaving at your
age, Sev. But he didn't have your eyelashes. Boy, the girls are
going to like you plenty."

Amy liked to drink and she liked to fool around. Torrins
could not forget Martine, and Amy didn't expect him to. She
was a relief to him in every way—a relief and a return to the
life he had been living before Martine, the life he might have
gone on living. She didn't read much but she had the snappy
smartness that a lot of readers, middle-class college types,
seemed to lose, as if the years of fine print dulled their wits
along with their eyes. She liked country music and that took
Torrins back to his youth in the Soo, when it was the music he
knew best—Hank Williams, Kitty Wells, Jimmie Rodgers—

and by taking him back there it helped him get over Martine, not by putting her behind him, which nothing could have done, but by putting her in front of him, years off in a future he might now forestall. Good old Amy. Over for the night, planted in front of the mirror slathering on lipstick and outrageous blue eye shadow while shaking her head and teasing her reflection—Aw come on, you old so-and-so—she would pick the family photo off the dresser and hold it up to her eyes, her other hand still swabbing with the applicator. Martine was a real looker all right and just see how Sev had grown in two years. Bryon there was going to look just like his dad—a real ladies' man.

Amy had been a waitress, then a hostess, then a manager at Muio's, and now she wanted a café of her own. She had a surprising nest egg tucked away. Torrins managed to get a loan by pledging the bungalow and camp as collateral, and in the spring of '80 the couple sank their pooled fortunes into a dingy diner on the main strip, Queen East, between an army surplus store and a prosthetics and oxygen outlet. The owners of the diner had been elderly and unwilling to keep the place going past suppertime, but Amy and Sam had big ideas. Since the Algoma cinema was across the street and the bingo hall next door, they would stay open late and give Muio's a run for its money with the night crowds. The Ancient Mariner Pub and Café. For atmosphere they brought in obsolete nautical paraphernalia— halyards and anchors, a ship's wheel, an old engine telegraph— that Torrins's ex-crewmate Cole Proudfoot got them for a song. They applied for a licence to serve beer. But strictly to boys with hair on their chins and the right credentials, Amy would say, winking at Sevigne, who would blush violently and with fleeting rage, as on the nights when she stayed over and Torrins's headboard would rap with accelerating insistence on the wall between bedrooms, a muffled duet of groans, husky sighs and soprano trills leaking through to him, hurtful and arousing. But then as she went on teasing him about his kiss curls and Elvis eyelashes he would feel a grin split his face as if the muscles there were spring-loaded, touched off by her affection. Amy could do that, she had the gift. She made no effort to step into Martine's shoes, which she would have split open anyway. She was more of a pal to Sevigne, or like one of those aunts only a few years your elder, the kind to drape an arm over your shoulder and whisper confidentially, give you a covert sip of beer or a drag on her smoke.

But over the next few years there was to be less of this companionship, because of Amy and Sam's long days at the café and Sevigne's withdrawal into his father's second-hand library, where the dog-eared cover of each book was a door opening on the trials of confident, quick-fisted men like Martin Eden, or a sluice in the dike of Jan de Hartog's Lost Sea, a hatchway into the smoking hold of young Marlowe's *Judea*, a turnstile at the customs post of countries where he must one day travel and live. And in imagination he scouted out new cities, new countries somewhere between Cairo and the Soo, as if to locate some neutral place where his parents might meet and reconcile.

Such private flights took him farther in spirit from his father's hard-nosed home town. Where a boy, to fit in, should play ice hockey and dream of quitting school for a berth on the Soo Greyhounds, and then maybe the Leafs, or at least a decent-paying job at Algoma Steel, like the older guys. The Soo was like Chicago minus the jazz, the jagged skyline, those terrific used-book stores and about a million women—so his father used to say. That left the broad shoulders, the broken teeth, and every year more dock and mill and factory workers wageless as another firm padlocked its doors. Bad place to be a dreamer and a "fem"—the sort of boy who's pondering the possible outcomes of the epic war between Tolkien's Orcs and the Dwarvish folk when the dodgeball slams him in the temple.

By the time Sevigne was fourteen and new to high school he was tearing through books at a rate of one or two a day. He sat at the back in every class so he could read them undetected, but soon enough his teachers—prone to direct questions hopefully or desperately his way—caught on. Then the other kids caught on, though nobody ever beat him up twice because he always fought back, clumsy yet furious, and his father had taught him how to cut his punch. In case you ever need to protect yourself, Torrins had said, eyeing him searchingly, Sevigne nodding but saying nothing.

He began to fill dime-store notebooks with poems and stories of his own, showing them to Torrins, who would write flattering responses on the last page in the awkward large caps and hickishly verbose style that were coming to make Sevigne embarrassed for him. "I always did intend to write a memoir of the Lakes," Torrins said one morning, handing back a war story. "About cooking on the freighters. And your grandpa Noel— there's a tome or two in that man's life. Guess I'll leave it to you to write them. Now for God's sake get outside and get some air."

"Long as you don't stick in any of your dad's recipes," Amy said. "Especially his coffee."

"Grounds for divorce," Torrins said, winking.

"I like you better in your cups, sugar."

"I like you better in *your* cups."

And Sevigne, more dreamy and serious by the day, would struggle, as he did in the schoolyard, to follow the repartee.

In Malton and Cairo he'd also been an outsider, but here it was worse. In Malton he'd always avoided the humiliation of being picked last for teams because in Malton that slot was the sinecure of the East Indian kids. He was grateful to them, so on principle, and by nature, he refused to laugh at the Paki jokes that ran through the schoolyard at recess. But then he seldom got the jokes anyway.

No Pakis in the Soo. The local jokes were about Indians,

drunken Indians, loose squaws, and the white "dirties" who hung out at the arena trying to pick up Greyhounds stars. But mainly Indians. The one Ojibway in Sevigne's gym class was tall and graceful, a lacrosse star who could run and fight, so he wasn't picked last. Yet Sevigne still avoided that stigma. He owed this surprising fact to Mr Kennan, a beaming, strapping, born-again ex-quarterback with the smug lacquered face of a Christian Soldier and a gold toupee that blew off at a football game in a heathen gust off Superior. Fresh from teacher's college down south, he had strode through the doors of Bawating High trailing the pennant of Progressive Ideas and an air of muscular, invincible rectitude. It was clear to Mr Kennan that the old system of choosing sides was cruel. He deemed that the degration of being picked last might be mitigated by standing the process on its head, and to this radical end the crusading Mr Kennan had the team captains pick each other's sides.

So Sevigne first tasted the glory of being one of the elect, of the chosen few, picked first among peers, for lacrosse. Eyes blind, voice broken, he found himself wishing for an influx of Pakistani immigrants, or for a local Indian who couldn't run or fight.

6

Giants in the Earth

I N TORONTO DURING THE SCHOOL YEAR Martine had
sometimes taken the boys to a small Catholic church off the
Kingsway, and up north in summer, if the mood took her,
she might drive them into town for the service at the Cathedral
of the Precious Blood. If Torrins happened to be docked in the
Soo he would wait out the service in Bellevue Park, where they
would meet him afterward for a picnic: cold roast chicken,
pears, French bread and red wine, even a drop for the boys,
who would hide out and play at being drunk and always wind
up in a "drunken brawl," wrestling and tumbling downhill together past their parents.

Martine's father had been a perfunctory Protestant, her
mother a Catholic Québécoise whom he had met outside Notre
Dame in Paris, where she was vacationing with her sisters. He
was a retired Swiss army officer in his mid-fifties, she a spinster
of thirty-nine. Settled with him near Lausanne—where she
was soon unhappy and increasingly unwell, but then came the
war, and the child, and there could be no thought of leaving—
she had clung to the skirts of the church as if it were the very
fabric of her past, and of her lost, far home. The townspeople
had never stopped laughing at her French. Even Martine,
teenaged and Byronic, had laughed at her French—and at her
piety. Yet after a few years in Paris, Martine had chosen her
mother's distant Montréal as a place to pursue her dancing; and
in the years that followed she would sometimes find herself

sitting in at mass, as if by chance, at Notre Dame de Montréal, or under the model-ship chandeliers of La Chapelle de Bon-secours, or later still in that church in Toronto, whenever the mood seized her, as it always did in November when the Great Lakes were riven by gales and she would drive the boys in for mass and seat them under a stained-glass window of Jesus standing, arms outstretched, in what looked like a birchbark canoe: "Christ Calmeth the Waters." The panicked apostles jammed in around Him seemed far too small, a tubful of toddlers, and Christ's face was botched too, saucer-eyed as if with fear, His upturned palms seeming to signal not benediction but a shrug of defeat. *Sorry, boys, you're on your own.*

Beside the window the clay head of a mitred patriarch butted from the wall like the figurehead of a schooner. "Eugenius Mallon, Bishop of Toronto, 1884–1891." Bishop Mallon's droopy eyelids and porridge-grey pallor gave him a macabre and guillotined mien; a dozen similar heads emerged martyr-like from the walls beneath the Stations of the Cross. Up in the apex of the building a fan spun in the murk, and the roof-vault of cedar strakes made him feel he was peering dizzily downward into the hold of the *Bluenose.* And when he looked back: his mother returning to the pew after one of her rare communions, not pushing ahead through the procession as she usually did through crowds, her heart-shaped face serene, sweetly dazed, as if she'd been perusing photographs of her youth or rereading letters from an old love.

Nomini patri. Regina coeli. The priest still intoned part of the mass in Latin. *Agnus Dei, qui tollis peccata mundi; miserere nobis.* Sevigne would rehearse the dark cadences under his breath with an occult thrill, as if casting a spell or reciting the names of exotic cities—Inchon, Seoul, Chicago, Honolulu, Geneva, Montréal—or the contraband monosyllables of the schoolyard, each one sharp and hard as a steel blade or shard of glass: *prick cock cunt fuck suck shit.*

"Bless me, Father, for I have sinned." Sevigne up north in the Cathedral of the Precious Blood, on a rare summer visit; he was kneeling on the worn slab in the confessional, head ducked away from the grille through which Father Moroni's wan face could be seen.

"How long has it been, my child," came the sweet, weary voice, "since your last confession?"

Sevigne never had been confessed. He was not even confirmed. Curious, he'd slipped into the cathedral ahead of his mother, who was still in the doorway, with Bryon, flirting in uproarious French with three smitten old tourists from Ottawa.

"It's been quite some time, Father. May I call you Father?"

"Certainly, my child, you must always! Go ahead now, tell me your sins."

"I think I no longer believe in God."

Silence from behind the grille save for an odd unplaceable clicking. Sevigne leaned forward and studied the priest's troubled profile, the jowly mouth working slowly, still silent. Then came an ardent whisper:

"But, my child, how can this be? Look at everything around you. Look at the wonder of God's creation. He made it all! Why, you yourself are proof of God!"

"That's the argument from design," Sevigne said gravely.

"My child?"

"Couldn't we have come from elsewhere?"

"But God is everything, my boy, there is nothing else!" A wheezy exhalation and that clicking again: a pastille against the priest's teeth. Father Moroni inclined his face to the grille.

"How old are you, my child?"

"Do you think Adam and Eve might have been Neanderthals?"

A harsh crunch and a blast of eucalyptus.

"I've been reading about Java Man too. And Australopithecus. It's all very interesting."

"Yes, my boy, no doubt, but perhaps you've been. . . . You read these books at school, I suppose?"

"They're my father's books. He's an atheist. I think I am too. Do you ever wonder about these things?"

"Do I wonder about God?"

"Evolution, I mean. Java Man, Peking Man and the apes. The evidence is very compelling."

"Perhaps so, my boy, but is that not—surely such evidence is evidence of God as well? Of all His works?"

"Then everything is evidence of God?"

"Precisely, my boy, everything!"

"What about the *Edmund Fitzgerald*?"

"Ah, the *Fitzgerald*, yes . . . Those poor young men . . ." For a moment the priest was silent except for the sound his fingers made unwrapping another pastille.

"Tell me, my boy, have you a bible at home?"

"There's a King James Bible on the shelf."

The priest sighed. "That will do for now. Please go home and reread the story of Noah in the flood—and of Adam and Eve. Say a decade of Hail Marys every night before bed, and your prayers, don't forget your prayers! And come to me again next week."

Sevigne read the stories, which he already knew, and was left more baffled than ever. If a hastily built wooden ark could ride out flood and ocean storm, what had happened on Superior? Science had rolled back superstition and sent astronauts to the moon and launched steel ships the size of stadiums, filling them with the latest gadgetry and with trained men—and still there were no guarantees. Last summer for no known reason a DC-9 had failed to take flight and crashed off the end of the runway at Malton; soon afterward he and Bryon had ridden out to the site on their bicycles. The jet with its jaunty insignia lay splayed and crumpled in a weedy ravine like the tattooed corpse of a giant—one of those biblical "giants in the earth" who, like adults, like the whole adult world, were looking frailer and less stable all the time.

7

The Deer-Bed

NO SPRING in the Soo—just winter, then winter's messy death-throes, then a week of thaw and flooded gutters as if the whole city were running with sap, while streets pinched narrow all winter by snowploughed ridges seem broad as Paris boulevards with the going of the snow. Behind the arena an abandoned Jimmy and a grey Dumpster emerge like frozen mammoths from the drifts; on the main drag you hear music again from the open windows of cars. Music and wolf-whistles, lewd hollers at the pale napes and knees and calves of the girls in denim dresses, who hoot back at tank-topped boys with phallic-veined forearms as sex erupts from its winter quarantine back into the streets. The season of heartbreak. The city's lone busker, warbling his way through one Neil Young tune after another, sits strumming in the sunlit doorway of the Peacock Garden, while a block east the Greek butcher in a bloodstained apron saunters from his shop puffing a cigar, his sallow face upturned to the steep, reprieving light....
Now like some squalid Oz the Soo changes from black and white to full colour, the air rings with the crying of flocks returning and the lowing of ship's horns in the locks of the river, mild, gyring winds churn up dirt and dead leaves and spread the odours of raw dank earth and thawing dogshit, sprills of oregano in countless Italian gardens, smut from the mills and tons of winter road-salt dusting the air and riming your lips, so for a week the Soo smells, and tastes, as briny as a seaport.

That summer Sevigne was sixteen, Meeka five months shy, having long since graduated from tarpaper to Dubble Bubble and her curls oddly fallen away, so her black hair hung page-boy straight to the shoulders of a long coltish tomboy body, a female version of Sevigne's. The whites of her unblinking brown eyes were painfully clear against her tan skin. When Sevigne went to welcome her back—she and her parents and grubby brothers spilling out of the Duster after their long trip—his eyes fixed on hers, everything around her was cancelled, gone, and he could only mumble and stutter when Jill Greene rushed up to embrace her "little nephew Sevi."

Meeka and her family lived down in Saginaw, Michigan, and came up to their camp every June. It was a crude, harsh, unpoetic place-name, Saginaw, a bustling grey sawmill of a word, but in his mind it would always ring with a bittersweet romance because it was where Meeka, in her chrysalis of sweaters, scarves, toques, and down parka, had come of age in the same winter he had, hundreds of miles away. As if their bodies, in distant synchrony, had been ripening, readying for each other.

The café was thriving now and open till one in the morning, so Amy and Sam slept mainly in town. Sevigne speedily bussed tables five days a week and spent his nights out at the camp, with Meeka, as late as her folks would allow, and with Bryon who'd arrived "home" for the summer a week after Meeka's return. For a few days after Bryon had come—with his sunbleached hair, desert tan, prep school garb and strange, sarcastic turns of phrase—Sevigne had been distant with him and tentative towards Meeka, sure she would drift to the older and bigger boy, who was still stoking a fire for her, clearly. But when the old Polygamites were together—often, in the first few days—Meeka gave no sign of a veering heart, and Sevigne soon realized, to his surprise and great joy, that Bryon had arrived too late.

He vowed to be kinder to his brother, to atone. It made matters worse. He didn't like to think of Bryon brooding alone in the cabin or at night on the dock, but when he suggested he spend more time at the Mariner, with him and Sam and Amy, Bryon snapped, "The woman is coarse, Sevigne, she's *vulgar*. Just like this town is. How can you stand seeing him living with an old waitress with varicose veins? I can't believe you want to stay here."

On Sevigne's days off, he and Meeka would hide out in the basement of the bungalow and wrestle half-naked on the itching, lumpy sofa to a hi-fi soundtrack of *Blood on the Tracks* and *London Calling* and Springsteen going down, down to the river. Or they were out at the camp, where Bryon had begun to hang out with the Strasser boys on the far side of Pointe Louise. Meeka was still game to race Sevigne from the dock to Dr Pacini's dock, or along the shore, to try to keep pace with the ships. She still meant to work on the ships. Often now Sevigne outswam her. Then under the dock as they laughed and panted she would smile, watching his face, feeling her power to move him as she peeled the cupped top of her bathing suit down off her small high breasts, the sun through the slats overhead tigering her nude torso with stripes of shadow and light.

One night in mid-July the brothers got supper in the Mariner. They sat in a booth at the back on red vinyl banquettes beside a shabby mural of the *Algonordic*. It was the first time they'd eaten together in a week. After Amy—puffing, her freckled forehead glazed with sweat—had brought them Cokes and steak sandwiches and poutine and bustled off with an "All right, gentlemen, start your engines, we'll fatten yous up yet," Bryon with one finger had pushed his plate aside and leaned over the table till his slitted eyes were close to Sevigne's, the pupils steely, tiny as the tips of ice picks. He was growing a moustache, cop style, sand-pale against the flaming cheeks.

"How can he stand it? You must have it worked out by now. Tell me."

"Lay off her, Bryon."

"What, you're hot for her too? *Her* too?"

Sevigne creased his brow and sat back in the booth. "What?"

"Like something you'd pick up outside the Algoma."

Oh, you mean Walt! Amy chaffing with a customer at the lunch counter, tucking her pencil behind her ear. Above her red perm a ceiling fan slapped at the smoky air; over much of the ceiling, centred on the fixture, a freighter's stern had been crudely painted so the fan would seem like the ship's prop. *Now, Walt's all right in his way, the trouble is he don't weigh much.*

"At least she's taking care of him," Sevigne said. "Take back what you said about the Algoma."

But smart as slacks, that lawyer he's got, Don Smiley. Now there's a man has a paddle in every pond.

"Taking care of him compared to who? You're comparing *her* to Mom? You should visit more than once a year, you don't even know who she is any more."

"Take it back, Bryon! Amy doesn't deserve this."

"Amy deserves a good ole boy in a Caterpillar cap."

Jenny, you want to give Ed's cup here a warm-up?

"Take it back, Bryon, take it back!"

"Fuck you, Sevigne. If you want her you can have her. The girl is all yours."

"What the hell are you . . . Have who?"

"Her. There. For your mom."

Sorry to snap at you, Jenny dear, it's my lady days, if you'll excuse me, Ed.

"And you," Sevigne heard himself utter with a cold thrill of disbelief, "you can take Everson for your dad."

"At least he can hold down a fucking job!"

"What about this café?"

"Café? This is a greasy spoon. You call cooking this shit a job? You can't even see how far things have slid. You're too close to see."

"I can see he's doing better than before."

"You should never have left, Sevigne."

"You're the ones who left!"

"We could have been a family."

Bryon visored his face with his hands, his shoulders shaking; after a few moments Sevigne reached out, averting his own eyes. As he touched his brother's shoulder he felt sharp movement, heard a muffled crack and looked up: Bryon had smashed the bake-dish of poutine against the mural, the pulpy, viscid remains inching down the wall as faces turned towards them in the silence.

Meeka and Sevigne were lying together on a wooded ridge above the river, a blast-furnace wind gusting up out of Michigan, keeping off the flies. Bryon was somewhere below on the river, furiously waterskiing with the Strassers. You could hear the buzzing of the outboard and the beery whoop and holler of the boys, now closer, now farther, and over the motor's drone a drowsy electric whining from the hotbird—the cicada—in the limbs of the pines. Meeka and Sevigne had found a spot at the edge of a meadow rimmed with poplar where a deer had lain in the goldenrod and flattened them a bed, and Meeka said it was a sign, the perfect place for them. They set a blanket down and lay there damp rib to rib in the cool dappling of shade, both thin as boys, naked and silent, and Sevigne could not believe it when he first felt himself inside her. The silken grip of her. Pushing themselves together they watched each other wide-eyed, open-mouthed, as if hearing at the same time some piece of amazing news from a place that had seemed impossibly foreign and remote.

He would wonder later if it had happened just then that Bryon—hanging on to the tow rope too long and slamming into the Strassers' dock—had been hurt. Bryon himself would have scoffed at the notion of such synchronicity. Or was it more like the radar of common blood? Or Bryon's blood anyway; the lovers heard nothing of his fall. After Meeka's first brief pain and tightness, they made love on and off all afternoon and left the deer-bed of sweet goldenrod moist with the fluids of their bodies. When finally at dusk, winds dying, mosquitoes out, they came down off the low ridge—off the mountain!—they could not go in file as two should go through that ravel of deadfall and bristling scrub, they had to go side by side in a dazed and stumbling embrace, flushed and clumsy with love, while scratching branches added painlessly to the marks their teeth and nails had left. And as if each kiss were now essential as breath, were breath itself, they could not go more than a few steps without stopping to kiss each other backwards into shuddering saplings or solid trunks, to clamp each other fiercely, to eat each other's words and air; to eat, devour, each other. With the river once again visible through the trees, Sevigne pressed her up against a boulder velvety with moss, they wriggled themselves waist-down naked and as he slowly pushed into her, her ankles locked behind him, at the base of his spine, buckling him in.

Just a half-hour later—a half-hour east of their ridgetop bower—they were rushing hand in hand up the bilious hallways of Sault Ste Marie General, in search of room B11. God did not give Cain land, He gave him an institution. With hallways smelling of sawdust and ammonia, meatloaf, puréed peas and Jell-O. . . . Sevigne stood by his brother's bed with Meeka beside him, the two trying not to link fingers, trying not to glow with the sun, the heat and their passion. Amy at the foot of the bed was jawing away perkily, patting the cast on Bryon's upslung leg, while he glowered at the ceiling. "So what's a handsome young stuntman like you doing in a place like this, eh? We saw him from Sam's dock, it was a triple axel he did when he hit."

Torrins had spent the day drinking beer in the sun. He looked woozy, red and ashamed. When he spoke it was in laboured bass tones of mock competence, control: "I'm afraid we'd better call your mother, son. In Cairo."

"That leg's going to knit up just pronto, kid," said Amy.

"Oh, Bry," Meeka said, "I'm real sorry we came so late."

"Why don't you shut up, Amy," said Bryon.

8

Look Homeward, Angel

THE RESIDUE of Sevigne's bad reputation as a brain and a browner and a fem and a spaz and a teacher's feel was always there, but it was going. He grew tall and rangy, he cultivated wispy sideburns and unruly hair, while the scratched and lustreless biker's jacket he'd bought at the Salvation Army came to seem a growth on him too—a pad-shouldered hide he bore in all seasons, sweltering through summer heat waves and freezing in the winter snows, keeping it on in every class. He learned to strut and spit and squint and stop reading books in class, quit answering questions. The in-crowd still left him out, but they left him alone.

He fell in with a clique of student activists, aspiring artists and songwriters, drama club devotees and other misfits and marginals. In the school's social economy they were a lower-middle caste—suspect, but not untouchable like the bespecta-cled gnomes of the chess and math and computer clubs, whom they themselves shunned. Sevigne's gang huddled ill-clad in the school doorways in the depth of winter and rolled joints, they were up on the latest bands and musical trends from Britain, they sneered at the in-crowd with their "Hockey Night in Canada" parties and loud, loutish, top-forty affini-ties. They ran the yearbook and the high school paper *high times*, where they published, along with poems and stories, la-boriously polysyllabic put-downs of "scumculture": TV shows like *Dallas* and *The Dukes of Hazzard*, Hollywood smash hits,

AC/DC and Black Sabbath, anything to do with ice hockey (which Sevigne secretly continued to watch with his father).

Scum-culture was the catch-phrase of Michael Korkola, editor of *high times* and before long Sevigne's closest friend. "Ed.," they called him. Eddy. He was six-three and wore minuscule wire-rimmed glasses and long scarves, his broad hanger-like shoulders holding up a second-hand suit coat, his big splayed-out feet squeezed into vintage wingtips. Like a concert pianist or a conductor he would toss back his blond forelocks in a fey, haughty manner that made arts types want to earn his respect and jocks want to shove that cigarette holder and fancy lighter down his throat. The son of two profs at the small local university, he was given to reciting from Beckett's *Godot*—he had played Estragon in the school production—and from *Monty Python's Flying Circus* skits, which he knew by heart and could perform with all the right accents. He was always affecting one accent or another. It was difficult to say what his own accent might be. Histrionic, high on coffee, he would lead the gang from diner to diner on Friday nights (slowed by Sevigne, who would stop and give change and encouragement to every bum) and finally across the windswept bridge to the American Soo, where they would spend the small hours phone-boothed into banquettes in The 66, a permissive roadhouse, swilling cheap bad American draft, smoking ardently and discussing Camus, Nicaragua, Ojibway land claims, Elvis Costello and Bryan Ferry (Eddy's heroes), or *The Catcher in the Rye*, which they'd read in English class, so that now anybody they disapproved of was "a phony."

Meanwhile Sevigne was adding another layer to his black leather camouflage by joining the Bawating High Boxing Club. His father seemed both relieved and nervous; Eddy and the young bohemians were appalled. "Oh, how very Hemingway," Eddy told him, drawing languidly on a Sweet Caporal. "Next you'll be deep-sea fishing. For marlins. Or going to

South Africa to join the war against apartheid, as you keep threatening."

One Friday night over coffee in the Mariner Sevigne pleaded the boxer's case to them, and he spoke loudly so that Torrins, still in the kitchen, might overhear. "If you just look at things objectively," he said, leaning far over the table, grasping at the smoke-filled air, "a good poem is—a poem is made from the same energy that, the same carefully controlled, channelled passion that counts in a fight."

"The same is true of hockey," said Sylvie Perrault, the solemn and intense yearbook editor, who now wore tiny spectacles like Eddy's. "And the object is to hurt someone, not to redeem the human spirit."

Sevigne reminded her that her big sister had a blue belt in karate.

"Karate is different. It's so mystical somehow. It's an *art*."

"It's a martial art! Like boxing!"

"Boxing is so macho, though. It's so primitive."

"It's scum-culture, I would have thought," drawled Eddy.

And Sevigne understood. This wasn't about art, or brutality, or blue belts, it was about blue collars. Boxing lived on the wrong side of the tracks. So he raised his voice even higher, taking his father's part—though his father by this time of night was likely slumped on his stool by the grill, a book and a bottle open on his lap, singing softly, a gin lullaby, *O what care I*. It was getting bad again. The whole city seemed to know. The edge of something cold and borderless nudged Sevigne from behind, like the snout of a glacier, and he shuddered. His eyes seemed set on betraying him with tears, but he babbled on, fervent and relentless, arraigning his friends for their élitism; blaming them for his fallen father.

"Oh *please*, Sevigne," Eddy finally cut in, "don't go all working-class-hero on us. You hate scum-culture as much as we do."

"You're not the kind to strike another human being in anger," Sylvie said.

"If you've got to strike a blow," Eddy said, "use *words*, like a civilized human being."

"And you might get injured, Sévi—brain-damaged."

"I've heard it has the same effect as drinking does over a long period," Eddy said with sudden enthusiasm. "Actually I was reading last week about uhh, how. . . ." He glanced towards the kitchen, tossing his hair back with an uncharacteristically awkward smile.

Sevigne's coach was the school woodshop teacher and ex-middleweight champion of Ontario, Leo "the Boomer" Hogeboom. Hogre the ogre, the boys called him, with affection. He'd gone utterly to seed. A great lager paunch distended his damp hooded sweatshirt, so it looked ready to burst at the seams, while at the back his sweat pants drooped down his buttockless rump, producing a pale and hairy décolletage. He had a slabby red face, scarred yet unwrinkled; he spoke fast but moved at a shuffle, only his hands still having the boxer's light irritable quickness—his left hitching up his pants or raking at a greasy comb-over, while his right wagged a cigarette through the air.

As the team ran along the gravel shoulder of the Trans-Canada Highway among hills atomic with autumn golds and scarlets, under a scalding Indian summer sun, Hogeboom, driving a few feet behind, would beat on the horn of his Volkswagen Beetle, his squinting face cocked out the open window, cigarette adroop. He was always edging the car closer, berating them in a shallow raspy voice, the result of a punch in the larynx years back: "Jesus, DeMarco, your ass there is waddling like a stripper's. McAlmon, keep those hands up! Hey, Kravchuk, quit riding the tram!" The boys would be trudging along in army boots, holding hand-weights. "Torrins, relax! No running ahead, we're a team here, understand? Quit trying so hard! Shorter strides! You move as gangly as a baby moose!"

In the gym, if Hogeboom caught a boy with his hands at his sides, he would give him a smart cuff on the ear with the blocker. "I told you, lad, keep those hands up!" Then a wink and a grin and he would shuffle on. Or his damp, veined face, every scar in high relief, would loom above, eclipsing a ceiling light as he bent over a supine recruit to pummel his gut with a medicine ball. "Torrins, you been doing your stomachs at home or writing more of that poetry?"

"Gene Tunney wrote poems, sir."

"Gene Tunney was a wimp! All science and no heart. You want heart in your poems, do your stomachs!"

Hogeboom knew the kid did his stomachs, and more. Green and eager, Sevigne had thrown himself into boxing with the same mix of methodical self-discipline and frenzied overexertion he'd brought to his reading, his writing, and his work at the Mariner. He was forever asking questions; he was always last to leave the gym. So that sometimes now he fell asleep over his books after supper or dragged his ass, Amy said, bussing tables. He dreamed boxing dreams, Olympic dreams—the long and lucid reveries of the new enthusiast. He clung to his faith that when the dust of his efforts and the fog of his fatigue had cleared, he would stand purged of his childhood, that pathetic past, and could safely return to his life and his books. And to Meeka, whom he didn't deserve, since no one could really want him as he was; sweet Meeka, whom he had to earn and re-earn like a flagellant or a chevalier.

His first fight came in early November. They matched him with a Finnish kid from the other high school—a pasty, stocky tenth-grader with decent strength but stubby arms and no footwork. It seemed almost too easy when Sevigne looked back on it—he'd simply followed Hogeboom's clear instructions, racking up points from the outside, tagging his slow opponent with long jabs and then slipping back. His father had been helping him at home with his block and parry; his opponent either hadn't learned to block or didn't care. The referee called it near the end of the second round after Sevigne scored with four straight jabs and the Finnish kid's eyes began to swell.

As Sevigne felt his hand raised, pride and contrition duked it out in his heart.

"Chappie there's been watching too much Sugar Ray," Hogeboom said after. "Thinks he doesn't need to protect himself. And he's out of shape. Bailey doesn't make his boys run, it's all weights, weights, weights, just like he used to train when I fought him way back in the Dark Ages before Christ. You did just fine, lad, but next time it'll be tougher."

A week before Christmas he fought again, against a club fighter at an exhibition meet across the river. The gym was ill-lit, cramped and smelly, a faded American flag draped from the girders above the ring. The club fighter was supposed to be a novice like Sevigne, and maybe he was, but he turned out to be twenty-four, not twenty, as promised, and with the build and co-ordination and confidence that only age can endow. Crew-cut, swarthy and hairy, he stood in his corner drumming on the grille of his abdomen with red gloves and spitting with force into the pail. His mouthguard was red, the first one Sevigne had ever seen; as if he'd just had his jaws buried in a fresh carcass. Sevigne tried to spit but his mouth was too dry. Hogeboom was uncharacteristically quiet, muttering to himself and fussing over Sevigne like a giant hen—though once the bell rang he began croaking with everything he had, "Keep him off with your jab now, Sev! Keep those hands high!" while the pony-tailed Ojibway ref pointed and snapped at Hogeboom to shut up.

The man was fast and strong and hungry and there was no keeping him off. As he charged in, lips pulled back in a snarl around the red mouthguard, Sevigne scored with a jab so pumped with fear that he felt it down to his boots and blood streamed from the man's nostrils to his snarling mouth, but it only piqued him. Thirty seconds into the fight he had Sevigne backed onto the ropes, where Sevigne panicked, forgot everything he knew, tucked fetal, eyes closing. The man flurried some hard hooks to the kidneys to draw down his guard and then he went to the temple with a shot Sevigne never saw. Left hook, Hogeboom said later. What a wind-up, lad. Must have felt like a wrecking ball.

Not really—just a hard thump, a blizzard of light blowing over the eyes with a sound like a sheet of foolscap tearing. Icy cold shooting down to the toes. Sevigne's eyes cleared just in time to see his attacker's red gloves blowing up in his face, left right left right, then a voice was barking *That's it that's all back off your man* and the ref was leading the trembling victor away while Hogeboom helped Sevigne off the ropes. "You can bet I'll be having a word with these people. I'll be damned. You all right, lad? We'll be having a word or two, I can tell you. Putting a goddamned Green Beret in with a schoolboy."

On Boxing Day—Sevigne, chastened in defeat, had to smile—he caught the Greyhound south over the river and down through the great timbered wilderness of the Upper Peninsula to Saginaw, and Meeka Greene. As early dark settled over the forests like a slow fall of ashen snow, he watched his reflection form in the window the way many young travellers before him had done, and like them he found the face's mournful dimness haunting, and he saw how snowy farms and hamlets seemed to flash through it like dreams flitting through his mind. Passing through larger towns, cities, the sad vicinities of untold foreign lives, he felt homeless yet somehow exalted by the romance of a journey he seemed to be recording from the outside: the young boxer with his black eye, black badge of courage, sipping coffee, blowing soft blues harp by the rimed window of a coach hurtling south through the snows to his lover's home town. Dashing urgent

stanzas on the endpapers of his books: Cohen's and Purdy's
Selected Poems, Of Time and the River, The Dharma Bums.

> *I can live this constant motion*
> *& the skimming of unknown lives, with you a reason*
> *for my roads, you the watched-for ocean-*
> *coast, bell's sound after the beating*
> *& the face of my arriving*

Kerouac had been a French Canadian, as he was, sort of.
One-quarter. His French was getting weak, *faible, tellement
faible*, so his mother had told him the day before, on the phone
from Cairo. She was horrified by the details of his boxing,
which he'd insisted on giving her; he knew she'd half hoped he
would be a dancer, at the Ballet Jazz in Montréal, he had the
willowy build for it, the sensitive, refined face. She had begged
him to spend the next summer with them in Cairo; he'd told
her he had a job lined up at the steel mill, good money and he
had to start saving for school. She said they would pay for him
to come over—and he should never worry about money for
the university! He told her he meant to do it without help, and
after hanging up he felt, for a few minutes, thrillingly right-
eous, autonomous and brave.

He found Meeka besieged by suitors. Having filled out
further and made the cut for the senior basketball squad, she'd
been deemed possibly acceptable and singled out as the latest
project of her high school's ruling class. Some Kim or Angie
had taken her under wing and taught her to snigger and roll
her eyes and wear kohl and tacky lip gloss. Corrupting her to a
state of respectability would take more than that—at heart she
was still spontaneous, curious, an earnest dreamer and reader
of books; first woman freighter captain on the Lakes! But the
World, which usually fucks up what it decides to acquire, had
trained its sights on her. Her friends were distant with Sevigne

and he wondered at times whether she was not the slightest bit ashamed of him.

They had no privacy, and no summer woods to light out for.

On their last night Mr Greene consented to let them go out in the Duster, although Sevigne's Canadian licence was only a few months old, and frankly, Greene said, he didn't seem the type for driving. Lakeboat Meeka was forbidden to drive until after graduation, but as soon as they were out of sight the two switched seats and they had some good laughs, summer laughs, Meeka gamely fumbling with the clutch while the car did comic moon-buggy lurches, Sevigne, her hands-on instructor, pretending to scold her. In the dark of the car as she smiled, the whites of her eyes had their old summer-night clarity, though her voice kept toying with new attitudes of sullenness and coolness.

They parked in a lonely lot by the frozen Saginaw and climbed into the back and under a blanket. At a tender moment—Sevigne entering her with his tongue as if to speak to her body directly—the car, windows frosted and steamed, filled with glaring light and there was a roaring and screeching as if a squad car were racing up. They groped for their clothes and scrambled into the front seats while doors slammed outside like shotgun blasts and low voices laughed roughly. "Jesus," Sevigne said. "Here, give me the keys." A hard rapping on the hood. *Knock knock who's there?* One-handed, Meeka was doing up clasps and buttons and with the other hand clearing a circle on the windshield. Sevigne fiddled for the keyhole. A face, toqued, stubbly and stupid, filled the circle and mooned up against the glass. *Hey, you going to let us just freeze out here?* The engine kicked in. Meeka rammed the heel of her palm against the glass and the obscenely flattened face recoiled, eyes and mouth forming wide zeros of mock surprise. *Boo!* As Sevigne floored it in reverse the man slid back off the hood like somebody sliding down a banister, no hands, laughing, his pals caught in the high beams, closing in as Sevigne did a jerky three-point turn, almost stalled, and aimed for the exit. Their way was blocked. The boys had swerved their own car sideways, sealing them in. Sevigne braked too fast and stalled. A drumming of fists on the trunk now, hands wrenching at the doors, somebody on the roof. Then the rocking started, lurchy and erratic but soon settling into a solid heaving rhythm, while a voice from overhead yelled, *Yeah! Ride 'em, man, try and throw me!*

Meeka tore open the glove compartment and grabbed the steel flashlight, clutching it to her breast. Her eyes were frightened, fierce and denying. He got the Duster going and popped the clutch, jolting them free amid shouting, swearing from outside and above. There was a lead of icy road between the ditch and the fender of the blocking car, and he steered for it as if they might squeeze through. As they rammed the car, he and Meeka flew forward, Sevigne gasping as his hurt ribs met the wheel. The other car was now at an angle on the icy road, the gap bigger. He backed up skidding and took another run at it, reversed again, stalled, popped free, and on the third run they jammed through. A rock smacked the rear window, webbing it with cracks. Fading voices pursued them: *Asshole! I'm going to do you, asshole . . . !* Gunning the Duster he hoped he'd done enough damage to the other car that they could not catch up.

As they roared away Meeka let her head droop, crossed her arms over her breasts and rocked in her seat, flicking the flashlight on and off repeatedly. After a minute he snapped at her to quit it. She looked over, her startled eyes narrowing. Clenching the wheel he tried to anchor himself, to stop the shaking; he was chilled, half dressed, and his lower half—pale boyish thighs pimpled with goose flesh, rumpled boxers, the cock inside visibly shrivelled, almost poking from the fly—

looked pitiful and silly. Mr Tough Guy. Mr Boxer Man. Protect her from anything.

Back at the house, he told Meeka's father they'd been coming out of the cinema parking lot when all of a sudden a dozen toqued goons with knives and tire irons . . . they'd had no choice. Bill Greene, in his bathrobe, holding a can of beer, stood dourly considering him—black-eyed, sheepish, handing back the keys to the car he'd just destroyed. As Greene called in a report to the police, Sevigne couldn't shake off the feeling that *he* was being reported and would shortly be picked up and taken in. Even Jill Greene was distant with him. Meeka took his hand defiantly in hers, but it was too late, they both knew the week had been a failure, and the bus back to the Soo left early the next day.

9

The Man Who Loved Islands

H E T H O U G H T of not going back into the gym after Christmas, a part of him wanted to quit, not just because of his last beating but because hitting and being hit were so foreign to him that Hogeboom was always having to tell him not to say sorry after rocking a teammate with a hard shot. But having committed himself to the battle he could see no way to back out—not with the world watching, or at least his father watching, and his coach and teammates and the athletic crowd at school, among whom his boxing had earned him a belated, increasing respect.

He wanted more of it. And being in the ring excited him. There, he'd said it. Not to his pacifist friends, but to his pacifist self. And that other passionate, pacifist weakling D.H. Lawrence—whose work he was now swallowing whole—surely he would have understood, would have seen and praised the fearful symmetries of the fighter in his sleek, syncopated dance, the lithe darting of the left jab like a striking cobra, right cross, left hook with the hand and elbow sweeping in front of the eyes as a dancer draws a cape over the face. There was a new fierceness in his eyes when he boxed his own reflection; it was the honesty, he thought, of wild animals. And he read how the wandering saint who'd brought the Buddha's teachings to Bhutan had arrived in that country on the back of a tiger.

He fought again in March, in a drafty, seedy parade hall in Sudbury. The spaces under the soaring rafters amplified every sound so that combinations echoed back down like jackhammer bursts, and the modest crowd, if you closed your eyes, was a roaring, bloodthirsty mob.

After seeing a teammate in his own weight-class get stopped in forty seconds by a terrific kid from North Bay named Carmine LaStarza, he climbed through the ropes to face a short, pug-nosed, slab-muscled fighter who'd made the 156-pound cut-off for light-middleweight but looked 10 pounds over. Sevigne was 149. As he and his opponent touched gloves, he could feel his testicles cringing up against his groin and he felt as he had before his last fight—cowed and outgunned. The guy had the buzzsaw-brushcut bullneck bullethead and fuck-you-faggot sneer of a locker room bully, an Airborne cadet, and on the ridged ball-turret of his right shoulder he bore a fresh-looking tattoo: the Grim Reaper in boxing gear.

"Hey, goof. Goof. I'm going to hurt you bad."

"Bailey, keep your kid quiet," Hogeboom was rasping, "no intimidation, you know the rules."

"Hey, goof. Yeah, you!"

In a querulous tenor the bald dwarfish referee was asking everybody to please shut up. The bell went for the first of three rounds. As Bailey's kid, Kevin Quade, moved in, Sevigne felt the fear in his sinews, the skittish involuntary shyings and flinchings of the schoolyard. And with them a desire to hurt his man. Quade, fighting out of a half-crouch, lurched forward, windmilling wild punches and whispering endearments, *Hey fuckhead, yeah, you!* while Sevigne danced and jabbed cautiously from the outside, landing some lefts and a solid right and waiting for the referee to shut Quade up.

Quade must have taken *Rocky* and *Raging Bull* for the real thing, he led with his face and didn't know how to back up. Sevigne tagged him with a sharp double jab, then felt the ropes at his back. Trying to dance free he got caught with a round-house right to the forehead that twisted his headgear half off, half-blinding him, and as he tucked his arms in, Quade pounced, heavy-bagging him with fast low hooks—poor punches, all arm, but solid enough, and Sevigne heard himself grunting and gasping as the breath was rocked out of him. The buffeting went on. Quade's patter was almost lost in his own panting, *hurt—you—goof*, and now Hogeboom was yelling "Hey, goof yourself! Just shut up and fight!" and Quade's coach Mack Bailey was shouting back at Hogeboom. Through his gloves Sevigne saw Quade wide open, his pumped veiny arms slowing, sinking, but when he tried to throw a combination of his own his arms felt dead from being hit and it served only to wake the guy up. Another flurry from Quade, then the warning bell: thirty seconds left. Quade backed off, exhausted, dropping his arms to get the blood flowing, trying to dance, a trained bear tottering through a burlesque of Ali. His eyes were dull now, drunk. It gave Sevigne hope and he came on, grunting loud with every jab. He landed two or three before the bell, each with more snap than the last.

Walking back to his stool he was numbly aware of Hogeboom and Bailey yammering at each other from their corners while the tiny ref speedwalked back and forth between them, palms raised, fed up.

"You have to feel for a guy," Sevigne said, slumped on the stool, "who *starts* his boxing career with brain damage."

"Quit the wisecracks and save your breath. He's not going to have a career, he's a punk. He's got no style and no gas. I mean none whatsoever. Hell, it's like Mack makes his boys smoke or some damned thing! Let him tire out a bit and then go to work on him upstairs. Jabs and straight rights now, got it? Go on. Get on him like stink."

Quade came storming out of his corner grunting the same mindless tirade, flailing wildly, trying to end it fast. "I told you, Bailey, shut your kid up!" And Bailey: "Screw off, Leo!" This time the referee gave Quade a warning. Sevigne drew him

along for thirty seconds just out of range and saw him start to
tire, his eyes hazing, but then Quade lunged at him and Sevigne stumbled back into a neutral corner. Quade was on him instantly, clubbing away at his tucked gloves, trying to open a
hole, then beating on his arms and elbows as if to pulverize
them and break through to the ribs. Real pain now in Sevigne's
bones. Rivets coming loose, and seams, he's going to bust
you up. The punches were echoing, thundering down off the
rafters, and over the sound of Quade's grunting came Sevigne's
own shallow breaths, like being up on a beach past Gros Cap in
storm weather, waves rearing onto their hind legs and ham-
mering you flat and every time you raise your head you get
battered again, your breath gone, blind in the breakers. He
slipped sideways, partly knocked by a wild right hook, he
was down on one knee and Quade with a vicious grimace took
a swing at him, either pulling up short or missing, it wasn't
clear. *Goof.* It sounded more like *goo*, and maybe it was just
an exhalation, a grunt of terminal fatigue. The ref gave Quade
another warning. Hogeboom was hollering for a disqualifica-
tion and Bailey, slapping a towel on the ropes, was yelling
back. The exasperated ref considered Sevigne as he rose to
his feet and put up his gloves. "All right. Box." Quade, de-
flated, backed off and went into his shuffling satire of Ali, dangling his arms and trying to dance. He seemed dizzy and almost fell. He was all used up. But Sevigne was leaden too and
though he moved forward his punches lacked snap and Quade
took them as they scored, sending small glistening showers
off his boar-bristle hair, his pug nose and lips turning bloody as
he backed away pawing at nothing. Thirty seconds. Quade
straightened and got pasted with a left and a right, he staggered
backwards, then returned, head down like a sleepwalker, to
wrap himself around Sevigne. He was wet and limp as a drowning man. Panting for air. Sevigne's eyes, close to Quade's
right shoulder, took in the winking Grim Reaper in his black-

hooded robe, bony fists held high. Would the bell never come? The referee broke the clinch with a testy warning and Sevigne caught Quade with a left to the solar plexus and an uppercut to the chin. It was all he had left. Quade retreated two steps and sat back on the canvas, cross-legged, with a sort of thoughtful delicacy, an uncanny grace he'd shown no sign of until then. He looked baffled, as if by a piece of unlikely information. Perhaps he realized he'd beaten himself.

As the referee signalled Quade out, Sevigne was aware of the coaches, like flabby tag-team wrestlers, kneeing their way through the ropes. He assumed they were coming for their fighters but they made straight for each other, puffing, braying, towels brandished like battle flags. The referee helped Quade to his feet before rushing off. As the fighters weakly embraced, the tiny man tried to separate their coaches swearing and shoving at the centre of the ring.

10

A Farewell to Arms

P ROUD of his hard hat and construction boots, those totems of North Ontario manhood, he worked shifts that spring and summer as a runner at Algoma Steel, couriering line-up and production schedules between hangars where blast furnaces howled and coke fires spat up like sunspots, torpedo cars with cargoes of magma roared under the oxygen lance, liquid steel streamed into ingot moulds and tailings smouldered in their mounting piles. The mill had a kind of terrible grandeur—he was there at the hot pumping heart of the world's business, a part of some huge, inexorable will—but finally the heat and the din and the titanic scale of it all weighed his soul down, even as he grew inured.

In May the returning geese passed overhead in their great formations like the wakes of grain ships reflected on the sky; tears in his father's eyes at their gabbling call. Then Meeka returned from the underworld of winter and the school year, home to summer, their season, though the only part of her he still seemed to know, and that still knew him, was her body in fleeting hours of shared passion. She'd been "dating" somebody in Saginaw, which was fine, of course, they'd agreed to that, dating was just perfectly fine—only he hadn't been interested in dating anyone, the memory of Meeka had more power to excite him than the actual girls in the hallways of his school. So he'd focused on his books and his poems and his boxing, and his nightly fantasies, waiting for summer to bring his reward.

But he was losing her. The last week of August had the same valedictory pathos as the August before, but this year the bitter far outweighed the sweet. They climbed onto the windless ridge above the river, and as a whining cloud of mosquitoes settled over their bodies like an anxious mood, he asked her to marry him, elope with him—to France! Carcassonne, Annecy.

"But Sevigne, we're still so young! I'm just not ready for it, for what my folks have." Some sudden thought made her roll her eyes, and the new persona he feared displaced, replaced her. "I mean, oh my God! My parents!"

"Meeka, if this were a few hundred years ago we'd be married already."

"But things are *different* now, Sev. I'm just not . . ."

"Not to me they aren't. I feel married to you now."

At Christmas she wrote to tell him her father's company was moving him to Germany, Frankfurt, and they were selling the camp. He wrote a long letter back and inscribed the address *Saginaw* for the last time. Funny name for a town, he used to think; now he saw the sag in it, the sadness, the see, seen, saw.

He threw himself into his training—sometimes mauling the heavy bag, gloveless, untill his knuckles bled through the hand-wraps—and into reading and writing, churning out essays and poems for Eddy's *high times* and Sylvie's yearbook, and for the first time sending his work to the literary journals he found in the public library. Two form-letter rejections limped back to him months later, one journal never bothered to respond, and the other two liked his energy and asked him to try again in a year. But he could hardly wait a year. He sent the poems out again, to different magazines, as soon as he got them back.

He hadn't done any real schoolwork in months. To pass Functions and Relations he copied shamelessly. He brooded over the loss of Meeka and grew obsessed with the gap between his front teeth, which seemed to be widening as his face matured—supposedly into manhood, yet the gap made him look more boyish. Or was it from getting hit in the ring? For a while he tried filling the gap with plugs of wadded tissue, but they would disintegrate and leave spittly rabid flecks on his lips and gums. Then he deployed white candle wax. Finally he taught himself to smile with his top lip covering his teeth, like a camel; or avoid smiling altogether.

With the city bled and shaken by the recession, things at the Mariner were slow. His father, drinking hard, was spending less and less time there, while Amy had all but stopped sleeping over at the house. Towards spring Torrins decided to let her buy him out of the business, they weren't having much luck working together any more, or being together, for that matter. Sevigne was not surprised to hear it—that was how it was with couples, love died—but he was grieved. He missed Amy, her mannish laughter, her smoky voice belting out Patsy Cline or Buck Owens songs off-key as she put on her make-up in the morning. Now he saw her only when he worked.

Now, in the ring, when he landed a punch, no apologies.

Sevigne "the Machine" Torrins won a close decision in May, and then in June, his last month of high school, Hogeboom chose him along with four others for the North Ontario finals, at home in the Soo. He won an easy bout in the light-middleweight quarters, then won his semi against a good fighter who'd been battling a cold and fell apart in the third round, Sevigne scoring three points in the final minute to win. Or had the guy just wanted to avoid meeting Carmine LaStarza in the finals? For the past year Hogeboom had been raving about LaStarza—a terrific prospect, he was bound for Detroit in the fall, they were giving him a tryout at the Kronk Gym.

Best not to be afraid of things, Sevigne's father once told him, what you fear most has a knack of finding its way to you. Good enough. But this made it worse, having Torrins there in

the front row waiting, swilling from a zinc flask, Eddy and
Sylvie and others of their gang trying not to stare but staring
all right as Torrins stopped Sevigne, on his way into the ring,
to mumble advice—"Keep your chin tucked in and your
hands up, boy, please"—the strong smell of rye on his breath
not masking the brassy stink of fear.

Physically LaStarza was unremarkable—medium height
and build, muscles undefined, the chest under his black fish-
net singlet a bit sunken. What scared you was that long narrow lupine face, unshaven, the Roberto Duran look, his black
stubble setting off eyes of husky blue. What scared you was
that cool ferocity—how he didn't need to flex and preen and
posture in his corner, only fix you with those terrible eyes.
Hogeboom insisted he be shaved, the stubble counted as intimidation, it was an amateur rule; but the ponytailed Ojibway
ref pointed at his watch, said the meet was running way late,
forget it.

The bell unchained LaStarza, who charged out of his corner meaning to end it fast, while Torrins started firing instructions from his seat as if the volley of words alone might ward
him off. "Work that jab, boy! Step right, step right!" Sevigne
jackknifed over as LaStarza stormed in, taking the first flurry
on his shoulders and back and the top of his head, trying to
hook LaStarza to the body. He landed one left to the belly with
decent force and felt something he'd never felt before: no give
at all, no weakness: like punching the stump of an oak. La-
Starza shoved him back and danced in snapping out beautiful
jabs Sevigne heard whizzing past his ducking head like fast-
balls and each in time with the guy's grunting exhalations: *ooss
ooss ooss*. Sevigne's own jab was his prize punch but LaStarza
was a beat faster and stole the point every time. Didn't feel
like a jab when it scored, it felt like a stiff right. "Letting your
head come up, boy!" Torrins was yelling, slurring, so that a
deeper flush flamed into Sevigne's face already red from the

blows and bleeding now too, he felt and smelled the hot salt flux under his nostrils as LaStarza tagged him with a right lead, a slap in the face to any boxer, *I can land anything I want*, it means, and *Shut up*, Sevigne was thinking, *Shut the fuck up, Dad*, and then his father yelling "If the bastard leads right again lay him out with a cross!" and Sevigne *Shut the fuck up, Dad, please!* and his father "Nice hook there, Sev, but you're mailing it," and Sevigne with a wave of rage planted a jab full on LaStarza's nose, lucky, the blue-eyed boy *like yours* got careless *Dad*, cocky, Sevigne felt the punch down to his toes and LaStarza's head lashed back, a silver cross spilling out from under his singlet, and sweet to see, all of it, the release of it, but now his father was hollering "Bravo! Bravo, boy!" and peripherally Sevigne—backing off as LaStarza came on firing furious multiple jabs—Sevigne saw that Torrins had leapt to his feet with both hands raised as if he were in the ring. Maybe thought he was. The crowd around him was frozen, numb. "Stop," Sevigne thought aloud, tears welling, "Jesus, stop," and LaStarza's wolfish eyes narrowed, sharpened. *Thinks I mean him.* The ropes like an electric fence touched Sevigne's back sending a jolt through him and he ducked low and delivered two, three good hooks to the steel hull of LaStarza's gut, useless, though the last one drew a groan. "Bravo, more hooks, boy! You're tiring him out!" Right. LaStarza landed a low shot to his temple and Sevigne, dizzied, hooked high, missed but twisted off the ropes, firing short rapid jabs as he backed away. "Now stand your ground, boy!" Damn it. Fuck it. Like to see you in here. See you in here now. *You and me.*

The round was done faster than any he could recall and he was slumped on the stool in the corner, Hogeboom swabbing his face with a towel, massaging his shoulders with clammy hands. "You're holding your own, lad. I've never seen you fight so hard. Stay careful and you'll last the full three."

The referee was leaning over the ropes having words with

Torrins, who had the dazed, wildly aggrieved air of a battered fighter being forced to stop early: "What the hell's your problem here, mister? I've always accorded respect to you people. I've got no animus there. This land was yours a hell of a long time before *we* ever. . . ." For a moment Sevigne, watching with growing horror, forgot about LaStarza. Then the bell clanged and his bowels refilled with ice water, his knees were soggy as he rose and Hogeboom patted him on the rump.

The second round was the first round replayed—Sevigne fighting gamely but getting backed around the ring, while his old man in the peanut gallery made asses of them both. Fear for his son hadn't sobered him, the adrenalin was working in him like an extra shot of rye, a double, that one too many there's no going back from. From this. There's no going back from this. A sharp combination from LaStarza: Sevigne, drained and wobbling, took a standing eight-count, but his father's inane babble during the count refuelled him and when it was done he went after LaStarza, throwing six crisp jabs in a row. Now for the first time he truly felt the animal come alive inside him. Towards the end of the round LaStarza was visibly frustrated, he wasn't used to going more than one, he was eager to put Sevigne away before the bell and it made him sloppy so that Sevigne landed a hook, more a slap, to the side of his face, then a straight hard right, and LaStarza in a rage flailed out driving him back towards his corner as the bell chimed: LaStarza freezing with his right hand raised: wincing with the strain of not letting fly.

"Lad, that nose doesn't look too good."

"Don't throw it in on me, sir. Please, sir. I've got to finish this."

"Let's have a look at that eye."

Now Torrins was there beside Hogeboom, his hand coming through the ropes for his son's shoulder. Sevigne would not turn to face him. Strong fingers dug into his flesh.

"Bravo, boy! Looks fucking great in there, doesn't he, Leo? Must be pretty even on the cards."

"Well, Sam," Hogeboom said gently.

"I'm getting creamed in there, Dad. Jesus."

"Turn this way, boy, let me see your face. That nose. Looks more like mine now, eh—less like Mart's. You ever meet Mart, Leo? Turn this way, boy! You take one in the ear or something?"

Sevigne sat stiffly, shoulders heaving, eyeing LaStarza.

"Thinks I'll worry for him," Torrins told Hogeboom in a seismic whisper. Then, with sudden force: "Thinks I've never seen a goddamn bloody nose till today! Well, as a matter of empirical fact, boy . . ."

"Better have a seat, Sam, the bell's coming."

Torrins was turning away, stooped and muttering. "Tolling's the word, Leo." He'd missed two of the back beltloops with his belt.

In the last round when LaStarza finally cornered him to open up with his full arsenal and Torrins, as if being hit himself, started braying in a pained shuddery voice, Sevigne felt again that jolt of nightmare disbelief that while the two of them were ringed by adults—the custodians of order, the good cops of childhood—both were being battered senseless, just boys, and nobody would lift a finger to stop it. Adults and their polite safe civilization, it was all a lie, a promise he'd clung to despite the evidence—in the end they would stand quietly watching, eyes rapt, while the lions loped from the forum pens. He kept throwing weak hooks, just enough to sway the referee from calling the fight, while he absorbed LaStarza's slowing punches and his father's endless blow-by-blow. A waft of garlic—LaStarza's sweat or breath—and Cairo and all his losses bore in on him. It kept him fighting. Then when he knew it couldn't go on a second longer, Hogeboom would towel the fight or the ref would step in, his father's voice surged louder, closer, my God he's approaching the ring, bellowing "That's it, I've had it, if you're looking for a fight you stubbly son of a bitch I'll give you one!" Sevigne came out of his tuck and hooked hard, swinging free of LaStarza and planting himself in open ground. LaStarza lurched towards him, eyes coldly furious, while behind him like a coach or some bloated shadow, gripping the ropes with huge fists, loomed Torrins. As the boys began exchanging blows, four meet-officials converged back of Torrins. LaStarza reached inside with a right to the heart and then a hook to the liver that doubled Sevigne over wheezing, though something pulled him back up punching feebly, yet *punching*, and over LaStarza's shoulder his father was being gently pulled, then tugged, then dragged off the ropes. "Leave me the fuck alone you sons of bitches you want to try me out try me one on one!" Each word was a blow to the chest far harder than LaStarza could land. The bell knifed through a haze of red beating sounds the smells of sweat and soaked leather the iron taste of blood, eyes scalded with sweat and blood, his father lost in the blur only his voice roaring on above the crowd, which anyway was silent, deathly still, and over the referee's sharp warnings *Break it up now boys enough enough*! Sevigne and LaStarza in the heart of the ring still toe to toe swinging wildly.

In the change room, cursing through swollen lips, he pitched his bloody handwraps and shoes and mouthpiece into the trash barrel. Later, by the river under the bridge to the States where he sat gazing up at the underbellies of cars, big rigs and Greyhounds whining over the high spans, while tears salted his cuts, he thought better of it; but when he went back to pick them out, they were gone.

11

A Raw Youth

LIKE HIS NEW HEROES Franny Glass and Sal Paradise, Sevigne knew the time had come for him to go out and wander the world with a rucksack full of breadcrumbs, to evolve from boxer to Bodhisattva, escape the diminishing gravity of his father's home town. Meeka was in Germany, Sylvie Perrault was bound for McGill on a scholarship, and Michael "Eddy" Korkola was fleeing "the Sewer" for a summer in Paris before starting at the University of Toronto.

Sam Torrins was going out to the Legion for "lunch." Sevigne was sick of it—sick of his own stuffy, cluttered bedroom, sick of the noise of Torrins retching in the toilet and gargling his mouth clean with vodka, sick of the camp, that decaying reminder of his mother and brother and his lost "Girl from the North Country." He could sing wistful on the dock, the way Torrins did in the evening, sure, but mostly now he sang angry. Why wouldn't the man stop? Or get help. Not the man's style to get help. But he kept promising. And time passed. Time passed in a town boasting custody of The World's Largest Handcarved Freestanding Cuckoo Clock. And that spring an east wind seemed to blow undesistingly so the paper mill fouled the air with a great month-long sulphur fart.

He wanted to be a highway saint, a Samaritan, like Kerouac or Camenzind; he wanted to see the country, see Europe, the Holy Land and the Pyramids; Meeka, somehow; and his family. After a month of double shifts at the Mariner and weekends pumping gas into powerboats and big American yachts he hitch-hiked two days to Montréal, where his parents had met and through whose streets the teenage poet Nelligan—his mother French, his father *un Anglais*—had wandered at the turn of the century, haunted by visions of Rimbaud, Baudelaire and the priest-forbidden absinthe of perfect rhyme, bottling shipwrecks in sonnets, his sanity unravelling. . . . Sevigne fell in with a group of travelling musicians from Halifax who were camped on the wooded slopes of Mont Royal and came down every night to jam in the pedestrian malls of Duluth and Prince-Arthur. He drank with them, at first lightly, and joined in with blues or folk harmonica, he served as a rusty interpreter, he showed them some of his poems and one was scored by two different guitarists, sung to different tunes, like a traditional, making the poem seem real and him a poet. *Piano playing through the rain, the drops in high notes falling.* His short nights were spent with the group's fiddler, the red-haired, cherub-faced, foul-mouthed Vicky, in a pup-tent under a camouflaging lean-to of deadfall. Squirrels and chickadees tittered around them, the wind made sighing green lungs of the trees, yet you could hear the city as well and if you climbed the ancient beech radiating above them, there was a patch of it: the copper-green head of Cartier, the city spired and flashing beyond him, a distant bridge with iron spans iridescing in the day's last light like a rainbow over the Seaway.

One night Vicky led him, wine bottle in hand, along a street weaving up the side of the Mountain, and pointed out a limestone mansion she'd heard was Leonard Cohen's. Passing a mouthful of wine back and forth to seal the pact, they agreed to knock on the door and ask if Cohen wanted to hear some of their songs. Laughing, full of their own goofy bravado, they rapped with the brass dog's head knocker and there was a high-pitched yowling, slow heavy footfalls, the sound of locks unfastened. The door edged open. A portly man with hairy feet, white bathrobe and permed silver hair squinted out at them, his TV remote control upheld gingerly like a detonator. A lap dog, quivering and indignant, glared from between the lapels of the man's robe where it was nestled like a monkey.

The door slammed shut in their faces.

Between Vicky and Sevigne there was a simple erotic fondness and warmth, but they were not in each other's breath and blood and she took it well—maybe a bit too well—when the time came for him to leave. He'd loved Montréal, but it had not turned out to be the soul-home he'd foreseen, he didn't really feel French and most of the strangers he'd informed about his Québécois quarter had replied in excellent, politely indifferent English.

Anyway, *The seeker must always be moving on, always touching new strangers and seeding goodwill through spontaneous acts of generosity and love.* He was sleeping little. He felt high on poetry, wine, and virtue, as Baudelaire had urged one must: "You must always be drunk!" But not in his father's way, no: much better to coast forever on the sweet, beatific high of the third or fourth drink when the breath in your lungs turns helium and your veins fill with sparkling wine. But you so loved the world that you always wanted one kiss more, lip to glass, you always would board that fresh thermal for a higher cloud and this time give gravity the slip. . . .

Each time that Sevigne drank (and as if to keep in touch with Torrins, keep faith with him out of guilt, the farther off he travelled the more he drank) it seemed *this* time he would slip the body's backlash and keep his soul on the rise like a harvest moon. Bad moon. Fool, he thought, sober, rereading poems written drunk. But now at least he seemed to understand his father more—the transcendence he'd been after, the freedom he still craved.

He thumbed east to the Maritimes and slept two nights on a storm-scoured, empty Prince Edward Island beach whose russet sand was like the sand along the St Marys River and whose salt waters were as icy. In the shallows under louring dramatic clouds scudding with time-lapse speed, he braced against the undertow and shadow-boxed the breakers, laughing, beckoning like Frazier, *Come on man, come on*, as he inhaled the wild North Atlantic winds lashing the hair into his eyes. The loneliness was exalting—as was the rush of connection when solitary drivers gave him lifts and opened up to him in the confessional of the car, he doing the same to them. He returned through Maine and the White and Green Mountains and the gothic, haunted dreamscape of upstate New York—dying towns where Vietnam veterans, obese and bearded, scowled from wheelchairs on the stoops of caving clapboard houses—then back up to the Soo, where Torrins, having sold the bungalow, was trying to winterize the cabin.

Sevigne tried not to see his father's move as a last stand, the last stage of a withdrawal from metropolis to small city to hovel on the edge of the wilds. For what did that leave? A pine cross and a graveplot overgrown in the forest. Autumn now. As they worked mornings under the cabin with a thermos of coffee and a transistor radio in the dirt between them, their breaths jetted out and mingled in the dank, static air. Afternoons they rested on the sunny porch, as Torrins had to—his punctual crash now striking Sevigne as a daily anticipation of death.

Just after the first snows flew, Sevigne hitch-hiked north up the Trans-Canada along the broken coastline of Superior. On a cliff north of Batchawana Bay he asked the driver to stop so he could get out and scan the lake for Rye Island. Might be visible from the road, Torrins had told him, on a clear day. It was clear all right—the sky stretched taut enough to fracture and glacial blue like the bed of a crevasse, the lake a deeper blue with sunlight quivering over it in myriad scales and the low mournful capes and mountains of the coast like slagfires of sulphur and ruby—but Sevigne could pick out no island to the west.

On then, spirits reviving. This was a country big enough to make brief heroes of all its travellers—the span and the scope and the open spaces did it, you losing the light as you drove over gold-bellied prairies pregnant with grain and then dawn coming as a slow avalanche of light down the eastern wall of the Rockies, a new world there on the wide screen of the windshield, the soundtrack of the radio making your trip an epic film with you, for a change, in the starring role. Your life meant something after all. It was encompassed by continental vastness and because you ranged within that vastness you were a part of it. The country with its rough lonesome reaches and protean landscape was a sprawling map, or mirror, of your soul. A mirror, yes, and you could not pull your eyes away.

Midnight a week later, high on lost sleep, money low: having "raced the roaring Fraser to the sea" he reached Vancouver where a fat, affable trucker in red one-piece thermal underwear dropped him at a Shell station and pointed west. He walked untiring block after block and at last strode downhill through the balmy mystical night air, air full of the sea, to wade straight out into English Bay, backpack still on, howling at the freighters anchored far off and lit up like floating carnivals. So this was it, the Pacific—Superior of oceans! He lay on the damp beach and closed his eyes to toast his arrival with a swig of gin. This was it, this was how to do it—no loitering in the wings of your own life like an understudy, a shadowy prompter, offstage in the Soo.

While still high on his passage he bluffed his way into a weekend job tending bar in a franchise pizzeria and found daywork in a used-book store off Davie Street. The Inferno (as he called it) was a cramped, mouldy warren of aisles as blind and looping as the *darbs* of old Cairo, where any lover of recondite volumes would gladly pass an eternity. It took up the first three floors of a five-floor grey weatherboard house much taller than it was wide or deep. The aisles between the lofty shelves were so narrow, they forced brief gymnastic intimacies on strangers picking through books ranked or piled or tossed promiscuously—the poets with the polemicists, the cartoonists with the caballists, mass-market spy thrillers with mildewed classics. And yet, as if the shop were a projection of his messily encyclopedic mind, Mr MacBeth—reddening at the bloody great ignorance of Americans—would tell you at once if he had a book (in his accent it rhymed with "kook"), lead you to the spot with brisk bandy-legged strides, point it out with trembling finger, and eye you through his lopsided horn-rims. He'd hired Sevigne after catechizing him on literature, then led him up steep, crotchety stairs on which thousands of other books were shelved, and on through the building's upper storeys, each murkier and dustier than the last.

The fourth floor was taken up with rooms to let, all empty; on the top floor Sevigne set his backpack down in the doorway of his first garret, a dormered attic with sloping walls—water-stained and scratched with graffiti—and a bare double mattress on the floor. In the sloping wall above the mattress someone had screwed two hooks and rigged up a mosquito net. For the bats, Mr MacBeth snapped at him matter-of-factly. The last bloody clerk was a queer one, mind, I canna say if it's true.

The room came free with the job and at first its Left Bank squalor squared perfectly with Sevigne's desires. He loved coming in at night and seeing his sleeping bag under the bat-net strewn with chapbooks, calf-bound classics, ravaged Penguins borrowed from the shop. Such fertile, febrile disarray, like the unalphabetized orgy below! And the card table crammed into the dormer-nook under the casement was also littered with books, and with sheets of manuscript weighed down by a two-litre jug of Calona Red and the old manual Remington he'd found on the stairs.

On the orange-crate night-stand was an ashtray bristling with lipstick-stained butts smaller than any butts he'd ever seen. Molly had a way of burning things up, paring them down to the bone. Her nails were bitten down that way, her eyebrows fiercely plucked, teeth stumpy and stained. She was a slender wistful-looking woman with a faded Welsh accent that grew fainter instead of stronger when she drank, though Sevigne—prone to take everything at face value, and anyway in love with the accent—didn't pursue things.

In a black porkpie hat pulled down to her brows, dark glasses and bride-of-death make-up, she'd come to the empty shop at closing time one day in November, nodding curtly and vanishing into the maze of shelves while Sevigne glanced at the clock. After a few minutes he'd heard a faint sound, like a sob of indrawn breath, and she'd rushed from the stacks all afluster, her dark glasses down her nose like bifocals, open book in her hands. Listen, she'd said, peering out of the opening under her hat-brim and above her glasses, isn't this lovely? And I thought I knew all of Pound! *As cool as the pale wet leaves of lily-of-the-valley she lay beside me in the dawn.*

"Alba," Sevigne said, delighted and a touch unnerved, so that he flushed and started babbling: It's one of my favourites. My father loves that poem. I don't know much of Pound, really, but I've seen that one in the anthologies. I'm surprised you've never . . . I mean. Since you know him so well.

She gave a scant, pursed smile.

Can I get you a coffee? he asked.

That would be lovely, dear. Extra sugar and cream.

Later, in his garret, they drank wine and talked, she sitting on the folding chair by the desk, he on the side of the mattress. She said she was twenty-seven, which made her eight years older; to Sevigne that seemed worlds older and lent their evolving liaison a kind of sleazy, illicit glamour. She said she was a poet and a graduate student in creative writing at the university.

By midnight, her black frock on the floor by the mattress, they were under the bat-net, but at first he could not make love. He was afraid of her age and experience and the metropolitan finesse he was quick to ascribe to her, reading her pallor and jittery manner as fashionably neurotic, hip; and she was leading him a fast dance. An older man might have sensed fear in her speed—the nervous speed of a Willy Loman fast-talking to close a much-needed deal—but to Sevigne it was all urban libido, urban chic. At first his failing seemed to agitate, or frighten her, but then as if by sudden resolve she grew composed and patient, and before long they were making love, then going on for much of the night—and in the weeks that followed, she would show up out of the blue and fuck him with the same terrifying, gratifying urgency, in orgasm crying out with a choked shattered voice that made his scalp freeze and his nape bristle. She would always be gone when he woke in the morning. Couldn't really sleep without her pills, she said. *So bring them with you, Moll. Please.* But then I'd sleep all day, love, I'd be underfoot. And he would wake alone to the smell of her on his body and in his bed, and once to a note by the ashtray crammed with stained butts like tiny, blood-flecked bones: *Sixteen nights 'til Christmas, luv. I shall bring you rarest things.*

During one of her disappearances he called the university—she'd told him she'd no phone at her flat, which was out in Kitsilano—but there was no Molly Davis at the department. Because I use my pen name there, she told him, two nights later. But never mind that, love. I want to keep things light between us. Simple. Names are just words, and where do they ever get us?

Just words, Sevigne said. But you're a poet!

Even so, love. Never mind. All in good time. Promise.

More and more he would range the misty downtown on the nights she failed to show, checking the cafés and thronged bars of Davie and Granville Streets and Gastown hoping to catch sight of her, yet afraid of finding her with somebody else. Or excited by the notion. Playing it out in his mind.

A husband, maybe that was it—a loveless marriage? Sevigne scanning faces in smoky blue barlight as if scouting among shades in the underworld; staring with a brooding intensity that some men read as a challenge, glaring back. Some nights he half courted that—the cleansing atonement of drawn blood. *A drunk and abusive husband is dragging Molly into a fogged alley when Sevigne appears, slipping the bigger man's punch to come up with a left hook under the ribs, right uppercut, left hook to the temple, right cross.* Saviour, slayer, slave. In love with her, he thought, he knew he could save her, whoever she was.

But as winter socked in—the low grey skies of coastal winter like a clammy palm pressed down on the city—there were days his bohemian digs failed to cheer him up, instead infecting him with a skittery dread. He saw no bats, though at night sometimes he thought he heard them or woke from a dead sleep with the sense that something had just brushed over his face. A woman's hand? Or hair—Molly's jet-black hair, taupe at the roots. His older workmates at the pizzeria were now smiling with a sort of mocking tolerance whenever he referred to her, and there were times, waking at night and finding her gone, when he half disbelieved in her too. His sleep was increasingly fitful; one night as she slipped out, he awoke and stalked her down through the night-lit levels of the store, a labyrinth of towering shelves he was starting to find so unnerving that sometimes coming in late from another vain search he would shoot looks back over his shoulder as he hurried through—though now, he realized with a stab of mean satisfaction, it was Molly who should look back in fear as something shadowed her through the shelves, those winding gauntlets of remaindered heroes, villains, bit players, all crying out, in clamorous silence, to be remembered.

From the front door he saw her get into a cab. Barefoot he ran out onto the wet sidewalk and looked around for another cab, meaning to follow her, like in the movies, but the street was empty. A pudgy teenaged girl in scuffed stiletto heels hobbled up and asked if there was something maybe he was looking for.

As the brackish damp of winter seeped through the walls and ceilings, re-mapping the plaster with insular stains, he kept to himself more and more. Mr MacBeth now treated him with a clumsy and nattering indulgence that must have cost him great effort. When Molly did appear, always at closing time, Sevigne would fuck her with a famished intensity almost matching her own, slurring ardent vows that seemed to frighten more than embarrass her, and which launched her into tirades where her accent would all but vanish: You mustn't crowd me, Sevigne. Love is not easy. I can't live with you here, I've told you that, I'm a highly private person, I need time for my art. . . .

The many poems he wrote that winter were rejected. As they straggled back to him in their self-addressed envelopes he reread them with faltering anger. Great souls were often misunderstood; but these, he soon saw, were not great poems and carried none of the power, the burning emotional voltage that had run through him as he wrote. He saw himself as pathetic, once more a schoolyard pariah rebuffed in his gambits for acceptance, approval. The well-groomed purposeful women he eyed as he roamed the streets (hunting, he thought, for poor Molly) looked through him as if he were a figment of the drizzle, the grey citizen of some duller, incorporeal plane.

Then a good day when his body scored him a hit of speed, out of season, like that ornamental cherry on Cardero Street blooming in February in the soft-falling snow. And the mountains shrugging clear of fog behind the city, and hours west beyond the Spanish Banks a plunging sun filled the narrow rift between the cloudline and the sea as if a crack had opened in a blast furnace—one of those sunsets that ransom the soul and redeem long weeks of winter gloom—Sevigne hunkered on the Seawall playing blues harp, his mood soaring, spirit weightless and yet vast and expansive. *Great souls were often misunderstood.*

By March on the nights when she did show up, after longer and longer absences, it would always be anticlimactic. He wanted to open her up, on the mattress he thought he did, but after her violent orgasms she would withdraw behind her smoke and her layered make-up (had he failed her in bed even so?), frown down at her watch (did he bore her?), or jabber about her poetry and her "forthcoming book," always staring off at the candle as she spoke, her stories more and more contradictory. Now and then she would dart a startled look his way, as if she'd only just noticed him—an eavesdropper in his own room. Excited and nervous he would read her his own poems; she said they were all very fine, but hers were never ready. For a long time that stubborn reserve made him sure she was brilliant.

Then one morning he woke up and she was still there beside him in the stale light, so terribly thin under the sheet, curled like a skeleton in a mesolithic grave. Her brow in sleep was furrowed hard. Under smudged make-up her face was yellow, creased. She looked twice his age; twice her own age. When she woke and found him staring she gave a breathless, caught sob, like that first sound he'd heard her make, downstairs. *Cool as the pale wet leaves of lily-of-the-valley. . . .* She was weeping. For the first time he was really seeing her, cruelly dismantled, not a grad student over from Cardiff and not the brilliant but reticent fellow poet he'd collaborated in creating. He'd known as much, he saw now, for some time. He lay back beside her and let his eyes drift over the stained, sloping wall. Love began with quivering nerve-ends and a buoyant heart and the answers to all the vital questions, then died with those same answers revoked and countless new ones to find. Disenthralled, he embraced her. *Don't cry. Molly? Don't cry, babe. I love you.* It was a lie. Which made her seem more frail and vulnerable, and him more responsible, attached.

On the beach a few nights later after tending bar he dropped acid with two of the waiters. When it kicked in he wandered off alone, back into the stammering circuitry of the urban grid: Morton Ave., Denman St., Deadman, Davie Jones. *Of his bones.* From a mile up looking down, modern cities were microchips, Cairo an army of camped pilgrims roasting meat over fires. *St Denman. Ave Morton, Ave Maria.* Rain was leprously dimpling his upturned palms and fingers until they melted before his eyes like paraffin. Each drop was separate and separately afraid: polychromatic krill fleeing the black yawning maw of the sky with teeth all stars and baleen of articulate constellations. An old bum in a buckskin jacket and werewolf beard weaves towards the Bodhisattva. *Hey bud. Brother.* Sevigne gently presses the rain into his hand like alms. The man shoves at him, misses. *Arsehead.* Huge pores in the gnarled nose sprout curling hairs. Sevigne backs away. . . . In the Inferno again up the darkened helix through the creaking tiers of Sheol, or is it a morgue with the city's million bodies filed behind printed spines? Through the panting labyrinth of Floor 3 casting looks behind and the fourth with ROOMS-TO-LET always vacant as craving. *I give birth to a centipede through the burning tip of my cock   Bosch a figure in his own canvas bending over pantless and farting out a cloud of bats*

The attic. A saucer-eyed infant in his hands, now a skeleton's hands paddling in sulphuric acid, X-rayed, dissolving. Molly's hands. *Love, who did this to you?*

She had not come back.

> *I know I am in a dark place because I*
> *cannot swallow*
> *and the wasps are weaving hives*
> *into the dead eyes*
> *of the streetlamps*

12

Nearing the Sea, Superior

THE STRONG died younger than the weak; they never felt the need to pace themselves until it was too late. Their bodies never registered wear and tear or gave early warning—then suddenly ulcers, chronic colds and flus, hangovers, loss of appetite, scaly blotches on the skin, incipient breasts, a fatigue that was not just superimposed over briefly truant health but which filled the body to its very bones and brim. Torrins still began swimming every year on the Victoria Day weekend, weeks before anyone else would dare, but in truth he'd been feeling the chill more acutely in recent years and would have preferred to wait until June. But pride held him to the ritual date. Pride and will. And fear. *Back off this year and you'll never go back.*

Drinking didn't much cure the fatigue but it made him feel a bit lighter. When Sevigne's exuberant letters arrived he would sit with the atlas, glass in hand, and chart the boy's progress through Europe. Better than brooding or conducting circular dialogues—his half aloud—with Martine or Amy (the Mariner was doing well again and she owed him something for that), or with his old pal Coleman Proudfoot, who'd let his wife discourage him from further dates with Torrins at the Legion. Better than tearing his phone out by the roots because it never rang and then sobbing like a pall-bearer as he fumbled to fix it. Or overturning that split decision in Winnipeg when he had "lost" to Ghislain Dufour and missed going to Rome, the Olympics, where he might have fought Clay; or *fighting* Clay and against all odds taking the gold.

Or fending off bears. Mornings it all seemed preposterous, but come evening sometimes he would turn off the lights and skulk from window to window, rifle in hand, peering out through the curtains. Dr Pacini, face white as birchbark, had rushed over the first time he'd fired a shot. In a sly whisper Torrins had confided that they were coming down off the ridge at dusk every night, in clans of three or four. You could only surmise what they might want down here. The shot had scared them off though.

He got a dog, for companionship and protection. Dog was a grey malamute with wolf in him and slate-grey eyes like Torrins's own and he would run along the shore when Torrins swam and charge barking into the shallows if a motorboat neared, as if to warn his master or scare the boat off. For days at a stretch he would vanish into the forest, returning to flop on the rag rug by the woodstove and sleep around the clock. Lovingly Torrins would bathe the caked blood from his jowls and ease black-barbed quills from his muzzle and throat.

Sevigne had written from Edinburgh and from the Orkneys, where he'd gone for an all-night festival on the summer solstice and "danced like a Druid." He'd written from Paris—a bit overwhelmed—and then from Carcassonne, Annecy, Frankfurt, where he'd looked up the Greenes and called, asking for Meeka, only to learn that she was back in the States, at college.

An aerogramme from Zurich, where Bryon was at business school. The boys had "spent a good day together." Just a single day! Bryon had not even added a note of his own. Come to think of it, Torrins had not heard from Bryon in over a year. In a letter from Alexandria, Sevigne reported how on the ferry he'd declined a wealthy old gentleman's offer of dinner when the man had found him up on deck cooking rice over a tin of Sterno "under a hobo's chandelier of stars."

A letter from Cairo put Torrins on edge. The boy seemed too eager to write of his ongoing quarrels with the "grossly materialistic" Everson Milne. Maybe they were getting along now after all. Torrins could see it coming. Martine was well, the boy wrote—then briskly changed the subject as if to protect his father from something. Like what? Feelings he no longer harboured? Torrins knew her "dance academy" was flourishing, he didn't need the boy's careful tact. "Mom is well." Eating well, no doubt. Living well. *Living hell.* As for Sevigne, he was writing poetry and reading of all things the Koran, somebody named Isabelle Eberhart, and those fussy desert windbags Larry Durrell and T. E. Lawrence. Loving them, apparently.

Writing back, Torrins reluctantly enclosed the latest rejection slips, as the boy had asked. Torrins had been touched to find the rejected poems handwritten on airmail paper, the writing clumsily seriffed and justified as if a schoolboy with a ballpoint pen had been trying to forge a report card.

The acceptance—typed on an old machine with a faded blue ribbon—turned up in late March, as the first ships of the season shunted and ground their way west through the ice-clogged channel.

Dear Sevine Torrins,

I am pleased indeed to accept one of the twenty-three poems you sent me (in future, no more than seven at a time, please) for publication in a future issue of Toronto Poetry Review. *I think "Sad Vicinities" a very fine poem, rich in feelings both stated and unspoken; and your subtle rhyming is a good surprise. You will be paid on publication at our usual rate of twenty-five dollars per poem. Welcome aboard!*

Yours sincerely,
Lois Jean Shapiro, Ed.

Torrins held on to the letter since Sevigne would soon be home. The morning of his arrival he brought it to the bus station and on the drive out to the camp he gave it over—sooner, in fact, than he'd meant to, a clever diversion, his emotion at the boy's return starting to choke him up. And the boy—till now listless and remote after two nights of sleepless travel—had read the letter with open mouth, cheeks reddening, then whooped and hooted and rolled down his window and thrust his face out into the wet, baptising wind, making a victory pennant of his hair. His torso began squeezing out through the window as if passengers on the roof had clutched him under the arms and were hoisting him aloft. In fact he'd twisted round and gripped the roof rack and—as Torrins slowed and told him Jesus to wise up—he'd heaved himself, still yipping and hollering, onto the roof. Torrins braked gently. A disembodied palm smacked the windshield. "Drive, Dad, keep driving! I'm lying flat, I've got a good hold!" Torrins grinned and shook his head, as much at his own irresponsible compliance as at the boy's pranks. His eyes were full of tears.

"They do this in Cairo all the time, Dad. On the buses. Yes! I'm published!"

Cairo again. "You're starting to like it there, aren't you," Torrins shouted.

"What? Up here?"

"In Cairo."

And Sevigne realized he was—his loyalties broadening, changing, his home shifting eastward, towards Martine. "It's great to be home, Dad!"

"'I met a traveller from an ancient land.'"

"An*tique* land. Shelley. 'Ozymandias'."

"Two points, our usual rate."

As if this acceptance were a sign that he truly was called, that his muse had not been crying wolf, Sevigne refused to apply himself when he went off to university in the fall, focusing instead on his writing. He had the marks to go to a better school in a bigger and more distant city, but Sudbury—with its smelter stench and lunar environs where the Apollo crews had trained for the moon landings—was the only place he could be on his own, yet close enough to visit and help his father.

Yet before long Torrins was worried about *him*. His calls and letters ran the gamut from breathless enthusiasm to withdrawn, misanthropic enervation. With spring came a self-dramatizing postcard written in the Ottawa jail where Sevigne and sixty other "students and workers" were spending the night after blocking roads and chaining themselves to gates, trying to prevent the Tories from putting on a huge arms exhibition and sale—China and El Salvador and other Fascist regimes cordially invited, he wrote. Torrins, who'd liked Thoreau and voted Liberal back when he still voted, tried to take his son's civil disobedience in stride, but wasn't China, he wanted to know one weekend, Communist, not "Fascist"? Sevigne was at the chopping block by the shed, cutting kindling. With a look of sorely tried patience he'd put down his axe and explained that Fascism was a state of mind that transcended conventional political taxonomies; it was a belief that the strong had a natural right to dominate and exploit the weak, and Sevigne hated it with all his heart. "You really ought to get up on that chopping stump while you orate," Torrins had snapped, trying to smile, and Sevigne had rolled his eyes and shook his head and begun splitting logs with furious energy.

At Christmas of his sophomore year he came home disturbingly thin. His eyes looked large and famished, he had a nervous tic in one cheek and the dark wispy beard of a desert hermit. The boy declared that North America was dying of Consumption—the modern consumerist strain—and starving the rest of the world in the process. Every night he made sure he could feel hunger pangs before he went to sleep. It was a way of grasping how the vast majority on the planet lived, and died.

If he could not feel the pangs, he took Dog for an expedition in the snow or stayed up reading—Tolstoy and Gogol and other Russians of solemn austerity and renunciation—until he could. His mind and body felt light, he said, and clear. His breath had a bitter smell, like burnt hops. Torrins watched him meditating at the end of the dock in a hooded parka, a hunched figure facing away over the frozen river, uncannily still amid the gusts of blown and falling snow that at times almost swallowed him.

He said he planned to spend his summer on Rye Island with a sack of brown rice and the Upanishads.

Come April, Torrins had to go to Sudbury to pick him up after his collapse during exams. He'd been trying to cram a term's worth of work into a couple of all-night sessions. He'd spent much of the year writing a novel—something about a young commerce student being bred for Bay Street who chucks it all and disappears on a vision quest into the Rockies. Torrins found it unreadable. For two weeks he stayed relatively sober while he cared and cooked for the boy, driving him in to the hospital for check-ups and filling mysterious prescriptions. Martine happened to be off on vacation in Kenya those two weeks—incommunicado, Torrins fumed—while she in a rage later claimed that she had sent a whole series of numbers where she could be reached, and he—naturally!—had lost them.

Or had he?

Once more the peacemaker, Sevigne assured them it was all a misunderstanding, nobody was at fault, he was fine now anyway. Sickness always ages you but sometimes in reverse; Sevigne now resembled a fourteen-year-old boy, huge eyes raw and withdrawn into a pale, pimpled face, his springy stride reduced to a cowed shuffle. And *thin*.

Though badly shaken, Torrins felt somehow bolstered, reprieved by this shift in the balance of power—this promotion back to his old rank of father, protector. But mostly he was afraid. In this world there were believers and there were scoffers, and the scoffers, he knew, wound up with the world in their pockets, bulging there like a billfold. Or call them spenders and hoarders. Sevigne was a believer, a spender, like him. "No pockets in a shroud," Noel had always declared, and no one could dispute it, but life's hoarders squirrelled it away all the same and gave nothing out in hopes of outliving everyone and taking it all down with them into that strongbox in the ground—and not only cash but generous energy, goodwill, love. Tight-lipped Mother scrimping up credit with her Presbyterian God, and only Noel, with his bottomless tumbler, showing any warmth or love, spreading cheer through the house like a currency the heart could use, so it seemed rye must be the very elixir of happiness. Ah well. Poor Mother. No wonder, he saw now. As for Mart, he could not make himself despise her because at heart she was a spender like him—live for tonight, squeeze the last brass drop out of the paycheque to throw a better supper and card party. So how did she abide Milne? There was a hoarder and a tightass if Torrins ever saw one and Torrins had seen plenty. But then she'd gone for the hoard in the end. No: she'd gone, she'd gone, she'd gone to get away from what he, Samuel Rayland Torrins, was turning into. Turning himself into. A man who'd once made her heart pound so hard under her breasts he could see them quivering through her shirt—could feel it, even now— in the back of a taxi pulling away from some lakeport at nightfall.

He'd murdered that man she'd loved. Poisoned him by the shot and the bottle. He knew how death felt. It was the paralysis of late evening, of lying on the chesterfield with your mouth ajar watching your son grieve at the window and everything blurred and beyond your powerless reach as if you were the corpse at a wake laid out and viewing it all through a shroud. Pocketless. He knew the sound of it too. You pick up the telephone expecting a dial tone, then the soft remote jingle

as it rings, then your boy's groggy morning Hello?—and
there's nothing. Dead line. There is no other silence like that.
Like a direct goddamn line into the tomb. Did you tear the
fucker out of the wall or did Ma Bell cut you off? And every
half-hour a freighter's horn—*O lost, and by the wind grieved,
ghost, come back!*—to serve notice that the world is getting on
with its errands and you a faint blip sliding off the screen.

They'd tossed him out of the Legion for taking a swing
at Mitch Haffy when Haffy had cut him off. And how many
rounds had Torrins bought the house over the years? How
many good stories told? He'd lost his licence on the reckless
drive home. Which made the cabin his only bar and Dog his
only audience. Then one morning he had found Dog shot in
the woods beside the cabin, still alive, sides heaving, slate eyes
hazed, the autumn snow beneath him a slush of blood. Some
fucking kid on a Ski-Doo, probably meant to rob Torrins, or
do him in. He hadn't heard the shot. He went into the cabin
with murder in his heart, knowing that all he could kill, must
now kill, was Dog, to put him out of his torment, but he
couldn't find the rifle—then there it was, propped beside the
table. Beside the window, dear God. Spent shell in the chamber. Loaded for bear.

And that night he had sat a half-hour staring down the barrel of the .30-06 as if to see who would blink first.

There was a last good time; there always is. Sevigne was home
and by autumn he was back on his feet, suntanned and fighting fit. He was Torrins's morning crowd and Torrins was the
boy's first reader. The boy was working at his writing with
stubborn dedication and Torrins took pleasure in his small
successes, the slowly improving ratio of acceptances to rejections. At the sound of the postwoman's arrival each morning—

gears downshifting, tires crunching to a stop in the gravel, the Pavlovian creak of the postbox opening—Sevigne was up from the table and out the door. From the kitchen window Torrins would watch him claw open his mail there by the box, even in winter, and he could read those letters line by line in the boy's changing face. His sunburst smiles, his wounded frowns. God, how wonderful to feel so impatient with life, to really want time to hurry up and bring on the future! To have real energy in your joy, and in your sadness too so the hurt of it would sting intensely and then pass, not just linger like this dull, daily weight.

To Torrins's disappointment Sevigne had no intention of going back to school. A Vancouver magazine had just picked up two of his stories, and Lois Shapiro meant to use five of the seven poems he'd last sent her. He was happy in his work, yet restless, his nascent confidence making him impatient with the very refuge where it had been nurtured to grow. Torrins tried to be encouraging when the boy spoke of maybe spending the winter down in Toronto, or somewhere, but in truth he was afraid of being alone again and the encouragement he offered each morning he mumbled away pathetically at night—helpless, it seemed, to stop. *Please don't go. Please.* Had he really said that last night? He saw himself shaking a bank-book in the boy's wavering face as he came in from his shift at the Mariner. *What's this? Saving money I see, while we eat like Biafrans here. You forgot the steaks again yesterday. I know you're antagonized now by a bit of honest blood but you need it. Too goddamned thin. You forgot the brandy too. See if you're going to reside at home and compose these sprawling epics of yours you'll fucking well have to . . .*

Too shameful, let it drift. Say nothing. He'll think you forgot.

By the following June, Torrins was having fits of dizziness on every swim. Swivelling his head up to the left to breathe, he felt the motion follow through in a whirling full rotation, as in high fever—something else he'd known nothing of until a few years back. He'd had to give up on his two-mile swims to the

Michigan shore and home. Just a mile now left him tired, not refreshed. He said nothing to the boy. A couple rounds after breakfast, boy? Nice and easy. A couple mugs of java and some fried eggs and he would be, for another hour, the man she had loved and he had done in. *Mountains divide us and the breadth of seas.* His brain was still a jukebox full of songs and quotations; the shakes were just shivering from the water. Colder this autumn than last. *And I can't cross o'er.* (It was warmer than usual. As both men knew.)

He was dropping weight for the first time in his life. Down through the classes he would go from heavy to light-heavy to middle to zero, nought. And now he'd lost his taste for lunch, like supper. After a recent "supper" he'd looked up woozily: the boy, turned away, was scraping unfinished food into the trash can and his thin shoulders were slumped, head drooping. Torrins had gone out onto the screened porch and poured his brandy through a knothole in the floor. (Faint trickling like a weak, old-mannish stream of piss as it spritzed the weeds.)

Within the hour he'd fetched another round. If only to toast his selfless act. Which surely counted for something! It was a step. It was *one drink less*. He still had the strength and the time to stop it all.

But there could be no stopping.

On a clear still morning in mid-September, Sam Torrins woke an hour past dawn and leapt stiffly out of bed, as if faking his old ways might revive them. He fumbled his bathing suit on, got his towel and goggles and stood swaying before the mirror. Jesus would you look at that. Jesus. Piece of shit. As if he'd been wearing the goggles all night. Or were they black eyes from yesterday morning? In their roped ring in the forest he'd missed with a wild right hook he'd forgotten to pull and the boy, angry, had caught him with a jolting double jab, then dropped his hands, crying "Sorry! I'm sorry, Dad!" and torn off his gloves and thrown them down and stalked away, shoulders shaking. So Torrins seemed to recall. . . . Everything had become so anchorless and dreamlike, no short-term memory clean-edged, certain, as his image in the mirror was, alas. Caving in. Red rheumy eyes and white stubble of a Queen Street drunk, nose cratered and veined, slack breasts. Gut soft, and the rotten old wineskin of his stomach scraped raw with a razor, or so it felt.

He padded out into the main room and eased open the bunkroom door. The boy was tucked in a ball under the blankets, mouth open, dark hair long on the pillow, like Martine's. Christ, what you felt sometimes. The love, winding you, blinding you like a punch. He had a painful flashback of the boy helping him into bed a few hours before, and then—had his son kissed him? Or he his son? But that was hardly the Torrins way. No sir and no use teaching an old dog. Or bothering the boy now.

Down by the dock, out of the old groundhog hole under the water pump, a gold-filled molar seemed to gleam. Canny precaution. Seldom needed in the dawn. But now the heart in him was pounding thin and weak and fast and hollow as if hung in a vacuum and the razor in his belly kept scraping away. He knelt and withdrew the mickey and drank. Not Seagram's VO as he had every right to expect, must have finished that one, this was cheap bad Liquor Board brandy, XXX. As the liquor hit home, the razored flesh in his guts thrilled with pain and he groaned, jackknifed and retched violently into the stripped blueberry brush by his knees. To swim now would be idiotic. But it was not the Torrins way to change plans. Back off once and it's all over, the slide begun, don't you know that much? And where that leads? He dives off the dock as always in a racer's whiplash start and even now the sting of impact and the icy cold are a good shock, bracing. But it wears off fast and he feels again the burning in his gut and tastes bile and cheap brandy and spits out foulness. His arms are dead weight: heavy as girders. Turning his face to gulp at the air he feels the whirling and vertigo commence. He thrashes west along the drop-off using the lip of the slope as his racing lane and sure enough the red scalloped marl of the riverbed *is* like a desert, sand-dunes glimpsed from miles above in Sevigne's new poem of flying into Cairo, the boy fusing his parents' landscapes as if to reunite them in words, poor boy, but now Torrins should leave the desert below and crawl out over the river's deeps as he always has, if only as a way of turning around, heading for home. His goggles seem to be misting up and he's coughing bile so he stops and tries to stand on the edge of the drop to clear himself out, but he's too dizzy to sound bottom, or out past the edge. He looks down. The river's plunging depths are a thick and viscous black, like stout, and his feet hover there horribly blanched and twitching. Now the burning in his gut turns to a strange flooding fullness and warmth, like the first belly-surge of falling in love, and as he coughs again underwater he sees a darker stream rise before his eyes. Blood. He has sunk a foot or two without feeling a thing. He flails to the surface gasping and choking and jabs at his goggles to push them off. His eyes are blurred but off towards the Michigan shore it seems a long, low, sombre ore barge is forging slowly upstream, the thrum of its engines like a giant heart in the river around him; or is it his own heart, hugely amplified. . . . He feels the current flowing down out of Superior nudging him home towards the camp and a wave of blind searing grief sweeps through him, and then, just as sudden, dumb joy in the knowing he has also been lucky, and, for a time at least, beloved. He sinks slowly, already at peace, dreaming the monarchs like sundown cirrus high over the ship and that time he was deep in the hold with Jazy and Proudfoot checking for seepage, sliding down a scree of pellets and near bottom finding the sign of a prior cargo, a sprig of wheatgrass—green as April in all that grey—sprouting delicate, defiant from the vast barrow of ore.

2

Cities of
the Dead

In the cream gilded cabin of his steam yacht
Mr Nixon advised me kindly, to advance with fewer
Dangers of delay . . .

EZRA POUND, "Hugh Selwyn Mauberley"

We turned our loneliness into cities,
our ambition into towers.

JEANNE TAKAMURA, *Heights of Folly*

I

The Islands of the Nile

THE WAKE was held at the cabin in late September. After everyone had left—Amy, Leo Hogeboom, Dr Pacini and a score of his father's old friends, hard-drinking laconic men Torrins hadn't spoken to in years but who still came to pay their respects—the place seemed more empty and desolate than Sevigne had ever known it. The loneliness was palpable, a physical thing. It smelled of woodrot, raked ashes in the chilly hull of the stove, air too little lived in—air breathed by just one person and fraught with the acrid, funereal incense of cedar smoke drifting down from the Pacinis'. It filled the small rooms like a sound, the remote roaring of a nautilus held to the ear. Not the ocean. Polar wind. The frail, fibrillating leaves of the birches turned yellow and an early gale off Superior stripped them bone-bare in a night.

At times he felt half crazy, afraid of another breakdown. He tried to write but in the cabin it was no use. He would sleep till noon, then spend afternoons at the Ancient Mariner helping Amy or drinking too much of her coffee and crumpling up elegies that went nowhere. Amy always cheered him up. Generous as ever, she'd made him accept a cheque for two thousand dollars, she'd been meaning to give it to Sam anyway seeing as the Mariner was going such great guns, all Sevigne had to do was some day give her a free copy of his racy novel and leave her the hell out of it. She had him over to the house some nights for supper with her boyfriend Wolf, a foreman at Algoma Steel, who would blush and beam over his shepherd's pie as Amy said, "He's older than me by a long shot but he's a game old geezer." Other times, alone at Muio's or the Peacock Garden, Sevigne would stretch a meal and a few beer into a night as he read and doodled in his notebooks and told himself he was sidewinding his way into a Big Novel. He was really just postponing the drive home. If the cabin could be called home. He owned it now, anyway.

Then one afternoon as he stood on the porch in the oblique, listless sunlight of late autumn, he realized his face had just assumed his father's afternoon rictus, he felt it in the muscles of his jaw and brow and he pictured it plainly in his mind's eye and knew he was brooding on the river and the far shore through his father's eyes. One freighter, Brazilian, downbound. Within an hour he had spoken to his mother in Cairo and a travel agent in the Soo. Before closing time he had sold the old Pontiac to a used-car dealership for two hundred dollars, then thumbed and walked back out to the cabin—which he would not sell, though for now it was unusable, uninhabitable. Like a crumbling family tomb, it was a memento of past and future deaths, it offered no shelter, required constant upkeep, and could not be sold and forgotten with a clear conscience. He flew east a week after Hallowe'en.

In Egypt many thousands did live in the tombs—in old or recent family tombs in the Cities of the Dead, on the south and east peripheries of Cairo, some people economizing by setting up in the opulent repositories of their forebears' bones, others squatting in the sepulchres of families who had moved away or long since died out. The Cities' broad avenues and neat straight *darbs* were canyoned by solid walls of false-fronts ornately carved in granite, limestone or marble; the tombs, built around courtyards like the houses of the rich, were miniature mansions, some now consecrated to such humble pursuits as the selling of groceries or the cooping of fowl. No quiet final rest for the departed; in the thriving necropolis, an endless wake.

It was in the shanty-cafés of the Eastern Cemetery that Sevigne drafted his novel. With his longing to create something of beauty now fuelled and focused by grief, with his sense that Egypt was again the site of his father's deepest absence, he would have to write of a dying father and the islands of the Nile. And he would write with a grief compounded by guilt—you weren't there to help at the last; you were there for freedom's sake half wished him gone anyway; you haven't grieved as deeply as you should. *For my father, Samuel Rayland Torrins, 1932–91.*

Early, before the sun commenced its daily reign of terror, he would slip downstairs through Everson Milne's chamber of garlic and out into the warm, windless dawn to lose himself in the waking *darbs* of Old Cairo. The day's first light, a sacramental damask, would be shining on the domes of the mosques and on the flocks of pigeons gusting high and silent over the citadel and minarets. Then first traffic: knots of tiny pugnacious cars like packs of yapping terriers, clinging-room-only buses hurtling past in an evil eructation of fumes, an old hearse pulled by a donkey whose eyelashes bat shyly over brown, doe-like eyes, with the *fellah* driver, in *galabeyya* and wool cap, hunkered on the hood holding the reins. (The hearse contains not a coffin but styrofoam coolers of crushed ice and syrup and soft drinks that the man will sell on his rounds.)

The streets of the Cities of the Dead fill with the living as the sun crowns out of the bouldery moonscape of the Muqqatam Hills. In the open gate of a medieval tomb, an old woman is framed in her inner courtyard, bent double beating a carpet with a broom. An engine snarls into life and as the gate of another tomb swings open a teenaged boy on a trail bike surges out, sunglassed, smoking, wearing a grease-stained T-shirt: CHICAGO BULLS. Mobs of children scoot past laughing as they follow a colossally fat blind man in a white robe and wraparound shades walking hand in hand with a monkey. Whenever the children draw too close, the monkey scrambles up the blind man's sides and perches on his shoulder facing backwards, chittering and scolding, while the man, smiling patiently, waits, the children charging in with happy shrieks and then dispersing.

Carnival. He was not a part of it, but with his hair-trigger grins and earnestly botched Arabic he was liked well enough, and he felt he belonged, felt he understood. He loved the way the dead and the living were not segregated here as in the West: no pine-box compartmentalization and abandonment, no wall between the two worlds. No barriers! In the Soo, without bothering to get the requisite licence, he had followed his father's wishes, taking the box of ashes out in the canoe one windless evening and strewing them over the border waters midstream.

The day of his arrival his mother and Everson had met him at the airport and driven him into Cairo through the tight-ranked dreary projects of Nasr City and the hunkered slums of the *zabalin*, junkyard dwellers who drew life from the city's refuse, jerry-building hovels in the vast nuisance-grounds and selling whatever they could salvage or rehash. Like writers they were scavengers of the social compost; but poorer than even a writer should be. The climate-control in the BMW sealed out the desert heat and city life swirling around them in all its clamour and malodorous vitality, so each window seemed to frame a silent documentary on Third World urban blight. Suddenly vexed, Sevigne lowered his automatic window, in regressive hope of baiting Everson. No use. The prodigal son was to be indulged. Still, he had to admit that it was good to be here, not there. Martine hadn't removed her sunglasses on first embracing him at the airport, but he'd felt the joy in her grip and the moist warmth of her cheek, and it had all seemed more like a homecoming than he'd expected.

Ah, bienvenu, mon petit! Que tu m'as manqué. . . !

"Sev? Your shot now, Sev."

"Come on, Sevigne, wake *up*."

They were on Gezirah, one of two large islands in the Nile in the heart of Cairo. Everson, Martine and Bryon were members of the Gezirah Sporting Club, once the exclusive fastness of the rich, the powerful, the white, but now open, Everson assured Sevigne, to anyone—though in practice the fees must suffice to debar the vast majority of Cairenes. They'd caught a cab to the island after Sevigne had had a shower and a rest. He might have begged off, seeing golf in such a setting as inappropriate, had it not been a special occasion: Martine's birthday, which had actually been the week before but they'd deferred the festivities, Everson told him, pending everyone's arrival. Bryon and his fiancée Tralee had flown in the day before from Istanbul, where Bryon was now a partner in a computer and business-supply firm targeting the new markets of the Middle East, while Tralee taught English to Turkish children.

Martine and Tralee were on the clay court playing tennis while the men golfed. The megaphonic echoes of the late-afternoon *adhan* were fading; over the palms, acacias and bougainvillaea fringing the immaculate course, and over lofty office buildings and luxury hotels, the Gezirah Tower shimmered in the heat. Sevigne teed up. He stood facing a distant colonnade of date palms and behind them the Nile, a glistering of low sun off its eastern channel. *Sun sets a torque of sapphire over the blue-veined wrist of the river. Sun wraps a torque of. A circlet. Over the blue-veined neck of the*

—he'd missed the ball by half a foot. With a gravely reflective expression he re-enacted the wild swing, as if he'd only been practising.

"It's about five hundred degrees out here, Sev," Bryon said. Over the last few holes he'd been growing impatient and touchy, his initial goodwill depleted; slumped over the golf cart's steering wheel, with his mirrored Ray-Bans and small sandy moustache, he looked like a tired cop on a long stake-out. "You mind taking your shot?"

"Now he's just getting the feel of it, Bry," Everson said, opening a bottle of Perrier. "Right, Sev, swing her through there nice and easy, *easy*, keep your eye on the ball the whole way and.... Yes! You've got it now! Outstanding!"

The ball soared straight and swift towards the distant flag, but then—as if sideswiped by a crossgust though the day was calm—it sliced sharply right towards the river and vanished in the rough.

Sevigne kicked at the tee.

"Now, now, Sev. It started very well indeed. One has to be patient out here."

"We all have to be patient," Bryon said.

"Here, let me drive now," Sevigne said. "Seeing as I'm on a roll." Though annoyed that he couldn't master the game instantly, by mere exercise of will, he did feel pleasantly buzzed with jetlag and the African sun and the three tins of lager he'd sipped on the course; perfectionism and hedonism battling for his soul. He squeezed in beside Bryon, who frowned and slid over to the passenger side of the bench seat.

"You're not really meant to be driving, Sevigne, you're not a member."

Sevigne eyed his brother aslant. Everson slipped into the back and set a lizardy, brown-speckled hand on each of the brothers' shoulders, as if trying to form a civil conduit between them. He had on a white cotton peaked cap and a peach Lacoste golf shirt. "I think it'd be fine, though, Bry, there're only a couple holes left to play. And we're members."

Bryon turned and took off his sunglasses. "You've never seen him drive, Ev. Dad wouldn't even get in the car with him. He almost killed me and Meeka on the way back to the cabin one time after dinner. And he was sober then."

"I'd only been driving a few weeks, Bryon—and I'm sober now."

"Let's be agreeable about this, boys. Just a couple more holes to play. Remember, this is a special day for your mother, and we're family."

Sevigne stepped on the pedal and the cart jerked ahead. From the west side of the river came a tardy *adhan*, the muezzin's quavery, distorted summons forcing, then filling, a brief silence between them. *Come to prayer, come to prosperity. Let the prayer begin. God is great; there is no other god but God.*

"You're just worried because I'm finding the range," Sevigne said, to lighten matters.

"I'm tired, that's all. Burned out. You just don't . . . I didn't know what work was until I had my own business." Then, with strained chumminess: "We usually have this Moroccan guy drive us around and caddy the clubs, help find the balls, but Ev thought we'd better not use him today because you've got a bee in your briefs about hired help."

"Well, it's been fine though, hasn't it?" Everson called out, setting his hands back on their shoulders. "Jilali probably appreciated the day off, it's not often this hot in November."

"People *want* to work, Ev," Bryon said, twisting around, "it's how they make a living. Sevigne! Watch it here, the ground cants off into the trap."

He steered them around the trap and stopped in the rough on the edge of a clump of tight tropical scrub and dwarf palms. As Sevigne began looking for his ball Everson took a pitching wedge and sauntered back towards the fairway in his white slacks and spatted golf shoes, whistling, using the club as a stylish cane.

"I'll go on ahead, boys. Sev? Don't forget to call 'fore'!"

"I'll keep an eye on him," Bryon said.

When Sevigne found his ball in the rough and tried to set up, facing west, the low sun shone directly into his eyes.

Currently opposed to sunglasses on the principle that they set
another synthetic barrier between the self and the elements—
and *homo sapiens* in a primordial state had flourished without
them—he squinted helplessly. Seeing Bryon slouched in the
cart watching Everson on the fairway, he nudged the ball with
his toe and kept nudging until he was placed so the fronds of a
dwarf palm served as an organic visor.

"Why don't you just dribble it another hundred yards or so
towards the flag," Bryon drawled, still scanning the distance
through his glasses. "I'll turn a blind eye. The way things are
going here, before we're done there'll be nothing but sand
blowing over mummies in a rusted cart."

Sevigne's shot whizzed off at a tangent and smacked into a
dwarf palm thirty feet from him, wedging fast in the pine-
apple-grid of the bark. Peripherally he saw Bryon burying
his face in his hands, then slowly removing one hand to check
his watch. After a few minutes' struggle he gave up trying to
pull, then pry, the ball free of the bark and started hacking
away at it with his five-iron. Stupid game. Their father, duff-
ing shots off the end of the dock, had let all within earshot
know it was one of those effete, patrician pastimes, like tennis
or polo, where money could buy you an advantage.

In silence he drove Bryon over the rough towards the spot
where they figured his, Bryon's, ball had landed, lateral to the
flag. Everson was on the green strolling around with a professional's nonchalant strides, the putter over his shoulder like a
fishing pole. Some anger seized Sevigne. There was a crashing from the underbrush beside the rough and as the brothers looked, a huge storklike bird—a sacred ibis?—rose into
the air on slow thudding wings and flew cawing into the sun
with sickle beak and long gangling legs in silhouette, an ascending myth, or fossil. For that moment the golf cart became a time
machine and the boys again children, gaping and whistling,
pursuing the bird with awed eyes.

The spell broke.

"Watch where the hell you're going, Sevigne!"

They were ploughing into the underbrush, Sevigne having swerved right as the bird crossed their path. For a moment he felt frozen, unable to brake or steer. Then as Bryon grabbed at the wheel he fought him for it, pushing the pedal to the floor and steering them between two dwarf palms, like pillars marking the entrance to a shrine. Stands of fig-sycamore, bamboo and eucalyptus and thickets of bristling scrub whipped past them in a dusk plumbed by thin shafts of sunlight. The ground was rough, the cart thudding, bucking them out of their seats.

"Brake, Sevigne, Jesus, take your foot off the metal! Watch the tree!"

"Hang on," Sevigne yelled over the scratching and snapping of branches on the hood. A tearing sound from above as the canvas sunroof was ripped open, pulled off. Head low, Bryon grabbed at the wheel again, then tried to jab the toe of his cleated shoe over Sevigne's and onto the brake. The cleats barked Sevigne's shin, a spiny bough raked over his forehead but he pushed on laughing. They were thumping down a slight grade with the river shimmering ahead through the trees. In the crotch of a sycamore sat a large nest with the tops of eggs glowing in the twilight like gathered golf balls—this seen in a freeze-frame, then gone. Bryon had given up trying to stop him. Hunched down pale and furious he had his arms locked straight out, his hands braced on the dashboard. They burst through another whipping, stinging thatch of scrub and Sevigne finally slowed, braking hard as they hit the riverbank—a thin rind of copper mud—with the front tires squelching in and the cart plunging on a few feet till it ground to a stop fender-down in the Nile.

Around them in the shaded shallows, reeds and tall stalks of halfa quivered in their backwash. A pair of swallows darted out of a brake and peeled off low across the water.

"The Nile, I presume," Sevigne said between spasms of laughter. The cart was settling in the shallows, warm, raw-smelling water gurgling over their shoes.

"Asshole," Bryon said, climbing out.

Upstream, traffic lurched in two directions over the 26 July Bridge and from under the bridge, past a bunker of cardboard shanties, came a felucca, its crew in the stern casting nets, swallow-wing sail afire with the dying light. Sevigne had no idea why he'd done it. It struck him how long it had been since he'd really laughed.

"Brothers devoured by crocodiles," he said, "during golf game on the Nile."

"Estranged brothers," Bryon said. "Now get out and give me a hand."

An hour later, showered and changed, they met the women in the swank revolving restaurant atop the Gezirah Tower, which rose from the southwest corner of the island half a mile from the clubhouse. Six hundred feet high, the tower looked like an outsized, high-tech minaret, its latticed concrete walls and ornamental spire tipped by a radio and TV mast. Everson explained casually that the new wave of fundamentalists had vowed to destroy it as a modern abomination.

The women were already at the table drinking champagne, Martine beaming, bronzed, in a strapless cream cocktail dress, grey curls cascading to freckled shoulders that struck Sevigne for the first time as vulnerably thin. Then he saw Tralee Monaghan—frazzled and pink from the clay oven of the courts, trapped in a chic black dress she must have borrowed from Martine—and he had to smile. She was twenty-three but looked sixteen, snub-nosed with freckles on the bridge, her eyes a guileless, unblinking blue. An Egyptian woman, sallow

but handsome, monumentally solid, rose to greet the men with
the air of an empress welcoming foreign dignitaries. "Yasmine
Salloum," she said. He reached to shake her hand—"My
mother has told me about you and your books," he said—and
she took his hand and tugged him to her and kissed him on
either cheek. She smelled like frankincense and bitter, dark
chocolate; somehow the bruised half-whorls under her eyes
did not make her seem exhausted but stately, seasoned, as if
they spoke of wisdom and dignity acquired through an epic
insomnia. Behind her through the slow-turning tower's tall
windows the city fanned out in unfolding panorama, Rhoda
Island to the south and the River Nile, shored with lights,
flowing in the falling dark along its ancient channel.

"We had a brilliant set!" Martine announced. "Tralee was
improving so fast."

"Except my serves kept going way out. Onto the croquet
lawn."

"Once she almost hit a prince!"

"That's nothing," Bryon said, falling into the chair next
to Tralee. He looked weary but relieved, mollified by her
presence.

"Love?"

"Compared to Sevigne on the golf course."

Everson, to his credit, was chuckling. "Our man Sev. Sev
Villeneuve. You play tennis with the girls just now, Yasmine?"

"Certainly not," she said.

"Oh," Sevigne burst out, "and we saw a sacred ibis on the
fairway!"

"Afraid they're extinct here, Sev," Everson said. "As I
mentioned in the showers." Then, to the table: "I figure it
must have been a great egret they saw, or maybe some kind
of heron."

"It was an ibis," Sevigne said. "It was! I know them from the
hieroglyphs, and the Egyptian Book of the Dead."

"You've been reading the Egyptian Book of the Dead?" Bryon said.

"According to some," Yasmine Salloum declared in her magisterial Oxbridge accent, "there are a few last specimens remaining; much like the coelacanth."

"Well, we saw one."

"So golf courses have a function after all," Bryon said wryly. "I mean as wildlife preserves."

"But groomed, watered greens in a country this short on . . ."

"It's a miracle such men can even reproduce themselves!" Martine was exclaiming at the end of the table, to Everson, in regard to something. Busboys were lighting the candles. Head to one side with a look of artless curiosity—a dreamy innocence as out of date as Yasmine Salloum's stolid dignity—Tralee sat watching Sevigne with clear blue eyes set far apart.

"My brother would rather box," Bryon said. "My brother keeps a warm place in his heart for caveman culture."

"Now, Muhammad Ali was a marvellous pugilist," Yasmine Salloum said. "And a true artist. He fought here once, at the pyramids."

"My father almost fought Ali!" Sevigne said.

"Here we go," Bryon said.

"It's true—he got robbed at the Olympic team trials!"

"Really?" Tralee said diplomatically.

"Of course Ali was Clay then," Salloum said. "Cassius Clay. A wonderful name, Cassius Clay."

"Bet it wasn't even close," Bryon said. "Dad just talked himself a big career. He always did, he was always a dreamer. You're crazy, you know that, Sevigne? You know he just purposely drove a golf cart into the river?"

"Everson just told me!" Martine called gaily from the end of the table.

"None of you would be so tickled," Bryon said, waving off

the waiter trying to fill his glass, "if it was your property people were writing off."

"Please!" Sevigne told the waiter. Bryon's refusal to drink made him want to drink hard, as if teetotalling were a kind of betrayal; as if not repeating a father's worst mistakes were a tacit denial of the man. As the tower revolved, the shuddery bass thrum of a large engine could be felt through the polished parquet floor. Eastward beyond the lights of the Old City, below a smattering of stars, the solid face of the Muqqatam Hills made an interlude of seamless dark.

". . . because the ring is so elemental," Sevigne was telling Yasmine Salloum, "in a . . . in such an artificial age."

"Of course, and as a poet one endeavours to stay as close as possible to the elementally real. Nevertheless, as a matter of paradox, good writing is highly artificial." Salloum smiled briefly, graciously, at Bryon, at Tralee. "Like golf, with its groomed greens. Like tennis. Of course art must begin with the raw heat of passion; but then such primitive energies must be submitted to the interposition of the critical will, and given form through artifice."

"You see why I've been wanting you to meet!" Martine said in a stage whisper, leaning across her friend's considerable lap to put her hand on Sevigne's wrist. Her wide eyes were heavily mascaraed, her small face at close range pursed with surprising new wrinkles. "Ah, it's Khalil!" she cried, tendering the hand to a moustachioed Egyptian in a white dinner jacket who bowed and kissed the hand unhurriedly, his upturned eyes sweeping over the party with a roguish twinkle.

"Est-ce Madame se porte bien ce soir?"

"Oui, oui, très bien!"

"Tonight's her birthday," Everson said, sprawling back in his chair with an expansive smile. The headwaiter gave Martine a look of shrewd, flirtatious scrutiny before offering his fantastically modest guesses as to which of Madame's

birthdays it might be. Martine wagged her finger at him as if
scolding a mischievous child. *Mais non, Monsieur Khalil, et
vous le savez très bien!* He leered outrageously. In the distance,
the serried concrete hives of Nasr City blazed with light, and
beyond them, giant, hellish pyres of rubbish burned in the
shanty towns of the *zabalin*. The day's sun and the champagne
had drugged Sevigne into a luxurious detachment, so for the
first time he felt himself implicated, like Gatsby, in the vast,
invincible apathy of the rich.

"Khalil is really such a doll," Martine said as the man roost-
ered off with their order. "I've always felt that men should lie
more often, but about different things."

Yasmine Salloum inclined towards Sevigne, her bruised,
heavy eyelids slowly blinking. "Your mother has told me that
you have published widely. Would you be so good as to let me
read some of your verse?"

"God, I'd love that," he said. "But I'm not sure it's ready.
I mean, I'm not really published widely. She tells me you're a
famous poet."

"I think, frankly, that it's much easier to be a famous poet
here than in your country."

"When Umm Kulthum died," Everson said, "back in '76—
it was '76 wasn't it, Yasmine?—the whole of Cairo came out to
mourn. People were trampled to death outside the embassy."

"It was in 1975. But Umm, I think, was more of a singer."

Sevigne said, "That wouldn't happen for a poet *or* a singer
back home."

"Now don't listen to Sev, Yas, he's doing very well indeed."
Everson extended his arm back of Tralee and put a hand on
Bryon's shoulder. "Imagine—Bry here's only twenty-five and
he's running his own successful business, and Sev is a published author. He'll be writing his first novel here before he
goes back to Sault Ste Marie."

"Toronto, I think."

"Now there's a city I could live in," Bryon said.

"Istanbul is so exciting, though," Tralee said. "I thought you were getting used to it?"

"I am. It's a bad sign. Toronto is like Zurich and London—people show up for their appointments. Things work."

Yasmine Salloum was carefully cutting up her greens with her knife and fork. With good humour she said, "Well, you must not have been much enamoured of living here, then. This is one of the first times I have known the revolving mechanism in the tower to work for more than an hour without fail."

Shubra Al-Khaymah appeared down the Nile towards the delta, its jewelled glitter answered from above by a tiara of autumn constellations: Andromeda, Cepheus, Cassiopeia: Triangulum like a celestial blueprint for the Great Pyramid. Tralee had picked up the candle burning between her and Sevigne and was holding it to her nose, sniffing, while amber wax dribbled onto the tablecloth. Bryon watched with what seemed to be accustomed irritation. "Bergamot and myrrh," she said, smiling at Bryon, then at Sevigne. Sevigne smiled back. The Pyramids Road, lined with nightclubs and cabarets like the main strip in Vegas, receded to the southwest where the Sphinx and pyramids, floodlit by dazzling ground spots, loomed huge even ten miles off. As a jazz combo set up on stage, a stag line of tuxedoed waiters emerged singing "Happy Birthday," led by Khalil bearing a cake bristling with spitting sparklers. It looked like a wedding cake. Martine was weepy with pleasure. When Bryon went around the table to give her a kiss, she leapt up and swept him off on a manic fox-trot straight through the line of grinning waiters, while the band, in tasselled fezzes and Guy Lombardo suits, kept picking up the tempo of "Desert Nomad" trying to catch her. Erect in her chair Yasmine Salloum clapped hands with the party, her dignity unbroken as she gave a wild shrill *zagharit*, or joy-cry, Egypt's earthy antithesis to the muezzin's numinous call.

The piece ending, Martine let Bryon go as they passed the table, a powerboat dropping a skier by a dock. He returned to his seat stroking his moustache with one finger as if to wipe away sweat or hide a smile; Sevigne was surprised by a wave of brotherly love, and déjà vu. From when? and where? It haunted and jarred him. Everson and Tralee were up and dancing close to the table, he attempting a complex jive but with Tralee trampling the toes of his oxfords and laughing it was more an Oktoberfest closing-time polka, and now Sevigne was joining his mother for another upbeat number, good old Fats Waller, "The Joint Is Jumpin'." This band is tight, this band is blowing hard. You can see how inspired they are to have people up and dancing so early in the evening, and such dancing, man, there isn't a step Martine doesn't know and love and the love is there on her face as she does them—look for scorch-marks on the parquet floor—rhumba, samba, salsa, freestyle, you can feel the fifty years scraping off her heels with every step, including the years squandered and lost, my God, Sévi, and for what! waiting for a break in that tawdry Malton townhouse. Why did she wait so long to dance free? Why does anyone? Till anyway all you can do is teach others, too old now, she says, to perform. . . .

He gave her a kiss and followed her lead as the champagne and narcotic fatigue swirled in circles around his brain and the lights of Cairo, blurred and faint-tailed as showering meteors, flickered far below. "Let's do the Sugar Foot Strut." All right. Maman was always right—flee heaviness, gravity, the cold killing depths of the Bergmanesque north, that black-and-white country of brooding abstractions; light out for the equator like Keats and Percy Bysshe and Mary Shelley and Lord Byron with their beakers full of the warm south. Oh, he knew, he'd known for years that Cairo was as much of an attraction to her as Everson was, but now in an instant—no barriers—he forgave.

Taking Tralee's hand he pulled her out on the dancefloor. They lost their footing and staggered, as if the floor of the restaurant had tilted; from beneath came a low-pitched grinding and juddering, like a tremor in the earth. The tower had ground to a stop. The jazzmen quit playing and looked around them, grinned sheepishly, shrugged—the piano player's fingers frozen over the keys as if poised for some apocalyptic chord—then jammed frenetically on. Inside Sevigne's head and body the tower's turning continued, but faster; the sunburned skin of Tralee's shoulder, where his chin grazed it by chance, seemed hot as a live coal. Then they were all at the table drinking toasts to Martine while their lamb and fig and sweet-pepper kebabs arrived and he felt the champagne tingling in his very veins.

You did right to come.

Across the vast starfield of lights, the upper dome of the Muhammad Ali Mosque glowed blue as a full moon on the rise, and beyond it, to the south and east, sparsely lit as some remote, older galaxy, dimly receded the Cities of the Dead.

Martine

In candlelight your face is still your own face, not that counterfeit encrustation that the years apply, by slow degrees: the make-up of mortality. Sometimes in harsh light and insolent mirrors your eyes peer out with a trapped, baffled look, the gaze of someone left stunned and humiliated in a circle of laughing onlookers, after the sort of practical joke that disabuses you of all illusions about the world's intentions.

They had returned from the Tower after midnight and Everson had fallen into bed and slumber with his usual facility, while an hour later Martine still sat at her dressing table in front of the mirror, candle burning. Reflected above her naked shoulder was Everson, asleep, the moon through the skylight bathing their king-sized bed and his sheeted body in silver light. As always he lay in state, rigidly supine; now and then his closed eyelids would twitch as if sensitive to the moonlight. He whimpered once and his head rolled on the pillow. He claimed never to remember his dreams; with feigned interest he would listen when she related her own dreams, which were many and all congregating loosely but conspicuously around the theme of time—its accelerating passage, its fleshly debits—and erotic love with its slow withdrawal into the past. Everson, who knew nothing if not his cues, would assure her that with time she grew ever more desirable and moreover had the legs of a woman half her age; and he would twitch his bushy eyebrows in silly, sexless innuendo. Anyway she knew about her legs and wasn't the point of flattery to be *dis*honest, not simply to state the known?

There were some dreams she kept to herself. She was in the enclosed garden under Sevigne's window and her first lover, a slim student with tiny glasses, prematurely greying hair and a shy yet somehow conquering smile, was bent down drinking from the fountain. He had been a student of politics at the Sorbonne, a scarf-and-espresso Marxist from Austria, and now when he stood up and spoke it was in his own tongue, yet she understood him perfectly. He told her that he had been dead for years and had been searching for her ever since leaving the earth. He was sorry for his fear of her love when they met, he should never have pulled away from her, breaking her heart. His glasses were wet from the fountain, hiding his eyes. They embraced, abruptly naked, but before she could guide him into her yearning body there was shouting from the street, a sound like firecrackers going off, sirens, and he backed away . . .

Constant dreams of unconsummation, but Nadir was real. Nadir, her "young lover"—though thirty-eight had once struck her as decidedly old, and besides that he looked older than his age. Marriage did give you exclusive rights to your spouse's body, she believed that and would have been crushed had Everson ever mustered the energy for infidelity. But over time a married person could forfeit those exclusive rights by failing to exercise them. Was she to live like someone's forgotten aunt, a homely cook in a convent, during the few years remaining to her when men might still approach? Life without physical love was unthinkable, yet of late Everson seemed not to think of it at all. Of late! It had been years. He was turning into an old man years too soon, his body now covered with grey hair, like a sort of moss, as Sam's had been. Sam, who since his death had also been paying her visits in dreams. . . . By ten o'clock every night Everson was in his pyjamas, not fighting off sleep as one might expect at such an hour but welcoming it, taking it into his arms like an irresistible mistress. Leaving her, his wife, to toss in the moonlight.

Moody Nadir in one of his gallant, emphatic moments, so rare these days, had declared that he wanted to make love to her on her fiftieth birthday, but with Sévi flying in, and Bryon and Tralee already arrived, there had been no occasion for a meeting. Though perhaps they might have arranged something for the morning? Yes, there had been some time, not much, but a small window (to use Everson's new favourite term) when they might have met at her academy, no classes then, and made love as before on an exercise mat beside the mirrored wall with only the red glow of the exit sign for candlelight, though it was a colder, deader light, and a reminder that one or the other would be exiting within the hour. And it struck her that in the early days of the affair—just fourteen months before—they would have arranged it. An American friend had once told her that affairs turned into marriages too. There was always a turning point. Perhaps he'd found a younger woman, or suffered an attack of renewed affection for his wife? In May when Martine had said, half joking, that she wanted him to make love to her at night under the stars on top of the Great Pyramid, his face had contorted in a bitter smile and he'd said that only a Western woman could suggest something so preposterous and vulgar. Furious, she'd lashed out at him and he'd raised his hands, palms out, laughing, and promised to take her somewhere truly private, a place on the edge of the desert where she would see more stars than ever in her life.

They drove south out of Cairo through the valley of the Nile and past El Ma'adi, and some miles farther he turned east onto a side track, not a road at all, and much rougher, he said, than he recalled. She was excited and slightly afraid. In bed Nadir was passionate and could also be tender, but at other times he was coldly formal, with periodic fits of pique; usually his English was fluent, yet on occasion it become garbled and impenetrably strange. As they drove up the rough track, she realized that almost nothing he might do now would surprise her. Perhaps that was the turning point? He stopped the car and turned out the headlights and instructed her to follow. The air outside was cold. The moon had not yet risen but the stars—more than she had ever seen in her life, as promised—gave actual light. She took his hand. A jagged absence of stars along the horizon showed their destination: a circle of trees and the huddled ruins of mud houses.

When Nadir was a child, he said, his father had used to bring him out here on holidays in the sidecar of his motorcycle. The village had been abandoned in the twenties when the spring began to dry up, but enough of a flow had remained to keep a handful of date palms and tamarisks alive. As a child Nadir had played among the ruins while his father, weary engineer, had rested in the shade of the trees, smoking and reading the papers, napping, or simply staring at the sky.

Now the moon came up over the desert to illumine the remains of the village and the skeletons of the dead palms and tamarisks. For in the past four years, since the last time Nadir had visited the oasis (she didn't ask what for), the spring had vanished altogether and the vegetation had died. The bed of the spring was a circle of dry mud wrinkled with deep cracks. Nadir seemed stern, angry, as if with her, as if she were somehow responsible for this state of affairs. Possibly he blamed "the West"—some local mining or water-diversion project, who could say? He blamed the West for so very much. She had had enough of it.

Was that the turning point, then—or was it the manner in which they made love? They'd gone ahead despite the mood of mutual disappointment, almost desolation, as if they were being given a sign as obvious as in her dreams of interrupted love; a sign they must contradict by means of a passion they did not feel. He fucked her with a kind of surly negligence, in the open under a voyeuristically attentive moon, and she kept sighing and talking to him, as she always did, waiting for the warmth to flood into his face and soften his eyes, as it always did. But it never came. That was the turning point. He stood brusquely and zipped himself up as if he had just had a piss, then stalked away and stood by the dead spring voraciously smoking. When he turned away, hiding the small red ember at the tip of his cigarette, she dressed quickly, shivering with the cold, and hurried back to the car to wait for him.

They had met again since then, but not often.

She rose on sore knees, blew out the night's last candle and walked to the bed heavy with a post-soirée sadness, her mind reverberant with voices and fragments of song and conversation. She crawled slowly onto Everson, straddling him, the sheet and his silly monogrammed silk pyjamas between them, and she seemed to feel a faint warmth on her back as she entered that frame of moonlight. He stirred under her weight but continued sleeping. She kissed his parted lips; the Veuve Cliquot had turned sour on his breath. She had an urge to seize him by his thin hair and shake him, to yell at him *Wake up, for God's sake, wake yourself!* and if he did wake up and look in the mirror across the room he would see her long back and buttocks and splayed thighs blue in the moonlight, straddling him. Yet he slept on as if she weighed nothing, were nothing, a spectre, as if they had forever, as if they were no longer in love. How had it happened, by what insidious instalments? To think that their illicit passion potent enough to shatter hearts and families could degenerate to this: this futile squirming, this wrestling with the dead, these soured, snoring breaths, and two bodies turning to stone under a shroud of moonlight.

A dying man, long since divorced, embarks with his son on a river cruise to the Valley of the Kings, Elephantine Island, Lake Nubia and Khartoum. Both know the next few weeks together will be their last. Prior to agreeing to make the trip, the two men have been estranged for six years, since the time the son fell in love with the wife of his wealthy older brother, and eloped with her. The father—a veteran of the lake boats and the Korean War now calcified into an inflexible moralist much given to stern verdicts, irreversible decisions—has had nothing to do with the new couple. The younger son and his lover are still racked with guilt, the older son with anger.

Diagnosed with terminal liver cancer, the father resolves to see his family reconciled before he dies. He asks both sons to join him on the cruise—a trip he has always wanted and planned to take, and which will force him and the boys to spend time together in close quarters, talking. The younger son, a musician, eagerly accepts; the older brother bitterly rejects the invitation, outraged that his father has forgiven the younger son and now wants him to forgive as well. With regret, but determined to go through with a journey he has dreamed of for so long, the father flies to Cairo with the younger son and they embark for the southern deserts, where they will have a chance to say those final, fundamental things so many parents and children leave unsaid.

In the course of a journey that will take them a good part of the way to the headwaters of the Nile at Lake Victoria, they talk and argue about the past and move back in time to the sources of the family's pain and conflict. Meanwhile the cruiseship bears them slowly south with stops at ruined cities, Pharaonic tombs, the sites of forgotten battles and the sad antiquities of vanished peoples. This parallel exploration and mapping of two arid landscapes turns up evidence over which the men heatedly argue, though the father is losing strength as they move deeper into the desert of their past with its sporadic but beautiful oases. Love, the father has come to believe, is the only true oasis, unlike competitive success and hoarded security, which turn out to be mirages, providing no real shade or sustenance; love is the underground force that here and there drives springs to the surface of life's quotidian waste—and so the son's mother and the woman whom he and his brother have both loved loom ever larger as characters despite their absence.

As the end of the journey nears, the narrative is quickened by the sense that time is running out, the father weakening. And now the key part of the story is told: in what circumstances the son and his brother's wife first fell in love, and how the father reacted with special disgust because—he now reveals—his own wife, the boys' mother, had left him for his best friend, not for a stranger as he told the boys when it happened years before.

The father's condition suddenly worsens and the ship's doctor insists he be disembarked for treatment at the field hospital of a Sudanese army base, on an island in Lake Nubia; he will be flown back to Cairo as soon as a helicopter becomes available. The son calls his brother in New York to warn him their father may die at any time and to urge him to fly in and meet them. It is the first time they have spoken together in six years. . . .

Sevigne took a seat in a café set up in the courtyard of a tomb in the Eastern City of the Dead. A large, drooping, soot-stained piece of canvas served as a roof. It was early March and early morning and a breeze out of the north had somehow found its way into that smelly, breathless labyrinth of streets, so the air had a bracing coolness as you drew it deep into you. In his four months in Cairo he'd drafted a half-dozen stories along with scores of poems combining archaic cadences inspired by Egypt's antiquities with the modern lingo of the metropolis: *Who sailed from Sidon, quinquiremes laden / with imperial sarcophagi, now / hearsed in a rusted Caddy, battery / dead and towed by asses . . .*

But over the winter he'd been pouring out the first draft of a novel he'd conceived in the fall, just after his arrival. Kept awake by thoughts of Tralee, who was in bed with Bryon in the next room, it had struck him that guilty fantasy was not the sole alternative to harmful reality. There was also fiction. A story had begun growing. By the time Tralee and Bryon had flown out, two days later, he was scribbling notes; today, with the last page in sight, he would complete the first draft. Unsuperstitious except with his writing, he'd returned for the final flurry of pages to this sepulchral café, where he'd written the first chapter in December, on that day sitting so long that by afternoon he was chilled and shivering despite the brazier fuming beside him and the warm fug of tobacco and hash smoke and the desert sun glowing through the canvas overhead.

He was not yet sure how the story would end, so for him the day held something of the reader's suspense and excitement as the final page nears. His need to discover the story in the telling would drive him to write with impatient, unselfconscious energy and haste, as he felt he had to write at first, before the slow meticulous grind of revision. Writing by hand in a kind of manic trance, at times not far off rapture and other times in panic, exhaustion, believing it all doomed, he pushed on extempore and by means of sheer momentum got something down. He didn't look back. He wrote the way the locals drove their small, smoggy cars, even through the streets of the Cities of the Dead—fast, straight ahead despite obstacles, in the wrong lane more often than not, and no looking in the mirror.

"Coffee," Sevigne said decisively. The proprietor set water to boil on a camp stove and switched on the television atop the humming, trembling refrigerator. There was the hoarse voice of a *muqri* reciting verses from the Koran, but the screen showed only static. The proprietor, with a trimmed Nasser moustache, flip-flops on his feet and a down vest over his dark *galabeyya*, calmly smashed the side of the set three times with a cricket bat. A grim visage appeared on the screen, mouth moving but mute. On the far side of the lambent brazier two men leaned together over steaming glasses of tea and a *tawlah* board.

The son sits with his unconscious father in a small white room under a ceiling fan reading or talking to him or softly singing his favourite songs. He eats with the medical staff and goes for short walks on the gibbous beach on the north side of the island, or explores the ruins of an ancient Egyptian outpost that once marked the frontier of the pharaohs' realm. There has been some kind of military presence here for millennia; and since his father was a soldier throughout his twenties, and with time turned himself into an island fortress through his refusal to forgive, his steady retreat into ancient grudges, his inner refighting of old, lost wars, the island base comes to figure in the son's mind as a model of his father's soul—or is it a model of what men in general turn into as they age? Shadow boxers. Certainly he and his brother seem headed the same way . . .

The noon *adhan* was sounding. The proprietor kept trying to clear away the four empty thimble-cups on the table but Sevigne liked to keep them lined up there, markers for the hours. He ordered an onion roll, sliced tomato, two hard-boiled eggs and a huge serving of pistachio baklava oozing with rosewater syrup and he wolfed it all down, hardly tasting. Soaring on caffeine and adrenalin he scribbled on, still picking up speed. The sun bore down on him through the canvas. In the street two snarling pariah dogs fought over a fish head. To keep his nerve-ends from shorting out altogether, he switched to mint tea.

The older brother arrives on the island, having chartered a small jet in Khartoum. The father, still unconscious, is to be flown out to Cairo the next day. After a night's silent vigil the brothers leave their father with a nurse and walk down to the beach at sunrise and share a cigarette, then begin to talk, but the mood of conciliation soon dissolves and they argue, the exhausted older brother accusing the younger of having destroyed what remained of the family through lust and his greed to have all the love for himself. When the younger brother, unwilling to hear more, finally turns and starts away, the elder in a rage plucks a fist-sized stone off the beach and strikes him down.

Sevigne looked up, shook his head. Not a stone. There had to be a weapon of some kind, the blow must echo back-wards through "Goodbye, My Brother" and the *Inferno* to Cain and Abel—a terracing of primordial, fraternal violence—but not a stone. Some other weapon. To make it new, modern.

The café was filling with boisterous young men in bell-bottom slacks, turtlenecks or old collared shirts, light jackets. The proprietor—now with a swallowtail coat over his *galabeyya*—brought braces of bottled Pepsi and Sprite and Orange Crush and, for a few of the men, Stella beer. All of the young men smoked. The proprietor's coattails shimmied as he stood on tiptoe clouting the TV set until the sound cut out and a picture came. The Egyptian flag filled the screen, then another flag, some tricolour impossible to identify because of the colour problems. A soccer field, mauve. The Egyptians versus the Dutch? The Irish? Some of the young men were glancing at Sevigne. He smiled, nodded, picked up his third cheap ballpoint of the day.

An old bottle, an empty left by a soldier on the beach. *Enraged by his brother's turning away, David clutched the bottle by its neck and swung it, pulling back at the last instant but connecting. There was a thunk and Luc collapsed to his knees and then turned in shock to look up at his brother still holding the cracked bottle. Luc's hand came away from the back of his head covered in blood. David stared down at him for a moment and then dropped the bottle in the sand and hurried off towards the hospital.* When the older brother gets back to the room he finds that the evacuation has begun, early, a helicopter will arrive in the next twenty minutes. The medics and nurses, wheeling the father out, say that they've been looking for the brothers. The father has regained consciousness in the bustle of transition and his son leans over the gurney speaking with him as they move outside.

But Dave . . . where's your brother?

Down on the beach. You know Luc. But he'll be here soon.

The young men were roaring, standing and embracing each other, exchanging kisses, as were the Egyptian players on the soundless screen. The air of the café was full of smoke and the light had faded. A sound of bells and gentle bleating as a herd of goats, framed by the tomb door, passed skittering in the street before their drover.

The younger son's brooding reverie on the beach—where he admits he has done wrong but would repeat every mistake, for Mera—is broken by the sound of a helicopter approaching from the north. He runs back to the hospital room and finds his father gone; a medic, standing by the bed writing on a clipboard, tells him to go at once to the helicopter pad across the compound, they have only just taken him, but the helicopter will not wait. *We were wondering where to find you. Your brother says you are down by the shore. Your father is waking again. Oh, are you injured?*

A collective groan of disbelief and dejection and on the screen a group of pale, light-haired men coalesced in an ecstatic scrum . . .

Still dizzy, blood drying in his hair, the brother runs across the compound towards the helicopter now lifting off the pad in the light of the rising sun; runs like a wounded soldier in danger of being left behind enemy lines in the haste of evacuation. Too late. The older brother is there at the edge of the pad, squinting upward, hair tossing in the furious propwash as the chopper lifts off. There is no room aboard for the brothers. Because of the noise they are unable to speak. They watch the camouflaged craft touched by sunlight recede in a blue abyss of desert sky until it winks out of sight, the way the morning star—last light in an eye exhausted by its vigil—blinks out at dawn.

Another detonation of joy and this time as the young men sprang to their feet one of the tables tipped over and several bottles exploded. Even the funereal proprietor was happy, a wide grin spreading under his moustache. The celebrations went on for some time. In a fog, half disbelieving after months of struggle, Sevigne skipped to the base of the page, leaving the lower half blank, and neatly printed THE END. (In fact he was still uncertain if the brothers should finally embrace or come to blows, but he could wait for that last detail to arrive.) Now his eyes teared up, not just with sadness—the layered sadness of a fictional death and its actual basis—but with relief. He let his head sink onto his folded hands amid smells of his own sweat and the acrid coffee-scent of his confined breath. Something pressed on his arm. Lifting his head he saw through blurred eyes one of the young Egyptians standing by the table, two of his friends and the proprietor watching to one side.

"We hope that you are not too decomposed that your country is defeated," he said gently. "They have played extremely very well. You may be proud."

The proprietor was making some kind of offer in a vehement tone.

"I'm sorry?" Sevigne said. "*Nahm?*"

"Would you take a beer?" the young man said. "The owner would be so kind if you would take a beer."

2

Queen Augusta

AN HOUR'S DRIVE short of the city, Highway 10 descends out of the Caledon Hills into the plain of the Great Lakes lowlands, and from the brow of the escarpment on a cloudless day you see Toronto and its tapering satellites ranged in a sixty-mile-wide strip along Lake Ontario. After dark, the dense galactic band of the lights seems a magnified reflection of the Milky Way—a mirage afloat on the blue-black waters of the lake. And at the heart of the mirage the CN Tower and the skyscrapers form a spiring cluster aglitter with the promise of any big city seen from afar.

From the cab of the pick-up truck that stopped for him at dusk—April Fool's Day, 1992—Sevigne gapes at the now remembered prospect. The big-boned woman at the wheel, fortyish, in baseball cap and buckskin jacket, grins as she sips her coffee.

"It's just a city, guy. You see this all the time coming down for the games."

Around them the fields form a dark ambit of raw loam, snow in the furrows lingering in long, ghostly striations like whitecaps in black water. Nights at sea the *Nanaimo* must have cruised in over rough waters to foreign ports lit up this way: Honolulu, Yokohama, San Francisco, Hong Kong.

"You ought to come along see the game," the woman says. "You ever been to a Leafs game?"

"My father took me and my brother once. A long time ago. God, it must be sixteen years now!"

"Ha. The Sittler era. Those were good times, eh."

"My father was a real fan."

They come down through the snowline into valleys where the air is milder, damper, mist heavy in the hollows; they pass through hamlets of stalwart Victorian houses, ramifying suburbs, flat-roofed defoliated industrial parks along the vast fen of the airport, where tail-lights taxi and rise through the fog like red will-o'-the-wisps. Their vision of the city's full extent falls far behind, but he'll remember it over the year to come and see it again most clearly in his mind's eye when reading of how Jude Fawley first glimpses, from a country road, the shining spires of Oxford.

The woman lets him off at a thronged intersection and drives on to the game, honking once, "Lovin' in Vain" twanging from her open window to mix with the quadraphonic cacophony of a downtown Saturday night. In the pick-up's flatbed as it roars away, a fugitive cargo of clean, north-country snow.

Sevigne stands on the windy corner of Yonge and Dundas peering up at the glass-and-steel tower of the Eaton Centre. He grips the straps of his duffel bag at chest level as if holding an old hat in his hands—a farmboy down to the city to plead Papa's case with the bankers. Two burly men, trenchcoats flapping open over their suits, veer around him on the sidewalk. One casts him a look of entitled irritation. Windblown cups and scraps of crumpled newspaper scurry past.

He's been absent from big North American cities for some time; his long hair seems out of style. Everyone his age has shaved heads, brush cuts, mid-length hair. Gangs of teenagers slouch around him wearing ragged layers of black on black and black hoods over gaunt, pallid faces. Once from amid the layers the bare navel of a girl winks out at him and makes him ache deep down. Decisive professionals hustle past, men, women, faces pinched and blanched by the wind, even the black faces ashen with cold and the Asians sallow—so many more of them now than in the seventies, he feels he's arriving in a city he has never known. Despite the cold everything is moving with feverish animation. Looking up he would not be surprised to see clouds scudding among the towers with hallucinatory speed, as in a time-lapse film.

A walk signal flashes and he starts across Dundas.

"Sorry," he says.

Jostling people with his bag.

"Sorry. Pardon me!"

Grimly hurrying strangers. For a moment in the crush he catches a glimpse of a hollow-eyed woman in arsenic make-up with a zipper-row of safety pins down the middle of her throat and a zombie's blank stare, as if she'd been opened up and stitched back together in some ghastly basement lab. Her eyes find his and lock onto them. He looks away. Across the street, searching for a pay phone, he passes a spindly man with smack-veined forearms hacking away at a drum kit. *You can't take it with you*, he hears—gruff, faint words seeming to emanate from the pavement or a sewer grate. He looks down. A snaggle-toothed woman in a soiled parka squats against a hydrant, holding out a popcorn box. "You can't take it with you," she repeats in a penetrating whisper, eyes squinted, maybe closed, but probably, he senses, not quite. She nods, smiles sagely. He drops a coin in the jingling box.

A pair of phone booths appears through the crowd. Just short of them he ducks past a shaggy rubicund giant perched on a small amplifier, microphone in hand, raving. His hair and scraggly brows and moustacheless beard are all bleached and unruly, as if the badly distorting amp had electrocuted him. Catching Sevigne's eye he begins hectoring him on the coming apocalypse and the new millennium. Sodomy and Gomorrah are the diseases of the age, AIDS truly stands for And I

Doom Sinners, all scaly sinners will feel the flaming finger of the Lord and the very streets and sidewalks that Sevigne treads upon will soon cleave and devour him as they did the ancient Israelis and their idle calves. . . . Sevigne squeezes into a glass booth with his huge duffel bag and digs in it for the letter of sympathy that Michael "Eddy" Korkola sent him last autumn. He dials Eddy's number while a siren caterwauls closer and closer, deafening him as it passes, the notes dropping a half-octave as if in sudden sorrow or fatigue.

"Hey there! You've reached 522-8134. If it's about the new mag, press star."

"For when God spake to Moses out of the pillar of salt, these words uttereth he . . ."

"If it's for me, I'm all tied up at the moment, but if you just leave your name and calling card number and the time you called . . ."

"All fornication must hath its price and the Bible sayeth 'Dry and without moisture shall be the fruit of thy . . .'"

Screeching feedback flares up and stops the voice dead. Sevigne cringes and covers his ear.

". . . and we'll see what happens. Hey, just kidding! Wait for the beep!"

Sevigne mumbles something flustered, trying to finish before the evangelist resumes. His own dim reflection, mouth working in shadow, frowns at him out of the glass; a block down Yonge Street a large skull-like mask gapes beside a neon sign, PANTAGES.

"So anyway, Eddy, I'll, um, I'll just leave and, call and leave a number when I uh, if I . . ."

"For behold Babylon is the horse who sitteth on many waters."

A hulking ghetto blaster with body and legs scuffs past humping out rap, "Re*spect* yourself and show your *self* re*spect*." Sevigne's voice falters. There's a click on the line.

"Sev? Sevigne? Is that you? Man, that's got to be the one

and only." The voice is breathless and rapid-fire yet somehow composed, in control, like a virtuoso on antic ragtime piano.

"Eddy?"

"Sev! Sevigne the machine!"

"Eddy? I thought you weren't—"

"Yeah, right, sorry. Let me turn this thing off. Just buried these days."

"What?"

"So how are you, dude? *Where* are you?"

"I'm on Yonge Street. Just off Dundas."

"You're here! That's excellent. You got my letter?"

"Yes, it came when I was—"

"Sev? Hang on a sec, got another call coming in. I'll just get rid of it, OK? Could be important. Be right back."

Another click and a recording kicks in midway through its loop: Eddy's coked-up voice gone FM, low and cool, talking about the city's newest literary mag and giving info for subscribers while a Muzak cover of "What's New, Pussycat" plays. Down Yonge Street, beneath the noseless mask, an elegant queue flows under a marquee into the theatre. PHANTOM.

"—Sevigne? Sorry about that. More magazine stuff. Things are really heating up. We haven't even named the thing yet and it's heating up. Hey, you can help us brainstorm a name! I'm on my way out the door now. You'd love some of the people I'm going to meet. Especially Una."

He rhymes off the name of a club and vague directions as if Sevigne must know the city by heart. It's too noisy to ask him to elaborate, and anyway Sevigne—prey to a temporary deafness whenever somebody gives instructions—wouldn't have absorbed them.

He approaches a fat, wry-faced bum in a pea jacket, red nose knurled with grog-blossoms, sitting Buddha-like in the alcove of a cash machine.

"I'm looking for Queen and Augusta, sir," Sevigne says,

putting a quarter in the man's ragged toque. "Would you happen to know . . ."

"Queen Augusta?" The man leers and spits. "Well ain't we all, son, ain't we all and join the fraternity amen. Why, you're a sunburned son of a bitch, ain't you? Where you been for that?"

"Cairo," Sevigne says. "But I'm from the Soo."

"No kidding! The Soo? So am I! Looks like you're doing a hell of a lot better down here than me."

Sevigne looks down at the pavement, the toes of his boots that he swabbed with dubbin before leaving the camp at daybreak. "Where are you from back home?" Sevigne says.

"Been years now. Lost count. At least winter don't lean so hard on you down here. By God, you're a sunburned son of a bitch! Where you been, down south for that?"

"Uh, Cairo. Egypt."

The man belches and stares up at him, unimpressed.

"There's your street right there," he says. "Bear right. It's dead easy. You'll find your Queen Augusta a few blocks on." And he tips the skimpy contents of his toque into his hand and starts counting.

Still no sign of the strip of nightclubs Eddy described. Against the lights he dekes across a six-lane avenue walled in by office buildings whose blockish façades amplify the traffic till it seems a motorcade of tractor-trailers must be bearing down on him. He rushes on, checking his watch. In front of a used clothing store a signboard is planted in his path:

SUPPLYING YOU WITH CAMP, KITSCH & IRONY
SINCE 1989 . . . CAUSE YOU NEED IT!

For a moment he stands staring blankly, as if the sign

displays runes or petroglyphs. Around him the crowds are thickening, younger now, surging cliques of them, tribally exuberant and territorial. In Cairo, where he knew he was an outsider, being excluded was part of the appeal; here he's supposed to belong. *Have You Seen This Child?* The lamp-posts and hydro poles all bear the same poster, some of their edges tattered and flapping like prayer flags in the wind.

Down a cross-street the CN Tower looms over the lower skyline, an immense secular minaret with warning lights blinking red, white, red, on a backdrop of scudding, sulphur-lit clouds. Two-second intervals. He's lost, and late. "Pages," the sign reads, and there's a tautening in his chest and his belly but he goes in. At the counter, behind a rampart of books on sale, a cashier in black lipstick perches on a high stool, chewing gum, her head back in an attitude of haughty ennui; or so it seems. One long leg is crossed over the other and her bare arms are folded under her breasts. He passes her with a shifty feeling, as if skulking past a customs post.

He's been hoping the few poems and stories that preceded him here and debuted in the glittering journals of the city will have served as letters of introduction, as vouchers of authenticity, so in literary salons his name will be known—known vaguely, perhaps, but known. But there are so many magazines (he's browsing now, his hands unsteady), so many other young writers. Again he's lost in a crowd. In the convex kleptomirror above the racks his face shows flushed and furtive, warped to homeliness, the nose swollen as after a fight. The cashier is watching him. Behind a stack of *Guise*—a magazine that has rejected him three times—he finds a lone copy of *Toronto Poetry Review*; he was expecting to find dozens. It's a newer issue, not the one he was in. There's a copy of *Re/sound* as well, but they've only just accepted his work and sure enough his story isn't there; but at the back of it, among the brief reviews, there is a piece by Michael B. Korkola.

He hurries out past the daunting cashier, although he meant to ask directions to the club. He passes bars, boutiques, bistros, cafés full of animated drinkers—a dazzling pair at a lantern-lit table clinking glasses, faces aglow, toasting the moment or some other success—and then across the street a couple embracing under banks of spotlights with large cameras and a film crew in attendance, bored cops, gathered bystanders. . . .

He's in a block of closed-up antique shops, textile stores, seedy take-outs; no more clubs. He's muttering about the bad directions—every rushed stride might be taking him farther from his goal—then there it is in front of him, finally, Augusta. He looks around in relief and expectation, but still there's no sign of the club. I mean, come on, Eddy. I mean where the *fuck*.

"Hey, Sev, Sevigne, what took you? Man, you look out of it!" He has blindsided Sevigne and now wraps him in a hug that somehow feels both ironic and genuine. There's a warm glow at Sevigne's ear—Eddy's cigarette. "Forgot the place doesn't have a sign, Sev. Everybody here just knows it. Man, you haven't changed a bit! Looks like you haven't even changed your clothes!" He's even taller than in high school and his hair is darker, shorter, swept back James Dean style so that his sharp bony features thrust out with a strong sense of forward momentum and energy. The tiny spectacles have been replaced with black horn-rims. His thin, crimson lips are the same, the big bobbing Adam's apple, baggy suit coat, huge wingtips splayed out when he walks.

He leads Sevigne into a high-ceilinged ballroom, dark scarlet and mahogany with large quattrocento-like tapestries, wrought-iron candelabra flickering and old landscapes fussily framed, like the wing of a vast gallery of Renaissance art; or a film set of one. At the back, people sit drinking at a long bar and three dancers—downturned faces sullen, self-absorbed—

move slowly, separately under mounted speakers. "Fuck it," he says, "more acid jazz. Have to have a word with Soraya." He drapes an arm over Sevigne's shoulder and steers him towards the bar. It's totally on him, he announces—the anonymous new mag will pay.

Not wanting to seem provincial, Sevigne orders a bourbon, neat.

"Straight up, you mean?" the bartender says. He's brush-cut, burly, his smirk framed by a black goatee.

"It's Soo talk," Eddy says, handing him a twenty. "Just a deuce back, Clay."

"Hang on, Eddy, that's just for mine?"

With his fingertips the smirking barman pushes the drink and change over the faux-marble bar. The werewolf hairiness of his hand and wrist where it meets the white cuff of his shirt makes a troubling contrast. Sevigne is seeing everything with hyperacute lucidity, as if high.

"Clay's not about to serve you white trash, Sev. And it's a double." Eddy nods tensely at the TV above the bar. "So?"

"Leafs are up two-zip," Clay says. "Wendell just bagged one."

"Excellent."

Sevigne looks from Eddy's face to the TV screen and back. In high school Eddy deemed all televised sports an unconscionable waste of time—scum-culture.

"Let's go, dude. We've got a table downstairs."

It's a pool table, apparently. In the smoky low-ceilinged basement are six burgundy-felt tables ringed with players, but Sevigne, descending the stairway, knows instantly which is theirs. Four players surround it—two men and a woman, standing with cues, watching a younger, black-haired woman in a low-cut dress stooped over the side-cushion taking aim. Her cleft breasts are bunched on the felt. Sevigne's grip on the handrail tightens. Whorls of tobacco smoke are marbling the cone of light from the lamp slung over the table and beyond it a portrait in brooding umbers hangs on the wall. Machiavelli, or some Medici. The woman's skewed, bouncing shot misses every ball on the table and she straightens and backs away laughing.

"Oh, I think we'll have to change the rules!"

"Air ball," says the man beside her. Black boots, black jeans, black T-shirt hanging off him, a week's worth of black stubble and a black bandana wrapped pirate-style around his head. The only white on him besides his drained face is the lettering on his T-shirt: NIKE *air*.

Eddy bills Sevigne as the Good Soomaritan. "And *this*"— with a droll flourish he indicates the young woman—"is the man of the hour, Una Sutherland. We launched her first book of poems this afternoon."

"We?" Una cries, cheerfully incensed. "*We* launched my book? What did you have to do with it, Michael B. Korkola?" She plumps down in a red velvet chair by a side table covered with bottles and jammed ashtrays and a half-eaten plate of something—nacho chips?—then sits with bare knees sprad-dled, both hands high on the cue, planting it like a rifle on the floor between her army boots. It's the poolhall tough-guy pose Sevigne used to see in the Algoma on the few occasions he went to play there with his father. Though it's barely spring she wears a floral summer dress; that hardy Highland blood, he supposes. Yet she doesn't look Upper Canada Scots. She's darker, with deep-set, coffee-coloured eyes and arched black brows and carved, flaring nostrils. The way she throws her head back when she laughs, her champing breathless patter and facial theatrics and each motion of her compact body all seem part of a semaphore of precocious success.

"Sevigne?" Eddy has his arm around the pirate. "Sevigne, meet the notorious Speed."

"Pleased to meet you," Sevigne says. "It's *Speed*?"

"As in velocity, yeah."

"And this is Dina—Dr Dina Brasov. Supervised my MA thesis back when."

Sighting down her cue with shrewd eyes magnified by cat's-eye glasses, she smiles with pinched lips and pockets a solid.

"And Ray Dennison, lest we forget. One of this country's very finest men of lit."

"Rhyming couplets now, is it, Mike?" says Ray.

"Maybe I'll do the bio-notes that way. In the mag anonymous."

"Not mine, mate."

The accent is faded East London, voice thin and raspy, like Eddy trying to do a cockney Mafioso. He's big-shouldered in a biker's jacket, older, maybe forty, with a combative squint and a widow's peak of dark thinning hair cropped short. Long sideburns. Big head lowered like a boxer he peers from under sardonically creased brows. As always when Sevigne sees a man exuding danger he begins sizing him up, as if for a fight; while another part of him wants to defuse and comfort and befriend.

"Your shot, Speed!" Una calls from a side table, heaping a nacho chip with parings of hot pepper.

Speed scowls, hits the cue ball too hard and muffs an easy shot, the striped blue rattling around the pocket but staying out.

"Rejected," he says. "Yessiree."

Una narrows her eyes at him. There's a laden silence. Eddy pushes Sevigne towards the side table and the food, saying, "Go on, dude, get something hot into you, looks like you haven't eaten in weeks."

It's Dante Alighieri, the man in the painting. As Sevigne sits across from Una she smiles, a bit wearily, then says with force, "These are ridiculous teams anyway. Here, take the cue, you play with Speed."

He nods, takes the cue, and to keep from ogling her he

addresses himself to the nachos—something he has never eaten—trying to detach a chip from the glutinous remains.

Pool is the game to help you forget. Pool is like watching the planets dance, on the emerald or indigo baize of the sky. Off the Big Bang of the break the balls crystallize into unrepeatable constellations, or archipelagos—smooth stones in a raked, rectangular Zen garden—while the soft clack of ball on ball and the hushed rolling of ball over baize make a muted music of the spheres. At college whenever the shadow-rap of words in his head got too agitating, he would go to the student union building or to a taproom downtown and shoot pool for an hour, alone. Coupled with beer, the game's meditative silence and the wordless calculation of angles were a welcome sedative. Times like that he began to grasp the attraction of calculus and theoretical astronomy and quantum physics and the other abstract fields his heart usually recoiled from; they meant freedom from the pathless jungle of language and from the slow rot of becoming—from life in all its chaotic flux and bustle, niggling or urgent details, scams and shamings, sucker-punch surprises. The inorganic beauty of theorems does have a draw when you've felt familial order slip into chaos, and, later, seen death—seen it there on the red banks of the river, a pale caul over a beloved, hated face. Now the boxing glove tattoo on the ankle and the meaty swimmer's arms count for nothing; a newborn baby has more strength than this hundred-and-ninety pound hulk of extinguished tissue. *No fights me taught the death to quell.* Anon, Dad. *Three points, boy. Tough one there.* And maybe it was your own fault after all—for wanting to leave, for craving your freedom, and he knew it? But they tell you no. You kneel beside him on the beach weeping and holding the cold hand clawing out from under the sheet, as if to lend some final warmth, while the cops and paramedics look away, cough into their fists, confer in subdued tones. Before surgery they pour ice water on a heart to stop it: red island in a freezing sea.

Pool's the game. Poker is too much like life with its bluffs and gambles and wild cards and bum deals. Boxing is no pure science. Golf courses are booby-trapped with gopher holes, loose deer, freak thermals, lightning. But pool—pure physics. Reckon right and you can't fail.

He buries another stripe ball in the corner pocket. He's on his fifth game. "Hey, nice going, Fats." Eddy hands him another glass and recites another exotic brand name—it's Scotch now. Another double. Down the hatch. The bravura of his play and his boozing might help cancel this stubborn sense of dislocation; sighting along the cue he shoots harder than he meant, omitting the back-spin and sewering the cue ball after sinking the called stripe.

Talisker.

". . . half Syrian," Una is telling him. "On my mother's side."

"So you're a poet?" Dina Brasov's accent is unplaceable, her tone dry, detached. Through her cat's-eye glasses she appraises him with amused, unsmiling eyes. "You look like a poet to me."

"That's just careful image management," Eddy says.

Ray, now running the table with clipped explosive shots, casts a sour glance Eddy's way. Speed is mumbling something, leaning close to Sevigne, but it's difficult to hear. It's after eleven. The din at the other tables is rising and upstairs the music has just been cranked, noise seeming to cascade down the broad carpeted stairway like a flood roaring from burst pipes. Across the room a balding young guy stripped to peace-sign boxer shorts is doing a high-wire stagger down the side-cushion of a table, his cue used for a balance pole. A stocky bouncer weaves towards him through the tables.

"Cetaceophallic tropes and constructs in *Moby Dick* and the movie *Jaws*," Dina is telling Eddy.

The waitress appears with another round. She stands on tiptoe, her tray fingertipped high overhead as she whispers in Eddy's ear. Eddy throws his head back in silent laughter. Closing hands together under his chin like a delighted MC he announces that Mick Jagger and entourage have just come in off the street. Word seems to be spreading. The poolroom crowd are deserting their tables and making for the stairs in a kind of delirious panic, as if a fire-alarm were ringing at a pitch only some can hear. Eddy—face morphing like a manic gurner—lifts mock-pious eyes and palms upward, then winks and turns around. Una with a copy of her book in hand bounds after him, collegially slipping an arm through his. In shambling pursuit Speed follows. Dina gives a cryptic, close-lipped smile and then she too strides off, in black tights and hunky platform heels.

From the top of the stairs Eddy and Una glance back, mime surprise, beckon emphatically. Sevigne picks a copy of Una's book off the pile by her chair and holds it up. *Go ahead, I've got more important things to do.* He always has shunned crowds in the grip of group manias—traffic-crash hoedowns, the human noose of rapt faces tightening around a bar room scrap—but now his shunning of the massed paparazzi strikes him as an act of radical maturity, higher criticism. Dante's gaunt countenance seems to peer down at him with fierce approval. For a moment he feels fully arrived.

He's drunk. Ray is ranging from table to deserted table finishing games and untouched pints. Sevigne returns his grin. It takes him a moment to focus on the book's cover—*No Eye That Does Not See You*, the words running above a simple line drawing of an archaic torso of Apollo. It's a good drawing, a handsome cover. On the back by the photograph of Una's dramatically sidelit face, a caption says she was born in Toronto, in 1970. Three years younger and with a book, and who can say how many more years it might take him? The honour roll of credits shows that the poems have premiered in more magazines than Sevigne has even sent his own work to. And in magazines that have stiffed him repeatedly. Then Lois Shapiro's *Toronto Poetry Review* appears in the list, and on the spine he reads Toronto Poetry Review Press; he'll have to tell Una that Lois has published him too.

Torn between desires—to be impressed by the poems so he can tell her so sincerely, to find fault with them and feel secretly disdainful—he starts reading. And there's no fooling your body. His body does respond, briefly, once with goose bumps and shivers, but he's in no condition to stay focused. He looks up. At the farthest pool table Ray stands toasting him with somebody's untouched pint. He lifts his own glass and follows it to his feet and he wanders past the stairway— spilling over at the top with the mob's rowdy overflow and a few people drifting back downstairs—then through an archway into a dark hall with a swinging kitchen door at one end, heavy red curtains at the other. The men's room opens off the hall. He walks in with his drink and Una's book still in his hands. He tries to put the book down by the sink with his Scotch, but the surface is wet; he tucks it a few inches under his belt and then stoops, throat parched, to gulp mouthfuls of the lukewarm, foul-tasting water. He rinses his face, checks himself in the mirror. Square those shoulders, boy. Shadow-box—a couple of jabs, a crisp right and now turn that hook like Frazier, hard. A little tag of hot pepper stuck to the top of a canine: winning smile for the ladies. Otherwise you're all right.

The door swings open. He spins from the mirror, snatches up his drink. Una. "What are *you* doing here?" she says with a moue of mock astonishment—the goosed starlet, the helpless

belle—though she seems anything but helpless and for a moment Sevigne, forgetting the urinal next to the sink, wonders
if he's in the wrong place. He shrugs. Her eyes light on the
book sticking out of his pants.

"Trying to make off with a free copy, I see. This way before
I alert the authorities."

Outside the door she takes him by the hand and leads him
up the hall towards the red curtains and through them, never
once glancing back or around, as Sevigne is doing. It's darker
on the other side but a door is visible to the right. She tries it.
It opens. A bare bulb clicks on. They're in a small storeroom
with a concrete floor, steel shelves stocked high with tinned
beans and coconut milk, curry paste, plum tomatoes, then the
door is closing and the bulb clicks off. Darkness spins around
him. Heart racing he reaches out for her but she isn't there. He
steps forward, groping, bumping into a shelf and almost
smashing the glass in his hand. He slides the glass screaking
onto the shelf. He's opening his mouth to say something, he
still doesn't know what, when she pounces on him from behind, her teeth on his shivering nape, arms twining around his
waist. He freezes. When the reaching hands touch the book still
stuck under his belt they pause, pat around, do a blind double-
take. She begins laughing and her breasts shake against his
back. He turns and grasps her. Her hands are in his hair, fingernails in his scalp, pulling him down to her. "You're wet,"
she says. "Your face." Her breath is peppery and her tongue in
his mouth tastes hot and sweet, like paprika. They stand for
some time mouths moving together, then he gets her dress
down off her shoulders and clumsily tugs her bra down onto
her belly, stooping to her breasts as they spill free. The edge of
her book under his belt keeps slipping lower, crimping the skin
of his groin. She winds a leg around him and he slides his hand
up under the dress, expecting to feel the hem of her panties,
but his hand keeps sliding, no resistance, nothing there. It's

dizzying, heady; a fall over the precipice to find yourself in flight. Una's book stays wedged between them like some weird instrument of chastity as she gropes with his belt, first cinching it painfully tight and then open, his zipper spreading open and he helps her slide the blue jeans down, the two of them swaying together in the darkness, last dance of the night. The book slips between them to the floor. Feeling for support, her hand upends his glass and it smashes by their feet. He leans back on a cold, creaking shelf, tins shifting behind him as they laugh and pant and he clutches her hips, a can of something falling to the floor, rolling away.

As she sits herself slowly onto him in sweet, aching stages, dress down off her breasts and up around her waist, they stop laughing, begin sighing, moaning, in unison, like doves.

Well she's not in the bathroom, Ray, I just asked the girl who came out. I already checked the men's.

Speed. The voice at first faint, outside the washroom or behind the curtains.

Look, Owen, get a grip, mate. You're right out of hand tonight. She's not going to be in the gents'.

I wouldn't put it past her. And where's the guy with the Pre-Raphaelite hair, Korkola's friend? He's not around either.

Reckon she's still upstairs, Owen. Just forget it.

Ragged footsteps approach, a hand rattles the doorknob. Sevigne freezes, eyes wide. "It's locked," Una whispers, still moving.

"Una!"

"Afraid I'm losing my patience here, Owen."

"Funny you should say that, Ray."

"I mean it, mate. It's high time you left her alone."

"Speed! Ray!" It's Eddy. "I was wondering where the hell you'd got to. Ray, you should have come up—man, what a scene! Everybody's crowding in and Jagger signing all these autographs and flirting with the crowd and then he takes this one gorgeous gothy woman and starts waltzing around with her, it's standing room only, people on other people's shoulders to see, then Una—who else?—Una cuts right in and starts dancing with him and pretty much *leads*, and then she gives him a signed copy of her book! I kid you not. So this tall guy with thick glasses, and standing way back, too, he yells, 'That's not Jagger—Jagger's older than this guy.' I guess there's a Stones cover band tonight at the Cameron and this guy's the lead? Dead ringer. Just sauntered up here on the break. Probably pulls this all the time. It was pure emperor's new clothes—as soon as this one guy broke the bubble everybody could see it. Some people were majorly pissed off. I love it! I mean, this could make a perfect intro for our first issue—you know, telling bogus art from the genuine. . . . Speed? Hey, what is it, man?"

"Afraid we better go after him, Mike."

Silence again but for the bass throb of music from upstairs and the muted, meaningless chatter and faint clack of balls from the pool tables, the sounds ebbing fainter and fainter in Sevigne's ears as Una Sutherland rides him into oblivion.

The two friends are sprawled at opposite ends of a scruffy, boneless chesterfield in Eddy's book-littered apartment, in a section of town he calls the Annex. Their legs are extended to the Victorian bay window, feet propped on the sill. In the near-dark Eddy in his black horn-rims paints oil onto a rolling paper with brisk, dexterous motions.

"Here, dude, you inaugurate. Sorry I'm all out of coke. I'm a bit strapped these days. No coke, no X."

"This beer here is fine, Eddy."

They're sipping tall tins of Heineken.

"*Beer*?" Eddy says, confused.

They pass the joint back and forth. On Eddy's good stereo

Nick Cave croons gloomily. Outside, past the leafless, up-reaching silhouette of a century maple, stars tremble in the clear freezing heavens, so much brighter than he'd thought to see here. They seem to form another city—a kind of celestial parody of the one below.

"Did I what?"

Using a pair of nail scissors as a roach-clip, Eddy makes sucking sounds, his slitted eyes fixed on Sevigne.

"With Una. Quit playing the ploughboy, Sev."

"God, I didn't think you knew." Hoping his blush can't be detected, he takes the glowing roach. "Wasn't sure if I should tell you."

"Oh come on, share away!"

"What? Oh . . . here."

"No, I meant—"

"God, Eddy, I've got to see her again!"

Eddy takes a drag, coughs, then nods in a knowing, diag-nostic way. "Listen, Sevver? About Una. She's a bit of a 'free spirit.' You've got to watch yourself around her, you know?" Sevigne opens his mouth to object but Eddy cuts him off. "Plus she's got a boyfriend—she's lived with him since she was seventeen."

"She told me, Eddy. He was sick, he couldn't come tonight."

"Sick?" Eddy sounds amused. "In a manner of speaking. He's one odd dude, is Thomas."

Sevver. Dude. Sevigne eyes his friend. His new style is manic, studded with hip witticisms and shorthand (LitCrit, CanLit, po-mo, goth), yet he seems to be saying about Una the kind of lowbrow thing he used to deplore when the hockey-heads back in Bawating High would mouth off. *She's a dirty. Real sleazehole.*

"But I'd *never* say that about Una!" Eddy bursts out. Sevigne must have been thinking aloud; he can't remember speaking. "Never! I love the woman! But Sev, listen, she follows every passion, like she'd hop on a plane tomorrow for Rio or the Big Easy if that took her fancy, she'd just charm a loan out of Dr Di and go. I'm not saying she always does what she did tonight—she was on a real roll—but it's not like you're the first passion she's ever followed. The woman is a law unto herself. That's what's so amazing about her! But this is the Big Smoke, my friend, you're not up in kayak country now, you've got to take some care. You used a condom?"

A needle-stab of heat as the roach burns through Sevigne's undershirt just over the belt. He has snipped the roach clean off. Wincing he plucks it up as the cinder dies.

"You aren't trying to tell me this guy has . . . you know. Is he *sick*?"

"Who, Wheatgrass Man? He'll never even leave the house at night in case he has to shake a hand and get microbes. He's an older guy, owns a health food store. Hides in the back painting New Age icons and stuffing oat bran into bags, lets his sales help fuck with the public."

"But why would someone like her want to . . ."

"Seems bizarre, I know, but it works for her. Or maybe she just doesn't know how to break free. He was, what, thirty when they met, doing the art-guru thing, and I guess she imprinted on him. Her father died when she was really small. Maybe she'll never leave."

Sevigne chafes the crumbling roach between his thumb and forefinger. Finally he says, "Were you saying you've been with her?"

"With Una? Ha! We'd laugh too much to pull it off. We're old pals. It's a civilized crowd, for sure, everybody's pretty much slept with everybody, but, you know."

"I guess that explains Speed." Sevigne drains the can, its bitter dregs. "I didn't realize they'd actually been . . . shit. I guess you have to feel for the guy."

"Don't. He's an asshole. Spend all your time here feeling

sorry for assholes and you won't have any time left for your friends." He cracks his knuckles loudly. "Let me tell you something. Just look at tonight as a one-off. It's like—like Hogtown just bought you a free lunch or something. See it as your red carpet and keys to the city. Your champagne toast. Forget Una. She's with Thomas. Speed couldn't figure that out and it's really done a number on him. He's stoned every day now and his thesis is caca."

Sevigne swallows hard, gazes up at the stars. The encounter was unsentimentally brief and basic but has left inside him a germ of sentiment, the kind another man might metabolize in a few days and forget, but which in him is more likely to metastasize swiftly and then erupt with the full range of untreatable symptoms. Character is fate, when all is said, and Sevigne has no pastimes—only obsessions. The idea of recreational anything, let alone recreational sex, strikes him as a shameful squandering of life's finite time, the supreme suburban lunacy, so that now—having had recreational sex—he has to poeticize it, to load it down with larger meanings and potentials. Una is the city now, and the coming spring. His new home. He has imprinted on her. And falling in love is like an orgasm: after a certain point there's no stopping.

"Besides, she's not the kind you want. Or I want, long-term. You came here to be a writer, right? And Una's a muse. You're thinking: Perfect. But you don't want a muse around when you're done for the day, you want some down-time to heal and recharge, believe me, I've been there. She'd just bring trouble into your life."

Trouble, Sevigne thinks. Ah, trouble.

"And quit staring at me like that." He sits up, fumbles for a cigarette, finds the pack empty and drops it on the floor. "We've known each other for years, Sev, don't try to snow me. You always wanted to shine, and big time too. And that's *fine*. When I finished the MA I decided I was going to make it down here, and once you decide that, you've got to proceed in a businesslike way with no Pardon me's or I'm sorry's. Success isn't a dirty word. This is now, Sev, act all retro-sentimental and you won't survive. Don't be shy about getting to know people who can give you a boost up or a blurb. Everyone does or they're nobody. Living here is a crash course in realpolitik."

"And give up verse," Sevigne says, "there's nothing in it."

"What?"

Sevigne coughs hard, clearing his scorched throat. "It's a . . . you know. A quotation. You *know* what it is."

Eddy squints at him, then slumps back into the chesterfield. It sags under his weight, its ruined springs giving off a languid echo. His pep talk seems to have tired him. He reclines with the empty beer tin balanced on his chest.

"The mag's going to be amazing, Sev. We just have to find a name for it. Consider yourself on the case, okay? And you'll give us something from your novel. . . . It's about Cairo, this novel? It should be. Not the Sewer. . . . You have to tell me about Cairo. . . ."

Within a minute he's unconscious, his great goiter of an Adam's apple quivering as he snores, the beer tin on his chest moving up and down. Sevigne—veins still volting from the input of the day's long journey and his red carpet arrival—seems helpless to prevent All Fools' Day night from stretching into dawn. The sky is growing lighter, stars fading. Twelve hours ago he did not even know of her existence and now her name, repeated, is a poem in itself, a tantric mantra. *Una, Una.* Say the word: the lips puckering, opening for a kiss.

He's still awake as the sun pulses up over the rooftops and glows like a heart in the midst of the great maple's vascular branchings, while Eddy snores beside him in the new light and he holds Una's book open to his face, wondering if he can smell her—them—faintly in the pages.

3

Sevigne in the
Season of Heartbreak

EDDY is always talking. Eddy is always gossiping, planning the magazine aloud, trying out possible names on Sevigne, telling him he should fly back to Cairo and squat in his City of the Dead if he isn't ready to fork out more than the four hundred bucks a month max he hopes to spend on an apartment. Four hundred rent and two hundred expenses and Sevigne's money will last, he hopes, until early fall, by which time he might be able to secure some kind of advance or arts grant with the next draft of his novel. Eddy is also urging him to get a job because Toronto is now a "world-class city" (a cock of the eyebrow, fingers framing quotation marks in the café's smoky air) and it costs like one.

"Here, I want you to review this book for our first issue. Hmmm—how about *The Issue* as a name for the mag?"

Sevigne considers for a few seconds, then says, "I do think it's better than *Retropolitan*. Yes, I like it."

"Hey, he likes it! Here, take the book, give me three hundred words. We pay sixty bucks on acceptance."

And he picks up the tab.

Over the ten days Sevigne has been camped out on Eddy's chesterfield, Eddy has picked up the tab in scores of cafés, bistros, prefab pubs, taverns and taprooms, diners, wine-bars piano-bars retro-bars hotel-lobby-lounges nightclubs and comedy cabarets basement-boozecans and other blind pigs and tigers and still Sevigne has managed to drop the incredible (to him) sum of three hundred dollars. He's picked up a few tabs himself. He tried coke and X, the new coke and X, and on a combination of Ecstasy and coffee that Eddy calls Ecspresso—and now prudently avoids—he stayed up fifty-five hours talking, singing, exploring the city with wide-eyed gusto, dancing at the Boom Boom Room (where the drugs drew the bass and the strobes right inside him, so the beat became a second heartbeat and the technopop he'd otherwise have loathed struck him as fantastic)—while acting almost frantically affectionate towards Eddy and the laconic Ray until, having worn them both out, he sat up scrawling engorged and humid odes allegedly for Una but in fact propositioning the metropolis. Though on crashing back to earth it was just Una he ached for—Una off on a publicity tour out west, and anyway she's spoken for, Sev, forget it.

Now at last passing out on the chesterfield while the stereo blasts Tom Waits and Eddy cooks penne in the kitchen, Sevigne is unable to call her face to mind. Like a word on the tip of his tongue while he writes—that elusive *mot juste*, always receding as he pursues it—she won't be summoned by an effort of will. Then on the edge of sleep he stops trying and there she is: the obsidian eyes, full lips he has kissed and sucked and bitten, sharp planed features like a face on a ship's prow. The smell of her returns to him too. A groan escapes him; and she's gone.

Next day after a dreamless, fathomless fourteen-hour sleep he walks with Eddy—Sevigne jogging a few steps every so often to keep up—a dozen blocks east on Queen to investigate a room in a rooming house, this one listed in the *Star* at two-sixty-five a month. His long stupor has left him aching, breathless and testy. He feels worked over, as on the morning after his last fight.

The unfurnished room has a sealed window giving on to

the hull of a Dumpster in a cul-de-sac; a floor of warped, filthy linoleum; a malodorous little sink yellowed by decades of beery piss. The walls and ceiling are defaced with savage patterns seemingly branded into the plaster with a blowtorch—howls made visible, a desperate transcription of the DTS. The dead air is tainted with squalor and decay. It's the last blow to Sevigne's bohemian resolve, though momentarily he thinks of renting the place simply to rebuke Eddy for his expressions of aloof disgust. And for being right, again.

He finds a bachelor flat on the eighth floor of a building at the corner of College and Bathurst. Eddy thinks it's a great deal for six fifty a month inclusive. Essentially one unfurnished room, it has a tiny bathroom walled off in one corner and a narrow nook of a kitchen in the other. But the sliding glass doors give onto a balcony and a panorama: southeast over a busy intersection towards the lake, the CN Tower and an impacted mass of skyscrapers—an aspiring cosmopolis rearing over the old provincial city of stolid, blocky red-brick buildings with aerials like high ladders climbing nowhere.

Standing on the balcony with hands clasped behind his back, as if surveying his domain, Eddy explains the Tower as a product of soaring seventies optimism. The top sections are the upper stages of an Apollo moonship, while the support part, flared towards the base, suggests a groovily elongated leg in bell-bottoms. Near the foot of the Tower, the SkyDome, dazzling white and fungally rounded, sprouts like an organic anomaly from the city's rigorous grid. (To Sevigne in his current fever it can only be yoni to the lingam of the tower.)

He sets up a card table in front of the glass door. Among the trees eight storeys down, an aquarelle gloss of pale green has appeared and is spreading day by day; from across the intersection, over the entrance to a bar, a cartoon skull with horns and corkscrew crazy eyes goggles up at him as he works.

Its expression varies with his mood. On a day with the words flowing and the sun spilling rivers of Pilsener light over his grimy broadloom, the skull seems jovial, a mascot of the city as year-round Mardi Gras where he will give his old self the slip and emerge from the crowds reborn. Days when his writing returns to him rejected and the acid rain pelts down, sealing him into his catacomb cell, the skull's rictus is sinister and the doorway a maw into which the city's hopeful youth bustle only to be expelled hours later like zombies, staggering, slurring tuneless songs or the usual brutish expletives, the sounds echoing up to Sevigne at his table.

The season of heartbreak hits early. In mid-April a freak heat wave blows in and overnight the city's cooped-up life brims over into the streets, sidewalk-cafés suddenly open and crowded, young couples everywhere. For him the ache is sharper because of Una—Una triumphantly returned from her book tour but nowhere to be seen, though he watches for her everywhere and one time just misses her at Pages, where the ink of her florid signature has barely dried in the stack of books on the counter. He can picture her bouncing with short, dynamic strides from store to store, signing dozens of copies, hundreds, a star on the rise, uncatchable. A few blocks west in Edwards'—where her signature actually smudges at his touch—they tell him that she left a few minutes ago, then they watch in mounting amusement as he rushes out and stands mid-stream in the surging ruck, craning his neck to see over the bobbing heads, even climbing onto the pedestal of a lamp-post and leaning off it, eyes shaded, a breathless frontier scout . . .

Eddy chides him gently, urges him not to call her, seeks to salve his masculine pride. "It's not a rejection, Sev, she really liked you, *likes* you, she just won't let anything jeopardize her long-term relationship. You've got to stop taking everything so seriously! Look, maybe she's worried she'd really fall for you if she saw you again, and she can't let that happen. Put that spin on the situation and it's like *flattering*, not a brush-off."

"You really think so?"

"Absolutely."

It's the wrong thing to say.

(For ISLANDS OF THE NILE, ch. 3) Luc's resolution—recalling moment he and Mera fell in love—"Learn to see everyone through the eyes of a lover"—the NECESSARY ASSUMPTION OF BEAUTY—somehow maintain fleeting state when eye is stripped naked, free of the cataracts of habit, so the beloved seems briefly sacred, flawless—(No not flawless but beautifully flawed, as in W. Stevens: 'The imperfect our Paradise')——

Last of April and the night air humid, balmy as August, the window open and the red-brick bell tower to the right of his window silent as it has been for years. It crowns what was once an Anglican church: now a community drop-in centre. A hundred feet down, another streetcar shudders east along College and Sevigne's computer jitters on the card table, as if struggling to process the welter of words he has fed into it since breakfast. He still isn't used to the machine—how it hums constantly as if impatient, how it blinks off if he doesn't touch a key for a few minutes, as if threatening to delete all his efforts should he fail to produce, produce faster. How if he stares too long into its glimmering depths it will stare back at him, like any abyss.

Eddy donated the Hyperion computer and a telephone answering machine, his outdated old ones. At first Sevigne declined to use either. Such devices interposed yet another layer of synthetic insulation between the self and others, between the self and the elements, those natural cycles from which

living art flowed. Eddy told him to put his theories into an
essay and maybe he could use it in *urban word* (his latest idea
for a name)—it was bound to piss people off and get them
writing in, Letters to the Ed and counter-essays and so on,
which was right on, but in the meantime would Sevigne please
crawl the fuck out of his time capsule, plug in and boot up?
"It's the nineties equivalent of that turning on, dropping out,
and tuning off thing. Or however it goes. Went. Hey, is that
Leary guy still with us?"

Eddy's computer turns out to be useful. The convulsive
first draft of "The Islands of the Nile" needs thorough revision. Yet for all the work that Sevigne has to do, the hardest
part is simply staying put in front of the screen when he knows
Una is out there somewhere, in a café or alone at the rail of the
ferry to Centre Island (this image of her ambushes, arouses
him) exposing her breasts to the breeze and the sun—breasts
he has cupped and kissed and tasted but not yet seen, the
storeroom was too dark. And the unbearable breezes soughing
in through his balcony door keep seducing him to leave his
unruly manuscript and Big Brother of a machine for the
streets below. He was planning to hole up like an anchorite in
a stone tower until the novel was rewritten, but the city's cen-
trifugal pull is forever drawing him out of his head, his novel,
his overheated flat. Often he bribes himself to persevere with
the promise of freedom in two or three more hours, then he is
up and out the door at a run, downstairs—he always takes the
stairs—to wander "aimlessly" north through neighbourhoods
of stately pillar-porched Victorian houses, their tulips votively
aflame, to the heart of the Annex where he haunts the aisles of
Holistica RealFoods and reads Gary Snyder or Wendell Berry
poems in the New Age journals, till finally—defeated in his
hope of seeing Una, or even Thomas—he buys a token bag of
rolled oats or a day-old muffin. The slouching cashier in bandana and 3M T-shirt smirks as he pulls out his tattered wallet,

coins cascading onto the counter and floor from a rip in the change-pouch.

Luc and his father and the others on the tour disembarked from the vessel for a portage by bus up through fertile terrace-lands from the base of the Aswan High Dam to the piers at the north end of Lake Nasser. They boarded a smaller boat and at sunset pushed off into the lake, cruising south over grey depths that had once been desert. Here the deepest sounding would be the old riverbed of the Nile, which, depending on your perspective, had either vanished under the lake caused by the dam or swollen into a vast new incarnation. That was what death did to people, Luc supposed: swallowed them so that nothing remained, yet made them loom larger than before—the very ground you walked on, the waters you traversed. Leaning over the taffrail, he thought of the cities they were gliding over—places that had once seemed to their citizens both current and eternal—and at times a shadow or ripple would startle him and he would picture jagged ruins, tombs, fortress turrets thrusting up like unmarked shoals.

Mera was always in his thoughts, just as he assured her in his cards and letters, though one time he found himself unable to call her face to mind. It was as if he'd spent only one night with her instead of five years. In alarm he pulled out his wallet and held her picture to his eyes.

As they moved southward the shores receded to either side, the sun slipped into the Western Desert and a light fog rose, swallowing the reaches, so the boat seemed to glide through a misty limbo, Luc at the rail and his father, drugged and dying, asleep in the cabin; safely tucked in before dark.

4

There Ought to Be Clowns

EDDY'S DINGY LITTLE OFFICE, crammed with book-piled desks, two word processors, a fax and antique Xerox machine, is squeezed between a computer graphics outfit and an agency that hires out live, balloon-bearing clowns. In the hallway whenever Eddy meets one of the interchangeably haggard, truculent clowns, who are always waddling in or out of the building, he greets them with glad-handing goodwill, tugging their polkadot ties or fat purple suspenders, tweaking red foam noses, popping balloons with his cigarette. The outfit is called There Ought to Be Clowns. Eddy has promised the owner he'll hire some of his staff for the launch of *Yonge St.* (his latest favourite name) at the museum during the medieval torture exhibit in June, and on the strength of that promise, and through sheer undesisting brio, he's managed to get the owner and three of the clowns to subscribe.

Eddy loves Suite 202. Loves the door with its frosted-glass window like the door of a *film noir* detective agency. Loves unlocking the place way too early in the morning, valiantly tired, rinsing his stubbled face in the sink under the mirror, sleeking back his hair, lighting a Winston and blowing the first puff at his winking image. Loves the dishevelled desk, loves those huddled masses of manuscript patiently awaiting him, loves his PC always on and purring like a getaway car at a curb. And when he hits another stinker of an opening—*Waking to the ding-a-ling of the alarm clock, it was all a dream*—he loves to

groan long-sufferingly and reach for the pink slip. The One
Competent Man. Mender, fixer, mover, shaker. Happily
under siege.

At nine when his student "interns" Marco and Janet come
in, they'll find him at his desk facing the door, a young po-mo
Citizen Kane with shirt sleeves rolled, body tensed before the
PC, face lit up and phone receiver clamped violin-style under
his chin. Varied hive-like hummings of the computers, the
copier, the fridge, the tiny espresso machine. Empty styrofoam cups crumpled on the desk and the remains of last night's
jalapeño salami sub or sushi take-out. Does he ever sleep?
He'll be evasive when they ask if he's gone home at all. *Oh,
sure, I caught a few hours, no worries.* Which is true. But said in a
tone that leaves them wondering.

And it's sweet to him, this thriving on crises of his own
making. Sweet, the rush of pulling something good, some real,
rare gem, out of the slush pile, a sapphire out of a septic tank,
and then—fuck formality—grabbing the phone and actually
calling the writer at home and calling back until he gets an
answer. Sweet, the stunned silence of the unpublished neo-
phytes, then their garbled replies full of elation and gratitude.
And racing the clock to an important deadline and winning
by seconds—sweet. He's hooked on the urgency, the adrenalin, the caffeine and nicotine, the excitement of getting something new off the ground and finding and charming potential
sponsors, he's hooked on taking on new projects and jobs when
he already has too much on the go, hooked on feeling heroi-
cally hassled, stressed out, asked for, asked out, asked up, written up, signed up, counted on, hit on, talked down, talked up,
smooth-talked, double-booked and schmoozed.

No longer, praise Jah, hooked on blow.

He's hooked—this is it in a phrase—on *making things
happen.*

With his right hand Eddy keys in an e-mail to the printers

assuring them he'll have the mag's title and title-font chosen by
Friday. With his left hand he swipes up the phone. If it were
possible to keep signing rejection slips by clenching a pen in his
teeth, he'd be doing that too. (On his lunch-hour workouts he
skims *Harper's* and *Brick* and *Spin* and keeps an eye on TSN and
MuchMusic while plodding up a sweat on the StairMaster.)
Now on his face he wears a harried frown. He feels terrific.
Phone clamped under his chin he fires off the e-mail and inserts
a disk—Sevigne's. Four rings and no answering machine. Two
more rings that take seemingly forever and he's about to hang
up when the receiver is clumsily uncoupled, dropped.

". . . Hello?"

"Sev! My God, you sound like Marianne Faithful on slow
play. You OK? Why aren't you using that answering machine?"

"I'm in the apartment, Eddy. Right beside the phone."

"You could have fooled me."

"I was sleeping." Long pause. "God, what time is it?"

"Way after nine, dude." Eddy winks at Marco and Janet,
who grin back. "When I called yesterday the machine wasn't
on either. And you never did pick up."

Sevigne exhales into the mouthpiece. "Sometimes I forget
to turn it on when I go out. You know how I feel about, you
know . . . people talking to machines."

"You and John Berger, Sev. Just put it in that essay. After
you've had a cuppa or two. I'm calling about your review." He
taps some keys and it comes up on the screen: 'Black Milk of
the Morning': A Review of David Greenberg's *Holocaustic.*

"Sev, it's good, but it's too long. Decidedly. I asked for
three hundred words, tops. This has got to be three thousand.
No, wait a sec." His forefinger pecks a key. "Three-thousand
two-hundred and sixteen."

"Your computer already told me, Eddy."

He shakes his head, grins. "'Books in Briefs,' Sev, 'Books
in Briefs'—you know we're trying to cover as many as we can.

Afraid we're going to have to make some cuts."

"Look, Eddy, I tried, but it's a complex book! I didn't feel I could tell the truth about it in just a few paragraphs."

"Of course, Sev. Don't get me wrong. I can see you read it carefully. Like maybe ten or twelve times."

"Three times."

"*Three* times. My point is we're not trying to be *The New York Review of Books* here. Good, yes, serious, absolutely, but serious doesn't have to mean solemn and long-winded." The interns are beaming at him. He's warming to the performance. "Solemn is fine if a mag just wants to ride on like, grants, or reputation? But we need a more modern thing happening here, Sev—more *post*modern if you will. More urban. Upbeat. This piece feels . . ." And it comes to him. It's beautiful. "*Too intelligent and not smart enough*. Not quite, Sev. I'm sorry. Can't you be a bit lighter? Quicker? Quotations are fine, but you've got about a dozen per page!"

"I'm not sure I even know what postmodern means, Eddy."

"Well *nobody* knows what 'postmodern' means—that's what's so postmodern about the term!" Marco and Janet crack up at their desks. Sevigne is silent. Eddy feels a flicker of guilt. "I mean, it's definitely got something to do with outing all the old sentimental constructs around 'love' and 'beauty' and 'heroism' and 'personal identity' and all that stuff. All attitudes in denial, Sev—all still in the closet. Hang out here a while more and you'll see what I'm saying."

"I knocked myself out writing that thing, Eddy."

"*Claro*, Sev, you're a trouper—I mean that. But listen, OK? Bottom line. You cannot make a living reading review-books over and over like they're Thomas Pynchon, then running every word you write through the machine a zillion times. You know we can only pay what we pay! Look, just let me cut it down for you. I'll be sensitive. And I'll only cut to like five hundred words."

Dead air. Sev's usual spark is definitely lacking. Maybe hungover? But finally he says, "Wasn't Pynchon just a name on a review-book himself at one time?"

Eddy shakes his head, smiles wryly. "All right, Sev. *Touché*."

"Fifteen hundred words," Sevigne says.

"Eight hundred."

"Twelve hundred. If I get to see your version."

Eddy's fingers are already twinkling over the keys.

"OK, big guy, you win. You'll be our feature review."

"Just leave as many of the quotations as possible, all right? And my argument about the 'syntax of sorrow'."

"You got it. I'll show you a printout Saturday night at Una's big reading. I finessed us free tickets. We'll all go out after the show, yeah? You *are* planning to come?"

5

The Sinking

HER READING—part of a spring literary festival to
mark the country's 125th year—is held in a theatre
in a luxurious shopping concourse on the waterfront.
Afterward a glittering conclave of authors, journalists, book-
sellers, impresarios and local publishers gather at a restaurant in the dining room of a docked ship a few blocks up
Queen's Quay. Not that all the authors glitter. Ray Dennison
is aggressively dressed down in a grey T-shirt and eroded
leather pants and jacket. Sevigne's intention was to glitter, but
in the black boots, black jeans and billowy white chest-laced
blouse he found in a second-hand boutique on Queen West
he looks, Eddy says, like someone auditioning for a remake of
Tom Jones.

"Gotta lose those bodice laces, Sev. Retro's fine, retro's in,
but don't overdo it. Like by three hundred years or so."

"I like this shirt, Eddy."

"So does Seinfeld. This is exactly why you should be
watching more TV."

In the wake of the morning mail's two rejection slips, he already feels like an impostor, an amateur among the pros; now
his face and neck begin to burn in earnest. Still, Eddy has chosen to sit next to him, instead of further up beside Una and
among the stars. With seeming nonchalance Eddy now indicates the stars: Canadian and American, British, Irish, a Swedish
couple, an Indian in a jade sari, the beret-wearing Czech and

the Québécoise who also read tonight. Sevigne has heard of most of them and at any other time would be eager to make their acquaintance, but now he can think only of Una. Installed in the heart of the pantheon she looks unbearably good, her sleek panther-black hair swept back off her face to expose strong clean bones, her body shining in a maraschino-red vinyl dress. Because the tablecloth is also red and the chairs are padded with crimson velvet and the floral carpet is aswirl with red motifs—and now waiters in scarlet jackets are filling the wine glasses with burgundy—Una in her radiant dress and lipstick seems the room's centre, its wellspring, the source of its crackling energy and rich, rubescent light. An elderly, plainly besotted Pulitzer laureate, leaning close, is speaking to her with urgent intimacy and she's beaming and wriggling at what must be a lavish compliment on her work. Now she throws her head back and her laughter fills the dining room and draws every eye, bright with desire or beady with envy, even hatred, and for a moment the jalapeño-red tip of her tongue flickers between her teeth. She is touching the laureate lightly on the wrist. The ebullient lilt and dip of her voice carries, though the words are unclear. Another heavily credentialled elder, a Swede who wears his greying hair back in a ponytail and has an earring, leans over the table and clinks his glass against hers while his blonde wife's flinty eyes narrow, first at him, then at her.

Thomas is again missing. But that is no help to Sevigne. After the reading, he stood in the long line waiting to have his copy of her book inscribed, and when at last he reached her she leapt up with eyes and mouth agog and cried, "Sevigne, thanks so much for coming!"—and leaned over the signing table to rest her hands on his shoulders and kiss him briskly.

"I love your shirt!"

"I got it for tonight, actually,"

"Oh." She looked down at the book he'd handed her, smiling with pleasure, yet clearly at a loss.

"So how was your tour?"

"Amazing!" Her cheeks dimpled and glowed, her eyes sparkled. "Especially Winnipeg and Saskatoon. Oh, and Vancouver went really well too. They're going to do a second printing of the book!"

"Una, listen, I was thinking . . ."

"Looks like this one's already signed."

"It's the one I stole from you," he said, "the night we met." He waited, in vain, then went on, "It's only your name though. I was hoping you'd add something more."

"Of course." She glanced over his shoulder at the still-lengthy queue. Squinting down at the book, she began writing with a bold, flowing hand. The hint of cleavage behind the jiggling pen made him feel sick with desire. Behind him the crowd shuffled. She handed the book back. "Well, I hope that's all right. God, I'm so glad you could make it!"

"Yeah."

She was looking over his shoulder again, saying, "Well, maybe we'll see you after, at the dinner?"

"Who's we?" he heard himself say. She frowned. He leaned close to her and said, "I was hoping we could talk."

"Of course," she said—almost snapped. "After. At the dinner." And some new light, a kind of early warning, brimmed into her eyes.

As he stumped away on shaky legs he heard her flirting casually with the next fan, whose name it seemed she was meant to know but had forgotten. He opened the book to the inscription that sprawled and spilled over the page:

To Sev—

> *In hopes and expectation that*
> *you'll soon be off on tours with your*

own first book!—And my warmest thanks for
helping make my launch night so special—
unlike Speed. (!)
                    Friends,
                         Una

So far in the shipboard restaurant she hasn't even acknowledged him. Now he says to Eddy, "It's like she made up this Thomas to give her an excuse to stay in at night."

"Una doesn't stay in at night," Eddy says in an automatic tone, as if he hadn't really heard Sevigne's words. Behind his glasses his eyes pace back and forth like penned, restless animals. And it hits Sevigne: Eddy is regretting having to sit here at the steerage end of the table with him, surly Ray, Dina Brasov with her captious, feline silences, and several younger unknowns. Up the table Una is laughing and Sevigne glances at her and she at him in mirror-unison and—far worse than looking away—she shifts her eyes one degree to starboard as if studying the bad nautical mural on the back wall. He pushes away his chowder, drains his wine glass and stands up.

Though surely no one "is reading" Hemingway. One reads him. At a sitting.

Anal sex? Oh, I just did that on the Internet!

Bullshit, mate—Ray to Eddy, about something—and you know it is.

He stalks along the table within inches of a dozen renowned heads and he doesn't give a God damn. He has an urge to yank that golden ring out of the Swede's earlobe. The man is hunching forward over the table to address Una and she's meeting him halfway, nodding intently, her face and the tops of her breasts aglow with candlelight. Heart thundering he stops behind the man's chair. Now it's apparent that his long greying hair, drawn tightly back in a ponytail, is meant to cover a bald spot—which gleams through anyway, beaded with sweat. His slabby back seems to ripple under the elbow-patched green corduroy blazer as if he were on top of Una and moving slowly. The balding head still blocks Sevigne's view of her. The Swede's wife, grey eyes averted, is mechanically spooning up chowder while other faces keep watch on Sevigne. Everyone is silent except Una and the Swede. Then the man sits back in his chair, lifting his hands palms out and roaring "Ah, well, but that's perfectly natural!"—and as Una sees Sevigne her attentive smile dissolves. He nods towards the door. She screws up her eyes and tilts her head once, frowning, *later, later*, but he feels she doesn't mean it, later she will be with these important people, courted by them, she prefers it that way. Perfectly natural. The Swede and the Pulitzer laureate are dismissing him with looks of mandarin disdain; he fires back his most menacing, pugilistic glare, then turns and walks with pressed dignity through the door.

Now who the hell was that?—the host's husky baritone—*I want that rude man's name.* An Indian accent: *One of the poets, I suppose?* And an English drawl: *For a moment there I rather thought we were to be run through with a rapier, Lars!*

The laughter is relieved, unanimous, conclusive.

A semi-spiral staircase climbs into darkness and he takes it two stairs at a time. The sound of his own breathing fills a low-ceilinged ballroom with scuffed pine floors, a bar at one end, tables along the sides stacked with chairs. Few things speak more forcefully of endings than a closed bar, a vacant ball-room. Out the porthole windows, over the calm surface of the harbour, the lights of a low wooded island.

Partway across the dance floor he freezes: the figure coming at him out of the dark is his own reflection in the square mirrored pillar centring the room. His swashbuckling blouse, palely luminous, now strikes him as an obvious mistake. Fuelled with anger his hands shoot at the mirror in lightning combinations and he grunts in time, reaching hard inside with his right, as if for a knockout—actually striking the glass.

The door beside the bar seems locked, but when he shoves experimentally it unsticks, swings open. Riserless steel steps lead upward like a ladder. He climbs into the pilothouse and stands before the locked ship's wheel, his bloodied hand gripping the engine telegraph frozen forever on Full Ahead. Almost nosing the snug of the quay, the bow aims northward up Yonge Street into the heart of the city, where two white towers loom like icebergs or giant waves. That was some performance all right. He is losing his grip; he is turning into Speed. Some time later he leaves, wanders back through the city to his bachelor cell, and with little hope works on the novel till dawn.

In darkness Luc stood at the bow as the ship cruised south against the current over a channelful of stars. Before long he would return to the cabin and check on his father. A memory shadowed him—that of his father home safe after danger, returned from the gales of '75 to sit on the floor between his sons' beds, drink in hand, and tell the story of the Big Fitz. If it was one the brothers could hear repeatedly, it was also one their father never wearied of repeating, that he seemed to rehearse out of some grim, inward necessity, and with the unshakeable certainty of a witness. There had been no witnesses, though their father was never in doubt. The authorities had tried to blame the lost crewmen for the sinking, arguing that high seas had flooded the ship through improperly fastened hatch-coamings, but that was a Goddamned lie.

The Fitz had been running before hurricane winds and driving snow and steep seas of twenty feet or more, the captain having taken them east into the lee of the Canadian shore and then south-east between Michipicoten and Caribou islands, bearing for Whitefish Bay and safety. It should have worked out. The shoal off Caribou was marked on the charts—but the charts, as another captain had noted and reported the previous autumn, did not agree. The two present versions centred Six Fathom Shoal in different spots—a matter of half a mile or so, that was all—but it would prove enough. In good weather her keel would still have cleared, but in those conditions, flying full ahead with the seas at her back and the hurricane on her and tons of taconite in her hold, she would have pitched down extra heavy between waves, drawing two extra fathoms for the second it took to shoal her. Boom. And with the whole ship shuddering and the storm screaming around her, nobody felt or heard a thing.

Now it's dusk and with the seas outrunning the ship and the cross-seas mounting and snow streaming past the wheelhouse almost horizontal, the Fitzgerald's *captain detects a list to starboard. He radios the nearest ship, the* Anderson: *he's lost two ballast tank vents and a fence rail and both pumps are on. "Will you shadow me down the lake?" The gouge isn't a big one but the lake treats it like a sluice-valve, gushing in at high pressure, and the pumps are helpless, the hold begins flooding and water is percolating up through the cargo like groundwater through gravel.*

The wheelhouse is over the bow and every time they plunge into a trough she digs herself out and shakes herself off a touch heavier, slower, maybe losing a quarter-inch each time. And with the ship riding a few lines lower, the wheelhouse windows get battered with spray like grapeshot and the bigger waves roll up her deck and bury it for seconds at a time, so if you're squinting aft for the next bad one, the deckhouse is a grey islet six hundred feet off in a boiling sea.

Now her radar gets torn off the wheelhouse roof and she has to rely on the Anderson—*still trying to catch up—for her course. At 7:00 p.m. the* Anderson *tells the* Fitz *she's within fifteen miles of the bay; at 7:10 the* Anderson *calls again and the captain of the* Fitz *says, "We are holding our own." But the bow under his feet is flooded, unresponsive, whenever they slide into a trough he and the first mate and the wheelsman all hold their breath waiting for the ship to dig herself out with a groan before the next sea flattens them. And somehow she does keep bouncing back, just half an hour and she'll be clear of the storm and safely grounded, but then come two giant seas, thirty-five feet each, and the first one teeters her stern high and puts her nose down and the men watch the lake hurtle towards them and they're waiting, Jesus, waiting to feel that first precious elevator-tug in the stomach as she buoys, but she won't, she's too heavy in the hull and crushed on her decks, and when the next sea surges over and tilts her stern higher she starts to dive. Now the freezing lake punches through the front windows of the wheelhouse, the side-windows explode from air-pressure and she picks up speed as those mountains of waterlogged ore topple forward and she's submarining straight down with her running lamps blazing red, yellow, green, as if guiding the way to the heart of the lake. For a moment her stern's levered high over the waves with the screw still spinning but then as her bow bottoms out ninety fathoms down the impact cracks her in two amidships. The boiler is still intact, burning in the stern, but deep in the lake it explodes like a depth-charge with a blinding flash of magnesium and a crump of muffled thunder. Then the muted hiss of air jetting out and upward from a thousand fissures in slowing arterial streams.*

Here Luc's father had always stopped, or segued into "The Ballad of Sir Patrick Spens," affecting a hammy Highland burr to conceal his emotion—*Half o'er, half o'er, to Aberdour, 'tis fifty fathoms deep*—but in photographs and drawings of the ship's remains Luc had found the tale's true ending, an epilogue of silence. Looming upright on the lakebed's desert plain the huge dented bow and eyeless wheelhouse, like the Sphinx, still clung in decay to a kind of baffled dignity; a few hundred feet off lay the rusted stern and between the halves the spilled cargo, like the viscera of some living thing torn apart.

6

Lilac Wine

I N EARLY MAY he receives from Amy Carson's lawyer a small package of his father's papers, including a 1909 government survey chart of Rye Island and the waters around it. "Spirit Island" is the actual name on the chart. To the Ojibway the island was sacred, a borderstone between Whitefish Bay and the "big sea water" of Kitchi Gumeeng, a site of ceremonies and special funerals; "Rye Island" must have been the bootleggers' waggish retranslation.

At first the map's arrival, along with another form rejection slip from a Toronto magazine, strikes him as a sign. For a day and a night he considers giving up his urban misadventure and returning north to spend summer and fall on the island, alone. But a retreat like that would shame him in his own eyes and, he feels certain, in the eyes of his friends. And in Una's eyes. He refuses to disappear like Speed, who has gone home to Montréal heartbroken, alcoholic, his thesis abandoned. Sevigne rolls up the map and stows it carefully in his duffel bag under the bed, vowing he will go to live and write on the island eventually, but for now he has to make a stand and work here.

So the "sign" is demoted to "coincidence," and forgotten.

And Sevigne does work. Though his mind, impulsive as Orpheus, keeps glancing back at its loss, he carries his novel forward with a will and a vengeance, determined to write something of durable beauty; unconsciously aiming to outdo

Una. And while his money is running low, there are prospects. One rainy afternoon as he sits in the Skull with the *Star* classifieds spread open on the bar, the bartender, in a reversed Blue Jays cap and an untucked Hawaiian shirt, brings him the telephone.

"It's for you, guy. More coffee?"

"Thanks."

He didn't even hear it ring. Pavlovian hopes, intestinal tailspins.

"Hey, Sev! It's Eddy. Man, you're easy to track down. So listen, I'm at the office, I can't really talk. You free Friday a.m. at nine?"

"Nine a.m.?"

"Rise and shine. I told you I'd scare up some jobs for you. What do you know about CD-ROM?"

"Let me see," Sevigne says.

"OK, listen, just go talk to Malachy's PA at nine sharp, he'll explain it all. I'm telling you, it's perfect! I'm doing jobs for them too. They give you the research materials, you retire to the comfort of your home, skim the stuff, fire off an essay. Or a book summary. Fifty words, a hundred, two hundred max."

"On what? A fifty-word essay?"

"On anything. Just last week I did *David Copperfield*— skimmed the introduction, reread an essay I wrote in Victorians 310, whipped off the summary next morning before I came in. A hundred bucks."

"You summarized *David Copperfield* in a hundred words?"

"It's CD-ROM, Sev, the CapsuleVersion is just a part of it. They run it along with visuals, clips from films of the book, reading lists, author images, snazzy graphics and blah blah blah. It's bullshit, Sev, pure Disney, it's like Coles' Notes for Netheads, but the money's good, and better you or me than some utter know-nothing, right?"

"I'd have to be pretty desperate before I drained the life out of *Madame Bovary* for a hundred bucks, Eddy."

"You are desperate."

Sevigne nods but says nothing.

"Another feature review then. You pick the book. And what about a paid reading? At the launch for the premiere issue of *On*. You know that show at the museum, 'Penal and Torture Devices from the Middle Ages'? Or whatever it's called. We're having it there to go with our—thanks, Janet, just put it here—with our photo-essay, on piercing. There's this new arts council fund for museum and publishing joint promos? Oh and this other outfit I moonlight for is looking for writers. They, uh, they publish sort of songs to go with like . . . short films. I'm going to call them today about you. Send them a CV, ASAP, OK?" And he fires off a Bay Street address.

A week later with his last stamps Sevigne mails off a humbling résumé and a half-hearted letter. He hears back within days. The caller is winded as if he's just made a dash for the telephone. Over an unplaceable rhythmic clangor, as of an assembly line, he tells Sevigne they've been hearing great things about him and he should come on down for a chat.

Then, on the Friday of the long weekend, he meets Ike.

She's starting her second set as he arrives. He never planned on coming in; he meant to keep writing until he fell apart, tonight the words were in easy reach, but he heard her voice faintly gusting up from the Skull's open door, weaving in and out of traffic sounds, distant horns and sirens, slipping through his balcony door. It kept stopping his one-finger typing mid-sentence.

He walks up front towards the stage. The tables here are empty, though there is a good crowd in the dark further back. He plants himself front row centre, leaning over his small round table, gripping the smoky Highland malt he rashly sprang for to go with her voice. She's impossible not to watch—wavy short dark hair and dark eyes, like Una, though much taller and with an older face, sadder, wiser, smiling to one side of her mouth when she smiles—but since she's older and stands above him on stage with the spotlit performer's air of belonging to a separate plane, he can't really think of her as a romantic prospect. Anyway Una still haunts him. He thinks she does; though as the night wears on, she haunts him less.

To her he looks endearingly serious. Sweet. When you teased him he'd always be a step or two behind, scrambling to catch up. She's seen a few guys like him before, the lone wolf types who move to the front tables and give you intense, brooding looks, as if wounded that you aren't singing only to them. *Lilac wine . . . I feel unsteady, where's my love?* There are the obsessive fans too, male and female, like the young albino guy with the Elvis sideburns and dark glasses who came to all her gigs for over a year and then never again. She worried about him, for a while. Some of the front-row types feel they're doing you a big favour, especially in bars where people just talk, or watch the hockey game, while you dig deep and throw everything into great old songs, and into your own songs, though most people would rather just hear the oldies, thanks anyway. No, she does have fans, more and more, according to Anson, and a "breakthrough deal" in the works, and now people asking for her songs at the encore. You eye all those things coolly when they've taken their sweet time getting to you.

Lone wolf hasn't heard her play before. He's responding to all the torch covers, when she sings "Frederick" he looks like he's going to rush the stage, but he's at sea when she plays her own stuff, his forehead furrowed hard as if he's trying to place a face or remember a name. Or just listening, hard.

After the set she lights a cigarette and crouches down beside the vocal amp, making adjustments. Peripherally she sees him approach the stage and take a CD from the pile on the table beside it. He holds it close to his face as if he needs glasses. When she turns to look at him directly, he whips the CD over, pretending he hasn't been studying the old photo of her on the front—three years ago, her thick wavy hair falling almost to her waist, navy pea jacket.

"Sorry I don't have a CD player," he says.

So "sorry" is his first word to her.

"Do you have any tapes?" he says.

She comes to the edge of the stage and squats on her biker-boot heels, blue jeans stretched taut over her thighs; in that position she's still above him, looking down, cigarette cocked next to her ear. She has on a snug black leather vest over a white T-shirt.

"We're clean out of tapes tonight," she says. Her husky voice can be used aggressively or suggestively, but lately it always seems to come out flat, detached. Except when she's up on stage—she hopes.

Sevigne assumes she's tired or indifferent.

"They're in the stores, though," she says.

"In the record stores? Wow, that's great!"

She smiles with the side of her mouth, a puff of smoke following. "You're surprised?"

Sevigne blushes at his slip, looks away. The afterimage of her eyes—slitted beneath heavy lids, dubious—mocks him. And they're green, not brown. Her bronze skeleton earrings, dangling like hanged men, startle him. To her his blush seems a quaint response, boyish—part of a kind of accidental charm. After a certain point, a certain number of slaps in the face, your cheeks have had enough of blushing and they grow immune. Except when you're in love. Always a mistake. Usually it isn't love anyway, in hindsight.

She sits down on the edge of the stage, boots hanging down, and with a wry grin sticks out her hand. When he smiles back, his mouth seems to mirror hers—the same gap between the front teeth. He shakes her hand tentatively the way men always do with a woman, even or especially if they're the type to crush other men's hands. She can tell he's a little intimidated and she likes that. And his manner—bashful, twitchy in her eyes' line of fire, brooding when he thinks she's looking elsewhere. Probably he'd be sweet, all that skittish, nervous energy, and eager to please, she can see that in him, yet she takes it all in coolly, as if from a distance. She seems to watch herself watch him and sees no softening in her face. Something has gone out of her recently. She wants so much more now, she's reluctant to risk wanting at all.

"Mikaela Chandler," she says. "But call me Ike."

"I'm Sevigne. It's Mi*kaela*? I once knew a Meeka . . ."

She smiles tolerantly and blows smoke from the side of her mouth. How old is he? Twenty? The open, emotive face and sudden exclamations make her feel prehistoric. She's thirty-four.

"I really loved that set," he says. "It was so eclectic. And your voice, I mean, God, it's just. . . . But I guess you've heard this sort of thing a million times."

"Only if you're a singer-songwriter who wants me to listen to his demo."

He eyes her like a colt at a fence unsure if your fist holds an apple or a stone. "No, no—not at all. I'm a writer. I mean, not of songs. Of books. Well, not books, yet. I'm trying to write a novel."

"But you know your music."

"My folks between them used to play everything under the sun. How did you know—"

"I could see when you knew one. You're not exactly poker-faced. It was nice to see."

"I really loved 'Lilac Wine'. And also, uh . . ."

"'Frederick'." His eyes widen. She feels the heat of her cigarette burning closer to her fingers and looks around for somewhere to butt out. She says, "You were mouthing the words. They're not on my records, those ones."

"But I liked your stuff too."

"And 'Ain't Life a Brook'." She grins. "Also not mine."

"Wasn't it? I'd never heard it before so I thought . . ."

"I could play a lot of songs you haven't heard."

"That one could tear the heart out of a boulder."

"I could see it really got to you."

"But I never saw you look down!"

"Trick of the trade," she says. "Or maybe it's just a male-female thing. You guys all have zero peripheral vision. Women don't have to stare to look." And she widens her bedroom eyes, inclining her head and torso towards him in a way he knows instantly as a burlesque of how he sat watching her. He pulls back but feels the draft of her approach and he smells her—a rich waft of her hair with its few grey strands, faint aura of smoke redolent of Vancouver nightclubs, neat whisky, sex; a sweet tang of sweat from her performance.

She slides off the stage and stands in front of him, earrings jingling. She's only an inch or so shorter.

"Well," she says.

"I'm going to get your tape," he says with ardour, as if voicing an oath of eternal love. As she struts off towards the bar, heels snapping, she looks back over her shoulder and nods and smiles in her cool, sidelong way. Unreadable. While she can read him, it seems, like a children's book. For a few seconds he watches her go, then realizes he's spotlit in front of the stage, a spectacle, the fawning fan or swain.

Going back to his table it hits him—he might have offered

to buy her a drink. Too late. She was just humouring him anyway, probably. He's glad to see some of the other front tables
being claimed, not just for her sake, but for his; his face feels
naked now, he wants to blend in with the crowd.

Eddy and Sevigne are in the Future Bakery, a sprawling, echoing, sun-filled cafeteria in the Annex. Side by side on high
stools they look out through retracted windows over a railed-in
patio full of young people drinking and smoking. An anorexic
woman with thanatic make-up and cyan spiked hair sits
sketching in the margins of *A Brief History of Time* as if illu-
minating a manuscript; at separate tables two sallow, edgy
college boys smoke rolled tobacco and scribble severely
in notebooks. Now and then they glance up at the street—
twinned profiles bristly and soulful, mutually unaware.

"'Ike the dyke,'" Eddy says. "I've seen her play a couple of
times, she's good, maybe a bit folksy."

"That's not granola she's got in her voice, Eddy. It's grit.
Pure gravel."

Eddy eyes him with what looks like surprised approval.
"Nicely put, dude. Now if we can just get you to stop saying
'oot' and 'aboot'."

"Anyway she's more blues and jazz than folk. I think if she
had a band with her instead of just her guitar that would be
more obvious."

Sevigne has just dispatched a huge serving of mashed yams
and kasha in mushroom gravy and is washing it down with a
pint of Rebellion—on Eddy. Eddy is sipping cappuccino,
smoking a cigarillo. Like the name of the city itself, everything
the literati smoke, drink, and eat seems to end with an O.

"She's gay?" Sevigne asks softly, as if saying the word with any force might make it true.

"Maybe bi. I don't know. I think she toured with Ferron. I don't know if the nickname ever meant that much. Isn't she a bit old for you?"

"I just hope she's not a, ah . . . a dyke."

"The Nazis of nomenclature can't hear you here, dude, say what you like."

"I'm just being respectful."

"Snore. I take it you didn't go home with her?"

Sevigne hangs his head. "I made an ass of myself."

"Hey, Simon!"

Up the sidewalk comes a guy with greasy black hair worn long at the back, tiny sunglasses with bottle-green lenses and a long black coat despite the season. Simon sniffs at Eddy— you can actually hear the sound—and stalks past them. Eddy shrugs, cracks his knuckles. "OK, let's look at your excerpt." He digs in his black satchel and pulls out the proofs for the first issue of *On*. Much as it irks Sevigne to see Eddy's head on its lengthy pivot of a neck always swivelling, registering each entry and exit like a shopping mall surveillance camera, he has to admire his professionalism.

"So what do you think, Sev? Nice, eh?"

Sevigne nods. "Can I make changes?"

"Typos, sure."

He tenses over the proofs and sets about rewriting the whole piece—"The Sinking." Yasmine Salloum in mind, he's trying to work the language so it doesn't just describe action but re-enacts it, in rhythm and sound; to make reading the words a physical experience. After some minutes of mumbling, scrib-bling, scratching out, he uncoils and frowns down at the mess. Eddy is tapping the business end of a fresh cigarillo on the counter and studying him with what seems fond amusement.

"So. You planning to see her again?"

"I'm going to her next show, Sunday, at the Free Times Café."

"Good plan. But proceed with caution, Sev. I was crazy about a singer in a band two summers ago, I mean, man, I was just totally . . ." Sevigne looks up from the page with surprise and interest, but Eddy has already changed channels. "Hey, here comes Ray! This should be newsworthy. Gabe Nyman's sitting right there by the rail—the guy who ripped *Fiercely Bereaved* apart, in the *Globe* in '88."

With a pained squint, his big forehead creased and yellow in the harsh light, Ray Dennison has just emerged from the Brunswick House and is hunching towards them with a drunk's stiff deliberation. Sevigne knows that gait. Ray's left arm is cradling a red motorcycle helmet like an enemy's gory head. Whoever the enemy is, Ray is muttering to him.

"Not now," Eddy says, grabbing Sevigne's rising hand. "He's in one of his states. He sits down, sooner or later he's going to go after me. Or maybe you, verbally. Or after Nyman again physically and wind up in court. Again."

Nyman—an older man, portly and dandified, with a patrician grey beard and small round spectacles—is shirking down into his seat, edging his *New York Times Book Review* higher. On the sidewalk Ray totters to a halt. Shifting his helmet to his right hand, he gropes in his pocket. The *New York Times Book Review* quivers, crackles. Ray flips a loonie over the flimsy parapet of the newspaper and the brassy coin jangles on a saucer. The pale hands holding the paper flinch; Ray with a chilling grin stands looking down. After a few seconds he nods, turns away and stumps on. Sevigne has never seen a man look so vulnerable and deadly at the same time, and a warning dose of adrenalin pumps through him.

7

The Interview

NEW GRUB STREET, *published in 1891 by English author George Gissing, traces the struggles of a young London novelist who in some important respects resembles Gissing himself (see MiniBio). Edwin Reardon, encouraged by the small success of his first novel, marries his beloved Amy and the young couple has a child. Reardon must then continue to produce three-volume novels—the kind required by the literary market of his day—at a frantic pace in order to survive. This effort compromises his health, his marriage, and the quality of his work, and he dies a broken man, unlike his friend Jasper Milvain, a cheerfully, frankly opportunistic journalist better suited to the competitive, careerist climate of their milieu. In the end the successful Milvain marries the widowed Amy, while Reardon and Milvain's mutual friend Biffen, disappointed by the failure of his own*

Sevigne taps a key and looks up: 141 words. Ridiculous. He has neglected central characters, whole subplots, to say nothing of major themes. With finances no longer just precarious but truly carious, like a mouthful of rotten teeth, he has agreed to undertake some CapsuleVersion Classics for the outfit Eddy works for. He feels himself becoming a ghost writer in a specialized new sense—a newer Grub Street hack who bleeds the substance out of a work of art and presents for the reader's disedification a leached husk, a spectre adrift in the virtual realm of a laptop screen. He feels increasingly

spectral himself. In Cairo, in the necropolises, even the dead
had a kind of half-life among the living; here most of the living
seem only half alive, glimpsed in the lobby in rushed departure or stooped down slipping a key into one of the morgue-
drawer mail-slots; a man in a high office across College at a
computer terminal working graveyard, static as a mannequin,
his generic face pallid in the glow of the screen and the glimmering overhead panels.

He calls Malachy Boyce CD-ROM Enterprises Inc. and tells
them he can't do it.

On a cool blustery day with a few high scuts of cloud blowing over a wind-scoured sky transported from the north country, he finds himself on Bay Street fighting the crowds of
lunch-time's mini rush hour, while the sun—as if artificial, another municipal amenity—beams directly down between tower
walls to light up the city floor. He's late. He locates the building, he runs inside, all the elevators are busy. He takes the
stairs. Scarecrowed in a March-of-Dimes zoot suit borrowed
from Eddy, he bursts breathless from stairwell 21 and through
a heavy oak door into the serene, spacious premises of Ritsos,
Moulton, Groen. He peels back one floppy coat cuff to check
the time. From between two aspidistras on the corners of her
desk a receptionist peers up, says Mr Moulton is expecting him.

As he enters the office he's blinded by light flooding
through the floor-to-ceiling glass of the south and west walls.
Outside, where bleached seabirds wheel in the gusts, ranks of
towers like massive solar panels recede southward to the lake.
The outer winds seem audible, a steady treble hum weirdly
accompanied by mechanical clicks and whirs, while from
somewhere comes the muted buzzing of a TV or radio. The
vista holds him; for a moment he fails to see Moulton in the
shadowy northwest corner where strip blinds are drawn behind the desk. "Please! Over here!" He seems to be standing
oddly, keenly hunched forward as if in obsequious welcome.

There are white flashes of unaccountable movement. Sevigne approaches, squinting: in a white mesh tank top, towel around his neck, Moulton is astride some sort of exer-cycle and pedalling strenuously. With a droning sound the machine's seat is lifting high and pumping down like a piston, over and over.

The man gives a square-jawed grin, exposing uncommonly clean, orderly teeth. Blue eyes sparkle in a seamed rugged face glazed with sweat. "My lunch-hour workout. I try not to eat lunch. You're Stan, right?"

"Sevigne."

"Right." He's panting, his voice stretched high and thin. "Glad you're bit late actually, Sevigne. Having a good one today."

"Sorry to interrupt, Mr Moulton."

"Give me a break. Just Kim. Have a seat." He nods a head of blond, flat-top bristles at a brown leather swivel chair. "If you don't mind I'll just. Finish up here. OK?"

Sevigne thinks the flicker of light from Moulton's left ear-lobe must be flying sweat, then realizes the man wears an earring. By his features, he looks to be in his forties. Fifties? Sevigne sits down, glances back over his shoulder. On a big screen set into the wall, a team of ant-like climbers is rap-pelling down the grungy inner face of what appears to be a bathtub. On the floor under the screen, an exercise mat, a skip-ping rope, dumb-bells.

"Thirty seconds!" cries Moulton, checking the control panel and accelerating. The whirring seat, apparently respond-ing to the heightened effort, jerks faster.

"That looks tough," Sevigne says.

"*Tough!*" puffs Moulton. The knobbly, coppered knees are churning, the basketball shoes flash. "Seat changes the. Angle of force. Works each. Separate muscle. Glutes to, thighs to, calves." There's a cluster of electronic beeps and the whirring

subsides, the seat bucking slower and slower like the saddle of
a carousel horse winding down. Moulton vaults clear, spryly
alighting back of his desk. He swabs his forehead with the
towel and cracks open a bottle of mineral water.

"Hey, thanks for waiting." He pauses for breath. "So. You
understand how things work here?"

"I'm not completely sure, Mr . . ."

"Kim, just Kim, OK?"

"Kim."

"Perfect."

"You see I was recommended to you, and Eddy's never all
that clear about things."

"Eddy. . . ? Oh, *Mike*—Mike Korkola! Yeah, he's been on
board with us for several projects now. A multifaceted talent,
Mike. I like him plenty." Moulton takes a lusty wallop of water.
"Hey, now I remember—he told me you were a boxer! Me too
I box. Every Saturday afternoon. A lot of partners and brokers
and so forth are getting into it. You know—*older* guys." He
grins. "It's one beautiful stress-buster."

He's shadow-boxing behind his desk. Noncommittally
Sevigne looks on. Propped by the telephone—turned outward, away from the man—is a framed photograph, apparently recent, of a beaming Moulton in a white tuxedo with his
bride, a tanned, frail platinum blonde who looks younger than
Sevigne.

"Mike told me you were an Ontario champ or something!
Said you could show me a few moves!"

Fingering mutinous lips, Sevigne tries to remould them
into a more serious configuration. Good old Eddy. He settles
deeper into the sumptuous-smelling leather. "Eddy exagger-
ates a bit sometimes, Kim, but I'd be happy to try."

"Great, great!" He spins his spinal-support chair around
and straddles it tough-guy style, brown rawhide arms folded
over the top of the backrest. This posture squeezes triceps,

biceps and forearm muscles into knotty high relief. The firm's work, he says, is simple. Or Sevigne's role in it anyway. If things work out. And Moulton has a feeling they will. RMG Images Inc. prepares the sort of compositions Sevigne must know from radio and TV ads. Jingles. Hasn't Mike—Eddy—even mentioned that much?

"He said I'd be writing songs. Lyrics for songs."

"Well, Sev, if everything goes, you will be writing songs. Or rewriting old standards. You remember that dreamy version of 'High Hopes' we put out for Wardair back in '86?"

Sevigne shrugs. "I keep telling myself I have to make more time for television, Mr . . . Kim."

"Bingo."

Moulton aims what looks like a small handgun at Sevigne's head. From behind Sevigne a burst of noise. He swivels round. The roped climbers are gone. A tiny periscope is surfacing in a toilet bowl and turning from side to side; a miniature submarine breaks surface while a seamen's chorus of deep voices with accordion backing trolls out a sea-chanty about U-Plunger, the Toilet Submersible. "*Your secret weapon in the war against germs!*" booms a skipperly baritone over the hearty background chorus. The dark vessel goes on cruising the bowl with aggressive vigilance. It looks repellently fecal.

"See, Sev, Bill and Cos and I have been around a while! Twenty years this May, in fact . . ." As Sevigne turns back, Moulton's eyes lock onto his with a kind of alert expectancy; Sevigne has a sense of missing some important cue. "I bet you remember the U-Plunger Shanty from back when you were, uhh. . . . How old are you now, Sev?"

"Twenty-five. In July." And it comes to him—he's meant to express surprise that Moulton could be that old, in business for so long.

"Young, yeah, younger than the others, but frankly I find some of the older writers a touch . . . overqualified would be the term, I guess. And between you and me? Out of touch with the realities of your generation."

Sevigne looks sheepishly at the tips of his fingers, barely emerging from the coat cuffs.

"OK, so that was the seventies. Let's forge ahead. Here's something new, something up to the minute—and more our speed these days." Again he aims and fires at the TV. Blurred shapes strobe across the screen while a menacing bass voice pumps out a bad imitation of Public Enemy. The shapes focus into a line of scowling giants in knee-length shorts leaping at a basket and slam-dunking in time with the stressed syllables in the rap, their psychedelic court-shoes flash-painting the air with parabolas of light. "I'm *in* your face like a *bas*ketball, I don't *like* you much, I don't *like* you at all. . . ." As the voice and the slam-dunking go on, the logo of a shoe manufacturer appears with the legend WHEN THE GOING GETS ROUGH . . . DO THEM UP RIGHT.

A click and the screen goes dark. With a faint hum two sliding doors of accordioned mahogany close over it, as over a coffin in a crematorium. Sevigne swivels slowly back round. A few feet from Moulton's shoulder, where the blinds end, a huge seagull hovers at the window, peering in.

"So you see why young guys like you are useful to us!"

"Sure."

"Mike informs me you're a gifted songwriter, Sev. Says you've written the lyrics for several hit songs, including that one last year by, hmm, what's-her-name . . . very simple? One syllable? Plays cool, kind of retro stuff."

"You don't mean Ike?"

"Bingo." Moulton tosses the remote up and swipes it from the air. Eddy, my Eddy; by the moment Sevigne feels more obliged to give the job a try. "Hit parade or not, though, we'll be requiring a sample lyric up front, Sev. Hope that's OK. We'll decide on the basis of that if we're right for each other.

Plus we ask that you sign a release form providing for our use of a modified version of the lyric in a future composition in case we decide not to take you on, which if we did do—take you on, I mean, and I feel pretty upbeat about that—would be on a contract-by-contract basis."

Sevigne nods, as if paying attention to the details. Behind Moulton the sunlit gull bobs on its urban thermal, bright wings making minuscule adjustments.

"Now if we do take you on, you're looking at about one assignment per month. Chances are, only the odd one'll actually make. That's just the way the business runs . . ." Moulton glances down at his hands—restless, ringless hands, lean and brown as a mummy's. "One doesn't make, you get a flat rate as a kill fee. One does, you get the same flat rate plus a hundred dollars per line plus a small royalty for each screening. A typical freelance lyricist makes between eight and fifteen grand per year, and for very little effort. I mean, when Cos was still writing jingles it hardly ever took him more than two days to nail one flat. As he used to say."

Again Sevigne nods, mouthing a silent *Wow*.

"Now, for your sample lyric. Here's the file with all the information. You have any questions at all, we talk, OK? I mean that. Any time. My card's in the file."

He puts up his dukes with a collegial grin. His earring glitters. The dazzling gull has vanished, a gap in the high air; obliged, amazed, and curious, Sevigne scoops up the file.

8

Souvenirs

Well, I don't remember how we met
When or where or what was said
And I don't remember how I felt
And I don't remember you

WHEN she recognizes him she's glad to have him there, front row centre again, she's trying out a new song and figures she can depend on his transparency. His face will signal what his heart hears. She gives him a smile as she plays the bridge between verses—picking it on a Takamine with a tone like her voice, no oil on the strings, plenty of rasp and roughness. His eyes seem to soften as she makes the chord change to E minor—it works, it works—and sings the next verse.

No, I don't recall the time or place
We first lay down and made our peace
And I won't remember how your face
Opened like a sea.
And I don't remember you,
And you don't remember me . . .

Les always sat front row centre when he came, unlike her busy new manager, Anson McWilliams, who rarely comes at all, which is fine with her, better. To think she started this song for Les and now doesn't even think of him as she sings it. The emotion as she sings is genuine, she can feel the quaver cut into her voice and the shivers zap up and down her spine, but it's all bizarrely impersonal. That's how it is these days. She's emotionally inert except when she sings, and when she is singing, her passion is for shadows, which she guesses are easier to love anyway. A week ago while having a drink with her old college friend, and one-time, fleeting lover, Nadine, she said yes, she'd thought she was in love with Les those five years but now she doubts she ever was—and Nadine cried foul, no way, you *can't* say that, you can't deny your love in hindsight! If you thought you were in love then, you were, and you have to honour that emotion.

Mikaela heard the history and unhealed wounds crowding into Nadine's speech, so she spoke gently when she answered. Maybe she'd just convinced herself she loved him, she said. I mean, you're supposed to love whoever you live with, right, and what can't you convince yourself of?

But with Les you've got issues, Nadine said, power issues, reproductive issues . . . they've severed the emotional continuum . . . your anger has toxified the memory. . . .

Mikaela always lost interest when Nadine laid on the self-help jargon—but maybe she was right. After all, just a year ago she was ready to start a family with the man! Or felt she was. He already had a son from an early marriage but he spoke vaguely of starting "a real family" with her, at some point, when the time was right for her "career-wise." At thirty-three and just beginning to get real air play and big festival invitations and interest from some of the major labels, it was hardly the right time for her, but when? Till the age of thirty she'd said (whenever her parents or friends with children would push and pry) that she never would have children, no interest, no time, too many friends and too much music to make and places to get to. Then there were those nasty ordeals her mom and her grandmother had gone through, the miscarriages and stillbirths and the "ossified fetus" (nobody would elaborate on that one) so that her grandmother hadn't had a live child till she was thirty-eight, and her mom had had only her, Mikaela Jane, at thirty-five.

Mikaela turned thirty, then thirty-one. She and her old folkie friends had been drifting apart and she was getting tired, no, bored, with the band, the late nights, the touring, their stale old ten-chord forty-song repertoire. So was it just boredom, this impatiently growing, embarrassing, unhip desire for a child? It didn't feel like boredom—it was more like the feeling of falling suddenly, irreversibly in love with someone who'd been around for years without stirring a flicker of interest.

Whether it was a good career move or not. She was now a solo artist and felt solo in other ways—in every way, really. For two years, while she wrote and performed, Les went on saying that now was not the time for a family, they were just getting her started, she should be patient, the breakthrough was imminent. *Soon, Ike, soon.* Only she was afraid she didn't have a few years, not when it came to the child. *The* child she was calling it now. Her desire became a fixation the way a new hope does when nothing else is working, and in her heart the crisis became a test of Les, who, she sensed, was scared not only by the strength of her desire but by its potential to spoil the career of one of his few promising clients. Which would put his own career in jeopardy. She wanted to believe—how naive it seems now, how self-destructive!—that his love for her was totally separate from those concerns. As if. As if *anyone*, in this world. He'd already lost his first career, as a folk-rock singer-guitarist in Greenwich Village in the early seventies. And when she finally served up her ultimatum he did a sudden fade, told her it was professional folly at this particular stage in her career (he always talked like a manager when the conversation got serious), and he couldn't in good conscience agree. Then, later, drunk: *I love you, Mikaela, and that is the reason I will not do this to you. Ruin everything you've worked for. Everything* we've *worked for.*

Then I'll have the baby without you.

Then I'll have to leave.

Then you're fired.

All the ways we loved have slipped my mind
Like the letters I forget to send
Souvenirs of grass and sand
Carried home from the sea.
And I don't remember you—
And you don't remember me.

In fact, in truth, she does not remember Les very well, and the ways they loved really are slipping her mind, or at least blurring into one dim, general impression glazed over with a sense of sadness and wasted time—and as for the letters, she wrote only that one angry one and she did send it. The irony is that "I Don't Remember You"—which she started just after firing him as manager, lover and friend—is going to be her breakout song. Her sounding board is swept up all right. She gives him another smile, this boy who might have made a pretty fling in another life, who she sees now as if seeing him from the moon. The way she sees the child now, too.

And I don't remember why you left
When or where or what was said
And I won't remember how I felt
Or what it's done to me.
And I don't remember you,
No, I don't remember you.
Oh, I don't remember you . . .
Do you still remember me?

9

Launch at the ROM

. . . like the viscera of some living thing torn apart. His brief reading of "The Sinking" ended, he spots a waitress in the crowd beneath the gallows from which a noose hangs swaying in drafts from the air-conditioning; by a display case full of hoods and masks for headsmen, hangmen and hands-on inquisitors he corners her and takes two over-full glasses of red. The wine sloshes, gouts splashing onto his boots. He opens his throat and drains a glass and fights the urge to smash it on the floor. It's over! A woman in a skin-tight grey dress smiles on the other side of the display case and he smiles back, then freezes: her dress is actually duct-tape, mummy-wrapped around her from just above the nipples to just below the crotch. A puffy blond man wearing a fat tie dotted with a skull-like motif appears and whisks her away. The tie's after-image niggles at Sevigne; then he knows the repeated motif as the tormented, howling figure in Edvard Munch's *The Scream*.

The elation of reprieve is fading. So he has survived his first reading. He was hoping to shine. He read too fast, he's sure of it, and he forgot, God *damn* it, forgot to introduce the next reader—who's now struggling at the microphone. Lucky Ike isn't here after all. Between her sets the other night when he spoke of the launch she said she already had a gig of her own, but break a leg, for her. Then—seemingly more touched than excited by his interest—she agreed to meet him for coffee, Friday. Tomorrow.

A TV crew is pushing through the crowd. Light floods into the display case and beams diabolically from the eyeholes of a dainty mask suspended inside. In a jittery soprano voice, the new reader tells a first-person story of a woman being raped by her drunken lover. Sevigne turns away as the camera noses in. The faces around him are lit blindingly and the heat on his nape intensifies.

"May we have a word with you?" A dramatic baritone, West Indian accent. He pivots on his heel and squints into the lights, pulse racing. A lanky handsome reporter in a suede jacket is interviewing Una, who apparently was standing within a few feet of him, Sevigne. She's nodding, looking up, laughing with her whole body as she listens to the man's question and then, brows earnestly pleated, weighs her response.

Hurrying off behind a showcase he lifts a glass from a passing tray and downs it. A node of sparkling guests opens, revealing a colossus: the wax model of a jailer or torturer on a low scaffold. Black hood, knee-length leather apron, hobnailed boots, meaty arms crossed over the barrel chest, lips warped in a sadistic leer. Glass eyes glinting from the eye-slits.

. . . ridiculous place for a launch though. Korkola's an asshole.

And I guess he had to lie to make it happen? Told them it was an academic journal for medievalists, "Round Table" or something.

So who was the Neil Young wannabe with the speed-reading?

They said he was from up north.

One of Korkola's old bumboys, I'd put money down.

That's how it happens.

Man, this woman is utterly overtime!

In an alcove leading into another room is a showcase full of rusted scalpels, pliers, thumbscrews, flaying tools and instruments of evisceration, and against the wall two standing coffins, one open—lid studded with spikes—one closed. Sevigne approaches. Behind him the audience evenly applauds as the woman in broken tones introduces the next reader. Looking in through the face-hole of the closed box, he recalls Father Moroni, and some vague boyhood sorrow revives in him; some faded shame. He pulls at the door of the box, pulls harder, feels it give. No spikes inside—it's a model, meant to show how they look when closed.

The peacefully dim alcove brightens. A camera is rolling in from the main hall, TV lights making the spikes of the other Iron Maiden gleam as on the spotlit stage-prop of an illusionist. He slips into the casket and pulls shut the lid. In his nostrils, odours of resin and sawdust and in his ears the aqualung rasping of his breaths. He's tipping his head to peer out the fist-sized porthole when a blinding beam lasers in. He ducks, looks up: countless particles swarm in that beam of light as if animated by the heat of it. The light vanishes. The sounds of the TV crew recede. Far away a monotonous male voice drones poetry, the voice lifting wistfully at the end of each line.

He's about to shove open the door when the porthole fills with a circle of white-whiskered cheek, then a squinting eye grotesquely magnified by a lens like a monocle. The eye blinks and swivels as if performing some kind of ophthalmic exercise. It's Gabriel Nyman, the "high-powered critic" Eddy introduced him to before the launch—also introducing him, at last, to Lois Shapiro. Yep, Sev was a comer. Sev was the real article. . . . The searching eye, seeing nothing, blinks and withdraws. After a few seconds Sevigne peers out through the hole: Nyman is striding back into the main hall. Pushing open the lid, Sevigne steps out and slips away.

A marble grand staircase describing a slow helix descends to a show on quantum electrodynamics and climbs back in time to the Egypt of the Pharaohs and the lost kingdoms of the Mediterranean. The stairs wind round a Nisga'a totem pole rising some hundred feet from the basement to the skylight, as if it were the building's axis. Climbing the stairs, Sevigne eyes the figures carved into the pole. Human, raven, grizzly, wolf—

the faces move him, their elemental fierceness and firmness tempered with calm dignity and compassion. There it is, the state he aspires to, while day by day he's being initiated deeper into the Scene and drifting farther from what he envisaged: the noble friendships, night-long confabulations about poetry, favourite artists, films and music, lovemaking, love. Instead, what others are doing and getting paid for it. Laid for it. How to get a foot in the door. And the carved eyes in the still centre of that world-tree regard him coolly, as they have countless other manic, grasping insects buzzing past on their upward or downward spirals; and while his heart keeps asserting its own difference—its kinship with the totems and with Spirit Island— the eyes go on demanding How so?

The mummies in the "Lives & Afterlives" show lie side by side in long glass cases, a dozen in each. Here and there visitors do the Louvre shuffle, glancing in at the bodies with dully speculative faces, as if viewing ceramic pots or bone arrow- heads. They seem that dead. Only the hair, which never was alive, is still lifelike. Across the room a man with shaved head and a leather jacket is stopping every few feet, as if examining each specimen with care. Back turned, he's big-shouldered but thin-shanked and geriatrically hunched, with the bur- dened, halting gait of a mourner. Sevigne looks away. The mummy in front of him bears a necklace of livid and puckered tissue, as if he was slashed in battle, or hanged. A spotlight shines directly on his face and through the eyeholes. The skull is empty as a dead hive, though once it swarmed with plans, de- sires, envies, the lifelong shadow-boxing exchange with one's selves or the dead or the lover who broke faith or the superior who shamed you in front of colleagues, scolded you as you laboured with chisel and mallet on a lintel of Nubian marble so the other masons and the slaves hauling blocks up from the Nile over boles of timber to the rising massif of the pyramid all look up—then look away, some in indifference, some in fatigue, some out of kindness, some to hide their pleasure. And as the day passes, your anger builds, and though the sun declines, the hot flush on your nape and your shaved scalp deepens like sunburn and you hammer absently at the face of the lintel now visibly marred, each blow echoing in your skull with the words you should have yelled at the long-hated foreman, and as they bubble to your barely moving lips, the mallet slips, slams your thumb and you bellow and curse and in a moment he is there, his shadow a great stain spreading over you. He's scolding you again, your hand better severed at the wrist your mother a shiftless whore, and something cracks inside you as when the mauled wedges finally cleave open a limestone slab, and you're on your feet with the chisel raised like a knife to his brow and the mallet bashing down on the end expertly and for the millionth time without consciousness or true volition. Like an axed sacrifice he crumples, his final curse dissolving with his breath. Now as the other masons gather round, and the slaves, ignoring the orders and the bullwhips of their foremen, drop their ropes and deepen the circle, you collapse beside the murdered man in the dusky shadow of the mob, your head drooped, the spattered mallet in your lap, sobbing for what you've done. No trial. Within an hour you're strung up, beside a slave executed at dawn, from a gallows overhanging the river. After darkfall your family comes to cut you down and see that you're dealt with as befits a skilled tradesman—mummified and buried with your tools, not tossed in a communal pit with the slaves.

And four millennia later here you are.

Christ, where did that come from? His gut is fisted, like his hands, as if the events have been real, the fatal drama his own.

"Heard you read, mate."

He looks up, startled. Ray's head is freshly shaved. The scalp has a lunar pallor and smoothness next to the sunned, seamed face; yet despite the biker's tan he looks haggard, unwell.

"So that was you over there," Sevigne says.

"Beats listening to that lot downstairs." Sevigne looks away, back at the mason. In a kind of grudging growl Ray adds, "Present company excepted."

"You don't need to say that."

"You're right. You read too fast. Read slower next time."

Awkward silence. Sevigne says, "You missed the get-together before the launch."

"I miss as much of Mike's extravaganzas as I can. Just not my thing, gala launches. Gala anything. Beware the word."

"But I was hoping you'd read."

"It's purest shite, my piece. Mike's truly fucked me over on this one. Shouldn't be in print. And I *told* him I'd changed my mind."

"Well—I loved it. Really. And *Fiercely Bereaved* . . . man, Eddy lent me his copy, last week. I would have bought one, but."

"But it's out of print." He turns his glower on the mummy's feet, the rotted, blackened toes like kernels of ancient corn shrivelled in the husk.

"Ray, listen, I can see you don't want to talk about it, about your piece, but I did really like it, and I think you have to . . . I think if you like someone's work you have to let them know because in this business, or what I've seen of it"—Ray is watching him, amusement flickering at the corners of his mouth—"there's more than enough rejection and—and *de*jection already and you need to hear those things. I mean, *one* needs to hear them."

Ray runs a hand over his iron-blue scalp. Sevigne eyes the mummy, its cartilaginous black lips retracted, brown teeth gritted in a snarl, shoulders seized up and arms tight to its sides as if bristling at some eternal outrage. Four thousand years out of the arena of competing dreams and the body is still one grisly semaphore of anger.

"You strike me as pretty young to have had a lot of rejection," Ray says. "Or you're speaking hypothetically. You're how old, twenty-two?"

"Twenty-five. Almost."

"Well, it's all pretty much hypothetical at that age, isn't it? Success and failure. Life, death—all that." Ray grins with clamped lips. "Right, we're even now, we've patronized each other. Let's get out of here, get a pint."

10

Let me be your shadow

NEXT NIGHT across the Annex in Mikaela's apartment—
first floor of a pillar-porched Victorian redbrick,
clematis and white lilac hemming in the porch like a
bower—Sevigne and Mikaela lie in bed by candlelight, Nina
Simone playing softly on the stereo, "Black is the colour of my
true love's hair." Breezes chuffing under the tapping ricepaper
blind raise gooseflesh; streetlamp-shadows of chestnut leaves
scutter over the blind like hands over a pale, undulating back.

He might be slapping himself for proof that he's conscious
if not for the touches, scratches, bites, sucks and long probing
kisses that keep reassuring him. He's struck dumb by his sudden reversal of fortune. Last night brooding over the mummies in their spotlit showcase, he felt sure that his "career" in
the city was defunct, and Ray's generosity in the Silver Rail
helped only for as long as the draft lager buoyed him. Then
today on the courtyard patio of the Bamboo Club he sat stiffly
in the sun's pooled heat, drained to the marrow, convinced she
would stand him up. She was late—ten, fifteen, twenty-five
minutes—then there she was, striding in, brow pinched above
her sunglasses, painted lips tight and tense. He was another
Thing to Do she would soon cross off a lengthy mental list.
But as she veered towards him, shopping bag in hand, her face
relaxed and she apologized for her lateness, embraced him
lightly as he leapt up, kissed him on either cheek.

"Why are you smiling like that?" he asked.

"Because you're blushing. Men don't do that here."

"Oh, am I? God, sorry."

"No, no. It's a sweet thing when a kiss pays off."

They started with coffee and then—quickly, unexpectedly taking flight in each other's company, filling the courtyard with surprised relieved laughter—they escalated to a bottle of cheap but icy cold rosé and then again to a bottle of good chablis. Ike's sunglasses and black cardigan had long since come off and a green satin sleeveless shirt showed off her tanned, freckled shoulders; she said she worked on her songs in the back garden when the weather was nice. They shared a platter of steamed mussels in a buttery, garlicky broth sopped up with hunks of crusty bread and washed down with more chablis and returned to her apartment at sunset.

Now he searches her face for any sign that this is all some elaborate prank. Dragging on a cigarette she narrows her eyes at him—hazel green, the heavy lids darker than the skin around them. "But I can't believe . . . I mean, you must have men, people approaching you all the time."

"Oh, are we at the fishing for compliments stage already? You men really are all alike." She smiles her sidewise smile, feeling for the ashtray and butting out. "Yes, I am joking, you can laugh now."

After a moment he says, "I have no sense of humour."

"Is that a warning?"

"No. A joke."

"Then you were right."

She watches his face cramp up, uncertain, then loosen into a smile. Already she loves to tease him. Kissing him hard she spreads his lips with her tongue, her fingers in his hair chording complex progressions. His eyes flash into hers, hands roaming over her back and buttocks. How do we live without this, she thinks, all the time it isn't happening?

The small hours slip towards morning. Overhead a storm

passes, rumbling, night trains on a high trestle. On the white blind the dense rain is shadowed like snowmelt coursing under ice. Then stillness. Thinking their lust exhausted they keep trying to go to sleep wrapped around each other only to find there is still more love to make. As she pulls him close, she feels again that ache of anticipation as good as any contact to follow, all of her, even her pores, wide open and greedy. With her hips she coaxes him to move harder. This is what she craves, the performer's holiday, to be taken this way or belly to the bed, pressed down, down with a weight and a fierceness, worked on instead of *being* on—on stage, on time, on top of every little detail, up above the crowd. The tireless doer.

Because you're different, if you want to know. More open. Pure of heart. I don't know. You don't fit any of the categories.

But neither do you, Ike!

Mikaela, I'm Mikaela. Ike's the one the others see. Not like this. I'm not pure of heart, though—I want to be.

You don't snigger, you don't know everything and sneer at everything.

And three nights later, he asleep in the bedroom and she naked in the front room with her guitar, heels tucked under her on the sofa, the sweetest drumbeat of a pulse between her thighs: Maybe you remind me a bit of me, the way I was ten years ago, no—twelve years?—when I was just starting in the business. Only I didn't call it that then. Maybe I do want to look out for you a little, is that such a problem? Let me. I'm not saying you're still a child. Everyone needs someone to look out for them, here. (She bends and scribbles a few words in a dollar notebook.) I've seen people change. Get hard too soon. Sell out, cash in. (She writes lines and crosses them out, strums chords, softly hums a phrase.) You know that story. Or maybe you don't, not yet. You want love to be your life's big motive, then you run out of fight.

Let me look out for you, let me be your eyes
Every closet's got its skeleton
Every turn a bad surprise
There's a map in the lines of my palm you'll
—There's a map in the lines of my face you'll follow
This is no street to walk down solo
Let me be your shadow and your eyes

In "The Islands of the Nile" Mera has grown older, grown several inches, and her eyes have lightened to hazel. What she does when she is not loving Luc has always been shadowy and undeveloped; Sevigne now decides that she's a musician. In the cabin on the weekend of their falling in love, Luc keeps hearing her singing snippets of songs he half knows while she makes her strong coffee for everyone. . . .

It happened on the last day. It was a calm August afternoon, hot, their father napping in the cabin, Luc sitting on the end of the dock with David and Mera, feet dangling in the current. They drank beer out of tall bottles pulled clattering from the ice-filled cooler. David— always tired on the few occasions he got away from the office—lay back, his feet still in the water, and dozed off. Mera shook her head and smiled to one side. Old man Dave, she said, laying a beach towel over his torso and face so that he wouldn't burn again, like yesterday. He didn't move. After a time, Mera—the faint down at the outer corners of her lips glossed with sweat—said she needed a swim and asked if you could go out as far as that sandy island. The islet was farther out than it looked, Luc said. If she wanted, though, he could take her out halfway, to where a sandbar rose within a foot or two of the surface, in dry summers breaking clear. You can sit there, he told her, with the river in your lap. The brothers had done it often in their teens.

As they swam, he angled them into the sluggish current, aiming upstream of the bleach-bottle buoy that marked the spot. As always the water was cold. She was a strong swimmer, and they were half racing each other out there, and then the sandbar humped out of the depths like the breaching back of a grey whale.

She knelt on the sandy crest; the current slid over her belly just under her navel. Cross-legged he sat close to her, since only a small ridge, like the top of a high dune, was near enough to the surface to sit on. The sun—its heat now welcome—beat down on their wet heads and bodies, and they watched the ravens revolving above the woods around the cabin. David was still asleep. They turned to see a freighter glide past on the far side of the islet though still so close they might have called out to the waving deck-hand. Luc asked Mera if she liked it here; as if he couldn't feel her answer already. He asked her to sing him something, and after some hesitation she did sing, "Black is the colour of my true love's hair," by the end of it her voice fraught with an extra quaver he assumed was from the river's chill. Unconsciously he edged closer and asked if she was cold. Lightly she touched the nearest part of him—the inside of his knee where it broke the surface—and said no. Their eyes met and held, his voice stalled in his throat, some strong new current was pushing him forward and tipping him into her eyes. He trembled as if the cold were in him now too. Nothing much could happen out here, yet everything already had. Downstream the ship that had passed them was droning its horn; peripherally he could see the cabin and the dock a few hundred yards off where his brother, feet limply dangling, lay like a husband murdered in bed, while the birds above him circled and called.

11

Beatrice & Grace

O N A DAY of sun and cloud and ephemeral rainbow showers he lopes westward along College Street into Little Italy where the street, straight until then, curves like a busy Venice canal flowing between walls of trattorias, small groceries, leather-goods stores; and nearby among the flower and fruit stands and the Dantean street signs ("Beatrice," "Grace") he finds the café Lois Shapiro has chosen.

She's sitting on the patio where the pergola still drips from the latest shower. Although hot sunlight sieves down through the vined trellis to fall sparkling among wet tables and chairs, she has a mauve cardigan around her hunched shoulders and she's smoking avidly, as if trying to draw warmth from the dim ember of the tip. In fact her whole being seems centred on the cigarette, fanning out from it as puckers around her lipsticked lips, deep concentric creases bracketing her mouth, the small bony nose, the smoke-coloured puff of hair, the slight circle of her shoulders. A martini in a glass with a lipsticked rim is on the table beside a heap of papers held down by a black, lozenge-shaped purse.

"I'm sorry I'm late," Sevigne says, panting.

"Oh, Sevigne, do sit down! How wonderful to meet you!"

"I was writing, I totally lost track of time."

"Nonsense. You know *I'm* always early. And I'm used to poets." Large tortoiseshell spectacles dwarf an already small, wrinkled face—a little-old-lady face, yet her voracious smoking and constant blinks and twitchings give a counterimpression of anxious, irritable vitality. Her magnified blue eyes are bright and unflinching and she leans way over the table as she speaks, the way Sevigne usually does himself, though this time, with Lois already in possession, he's obliged to hang back. She's renowned for the toughness of her editing and her sleepless dedication to her writers—*her* writers, Eddy says she calls them, the many she publishes in *Toronto Poetry Review*, the new ones she mentors with sherry-stained letters, the timid ones she kid-gloves into further submissions, the impossible dawdlers she rebukes and cajoles into writing full books, which she goes on to publish, and then to promote with feisty, testy calls from the antique black rotary phone on her desk. A reading here, a review there—far more reviews than poetry books usually get nowadays. Book-page editors soon discover the only way to get Lois off their backs is to yield.

"Now I won't beat around the bush and waste your time, Sevigne Torrins. It's said you're working on a novel."

His heart quickens; maybe she does novels now too. "I just came from working on it," he says.

"A bad idea. Too many poets nowadays waste their talent on novels. An inferior form, in my view." With bulging eyes she grips her martini and takes an audible sip; her fingernails are bitten to the quick, the fingers ink-stained. "A good career move, of course, and that's the full extent of it. Keep your poetry in your poems, Sevigne. You know how very fond I am of your poems! You are still writing poems?"

"More than ever," he says. "Love poems."

She coughs with violence, smoke jetting from her mouth. She goes on coughing and hacking and the loose cords of her throat tremble. He moves to help her but she waves him back, magnified eyes wide and forbidding; when the convulsion passes she resumes smoking with undampened fervour.

". . . are you all right, Ms Shapiro?"

"Lois. Yes, yes. Love poems, you said? So you're in love."

"For two weeks now."

"Newly in love and still forging ahead with a novel!" Raucous laughter shakes her frail bones. "How very like a man!" The laughter reverts to coughing. He looks on, helpless, and also bothered by her words. The waiter is still out of sight. After a few seconds she clears her throat and croaks, "I mean . . . I mean to take on love as if it were a hobby or a part-time job. Rather than a vocation."

"I *am* in love," he says staunchly.

"Oh, I'm sorry, Sevigne, you misunderstand. I *admire* that trait in men, really. It's much the safer approach, on the whole. Much wiser."

Then wisdom is unwise, he wants to say; but she's speaking.

"Now I wonder—have we enough poems for a book?"

In his mind he has put similar words into her mouth, not expecting to hear them. *Would you care to review for us? Mop down the office floor?* "Enough for a book," he says now. "Well . . ."

"Well, *what*? Don't be such a wallflower, Sevigne! You know how I feel about your poems."

"I meant," he says, "I think I do have enough, I was just trying to sort them out and get them ready to submit to places. You're serious about this?"

"You were going to show them to me first, I hope."

"I'm not very well known," he says, testing her, testing the gods to see if this is the latest tantalizing hoax. She scowls and crumples her butt in the ashtray. "You're not known around here, period. That's for me to address. Your concern should be putting a manuscript into these wizened hands, and soon. It won't be good enough, of course. We'll meet and I'll ask you to cut much of the material and to write more. It always works this way. Pare down, pare down. Publish in haste, regret at leisure. Let's think next spring at the earliest for publication."

"Next spring!" He's stunned, punch-drunk with joy, yet it seems unbearably distant.

"At the earliest. But the time will pass, you'll see. Some of the other houses are booked into the mid-nineties!"

"Really. . . ?" He's leaning over the table, as is she, so they might look to the approaching waiter like a pair of spring and winter lovers, Harold and Maude, heads together contriving an elopement or some other subversive caper.

The waiter inserts his shadow between them.

"Champagne," Sevigne bursts out, then turns to Lois. "God, I've always wanted to order champagne! Would you bring us your champagne list?"

Out of the side of his mouth the man says, "Would the ah . . .wine list do, sir?"

12

Summertime

ARTINE always said he should not worry about being thin, he would begin to gain weight as soon as he met the right woman. It would be a sign. And now at last he is filling out, bones padded by the lovers' banquets that he and Ike prepare each other several nights a week in her speckless, galley-cramped kitchen: dishes like *pad Thai* and chicken *mole* that she, sipping wine and peacefully smoking, makes step by step from recipes in books of international cuisine; the one-pot proletarian stews, slumgullions and stir-fries that he improvises while guzzling beer and shuffling at the white-tiled counter in a kind of jig, hands reaching, stirring, spicing, soundtrack for the action by Lou Reed or the Pogues, set design by Jackson Pollock.

They fall in love much harder and faster than either could have expected. Mikaela has grown cynical about romance, coming to believe that if you aren't actually looking for it, it won't happen, it's something you bring on yourself when you need a big change, consciously or un—it's definitely not this abrupt, unappealable verdict. Sevigne believed he'd been deeply in love three times already, so that now, as he falls deeply in love, the feeling is a surprise and a revelation. Now he's sure that he never did love Una, truly, never has loved truly since Meeka Greene. Eros the cagey and indirect has been guiding him upward through his vision of Una, a flickering adumbration of outgrown desires, home to the bed and the warm, comprehending embrace of Mikaela Jane Chandler.

Becoming Ike's man brings him not only a new lover's elation but also new confidence in his writing—oddly, since so far she's only taking him seriously in bed. All she knows of his work is the Xerxes ExtraSensitive jingle he quoted once to lighten a necessary interruption—*Because she'll love a man in uniform . . . Only one thing should ever come between you*—and a few lines from a still-unfinished poem, for her.

Before long he's staying over almost nightly, the lovers naked and sheetless in the muggy heat, an antique fan stirring the kilims and cast-off Persian runners draping the walls so that her bedroom—candle-washed in maroon light—seems some inner island of privacy and grace. Here is the life hospitable to the heart and the senses that he was missing without knowing it when he and Bryon surveyed Malton's industrial parks and projects from the weedy crest of a ski-hill made of garbage (Sevigne plotting to seal up its gas-vents to make a volcano); in the cabin in the Soo where his father was sinking by the bottle; in the Spartan bachelor flat where he still spends his days. It feels like an office now—an office, yes, for a ratified writer with a contract for one book and a second almost ready to show around.

One day as he hurries along Bloor after another jag of reckless overspending (a twenty-sixer of gin, limes to squeeze in it, a warm loaf of caraway rye, a wedge of sachertorte for her) he spots her across Huron Street in a crowd hustling towards him. He freezes in mid-step, for a moment unable to believe in their connection. She seems so much taller than the women around her and than most of the men; she has on faded blue jeans, a man's white shirt, that snug leather vest she was wearing the night they met. Strands of hair are blowing over her brown, sunlit forehead, she's walking briskly and smoking in a don't-mess-with-me way and it seems some of the people around her do double-takes when they look. His stomach floods with warmth. He wants to run to her, as across a field or a heath. The light changes, the crowd advances, a few feet on she sees him and flicks her butt away and smiles, not wryly but open-mouthed and with everything she has. She stutter-steps—an involuntary quick little skip as if she's having to stop herself from breaking into a run. Mid-street they embrace while strangers barge and jostle past them and they don't un-clinch, laughing, until the honking begins.

In July, when Martine writes to tell him that things have finally arranged themselves, Bryon and Tralee have decided to marry at Christmas and would he reserve his ticket soon, he feels no twinges of envy—only joy. Perhaps Ike can fly with him to Cairo, they could even get married there, *en sourdine*, after Bryon's wedding is over. Money is the only catch. He's surviving on reviews for Eddy, a thousand-dollar grant Lois Shapiro pushed his way after he signed his contract, and the promise of a cheque when he completes his next ditty for Moulton. But it's all right. The money will come now, he feels it. Besides, he and Ike are talking about his moving in with her in the fall, allowing him to give up his place and share her rent, save them both money.

Sometimes thoughts of their plan will catch Mikaela in the belly with a jolt a little like the womb-tugs she's been feeling for a few years at the sight of babies in strollers or in their mothers' arms. She offered on impulse, in the heat of the moment. She knows he's almost broke and she loves being with him, but it is a small place and Sevigne, though not a huge guy, somehow takes up a lot of room. Actually her own offer has caught her by surprise—she feels, at times, half out of control, another part of her seems to be calling the shots. About him a voice in her ear keeps whispering *mistake*. But so often what passes for intuition is just old, ingrown fears pinching at your heart, trying to keep you from growing or enjoying a U-turn in your luck.

And now everything is going her way. The sessions are set for late August in Montreal, good studio-musicians hired, the final song record-ready but for the instrumental (which *still* feels clichéd even though she's reworked it four times, experimenting with chords she's never tried before, a thirteenth, an augmented fifth). Anson McWilliams played a demo of three of the tracks to some key people at the new label and he said they were "more excited than ever." You have to take whatever Anson says with a grain of salt, but they're good songs after all. And she's in love.

Against all odds in love—
Never knew I was dreaming of
The things you'd bring, when you snuck up on me
Like summer, you took me by storm, lover,
Took me by surprise,
You lover against all odds.

And, no, she isn't stringing him along. It's not her style. She told him three weeks into it that she meant to have a baby at some point, and before things got more serious he ought to know. He should feel no pressure, she'd been serious about doing it alone if she had to, and she would. But he had to know. Not this year or the next, maybe, but before too long.

Which isn't really how she feels. In fact she's edgy about stalling for even a year, haunted by her mother's stories, by those pieces on infertility she keeps noticing in the newspapers and magazines, by glimpses of herself as an aging, childless lounge-singer in too much henna Flirt and eye shadow playing gigs in airport hotels with nothing to go back to but a pre-fab room, the soundman and a cheap bottle.

Sevigne might be the man for her, but how can she tell? His boyish enthusiasms sometimes rub her the wrong way, seem almost pushy, territorial, make her withdraw inward to a kind of cynical niche she has to struggle not to speak from. Yet she is touched and (no, there's no denying it) excited by his attitude. He says he never thought much about it before, but now the idea of having children, with her, inspires him. Imagine how loved the children would be, how surrounded by good food and music, books and conversation! They could travel together, live in other cities, New Orleans, Dublin, Tangiers. . . . So now she, who has already thought things through and knows simply that she wants a child and means to have one, one way or another—she finds herself backed into the unflattering role of urging caution and wary thought.

He tells her he's open to wherever his love for her steers him next. Nice, Sevigne, but. But . . . she does love him, against all odds, loves those alert, curious eyes, dark yet see-through in their sudden mood shifts, even in sleep his face always changing, his body when awake never still.

Having nursed Les Kravchuk through many a night of beery reminiscing over near-success and eventual disappointment, she's in no rush to get involved with another man who sees himself as a failure, or will come to. It's a relief to find that Sevigne has talent. She likes his poems, especially the ones for her (how could she not?) and the parts of his novel she's just read really make her feel the book will do well. Now he even has a contract for a book. This last development has finally convinced her friend Nadine that Mikaela is not being "totally self-sabotaging" in initiating a relationship with a twenty-something male fan. Earlier assurances that he was a talented, promising writer had not spoken to Nadine's concerns. Everyone in the Annex was a talented promising something, and most of them were highly emotionally dysfunctional, locked into toxic post-adolescent patterns, and deeply in denial. *I wonder if you're having some kind of pre-mid-life crisis here, Mikaela? Or unconsciously using him to have the baby. I think there are some pretty major reverse power issues to address here.* (Nadine by e-mail. The friends haven't actually managed to meet face to face in months; another sign, Mikaela guesses, of aging.)

In the middle of a hot, breezy, aromatic night, as if on some subliminal cue, they wake together both aching with lust and make love with bodies that seem to move autonomous of their wills. Sleep has stripped them of the day-world's protective, numbing second skin, so now their truly bare flesh seems to flare, to flower and shiver with exposed nerve-ends, every sense is quickened as in a sexual dream and without a word they go on, no pausing.

Afterward as they lie slicked with the clean sweat of sex, her cunt still clasping his soft cock as if unwilling to let go, he tells her not to worry, he will be happy whatever happens. So will I, she says, and he has to kiss her smile instantly. Her warm lips respond but he can feel the rest of her beginning to cool, to ease from his unavailing grasp back to that other place. Momentarily he hates sleep, a rival who will possess her nightly no matter how he fights.

Go to sleep now, he tells her. I know you're tired.

But stay, Sev. There. Like that. I want to wake up this way.

He nestles closer, whispering into her open mouth.

Mmm, she says. And me you. So much. My sweet Sevigne.

13

Fiercely Bereaved

N LATE AUGUST he and Ray ride east out of the downtown on the lovingly maintained Norton Commando
Interstate that Ray bought new when he was twenty, two
years after coming to Canada and taking a day job in a paint
factory and night work as a warehouse security guard. He has
told Sevigne how he saved resolutely for the bike, dreaming of
taking it west across the country and then down the American
coast to Mexico, maybe even South America. He got as far as
Cuernavaca, where he spent eight months in the cantinas self-
consciously communing with the shade of Malcolm Lowry
while drafting a turgid, derivative novel. The experience was
pivotal. He returned to Vancouver determined to stop drinking and to begin writing in a cooler, more objective voice, like
Alan Sillitoe, another hero of his adolescent reading.

Now Ray wears the abraded black leather jacket he first
took on that Mexican journey, Sevigne wears his own jacket
and a pair of tobacco-brown leather pants he found in Ike's
closet. He's staying nights in her apartment while she records
her album in Montreal.

Sleeping alone on the bed they've shared and will share
again—burrowing his face into pillows still redolent of her
skin and hair—combines for him the pleasures of intimacy
with the freedoms of solitude. Then there's the *frisson* of private discovery, the maturing writer in him as much as the lover
eager to explore a space that must form a kind of self-portrait

in material possessions. Sometimes he plays her own two albums on her excellent stereo and roams the carefully cluttered
rooms examining her stuff. Each object, each foreign particu-
larity, marks the space where another unknowable chapter lies
dormant, oblivious to him—chapters of a life that, at moments
of ecstatic union, he has felt he grasped. A sprawling collection
of records, cassettes and CDs from Leadbelly to k.d. lang, Rach-
maninoff to U2, a Henry Holt upright piano, two shelves of
novels mainly by contemporary women, a monogrammed silver cigar case full of picks, slides and capos on the TV with ceramic busts of Roy Orbison and Billie Holliday, countless
pieces of sheet music piled in the sealed fireplace, a Tascam
four-track tape recorder and, in a wicker rack between the bathtub and toilet, water-warped issues of *Rolling Stone*, *Vanity Fair*,
Toronto Life.

He'll be moving in on the first of September.

A calm sultry Sunday and the city has a paranormal air, its
streets and freeways almost deserted, great grooved columns
of afternoon light slanting onto the lake out of palatial cloud
banks. As they leave the downtown behind, the sky widens,
Ray opens the throttle and the cherry and chrome Commando
growls and lunges beneath them. Locks of wind-whipped hair
sting Sevigne's stubbled cheeks and chin and throat as the bike
zooms past freighters docked under concrete silos, gutted
warehouses, dead refineries with high blackened chimneys
like obelisks for a vanished age. Ray has told him they're
driving to a spot he knows of to talk about the novel, which
Sevigne completed just before Ike went away, giving copies to
her, Ray, Eddy, and the insistent Lois Shapiro.

"It's true you wrote that number on the radio, for the safes
ad?" Strained over the blasting of wind and engine, Ray's voice
seems thinner, older.

"I did write the words," Sevigne yells. "What do you think?"

"Purest shite, mate."

"Shite . . . ?"

"Your novel's another matter."

Beyond a subdivision of cloned houses Ray pulls off the road and noses the machine onto a dirt trail leading into a green belt. Telling Sevigne to duck, he hunches down over the handlebars and steers them up the path, braking as an archway of open space appears ahead—the sky over the lip of a cliff, Lake Ontario beyond. They dismount and walk to the precipice. The packed sand bluffs, like the steep runnelled walls of a mesa, drop away three hundred feet to the shore where a beached railway tie lies like an oily toothpick. Just over the edge an ancient sign pokes slantwise out of the slope:

ANGER NO AC ESS   KE P AWAY

"Scarborough Bluffs," Ray says, handing Sevigne a can of Danish lager the size of a shell casing. Far below, a lake the colour of oxidized copper dozes under a doldrum haze; sailboats in a regatta miles offshore seem becalmed. "After reading your book I reckoned you might like it here."

"I love it."

"Here's to it then. Beats toasting you in the Horseshoe, doesn't it?"

"So you don't think it's purest. . . ?"

"Partial shite only. But that can be fixed. Much of it's good. Strong. Not sure you've finished things off right, though, between the brothers. And some other chapters need a turn of the wrench. Pretty prose is a selling point these days, and a bit of that's fine, but you want to avoid page after page of it because that just isn't true. Assuming you want to tell the truth. And I do assume that. I mean, the world would rather be fooled, right?" Ray steps to the edge of the bluff and with the toe of his boot nudges a small stone over. "Not that you should start writing the way I do. I mean, look where it's got me."

"So how's it going?" Sevigne asks, though eager to go on discussing his own book. He knows from Eddy that Ray is close to finishing his novel; he writes nights on his shifts as a watchman in an electronics warehouse.

"Fuck my book for a game of soldiers. I brought you here to toast yours." He runs the can over his furrowed forehead, the widow's peak of short thinning hair sweaty, plastered to his scalp.

They walk along the rim of the bluff under hardwoods lushly in leaf and emerge on the edge of a golf course. Backs against a red maple with a view of the lake, they sit drinking beer. On the tended lawn between the clubhouse and the bluff, wedding guests in tuxedos and pastel gowns circulate while men in white livery slip among them. The muted sounds, the heat, the muzzy haze over the lake—the air itself seems buzzed as if from too much champagne.

"It's true Una's leaving her marriage?" Ray says.

Sevigne nods. "Eddy's helping her move into a new place."

"Or whatever it was they had."

"They were together years," Sevigne says softly. "Eddy tells me the guy has been getting more and more reclusive, always meditating and fasting. . ." He takes a slow, pensive pull on his beer. "I'm moving in with Ike."

"You're having me on."

"I know, it's fast. We'll look for a bigger place next year. If everything works out. Or I'll rent a small office if I can sell the novel . . ." *If*, he says, in deference to Ray, but the word in his heart is *when*.

"Jesus," Ray says.

"I do think she's a bit nervous."

"And you're not?"

"No, I think it's great! I've never felt this way before. I've never felt ready to stay in one *place* before. And the timing, Ray—even that feels perfect! Like a sign. I thought you liked her?"

Ray watches with his usual searching scowl, though his eyes have softened. "I do like her. Very much. She's the real article. You're a lucky man."

"Then what is it?"

"How old is she?"

"Thirty-four."

"And you're twenty-four."

"Twenty-five."

"Right. And ten years these days makes a generation—mentally, I mean. With everything so sped up now. And a generation makes all the difference, doesn't it? Before long you'll be wanting different things. I reckon you want different things now, only you don't know it."

Sevigne opens his mouth, urgently lifts his hand, but Ray cuts him off. "Look, mate, forget it, all right? Don't listen to me. I know *nothing* about these things. Made a mess of every one I ever had. When I was twenty-six I was living with a woman in Vancouver, and I got her pregnant. I wanted her to abort it, I was working two jobs and trying to write, I knew I wasn't ready for the family thing." His grin is ghastly. "Bit of an understatement there. Vicky wanted to have the child, get married, all that. I can tell you it wouldn't have been a wedding like this one."

The groom and the best man have just joined the bride and the bridesmaids for a picture. A photographer in a safari suit kneels heavily in front of them, crooning encouragement, switching cameras.

"Vic had the child and I tried to make a go of it. The jobs, the trying to write, my son. Philip Raymond. I felt half crazy most of the time, and the rest, completely. After a year I gave up. Came east on the bike. On the prairies I'd ride the slip-stream of the big lorries until a second one came at me in the other lane. Just before they passed each other I'd veer out round the one I was trailing and gun it through the wind tunnel they'd form between them for a second—or not even that.

Lovely. Shooting out into the sun on the other side I'd feel. . . .
I don't know quite what. Like I'd offered myself and been
spared. Tried and exonerated. I could look ahead again. By the
end of the day the feeling would have built back up, next day
I'd have to pull the same bloody trick."

Ray might be on the bike now—his averted eyes are tight
slits, shoulders hunched up as if with cold, veined hand a fist
round the grip of the can. Which he crushes.

"Never did see Vic again. Or Philip. Sent them money,
that's all, when I had it. She got married two years later, had
another boy. I reckon that's best. I'm happy for her. I reckon
some men could have done both, the writing life and a family,
but not me. And it gets to you sometimes. You see a father and
son sometimes and you think, right, you've traded *that* in for
two books that took years, years off your life and went out of
print in less time than it took to write them."

"But they still matter, Ray—they're great books!"

"Can't see how, really."

"Eddy says"—Sevigne pauses, then pushes on—"Eddy figures it's just that you're caught in the middle—you're not
a 'hot new property,' but you're not yet one of those older,
established figures either. And I can see what he's—"

"What do you know, mate?" Ray's pupils are minuscule
and remote; his bristly jaw trembles, his index finger punc-
tures the air in cadence with his words. "You or Mike? You
don't see how young you are. You think this is the big city. You
haven't been to Mexico City, or Los Angeles, or London, and
already you're chafing to settle down. This place is an overgrown suburb, Sevigne. And your 'bohemian' Annex? A flashy
costume. Camouflage over the body of a ghost."

"But Ray, you know I've been in other—"

"Nice, though, having someone of your experience to in-
struct me on the nature of Great Books."

"So what are you trying to tell me?" Sevigne speaks sharply;

Ray's blue eyes widen, focus, as if he'd just been slapped out of a trance. The sheeny skin of his temples where the hair is gone flushes deeply; a vein there shaped like lightning throbs. After a moment he says, "Shit, mate, nothing. Nothing is what I'm telling you." He shakes his head. "I get carried away some-times, you've seen me. Guess I worry for you sometimes, that's all, you're so . . . I don't know what. Trusting. Serious."

Sevigne shrugs. "Ike tells me the same thing."

Ray grips his shoulder with a strained smile, as if congratu-lating a rival who has just won a coveted prize. "Drink up. It's time to toast your novel properly. Your novel and your new life. I know just the stuff."

He gets stiffly to his feet. Signalling Sevigne to wait he shambles off towards the wedding party, bow-legged in his grubby leathers, a lanky outlaw off the range approaching a church supper of frock-coated townsmen. A small waiter comes out to meet him. Briefly the two men, tall and short, confer. The waiter points at the Tudor clubhouse and Ray nods and walks towards it.

Sevigne sits down on the edge of the bluff and watches the far yachts crawling over the lake. Ray's son, Philip something, will be a teenager now; if Ray in the wrong condition stum-bled into him in the street, he might provoke a tragic scene, snapping, lashing out, as if at a stranger. Which he would be. Sevigne wonders if he should tell Ray that Ike's period is two weeks late. On the line from Montréal she is sounding excited, anxious, a bit overwrought with the pressures of her day and the possibilities of the future. He feels both excited and at ease. Wherever the wind blows, wherever the horse leads, that had been Don Quixote's motto, and a good one. The human will, snarling smoggy engine of the West, fuelled by fear of time and by greed, has wreaked such damage on the world. He will be fuelled only by Love. The litre of beer is kicking in. A puff of smugness surprises him as he realizes Ray's outburst was born of envy—for hasn't he admitted "The Islands of the Nile" is good? And Ike a wonderful woman? Probably his words about the city are just bitterness too. Sevigne is on the verge of succeeding, and young, in the very realms Ray himself has failed to reconcile.

"Here you are, mate. But save some, all right?"

Sevigne leaps up, shamefaced, and takes the flute of champagne—a spitting, sunlit fountain in a glass. "But how did you. . . ?"

"Don't ask. Come." Ray leads him back to the Commando and asks him to hold his flute as well. They mount up, pull on their helmets. Ray starts the engine and eases them back up the path skirting the bluff towards the golf course. Sevigne holds the flutes carefully, one in each hand, darting looks over the precipice as they jounce over exposed tree roots like asphalt speed bumps. They roll onto the emerald hem of the golf course—you can feel the silken softness through the springs—and Ray, shouting "Hang on, mate!" accelerates along the edge of the bluff towards the wedding.

"Jesus, Ray, what are you . . ."

"Just something to remember," Ray yells, "after they've forgotten uncle Dick's endless speech and whether it was beef or chicken."

He feels himself grin, he lets go a holler. Karmic requital for Gezirah. He and Ray now have the utterly undivided attention of the wedding party, a feat even the bride and groom repeating their vows at the altar an hour before could not have achieved. Guests and waiters—some screaming, some laughing—scatter inland over the lawns. The maître d' is running towards them, gesturing, while the photographer in the safari suit snaps pictures. Beside them a strip of grass no wider than a sidewalk blurs past and the lake far below is like sky beneath their tires. Ray slows for a bald bearded man in a swallowtail coat, isolated on the cliff-edge with palms upraised. When the man bolts inland, swallowtail flying, Ray opens the throttle, the flutes angle back in Sevigne's hands and a slipstream of champagne sprays his face and flows out behind. "Glass!" Ray calls. Sevigne puts a flute into the hand that Ray reaches back over his shoulder. "Cheers and may your book take wing!" Sevigne clinks the flute with his own. Ray's helmet jerks back as he swigs, then he lobs the glass over the handlebars into the abyss, Sevigne doing the same, their flutes' meteoric arcs traced in a trail of droplets and the flash-cube detonations of sun on glass.

Now the downdrafts of the huge rotor felt like an oppressive hand forcing Luc to his knees, but he stayed on his feet. His brother's face, squinting grimly upward, had a gaunt and fisted hardness and for a moment Luc saw him clearly as an old man. Then everything went out of focus. He was still dazed and angry from the blow to the back of the skull. The camouflaged helicopter flew south and then circled around, roaring north into the broad cloudless skies over the river; touched by the morning sun it receded until it blinked out of sight, leaving the brothers, on the edge of the painted tarmac circle, with only each other to turn to, or on. Their embrace when it came was not an embrace but the clinching of two tired, bloodied boxers, unsure whether to hang on or to shove apart and resume punching, and no one watching them struggle on the edge of that painted ring could have guessed when the clinch would end, or how.

14

Ghosts on the Line

O N HIS WAY to Union Station to meet Ike's train,
he drops off copies of "The Islands of the Nile" at
the offices of three of the bigger publishers. In the
process he walks two hours over mobbed pavements miraged
by the heat, further earning what he hopes is his impending reward. After hearing Ray's praise he was too excited to hold
back on the submission; with each photocopy he has included a
letter saying that this is not a final draft, he will be paring and
polishing in the months to come. So that when and if the book
is accepted he'll have the finished draft in hand, and maybe it
can appear by next fall, which would mean a book, a child, a
second book in one year. And Ike's new album. What a year
that would be.

"Eddy?"

"Sev! Where are you? Sounds like Union Station."

"I'm waiting for Ike's train. Listen, Eddy, I wanted to tell
you not to rush your comments on my manuscript, I dropped
it off today at Penguin, Putnam, and Ellis & Erson."

"Already? Wow, the big guns. You know I'm dying to get
to it but I've been swamped trying to get the web site ready
and *On 3* in the can. Next week for sure."

"Sure, whatever."

"No, I told you, I *want* to pick an excerpt, I just have to find
a window to read the whole thing. Oh, and by the way, your
reviews for *On 3* are perfect, nice and concise, and did I tell you

who Dina's going to be eviscerating . . ." Sevigne loses track of the words, his attention gripped by a family climbing the stairs from the underground level. The mother leads the way, a tall gaunt Asian woman in a paisley dress that hangs off her, slack and wrinkled. She lugs two battered, swollen suitcases. The obese white father struggles behind, both hands on the rail, his sparse auburn comb-over greasy or damp. Last comes the child. In a Lion King sweat suit he moves lightly on the stairs, then at the top he starts imitating his father's pronounced limp, his pudgy face solemn, intent on the task. Sevigne tears a strip from the phone directory and starts scribbling.

". . . so I guess you didn't call that agent I mentioned?"

"Sorry? Oh. No, I decided I couldn't afford to lose the uh, the commission, on the sale. I mean if the book sells. Especially now I'm moving in with Ike . . ." Guiltily Sevigne is still writing, trying to record the image of the little family parade now straggling out the main doors. He doesn't know what it means, but he senses some import. Tall and straight, short and stooped, tiny and hobbling, *like a flow-diagram of human evolution brought to life*. "I mean, I've got to be pulling my own weight when we're, you know . . ." As he speaks and scribbles, a faint ticking comes over the line—Eddy must be tapping keys on his computer.

"So Sev, listen . . . having an agent can, um . . . make the difference between the book selling or no." *Tick tick tick tick tick*. "Ray didn't have one for his first two books, they were harder to get then. Might have changed everything." *Tick tick. Tick. Tick.* "Now it's a feeding frenzy out there, Una just got snapped up, but no agent'll touch him."

"I know, I know." *Maybe subconsciously seems a betrayal not to imitate father in his failings? Maybe sons must always, willing or not, follow fathers down their*

"So Sev . . . what's your latest for Moulton?" *Tick tick*. "You still on that infomercial for exercise equipment?"

But there must be happy families too, even if "all alike."

"I was thinking of quitting," Sevigne says—"I want to quit, but like I said I've got to hold up my end now. Moulton rejected the last one, said it made the MC look a bit stupid. But my replacement opus is almost done." He feels his face warping into a smirk—something it's coming to do with growing facility.

"So sneak me a preview."

Pocketing his notes Sevigne chants, "'Being your best means being yourself, but *better*—because your body can be art. With AbArtist. . .' And so on, and so on. The old mnemonic alliteration thing."

"Got to fit 'Beauty' in there somewhere too, Sev."

"We're workin' on it."

As Eddy laughs, Sevigne glances up and the smirk dies on his face. A crowd strangely silent but for the echoing slap of soles on the marble floor is spilling towards him out of a far archway and Ike is at the head of it, looking around, seemingly trying to get free of the ruck. She has a suitcase in one hand and her guitar in the other. His limbs are loosening, tingling with love, yet he droops as if caught in the act of telling a lie or denouncing a good friend. *You bet, you bet . . . you can be your best.* That old sense of unworthiness and imposture.

"Eddy? She's just arrived."

"OK, Sev, but don't be a stranger, hey?"

There's an oddly plaintive note in his voice.

One hand still on the receiver, Sevigne waves and calls out with more force than intended, Mikaela's stage name resounding like a public announcement in the grand, high ceiling's vaults and coffers.

When Mikaela and Les first became lovers they made love every day, at his place or hers, or in motel rooms here and there when she was playing out-of-town gigs, and often they made love several times a day. Then they moved in together (it was the upstairs of a roomy old redbrick in The Beaches) and everything changed. They still made love, but less often and with noticeably decreased passion. Mikaela guessed it was because their new availability made them see each other not as gifts but as givens—when they'd lived apart the constant sex in greeting or in leavetaking had been a way of staking claim to each other, marking each other until next time. Living together there was always tomorrow, or next week, or next month.

She hopes to avoid that loss of passion in her relationship with Sevigne, though the toughened skeptic in her insists it's impossible, the moon in honeymoon means month, one month. You might as well wish on a falling star that summer won't turn into fall, as it is doing now. But the problem isn't so much the passing months or their cramped cohabitation as it is her own physical state. She's a professional and a perfectionist, so in the studio in Montreal she concentrated all her energies and overcame her queasiness and flu-like fatigue, and with less help from coffee or cigarettes, she'd cut way back on both. Then on coming home she went cold turkey. It left her exhausted yet jittery, like someone doubling up on Valium and speed— dragging herself out the door to meet Anson McWilliams or play her regular gigs at the Free Times and the El Mocambo. Now even her appetite, always good, is gone. Even for chocolate and for the ripe, tart apricots out of the back garden. Twice now she has snapped at Sevigne. The nausea and insomnia keep worsening. This must mean that the pregnancy has "taken"; her doctor says only that the symptoms will pass.

On her return to Toronto, as drained as she's ever been in her life, she finds his clothes taking up a quarter of the hanger space in the closet, turning her own already crowded space into a blouse-and-minidress mosh pit where no one item is findable without a struggle. His razor and toothbrush and comb, placed with maddening modesty in a cup on the floor under the sink, are an inadvertent reminder of how her own toiletries have been multiplying, jamming the cabinet, and what that means—the concealers and anti-wrinkle creams, the strip-waxes, assorted tweezers, the Tylenol and Midol and antacids and anti-gas tablets and prescription sleeping pills. And then his computer squatting on the corner of her only table, as if to show how eager it is not to take up any more space than necessary, which just draws attention to how it takes up space.

Still, by the time he actually moves in two days later she's feeling slightly better in body, and far more positive in mind. Ready for their new life. And if in fact over the following weeks they do not make love as often, it's not because they are taking each other for granted but because of her symptoms. Which the doctor assures her will pass. Sevigne is understanding, he's almost comically concerned, always asking how she feels, rubbing her back with his large strong hands, supplying the canned laughter while she slumps in front of the TV cracking remarks about the MuchMusic videos. He keeps buying and brewing teas for her stomach and her nerves. When he cooks, now almost every night, he plays the music softly and spices with restraint.

But like Les he knows next to nothing about other domestic matters. He seems to think that if he showers every day (in one of his two pairs of boxer shorts, soaping them to save on trips to the laundromat) the cleanliness will spread, the way dirt spreads, outward into his surroundings. She has seen him working on his poetry for Lois Shapiro, he will tell her with a kind of bashful pride that he can spend a half-hour focusing on a single key comma, deleting or shifting it. Yet he can't see a sport sock on the burgundy hemp rug two steps in front of him. Reluctantly but steadily he's polishing a new jingle about bathtub rings, yet he doesn't seem to realize they exist in the real world.

Like the rings of Saturn, that they are something mysterious and ethereal until Mikaela, achy and ill, points one out in her cherished old clawfoot tub. *Our* tub, she says, hating it when Sevigne refers to the apartment as hers instead of theirs, but at times of irritation finding she does still think of it that way.

He says life is too short to worry about bathtub rings, she thinks life is too short to live in squalor and chaos—as if the world outside their apartment weren't chaotic enough! The place should be a sanctuary of order. Order and love. And because they are in love their negotiations often lead to the bedroom, and always, finally, to some affectionate compromise, Sevigne for the first time ever (he claims) on his knees in the bathroom using the same baking soda whose scouring properties he's being paid to extol.

She makes compromises too. They come at a higher psychic price for every year she has lived alone. But she's willing to do it—lower her domestic standards, invisibly take up slack. It scares her how willing. Shames her. How badly she wants to make this work. A few times already she has faked desire and made love to the chronically eager Sevigne when she feels unwell and worried and fat and knows that she looks like shit and yearns only to go to sleep in his arms. Then, in late September—the anniversary of his father's death—he becomes moody and private himself, pacing the rooms or the porch or the back yard with a bottomless glass, so for a few days they live together like sexless, melancholy friends.

Awake in the night she sits propped against pillows, dying for a smoke, seeming to feel herself age for every minute she is not asleep. The glare of the streetlamp on the paper blind casts the shadows of slow-falling leaves. Sevigne, curled into himself, is sleeping hard. It makes her feel protective, and angry.

By now she's used to being forced awake in the night by waves of nausea, so at first when she finds her eyes open and again staring into the dark, she isn't frightened but frustrated. She had some pain at bedtime—light waves of it—but assured herself it was nothing and focused on relaxing, on sneaking her body into sleep. Now the pain wells up again, not lightly, not in the stomach but deep in the groin, like the cramping of her period but much worse, and she moans, rolls onto her side and shakes his shoulder.

"Sev, Sevigne, wake up!"

He opens his eyes, reaches for the light. He's been watching a man in a black coat limp backwards through a muskeg studded with charred, gutted stumps. Ike's face is distorted, years older, her mouth open as if to wail. No sound comes. He throws back the quilt. A large poppy of blood darkens the sheet beside her thigh. Wide-eyed and gasping, she sits up, then tries to rise; he grips her arm to restrain her and she cries out "No, I have to!" and brushes feebly at his hand, then doubles over with a cry. He rushes into the adjoining bathroom, yanks a towel from the rack and drops it—damp, dirty—then grabs a fresh one from the wicker basket. Through the high vent to the outside, as if from another world, ring drunken hollers of triumph. Blue Jays again. He hurries back to her. She's curled up on her side, motionless, both hands squeezed between her legs like a child trying not to wet the bed.

"Get help Sev, now. Call."

"I am, Ike! Don't worry."

"Pack me some things. Black bag. Floor of the closet."

Drawing up in sinister silence the ambulance rakes the room with its pulsing light. The paramedics let him ride because she has no car for him to follow in, and he's adamant, and they're in good humour, it seems, because of the World Series. She weeps as he holds her hand. Ike with all her calm swagger broken. He has never thought to see her so defenceless.

"We're nearly there, love, hang on, all right?"

"I'm like my mother, Sev." She winces, averting her face. "Waited too late. Fuck it. I can't start over."

"Just hang on."

"Can't go through this again."

"For Christ's sake, can't you do something for her? It's going to be all right, love. Okay? I promise you. It's going to be fine."

With growing concern at his inability to comfort her, he watches her brood in the apartment. She's smoking again, heavily—so much that for the first time he's truly bothered by the fumes. He knows she's not so much mourning that tiny, blue-gilled, inchoate creature that has vanished, as the future lives she feels likely to lose. Or never to conceive.

As the dead vastly outnumber the living, so the unmarked, invisible dead outnumber those known and named ones under dated stones or crosses or kept in familial sepulchres of the Cities of the Dead. The oceans are giant urns, the mountains cenotaphs, the soil an indiscriminate plot. Each island is a tumulus overgrown with asphodels for some forgotten child.

Together they listen to the preliminary mix of *Against All Odds*, Mikaela chain-smoking, quietly making notes about changes for a final remix. It's a March release, the party already planned. She knows the record is better than the first two, good, it's very good and she knows it, but that knowledge comes in tandem with a numbness. The satisfaction would have to be cancelled out by a new heartbreak, wouldn't it? Oh fuck, she thinks, it's happening, just like they say it does, the turning bitter as you go grey—dark rings under the eyes now too, your mother's eyes, your mother's rings. Soon you'll look more like her than you do like you.

Soon he'll be wanting somebody his own age.

For some goals it seems determination and overtime aren't enough. She senses his determination rapidly returning, though he tries, transparently, to put a damper on it and keep his mood in synch with hers. Every day before going to the cafés to work on his poems (to give her the privacy she craves? to be around livelier people?) he checks the mailbox with poorly disguised impatience. One day a letter comes from his mother in Cairo—his brother's wedding is off, the couple separating again. Sevigne does seem disappointed, yet also relieved that he won't have to scrabble together money for the flight, or accept his mother's charity. Or Mikaela's. He says they'll fly together to Egypt next spring, on him, when he has money from his novel. (This though one of the three publishers has just sent it back.)

Her doctor says they can begin trying again after New Year's. Sevigne is eager; she seems, to him, wary and noncommittal. Even as she recovers and throws herself into the final production stages, she seems wary. He thinks he understands but he's troubled, at times he feels in over his head—somehow responsible for her pain and yet helpless to salve it. At moments of lowered guard a vague unease flits at the edges of his awareness, like a small running thing seen out of the corner of his eye.

Then November ushers in its rains and sleet and low, hovering, miasmic gloom. Winds from home denude the apricot tree of its last blackening leaves, leaving it as bony and lonesome-looking as a bleached rack of antlers on a northern shore. One day with the winds gusting to ninety kilometres an hour, he hears on the radio that in rough weather the CN Tower's upper stages can heel up to a seven feet off centre; that night in a dream he sees the tower bent to breaking point, then feels himself up there high on the radio mast, paralysed with vertigo, the city tiny as if viewed from a spy plane ten miles above.

He is safe on earth, in bed beside Ike. The violent winds of his dream rattle gently at the window. He nestles against her back, kisses her downed, salty nape—kisses lightly so as not to wake her. She stirs and he realizes he was hoping she would. With a sleepy smile and a waft of musky warmth she turns over and they make love with their former passion, even coming together, eyes wide open, O you you you you You.

15

The Bat

H E HAS ARRANGED to meet Ray upstairs at the Skull. It's usually pretty quiet Tuesday nights, no bands booked, yet the place is crowded. On stage, two guitars sit on stands by the amplifier and there's a mike stand and a boom stand with them. With Ray late as usual, he sits at the bar watching the much improved Maple Leafs overwhelm the Bruins in Boston Garden; somewhere Eddy will be watching too, animated, theatrical in his support, as if he'd been a fan all his life, like Sam Torrins.

Better to inspect the decorated honour guard of bottles ranked along the mirror back of the bar. The rye, Irish, bourbon and Scotch bottles all hold what looks to be a liquid pressed from gold bullion and tasting that way, especially the rye—cool and smooth and with a rich, metallic tang.

He and Ike's mutual resolution for 1993 has been to make a song—she the music, he the words—and a baby. A few days into the New Year they got to work on both. And his uneasiness grew. Among other things he was almost broke. In late December she had uncomplainingly, in fact invisibly, paid the full rent, and then on their first grocery outing of the New Year she'd overstocked the cart with an embarrassment of expensive items. Perhaps she simply meant to start the New Year well supplied. That's what she said she was doing. But when she tossed in a six-dollar carton of Swedish ice cream between the Stilton and the Pacific salmon steaks, he began to wonder if she wasn't trying to make a point. He tried to pay his half of the huge bill with his remaining cash; she begged him not to. She knew how things were with him, a couple of cheques late, one due from Moulton any day. . . .

Now in his shamed pride even the song collaboration strikes him as alms. Without income or a book (the second publisher has just returned it with a brief, perfunctory note) he will end up a phantom accessory to her career, in the shadows at the back of the stage rattling a cymbal, tootling blues-harp—officially involved but his contribution publicly doubted, disdained. Lost inside her life.

His cheque just in from Moulton he orders a third shot of Crown Royal. *Tired of scoffers, Luc had chosen to believe* . . . in StrongArm baking soda. *Rye and soda.* On a napkin he scribbles *Three-tiered array of bottles a set of elaborate psychedelic organ pipes, waiting for the touch of a hand flamboyant with great jewelled rings—Elton John or Liberace—Bach on acid.*

And he stares. Stares till that static geometric composition of forms and rich colours like a billiards table laid for a match yields inklings of the music of the spheres, briefly stifling the simian chatter in the zoo of his brain. No wonder so many writers drink—it's not only an analgesic for the constant rejection, it sedates the brain's manic left hemisphere, consciousness with its unremitting whims and worries, scruples, quarrels, neurotic tics and tinkering. The overexamined life. He has read somewhere that painters and musicians outlive writers on average by about seven years, and it's beginning to make sense. A painter would capture that pipe organ with a brain uncluttered by words and a body active; a singer belting out a love song would breathe fresh life into language with melody and pulsing rhythm while every face in the club paid her back. To be a writer is to be trapped in the garret of the skull, the solitary confinement of selfconsciousness. Only sex, drink, the summer sun, grant fleeting parole.

Drink.

The sound of a guitar being tuned. He spins around. "Hi there, I'm back and you're all still here by the looks of it." It's obvious now, those guitars, he thought there was something about tonight's date and now it hits him—a week ago she told him she would be filling in for somebody at Sneaky Dee's, this place he calls the Skull. Has he known all along? She will have no idea he's out here, moved to see her from a stranger's vantage and shocked yet again that such a woman has chosen to give him her love. Yet the woman on stage is Ike; he lives with Mikaela. Ike is introducing her next set with that sexy smile and sassy banter; Mikaela is brooding on the onset of her latest period and fearing that her other dream, their dream of family, is doomed.

This time when the blood came, he suffered an access of regret and relief so seamlessly fused they formed a single new emotion. Now she is singing "Wild Is the Wind" with unstaged, raw emotion of her own, her eyes scrunched closed, face contorted with a passion he hasn't seen or felt in her lately when they make love—every two days like clockwork—she afterwards on her back lying very still, knees tucked to her splayed breasts. Is this what living together does to people? Makes them save all their passion and beauty and charm for outsiders—friends, fans, utter strangers? As Una once showed him her passion and beauty, while she drifted from the man she lived with.

Sevigne has been taking Ike a bit for granted too, but now watching her secretly—as if he's living with Mikaela and seeing Ike on the side—reminds him of what she is to him. And what an artist. Tonight her fingerwork is full of those gritty, raspy imperfections that give a riff its character, her phrasing deftly delayed, words brimming over into the next line as if on a stream of bourbon tears. Twenty times at least he has heard her play "I Don't Remember You" and now it's choking him up again. *No, I don't recall the time or place we . . . first lay down and . . . made our peace.*

Sevigne turns away. A man with a brushy auburn moustache and watery eyes, tie loose, mouth slack and moist, leans
close and says in a chummy undertone, "She's nice, eh?" His
jacket and gold cuff-links and Rolex watch serve notice of
money, but there's something cut-rate in the tongue-filled
grin, the wriggly, sly, confiding manner.

"Roger," the man says, offering his hand, sliding a pack of
menthol cigarettes over the bar. His hand is clammy from a
glass of something on the rocks.

"Sevigne."

"Now there's a handle." With a small gold lighter Roger
lights Sevigne's cigarette, then his own. "Sev-*een*?"

"It's French, bastardized French."

The man stares into his eyes, then blinks twice.

"Another rye," Sevigne calls to the bartender.

"On me," Roger says. "And I'll have another run too.
Johnnie Walker Black. She's nice, eh, that Ike? I've caught her
a couple of times."

"I live with her," Sevigne says.

Roger blinks again. A loose, slow, tonguey smile reconfig-
ures his freckles. "Right! Man, you almost had me there for a
sec, you played it so straight."

"No, I'm serious. We live together. She's having my child."

The pale eyebrows twitch and lift.

"And this song of hers now, 'Like Fire'? It's ours."

Roger glances at Ike, then back at Sevigne. He squints his
eyes, shrewdly amused. "But you look young enough to *be* her
child! Now come on, that's a *compliment*. Get to my age and you'll
agree, I guarantee ya." Roger watches Sevigne obliquely as if trying to decide whether to be offended by the lack of response.
Then his eyes light up. "Hey, speaking of kids, have a look here!"

From his back pocket he draws a scaly brown wallet and
picks out a small photograph. Sevigne, disarmed, takes it and
holds it to his eyes—angling it towards the TV for light—then

jerks back with a little jolt of horror. For a moment it's the blurry image of a child's skeleton curled on its side in a shallow, flooded grave; then he does not know what it is.

"Ultrasound," Roger says, his mouth close to Sevigne's ear, breath pleasantly mentholated. "Taken at five months. The boy's due in May. Now isn't that something?"

Sevigne returns the image, nodding numbly. *Like fire, I feel you under my skin like fire.* Roger's watery eyes shine with emotion. Sevigne tries to pay for his last drink but the man—clearly concerned—won't hear of it, students ride for free.

Sevigne stumbles, suddenly drunk, downstairs to wait at the door. When Ray appears, Sevigne tells him he'd rather go elsewhere, Ike is playing upstairs.

"What's wrong, you and your lady at odds tonight?"

Sevigne shakes his head.

"Like to hear her sing when I can, that's all. Most women singers these days are so ethereal. Your Mikaela has guts."

"I *know*," Sevigne says gruffly, and Ray eyes him, taken aback; then affronted. And it goes on that way, the two men moodily touring the bars, Sevigne determined to drown consciousness in a butt of malmsey, or whatever will serve. The moon rises full over the frozen metropolis. On the snow-dunes of Hamilton Park it glows like a lunar module's arc-light in the Sea of Fertility, moon making moonscape of the dormant earth while each month a tiny full moon tracks its sterile arc through the firmament of a woman's belly.

Ray, your book, is it finished?

Good word, that. Already have it back from three publishers. Ellis & Erson most recently. Friday.

Fuck them, Sevigne says supportively—as if E & E were not his own last hope. They're idiots, Ray.

Their boots crunch and squeak on the packed snow.

And how's Lois then? Heard she was sick.

I called, she's doing better now, it's only pneumonia.

Good title, that—"Only pneumonia." Has a nice existen-tialist ring to it. Yes, I shall have to ferret that one away.

They're lurching up the middle of snowy Palmerston. Flakes sift solemnly out of a windless sky; low lamps ranked like torches make the street a stoa of standing flame. And a door bursts open. A barefoot man in grey pyjamas charges onto his porch and down the steps holding something before him at arm's length as if it might explode—a blanket with some of the fabric choked into a bulb above his fist. A bathrobed woman stands in the doorway behind him, hands over her mouth, eyes wide. Grunting with disgust the man shakes out the blanket. For a moment there's nothing—then a small black form flittering just over the sidewalk and rising into the snow-swarmed nimbus of the streetlamp. As the man retreats through the doorway and slams the door, the bat begins flying in tightening circles broken now and again as it darts out of its orbit, as if for prey; its sonar is telling it that from the night-mare of capture it has emerged into a cloud of flying insects, a bat paradise whose bounty is endless, but the bat is confused, frantic, every insect it catches is tasteless and melts to nothing on the tongue.

For a while as snow settles into the footprints of the house-owner they stand watching the bat circle—veering and swoop-ing as it tries to locate in that vast constellation of promise the one thing it can use.

16

The Green Light

I F ONLY she carried a cellphone. She's out until dinner, meeting record and video people, unreachable, and he has to tell somebody. He reaches Eddy at the office. He has to tell somebody the scoffers are again dead wrong, it's no anticlimax when at last your ship comes in, some greasy Erie Canal coaltub—no, it's a gleaming Great Lakes schooner, a Nile cruise boat upbound for the islands.

"Ellis & Erson? Holy shit, Sev, that's amazing!"

"I know, I know—but I haven't signed anything yet, so keep it quiet, OK?"

Eddy lowers his voice masonically. "Wild horses, Sev, you know me. What are they offering?"

"De Vos didn't give me a figure, he's trying to get a big New York publisher in on the deal. I guess they're hoping—"

"Man oh man! And if anyone can convince 'em, it's da Bossman, he's a pro. And Tahlia Erson . . . deep, deep pockets. I tell you, Sev, this is major league!"

"But it's all still kind of up in the air, so don't say anything, all right?"

"Aaa, de Vos or his people will leak it anyway. These things always get out. Did he say anything about movie rights? Man, I've got to throw you a party! And the printers—I've got to e-mail the printers right now, try to squeeze a change into your *On* bio. '*Islands in the Nile* will soon appear in Canada with E & E and Stateside with Huge, Prestigious & Sons.'"

Something like that. Piss off your enemies big time."

"*Of* the Nile. But don't, Eddy, please, all right? And no parties? He's away till April, he's going to some book fairs and on holiday in Europe, I won't be able to meet him and clarify things till then. And it's not totally nailed down."

"Whatever, Sev. *When*ever. Just give me a call Friday, we'll go out and celebrate, OK? Quit being such a stranger."

In fact Sevigne is now much closer to Ray, but he doesn't call him with the news even after speaking to Eddy. In the kitchen, with a jumpy hand, he pours himself a double rye. It will be cocktail hour in the City of the Dead. In the backyard, barefoot on the gravel path in rain-pocked slush, he lifts his glass by the skeletal apricot, twigs beaded with gelid drops like incipient silver fruit. *For you*, he whispers as rain rills slowly down his forehead and cheeks, chill baptism into the next stage of his life. Tears follow like warm spring rain.

From the doorway of the kitchen Mikaela watches a tall red-head in a tight shift with a cheetah motif standing at the edge of the group clumped around Sevigne in Eddy Korkola's main room. The woman, all legs and cheek-bones, is writing on something in the palm of her hand—a business card?—then she slips into that circle of writers, agents and publishers and says something to Sevigne. Everyone laughs. With a cigar clamped between his teeth like a tycoon, Eddy drapes his arm around the woman while Sevigne's old flame Una continues to laugh, her head tipped way back. Everybody's here except Ray. Cheetah Woman takes Sevigne's hand in both of hers and she folds his fingers closed over something. Through sheer force of glaring Mikaela manages to draw her batting eyes, and the woman flinches, ducks out of the circle and joins another by the bookshelves.

Sevigne's voice has been getting bigger by the drink and now he's making breezy chatter with two agents, a man and a woman both plying him with business cards and invitations. Small talk, party talk—she accepts it as part of life and she does it herself, more often than she likes, but she isn't used to hearing him participate and doesn't want to get used to it. His face has a feverish glow and he's nodding and smiling too much. Maybe it's the drinks. He *was* more awkward when they first arrived here, supposedly for a quiet dinner. His fist still holds whatever Cheetah Woman gave him. But now as the agents turn to each other, drolly squabbling, she sees him peer down and open his hand. It's a cigarette. He lifts it to his narrowed, darting eyes, and blushes. Some unreadable thought creases his smooth face; then he gazes around, locates Mikaela and fights his way towards her.

"God," he says, his voice loud and thin, "did you. . . ?"

She nods, drawing her mouth up to one side. Shaking his head, he holds out the cigarette. *You're Hot!* it reads in neat tiny script, and there's a phone number with an Annex exchange. "And now all the talk over there is that the New York sale is happening!" As he kisses her she can feel the heat wafting off his face. She lights the cigarette, has a drag, takes and sticks it in his mouth.

"I'm sorry," he tells Lois Shapiro, "that you couldn't make it to the party."

"Well I'm not sure I wouldn't have picketed it instead." From the dwarfing depths of her violet plush wing-chair she roasts him with magnified eyes. "I thought we had an understanding, Sevigne."

He looks down at the empty thimble-glass in his one hand, a gnawed biscuit in the other. The scuffed silver tray on the coffee table is engraved *Trinity College '46*. Five-ten by his new watch; through the apartment's yellowed gauze curtains, churning fog blots out the view.

"Eddy told me you were mad," he says.

"Angry, I suppose you mean." Una laughs, covers her mouth. Eddy winks. Lois plucks up a cigarette, then turns to glare at the large nurse trundling towards her out of the kitchen. "Oh, Angie, do give us a moment's peace, for *crying* out loud." Angie stands her ground in imperturbable silence. She is not so much fat as monolithic, her ruddy face liplessly grim, her uniform a fiercely laundered white. After a few seconds Lois sighs and lays the cigarette back on the table beside her glass of Tio Pepe. With no easing of countenance Angie recedes.

"They have me down to four a day," Lois says. "Apparently lung cancer is the one form of pulmonary affliction I don't as yet have." She widens her blue eyes behind the lenses, as if recalling a missed appointment, and cuts loose with a sequence of wet rapid coughs. Again in the kitchen doorway the nurse appears, the tip of a glacier, advancing. When the attack subsides she pulls back.

"Now," Lois says hoarsely, eyes bloodshot, "the reason I was so vexed is that you'd given me your novel to read, so naturally I assumed—since I already have your poetry book— that you wanted me to do it as well."

"But I didn't know you published novels."

"Then you know precious little about my list."

"You told me you thought they were an inferior form!" His own lack of deference surprises him.

"I do," she says tartly. "But not an utterly invalid one. And publishing one or two a year helps me keep afloat."

"I wasn't trying to mislead you," he says, "I thought I—"

"I told her it's not your style, Sev—she believes me."

"It's all the other young writers," Una says, "who won't."

"What's that supposed to mean?"

"You know how folks is," Eddy says, shrugging. "You start to make it, they want to tear you off the trophy wall. They start looking for a reason. And there's always some 'reason.' That's the whole principle of the gossip column. But don't worry, I wouldn't put a friend in mine."

Sevigne, refilling glasses, eyes Eddy blankly.

"Looks like I'll be doing one for *Frank*," he explains. "You three have diplomatic immunity."

Lois takes a curt, testy sip. "These days I seem to require considerably more than that."

"You're looking good though, Lo."

"Yes!" Sevigne and Una chime in like a Sophoclean chorus; some new current seems to flow between them, repelling, attracting.

"Nonsense," she says, "and you all know it. But there really is no retiring from a vocation, is there? Coffin nails or no. Don't worry, Sevigne, slowly but surely your book of poems . . ."

"Oh, *please* don't worry about that!"

"I did like your novel, mostly. You'll just have to learn to conduct your affairs more professionally. Though matters may have turned out for the best; I wouldn't have been able to do the novel for years, what with everything so backed up."

Again he checks his watch—he's meeting Ike for an early dinner—then drains his too-small glass and begs Lois not to get up. Eddy and Una check their watches too. "I'm sorry," he says, bowing to kiss Lois's caved, papery cheek (sweet odours of rouge and tobacco and some faint emollient, Noxzema?) while she clasps his hand tightly and says, "Now we won't worry about that any more."

He hurries out and down the hallway past the elevator towards the Exit sign over the fire door. For some time he sits in the stairwell. Lois isn't alone in his thoughts. Two days after the good news came—though before Eddy organized the party—Ray, knowing nothing, showed up at the apartment at dawn. Ike slept through the rapping; Sevigne wasn't asleep anyway. Ray had been up all night in a Chinese restaurant rereading his own manuscript and trying to decide, he said, between execution and clemency. In the harsh light of the kitchen where they huddled over coffee he looked ragged and desperate. His breath stank. He was meaning to ride down to Buffalo that day, just to get out of here, spend some time with a friend there. Then maybe pack up his flat and clear off for good. West.

As a boxer Sevigne trained by running stairs and stadium bleachers and now, gripping the handrail to corner on the landings, he pounds down twenty-one echoing zigzag flights, inhaling dank air laced with the concrete's chalky dust. *Asshole fobbed off a bad book of poems on dear old Lois, then scored elsewhere, big time, with his novel.*

Or said he did, when nothing was sure.

And said nothing to Ray.

He emerges into the foyer. With a bing! a green light blinks on above the elevator doors. They shudder open, steel curtains revealing Una, who smiles open-mouthed with her delicate small white teeth.

"What are you doing lurking down here, Sevigne Torrins?"

She must think he's been waiting for her.

"I took the stairs," he says. "Slowly."

On the threshold of the elevator shaft they embrace. It's harmless, the contact congratulatory, a brief remission of his sense that things are starting to boulder downward, exempt of his control. Their one kiss is chaste, yet charged. He has no idea why he feels this sudden backwards pull. The elevator doors, in their stupid, stubborn rhythm, keep trying to close against them.

17

The Ace of All Disorder

COUNTING THE DAYS, impatient to meet Laurence de Vos, he can set his mind to nothing. He wants to re-work the novel but thinks he should wait for de Vos's comments; several times he almost calls the man's assistant just to assure himself that she and the firm are for real. He rereads the letter repeatedly, as though it were a billet-doux and he a lover devoured by doubt. Troubled by thoughts of Ike, Una, Lois, Ray, and de Vos, his sleep is shredded, and often he lies awake on his side, watching Ike. One night she begins to sing in her sleep, her lips barely twitching, the lyrics slurred and unknown to him.

Just two weeks since the letter and already the old misgivings have returned and new ones reared up, the way the mind, that stubborn fighter, revives just moments after the knockout of orgasm. Maybe the scoffers are right after all. His Ship of Gold has appeared but dropped anchor inaccessibly off-shore—or foundered there, like Crusoe's ship. (Obeying some impulse of boyhood nostalgia, he has bought a copy of *Robinson Crusoe* and is rereading it in the night.) After getting the letter he was zealous again about starting a family, but somehow the feeling waned, as if a negative verdict had been reached inside him by a jury of strangers, *in camera*, closed chambers of the heart. Now Ike's tension about her coming release party and tour makes him tense, her anxiety about conceiving makes him anxious. More and more he wonders what she will become in time—in her forties, her fifties—if she never has this child, and what will become of him if she does. The quick first conception now strikes both of them as a fluke. Before long it will be fertility drugs—twins, triplets—his writerly stride broken at the moment of being found.

In his journal he writes constantly as if trying to scrawl his way to the heart of things. *Poignancy of fucking lies partly in repeated motion—that joining & withdrawing, joining & withdrawing—which not only mirrors how couples draw together & apart over time, but also shows dual determination: to merge into one & yet also to pull back, stay separate.*

Over the three days before Ike's release party he calls Ray over and over but gets no response. He avoids any place where he might encounter Una; their embrace and kiss under the elevator's green light are still with him, a gnawing ulcer of guilt and desire.

Love isn't blind, Mikaela thinks, it's drunk. Now there's a line for a song. One of those funny, self-mockingly corny c & w songs you hear these days. It is like being drunk, you're flying, for a while anything seems possible, but the blues always come, you come down hard, you get hung-over. Maybe Nadine was right and she'd acted too fast in the haze of the high, and for all the wrong reasons. One of a million maybes. Not that she doesn't still love Sevigne. She does—she *does*—and that frightens her too, because if you can love somebody this much and still find it a trial to live with him, what hope is there for the future? With him or anybody else? Maybe they just need a bigger place, or maybe summer will open things up, turn them around. Maybe no place will be big enough if it's shared—could she have reached that point in life already? Maybe it's him, not her, and he is too young, his virtues too paired with his faults, like the high spirits that make him play her stereo way too loud so she turns it down as she walks by and he turns it back up and three times now they've clashed over it. And the drinking. Since his book got accepted it's been worse, not better. She can see he's full of doubts about fathering a child—so full of his own doubts he senses nothing of hers—but she can't seem to bring herself to broach the topic. Likewise as the time for her period nears, she finds herself avoiding quick motions, inventive sex, finds herself holding her breath in, getting up and sitting down with special care, as if any of that could make a difference.

On the 401 east of Toronto there are two exits a few miles apart, one for Liberty Street, one for Harmony Road. (For a long time she's meant to write a song.) She once asked Les, Which exit would you take if you had to choose just one? They were driving to Kingston for Christmas dinner with her parents two months before her papa died. Les said, I guess there's hardly a man in the world who wouldn't choose Liberty Street, I mean if he had to choose just one. And Mikaela: After a certain age I think most women would pick Harmony. Les chuckled caustically and pointed out that both exits were now well behind them.

Locked in the bathroom applying her make-up before the pre-party dinner, she's hit by a wave of nausea—or something more like a dizzy spell in the stomach—and momentarily her lipstick has a sickly odour, like a wilted rose. An attack of nerves. Yet the hope that it's the start of another difficult, un-pleasant pregnancy is overwhelming, even now.

Sevigne stands by the doors of the Bamboo Club with his fourth complimentary rye. The place—as he'd hoped, prayed for her—is filled, the tables along the walls long since occu-pied, while on the black-varnished pine floor, formations of guests and paparazzi swell up and churn and diffuse like the smoke clouds hovering above them. Now and then the lightning flare of a flash: Ike trading kisses with a rangy goateed man in a suit, an American singer whose craggy features Sevigne knows but whose name he can't recall. Is she flirting with him? Another kiss Sevigne feels in his gut. She has introduced him to some of the guests but most of them glazed over on learning he wasn't in the business (or so it seemed) and now clouds of them are swirling, spiriting her off to other parts of the club so at times he can't pick her out, only sense her as a certain buzz and realignment in the crowd. Yet her voice surrounds him, and her image—that giant album-cover blow-up beside the bar, her touched-up likeness wearing a look of sly, sexy reserve.

The eyes don't follow him. They look beyond him.

Like a doorman he's there to greet Ray as he stomps in, smelling of the cold night. A caul of snow is melting into the black bandana on his head. He's been riding: his face is damp and white, eyes bloodshot, snowflakes tipping the lashes. He drapes a heavy arm over Sevigne's shoulder and with his free hand pinches Sevigne's rye, shoots it back.

"Ta, mate. Nice suit." A tight-lipped grin, his pupils glinting sharp and tiny as the tips of ice picks. Sevigne recoils but the arm holds him fast. "Reckon we'll have to grab the next waiter. We'll both need a shot if I'm to toast you properly on your latest literary triumph."

"I've been meaning to tell you, Ray—I've been trying to reach you all week."

"You had ample occasion. We spent a whole morning in your lady's kitchen, drinking coffee and chatting, the way friends might be expected to—then Tuesday I make my return and in the Brunswick an acquaintance tells me it's been in the can for a month."

"Not a month," Sevigne cries, "two weeks. At the very

most! And Ray, Jesus, I haven't even signed anything yet. But I'm sorry if you—"

"Why be sorry? This is tremendous news. Ellis & Erson too! I toast you with my empty glass." He lets it fall to the floor. It cracks but doesn't shatter.

"It was a bad time," Sevigne says, "that morning we were in Ike's kitchen."

"Bad for me, but you must have been feeling chuffed." He grinds the glass into the floor with his boot. Guests at a nearby table turn. Ray yanks him closer and butts his pale, unshaven face towards him, breath sour and hot. "That was a slap in the face, arsehole. What sort of man do you think I am? You think I can't rejoice for my friends? You think my world pivots around you and your petty falls and rises?"

"Maybe we should talk outside, Ray."

"Are you asking me to step outside?"

"Don't be ridiculous, Ray—I just don't want to make a scene at Ike's launch."

Too late. Dapper guests at the nearby table gape from their ringside seats. A sick, scared feeling plummets through him and pools in his wobbly knees.

"None of this matters anyway, Sevigne. I mean none of this posh gala shite. It's the work on the page that matters and all the rest only pretends to. The jury remains out on me, and it most certainly remains out on you—it's out for the next half-century."

Sevigne sets his palm on the small of Ray's back and steers him gently towards the door. Ray's splintery treads crunch and grate. In the doorway he wheels around and sticks a finger under Sevigne's nose. "You treated me with disrespect, Torrins—as if I were some callow schoolboy. Do it again and I will smack you. A few months ago you *showed* me that novel of yours and I helped you with it. You fixed the things I mentioned?"

"Not yet, Ray, I was waiting for . . ."

Ray grabs the loose shoulder of his suit and hauls him outside into the snowy courtyard. "Waste of my fucking time!" He shoves Sevigne up against the window. A few late guests enter the courtyard laughing and freeze in their tracks. They must think Sevigne is being bounced. Ray clutches his tie knot, Eddy's tie.

"Would you—*stop* this now Ray?" A thin, throttled tenor. "If I fucked up—I'm sorry."

Ray chokes his fist higher, crushing the Adam's apple, and Sevigne gasps, chops up with his forearm, breaks Ray's hold, shoves him back. Under clenched brows the bulging eyes seem focused yet unseeing—not seeing a friend's face but others, the layered features of the entitled and the rebuffing ranked backwards into a distant past yet by the day more present. Ray thrusts him into the rattling window and lashes out, a hook to the heart Sevigne sees and half blocks. It's not a hard blow, the fist neither tempered nor fully driven but already, unconsciously, Sevigne is punching, landing one square in the face, an eyeball soft under his knuckles. Grunting like a bull Ray punches back. Sevigne ducks under a fist that smacks the window and he drives a hook into the layers of leather and sweater over Ray's belly. A knee bucks up into Sevigne's nose, snapping back his head, and he gets off one last furious hook, his fist seeming to shatter on impact. Ray is sprawled on the icy flags. Under the window Sevigne slumps dazed and trembling, an aura of red, radiant pain seeming to pulsate around his head. He swallows ammonia. Ray is rising to his knees, bandana ripped half off, eye closing, blood from the nose; he's grinning, stumpy yellow teeth glazed with blood. "Nice stuff, Sevigne." In wary fascination the guests look on while Ike's muted voice drifts around them in the courtyard, *A map in the lines of my face you'll follow . . . this is no street to walk solo. . . .*

Ray raises his eyes from Sevigne's to the cracked window. Ferocious delight contorts his face. In a slurry voice that repercusses through the courtyard he bellows, "So what the fuck are you grand wankers all looking at, then? Leave us the fuck alone!"

Loath to cause even more of a disruption or embarrassment for Ike by looking for her in his state, he leaves a message at the door (with a breezy waiter who seems to doubt he really knows her) and rides with Ray to the Silver Rail. Large snowflakes feather down out of a low, soft sky. Ray makes no concession to the state of the roads and wears no helmet; the wet whorl of thin dark hair on his crown is like a hurricane's eye on a satellite map.

They slump in a booth, drinking draft beer, taking aspirin cadged from the bartender. As in a slow, sequential anxiety dream Sevigne feels paralysed—Ray needs him here, but he should be back at the party, yet he can't return in this condition. Yet he has to return, now.

He convinces Ray to go home in a cab. He flags one down and sees him into the rear seat, but five minutes later on his weaving trot back to the launch he has a hunch and retraces his steps. The Commando is gone. Ray will be home by now—at home or in some gutter, a black leather body-bag of shattered bones. He goes into the bar and dials his number from the pay-phone. After nine rings a thick but unmistakable *Yeah?*

Sevigne hangs up.

18

Have You Seen This Child?

S HE'S PLAYING the Commodore in Vancouver, its stage
lights more intense than in the Toronto clubs so it's impossible to see more than head-and-shoulder silhouettes
of people at the front tables. It sets her back on her heels. Flaring lighters and cigarettes appear sometimes too, and that's
difficult for other reasons. Still, as her nerves settle and she
digs deeper into her first set, she becomes aware of Sevigne at
one of the front tables, sitting alone. It can't be him, of course,
but the illusion is riveting—the long-haired silhouette, square
shoulders bunched up as he leans forward over the table,
motionless, impatient, bodily involved. As she sings their
unrecorded collaboration "Under My Skin Like Fire," she
stares at and *into* the silhouette, trying to make out the features, but it's impossible. Still, she's moved, it lends her voice
to the song in a deeper way until she's drawing gooseflesh from
her own forearms and the fresh-cropped nape of her neck.
The ovation afterward is powerful. Sevigne seems to clap
without changing the attentive posture of his shoulders and
head.

During her second set, relaxed but intense, she can't pick
him out, others have crowded around the table. After the
show as she sits on the edge of the stage signing CDs and pressing flesh and smoking—even so—the one necessary cigarette,
she keeps glancing at people milling around there, coming
towards her or heading for the door. His table is deserted, just

empty bottles and glasses, and now the nightclub staff coming to clear it all into buspans and stack the chairs.

After seeing Ike off at the airport he returns to the apartment and pours himself a stiff one. The place feels less like his home now than in his first days alone there. An image comes—of a small room so pared of possessions that it resonates when he speaks, as he does when writing, trying his words out on the air to test their veracity. Ike's place is so muffled with dark hangings, throw rugs, old soft chairs and stacked recordings of famous strangers' voices that when he calls out, no vibration returns. The rooms echo only their owner's dreams and fears. In the bottom of the closet her green suede flats are the shoes of a child hiding, in play or terror, back of their mingled clothes.

A groundless jealousy has been growing in him since the night of her launch. She's too good for him, big for him. If she has no lover now, she soon might—some older, classier guy— some new Everson Milne.

How can you know a child is yours?

He keeps trying to reach Ray. Maybe he's writing, when he writes he takes the receiver off the hook. It's been busy for three days. Eddy hasn't been able to get him either, and he's been trying, having heard all the brutal details of the fight and hoping to encourage him by asking to run an excerpt—not seeing that this is exactly the kind of coddling solicitude that helped cause the fight in the first place. But there's more, worse. Eddy has heard that yesterday de Vos's PA Kara Schneider opened a package from Ray and found a charred, crumbling typescript. Auto da fé. Was it the original? Eddy isn't sure. Everybody's saying so. Sevigne thinks Ray must have kept a copy, but Eddy has his doubts. *You know what he's like,*

Sev—not the type to play it safe or by halves. The man believes in burning bridges.

He runs through the icy rain to Ray's apartment block. The Commando is not in the shed around the back under its black vinyl caparison. Could he have left already for the west? While rain clatters on the shed's corrugated plastic roof, Sevigne stares at the plot of oily dirt where the machine should be. He takes a nervous piss at the back of the shed and crouches at the entrance to wait out the storm. Across the chipped, sulphur-coloured bricks of the building's posterior, someone with orange spraypaint has spattered "*It's not like on TV, it's a bad feeling.*"

Ray, if anyone, could tell him what to do. Tomorrow he's seeing Una for coffee.

They meet in a little chrome- and zinc-filled bistro in pricey Yorkville. Efficiently they've selected it over the phone without ever alluding to their criteria—that it be far enough off the bohemian circuit that they're unlikely to see acquaintances, but not so far off that if they're spotted it will seem suspicious. And it's not suspicious! They're meeting for *coffee*, and in the middle of a weekday! Not even a drink. Though Sevigne right now would kill for a drink. She's late, as he knew she would be, and he begins to hope she won't show, he thinks seriously of leaving, he has no idea why he's here, then she's barging in, drenched and elated, explaining how she was tied up on the phone with people from New York who are having her down to read.

"My God, Sevigne, you look terrible! Your eyes!"

"You look great, as usual." He still desires her, but feels little more. Too little. But such desire.

"And you're *smoking*."

"Only when I drink. Shall we have a drink?"

He shouldn't be here, for any number of reasons. She leans over the round zinc table dabbing the bruised flesh under his eyes with her pinkie as if applying a salve. She's fascinated. Their faces, close together, are indistinctly pooled in the zinc.

"So?" she says.

"Ray and I have been sparring a bit."

"Oh, everybody knows about that! I meant, have you—"

"Have *you* spoken to him?"

She studies him, then asks what's wrong. He tells her the full story, looking down as he talks, his fogged reflection rolling two lumpy cigarettes. When he looks up, her olive brow is furrowed, her black eyes grave. "Whatever you do," she says sincerely, importantly, "don't blame yourself for this. You'll get used to others having problems with your success— you'll have to! Envy is the air we breathe. And I know how it tastes, Sevigne, believe me. We'll call Ray later, okay?" Then with force: "We'll drop by with some take-out curry and imported beer!" A small smile dimples her cheeks with innocent satisfaction, as if her planned largesse has already excised a hurt rooted years in the past. Now in her he catches a clear glimpse of himself. Seeing himself, seeing himself—just a year ago on his arrival he simply, impetuously was, now he is and is always watching what he is. Hell, he thinks, is a hall of mirrors, always drawing you further in. With grim fascination he watches his descent.

Strolling down Yorkville in the sudden first sunshine in days they keep bumping into each other, as if their hips are magnetized. He's walking her home. A gentleman! A few nights after their visit to Lois Shapiro, as he lay awake with *Robinson Crusoe*, his attention caught at the lines "Though I had several times loud calls from my reason and my more composed judgement to go home, yet I had no power to do it. I know not what to call this, nor will I urge that it is a secret overruling decree that hurries us on to be the instruments of our own destruction, even though it be before us, and that we push upon it with our eyes open . . ." As if eavesdropping on some squalid couple he overhears his own coy assent when she invites him up so they can see about reaching Ray. Everything is fixed. They're only going through the motions, shadow-boxing. Ray's line is no longer busy, there's no answer but the receiver is back on the hook, and that seems promising, and their relief and honest concern forge between them an extenuating new bond.

They sit apart on a futon-sofa in her flamboyantly cluttered den, drinking something exotically new to him, Campari and orange juice. In the late afternoon light the drinks are the vibrant vermilion of an equatorial flower. A feeling of peace steals over him. They're talking books, favourite writers, a good number of them shared; their lists of films and musicians overlap as well. Then she asks him about Ike—what cities she'll be playing on her tour, how long the tour will last—as if he were Ike's fan, or manager, not her lover. The Campari turns to bile on his tongue. She has snapped the spell. Yet her expression is guileless, simply curious.

"What is it, Sevigne, what's wrong?"

"I have to go."

"Oh, Sevigne, you're not doing anything bad—you're just following your heart!"

In the toils of some strange moral inertia, he doesn't budge. He'll finish his third drink. Boldly defined by setting sun and deep shadow, her face is classically statuesque . . . superseding time . . . beyond the codes and prohibitions of the daily. The sun is gone. From moment to moment, evening steeps the room in twilight, darkness, neither reaching for a lamp.

Her lips and tongue taste to him of bitter herbs.

Another moment comes when he might still pull back and

leave—as they pass from the den through her study to the bedroom. On the desk her computer is humming. Abstract motifs, evolving, dissolving back into the screen, half-light the room like a flickering aurora. In that polar glow he sees, covering the walls of the room, framed photographs, sketches, paintings, all of Una: Una in profile, Una face-on, Una with a squinty long-haired man in a snowy pine forest, Una on stage somewhere, reading, Una on a roan horse by the sea. Something closes like a lid or a door in the place under his heart where fondness, irrigated with Campari, has been nurtured for hours. But it's not just her. It's his own self, borne in on himself.

MYSELF
Myself am Hell.
The blind bard?
Full points.
There can be no thought of stopping.

Rushing home through a pre-dawn darkness littered with objects that arraign him—Dumpsters like gutted landing craft after the Dieppe betrayal, the face of the girl-slayer Bernardo gloating from a *Sun* vending cage, leached, puckered handbills about a lost child on every power pole and hoarding—he offers himself congratulations on having at least "made it safe." *Because she'll love a man. Only one thing should ever.* Once in the night he snapped awake to find her sleeping in his arms, lips parted, brow crimped and nose twitching, as with a child's aversion to something in a dream. Sleep was a kind of island; she was a blameless citizen of whatever island she lay on in the circle of his arms. Cyprus, he thought, or Mallorca, while he was torn between Spirit and the red-soiled islands of the Nile. Those pictures in her study showed only that she loved her life. A gust of love surprised him, and he kissed her. "I love you," he said, softly, to see if the words might ring true and justify everything, and her eyes startled him by half-opening, closing.

Now sober, sated, weary, he climbs the groaning porch steps. The apartment knows everything and at every turn serves sullen notice of his coming eviction. Scalp prickling, he sees them on her bed, spanning the full gamut of sexual postures as in a telescoped honeymoon; he sees them locked in a private co-celebration of their precocious success, consummation of a royal wedding in the puny kingdom of letters. He sees them fucking in front of the mirror and recalls how his fatuous smile, framed there as in a tabloid exposé, had sickened him. Voyeur of his own trophy coupling; crown witness. He goes back to her bed the next night.

He is walking up the median of a lonesome highway in the Shield country. Night is falling and the dark stockades of cedar and hemlock fir lining the shoulders seem to close in tighter and stab at the stars. He passes a lampless suburban house set into the forest, then feels the approach of somebody on the road. Too dark to see but he hears and feels the stranger nearing. Ike, he knows it's Ike! He runs to meet her with that same champagne-tingle he gets in his limbs and belly whenever he spies her in the distance, coming towards him or moving away, and then she's in his arms and he's embracing her but she doesn't respond. From a long way behind him on the highway he hears her calling his name. He cries out and recoils from the stranger in his arms, whom he now knows to be a man, and evil, perhaps himself.

19

The City of the End of Things

W EARY BUT UPBEAT after her tour she takes an afternoon flight home from Boston. The venues she played were hardly big ones, but the crowds were respectable and the reviews of the shows and the CD have been even better. She's pregnant, she's almost sure of it. And her time away from Sevigne has refreshed her, she's eager to see him again and hold him close and take it all from the top.

Her heart slips a notch as she hurries through the airport's glazed sliding doors and picks him from the crowd. Instantly she feels concerned and yet *exasperated*, it's obvious he's been drinking hard, like Les towards the end whenever she went away, and why do men all have to do this, self-destruct on a small scale and then demand your feminine sympathy and nurture? The bruises around his eyes have faded to a greenish-yellow that complements the rest of his complexion nicely. Thin, nervous, worry-worn, he's the picture of a starving poet.

A freckled, brushcut guy with a backpack and a guitar case rushes up to tell her he loves the new CD and ask for her autograph. Sevigne stands to one side waiting—politely waiting at a time like this!—as she impatiently signs her name. The guy thanks her, then turns to Sevigne with a toothy grin and says, "Okay, dude, you're next."

That night when they make love it takes him forever to come. For a while that's sweet for her, but she *is* tired, and after a weak second orgasm she's had plenty and starts to wonder what's wrong. She can see he's exhausted. And his meeting with the publisher is coming up, he's got that "deal is too good to be true" feeling, every time the phone rings he jumps halfway out of his skin. But what really saddens her is his fear that she's pregnant. It's obvious, even though he assured her again that he'll be happy whatever happens. And opened a bottle of red wine and drank most of it while fixing her an elaborate, delicious *pad Thai*, and from a recipe no less. Finally she pushes him off her onto his back and starts giving him head, but after a moment he pulls away, his penis softening, says No, not now, he knows how tired she must be. Never, she lies, and clutches his bony hips. Like an animal caught and injected with venom he resists for a few seconds, then groans, shudders, goes very still.

When he finally comes his cry is strange to her, strangled and pained.

Una and Sevigne are in a run-down, unromantic Greek taverna on the Danforth washing down gristly souvlaki and feta salad with glasses of retsina. The fluorescent trays overhead give the skewered bell peppers an uncanny, acrylic lustre, and he's dazzled by the lurid brightness of things, like a man in a sleep-deprivation experiment at 4 a.m. the third morning. He's slept little for days. Una eats with appetite and is impatient with the waiter in a way hateful to Sevigne, with his terror of others' humiliation. Ike will just be finishing her first set at the Skull. He picks at his souvlaki and guzzles wine; it has the aromatic tang summer sunlight draws out of pine needles on a northern trail.

Mikaela, she's saying something about Mikaela—how people change, how couples' destinies diverge, how sometimes you have to break away. He asks her to lower her voice. He *hates* it when she uses Ike's real name. How dare she . . . how dare she remind him that he's betraying a flesh-and-blood woman, not some affluent, impervious public icon. A table of students at the back seems to be watching them. Perhaps they know of Una. And he'd thought this place was safe. *You'll have to learn to conduct your affairs more professionally, Mr Torrins.*

"And then he completely lost his drive and purpose," she's going on, "it was terrible what he turned into! But I feel like we're the same, we're both ambitious, I mean in the best sense of the word—restless to make the most of ourselves and our talent."

Behind her a warty, white-stubbled man in a scruffy blazer and Greek fisherman's cap grins gap-toothed as a roasted goat's head is set on his table. Its one visible eye regards Sevigne with sinister fixity. The horns steam and smoke. God, it's so clear now—Sevigne's fears of betrayal are absurd! A troubled mind can make anything plausible. Last year in his mind he spent night after night insatiably with Una, and yet already, after just four meetings, he has had enough. He has to break things off and somehow confess to Ike, although he senses jilting Una will activate certain energies he won't be able to contain.

". . . but I think now that only another writer can really comprehend what a writer needs and feels . . ."

On his way to the men's room he passes the table of students, their huddled faces and hushed voices unnerving. On a whim he stops at the payphone and dials Ray's number. It rings and rings. Taped up beside the telephone is another of those posters—*Have You Seen This Child?*—showing the face of an East Indian boy with jug ears and a buck-toothed smile.

"Yeah?"

"Ray!" Sevigne almost shouts, "you're there!"

"Sevigne. Had a hunch it might be you. Wouldn't have picked up otherwise."

"Where've you been, Ray?"

"Buffalo, mostly. I'm just back to pick up a few things. It's good to hear your voice, mate. I'll miss it."

"So you're heading west. . ."

"Are you drunk, Sevigne?"

"God, Ray, there's so much I want to tell you."

"Out to the coast, yeah. I reckon through the States. Everything's finished here."

"I'm sorry."

Silence for a few seconds, then: "Forget it. It's not you."

"We've got to get together," Sevigne says. "You're still pissed off, I know, but . . ."

"I'm not, now. Pissed. Well, I am, but. You know. Not angry. Forget it. Forget it all, Sevigne." He coughs hollowly into the phone; he sounds ill. *Ruchir* is the missing child's name.

"You still have a copy of your novel?" Sevigne asks urgently, remembering. "We heard what happened."

"It was a bad book, Sevigne, why would the Xerox have been any better?"

Sevigne lets his forehead fall against the clammy steel of the coin panel.

"Whatever was good in it I've still got upstairs. In my head. Maybe I'll start over."

Sevigne likes the sound of that—start over—and for a moment relief sweeps away his guilt and he forgets what it means for Ray to have destroyed four years of effort.

"Tomorrow morning," Sevigne says. "Let me come by."

A sound of phlegmy breathing. "No, I don't reckon there's time. I'm in a spot of trouble as well. I'd better leave tonight. Once I pack and have some coffee. I'll try to ring you from Seattle, all right? Or maybe Vancouver."

Whatever my number will be.

By the time he returns to Una with the news that Ray is in one piece, though leaving town, the man in the Greek cap has picked the head nearly clean, a row of teeth exposed under the eye socket like yellowing keys on an old piano.

Short, tanned, fit, with tight-trimmed pewter beard and hair, white shirt, pressed khakis, penny loafers, Laurence de Vos is light on his small feet, cat-like. Leading Sevigne into a perplex of office-lined hallways, delivering the tour-guide spiel, he doesn't turn his face but for the occasional quick, wary glance. His smiles are frequent and too courteous. Now and then he whistles brief bits of some tune.

"Here, Sevigne, through here, please. I can't get over how young you are! We were expecting someone older. Please, have a seat."

The room, walled with loaded bookshelves like an academic office, transports him: he's back at school anxiously meeting a professor about a disputed mark. But the spines of these books are unprofessorially bright and dustless, each distinguished by the elegant E & E colophon. Everything in here seems vibrantly new, while outside, through the drizzled window, silent traffic bumpers along in a shuddering old black-and-white film.

"Well," de Vos says, spreading his hands open, clamping them closed, "where to begin?" On the desk a cleanly squared stack of typescript on which reading glasses rest; an in-tray/out-tray; a laptop computer; a complicated telephone, one of its many buttons blinking red. "I'm very pleased that we're finally meeting face to face." His very white smile does not look pleased.

"How was your trip?" Sevigne asks in mounting panic. "You look like you were somewhere warm."

"Yes! Malta!" His eyes light up, his shoulders unlock. "It was *wonderful*. The second week, anyhow. I'm afraid the island is rather . . . *dense* with family, on my mother's side, so at first it wasn't much of a respite." He stops, looks down at his neat hands, steeples the tan, ringed fingers over the stack of type-script. "Would you care for some coffee or tea? Maybe water?"

"No thanks," Sevigne says, thinking *Irish coffee. Rye and water.*

De Vos with a pained frown says, "Well, I can't in good conscience talk around the issue. A writer of your talent de-serves better." Again he opens his hands, claps them closed; the void giveth, the void taketh away. "I'm afraid I may have been somewhat . . . prematurely optimistic in my letter to you. I do love your "Islands of the Nile", you see—in fact I think it's largely brilliant, and I'm most anxious to publish."

But. (The red light keeps winking.)

"But in my absence the situation has changed. In fact it's been changing for some time now. Kara also admired the novel, as did Tahlia Erson—though with some reservations about the ending, which I do frankly share—but she and the people at sales and marketing, given my lack of success con-vincing our New York associates to co-publish—and I did mention in my letter how important that was?—well—they now feel that doing it ourselves would present some rather serious difficulties. For now. I'm afraid Ms Erson and I got our wires crossed—I thought I still had *carte blanche* until the end of the year, *she* thought she had made it clear that because of our, what, our bottom line, and last year's disappointments with several first novelists. . . . Well. You get the picture."

With a look of genuine distress, Laurence de Vos splays his empty palms again, as if to plead that he and the company are dead broke. Next he will be rising to pull out his pants pock-ets. Sevigne is gripped by the irrational conviction that he has brought this on himself.

"It's not as if all is lost, though"—de Vos leaning forward over the telephone on which a second light now winks—"not at all! Things may well change here, and in the near future.

First novelists have been hot property before. I believe they will be again. And maybe soon. We *will* be in touch. As for the present . . . I feel your best course of action would be to place the book with a, with a—with a what? A more 'literary' imprint, shall we say? Maybe Lois Shapiro. She *is* doing your poetry collection, isn't she?"

He has a few hours to kill before meeting Una. Now that he has seen de Vos, he knows for certain he can carry through on his decision to end the affair. Pass the rejection down the line like bad karma; pay a long overdue visit to his employer, Kim "the Money" Moulton; then homeward to tell Ike. Ike and the baby. Her period is twelve days late, which for her is not unheard of, but there are other symptoms, as before. Today she's seeing her doctor. He could call the apartment now for the results—she might well be home—but he's afraid of what he'll hear, either way.

In a Bloor Street diner he orders rye with a beer chaser, then the same again. It's afternoon and the place is full of quietly, unobtrusively ruined old guys propped singly at tables too big for them, pulling at bottles of beer. Officially the place is a restaurant but no one is eating. Outside the skies begin to clear, warm sunlight slopes in, the pickled eggs and sausages in gallon jars on the bartop are luminous embryos, grey viscera in formaldehyde. Everything is dusty and out of date. A hairless, browless man with hideously tight, glossy burned skin watches him drink, and for a moment Sevigne hates the man—hates those wide-set baby blues peering from slits in a red laminate devil's mask. The burned man—yes, this is it—forcibly reminds him of his own banal ingratitude and the unheroic littleness of his trials and burdens; as if reminders ever did any good.

So little sleep and food for several days. The booze lighting into him hard, he steps down to straight beer and sips just enough to keep the demons sedated but not so much as to dilute his resolve. His pulse is rapid, erratic. The burned man's stares, frank and constant and (he sees now) wistfully sexual, finally force him out onto the street, where the harsh interrogating sunlight drives him down into the first subway station he comes to and onto a train, where the eyes of passengers push him to the back of the car. Backward, downward, but still not far enough. He has to bottom out, he even craves it. Above the grotesque faces—all sallow, snouty as if convexly mirrored, louchely watchful—postered ads run like the cartoon-bubbled thoughts of the heads below. *Shop Rite: Your guide to the City's shopping meccas.* He begins to laugh. The sun-glassed kid in the open puffer jacket turns. On his T-shirt, cartoon skeletons copulate in every possible posture, doomed lovers caught by hidden X-ray camera.

He gets off at Union Station. A rumbling confluence of crowds bears him up echoing flights and escalators from deep underground. *Have You Seen This Child?* The posters are on every wall. He emerges into the same hard sunlight and the flightless moonship of the tower is reared straight above him, puncturing the purged-to-vapourless sky. At street level something feels wrong and then it hits him: the shadows—of taxis, statues, bratwurst vendors, harried pedestrians—are all pointing the wrong way. The true sun hidden behind the station is reflected lifesize in the glass façade of a copper-coloured bank tower, a counterfeit sun whose lustre has a liquid, dreamlike cast, whose amber shadows are less defined.

The taproom of the Strathcona Hotel is windowless, always dark. Its regulars—stringy codgers in billed caps and flannel check shirts, their leaky eyes fixed on the big screen or the door—are never reproached by daylight while sprinkling salt into dollar hourglasses of draft.

Well, he passed away. That fella with the big tumour in his side.

So it took him, then?

Sevigne gets coffee, then a refill. He's early. Then Una is late. On the blurry big screen a greased man in a bandana and chaps grapples with a Native giant in Plains costume while the live audience screams. Sevigne rolls a nervous smoke. She enters in a black skirt and army boots, biker jacket flapping open over a snug, scoop-neck mocha shirt, and the old men sit up and watch with the aroused but resigned eyes of sprawled hounds spotting mailmen in the heat. *We would like to get up and cause some trouble, but under the circumstances. . . .*

He stands, gives her a preoccupied kiss. She plumps down in a rust-red swivel chair and ponders him, black eyebrows lowered.

"You're still agonizing," she says.

"I guess I am."

"You're telling yourself lies, Sevigne." She can't hide her impatience, or anything else. "You know what you want deep down."

"I'm starting to think I do. Should we have a beer?"

"It'll just be that awful draft in here, won't it?"

He glances around.

"And there you go again, worried about the neighbours! I'm starting to think that's your problem, Sevigne. You're worried about what people will say if you leave Mikaela." In one motion she rollers her chair forward and leans over the table, planting elbows, framing her face with her hands. Every eye in the tap-room has a bead drawn on them. "But it's your life."

"It's not that simple, Una."

"It is that simple—love is so simple! Then people like you complicate everything by thinking about it!"

"You don't know," he says, "how I love her"—his voice pitched low in hopes of tempering hers, but it's no use at all, for better or worse, supremely herself, she won't be influenced.

"I don't know if I believe it, is all."

"And she really wants a child."

"That's not your problem, Sevigne!"

"Seems everything is somebody else's problem down here."

"God, don't *do* that—don't mistake compassion for love, I did that for too long, Sevigne, believe me, it's a blind alley."

"Una. Listen to me."

Something in his face stops her. "Oh, God, no."

He nods. "We're almost sure of it."

"But you told me you've been afraid of having a child! You don't mean to tell me you've actually been trying? You're not ready for that and you know it. God, Sevigne, your capacity for compromise!"

"It's not compromise, Una, she's my . . ."

"What?"

He stares, tongue frozen.

"And what the hell are you doing here with me?"

He flicks his butt into the mug. "What about the compromises you made with Thomas?"

"Oh, fuck—*fuck* what you call love!" Near-silence in the taproom. In a softened, surging voice she tells him that love is what he felt with her the other night, in the Parthenon and afterward, what she made him feel, not *Oh well, I guess I owe it to them to be whatever they want me to be*—that's a travesty, it's pathetic and she is never going back. It's how most people give away their lives—like her mother and stepfather, years of joyless coping and compromise—but the two of them can be different, they can stick together, they can keep each other awake. They'll leave here for somewhere older, warmer, Tuscany, maybe, Andalusia. . . . And it hits him, finally, what's wrong. They're too much alike. Not to flee her would be to remain with what he is.

In sudden fatigue, as if hung-over in advance, he clasps her small hand and shakes his head.

"If this thing about her being pregnant is a lie, Sevigne Torrins, I swear to God I will make you wish—"

"You can probably leave that to her."

"As if she would!" She twists her hand free. "I saw that interview in *Now* last year. She sounded so flat and tired and whiny, as if she was just fed up with life. Maybe that's it— maybe it's just safer with somebody like that."

"You leave her out of this"—he brings the ash-filled mug down on the Formica—"you don't know anything about her life."

Another silence that balloons to fill every corner of the tap-room but for the sportscaster's faint buzzing; at some point in their clash the volume has been turned down. His numb hands lie like slain things on either side of the mug. Surreal jeaned lap, glint of zipper, bulge of wallet in the coffee-stained front pocket.

"I'm sorry, Una. And this isn't just about her."

"No, but you will be," she says. "When it's too damned late. Too late for both of us! Or was this all just some sort of emotional safari for you? No—I can't believe that, I've felt where you are!"

"And you," he says hoarsely, hunching forward so their noses almost meet, "where were you last year when I was lying awake every night making love to you in my mind?"

She recoils, eyes wide. "What is this, some sort of revenge thing?"

"No!"

"Oh, my God," she says.

"And then—suddenly then I'm the hot new thing with the big novel and you were all over me."

"It was you!" she says, voice full of conviction, eyes full of doubt. After a moment she says, softly, "It was both of us."

"I've lost the book."

As he explains, she listens with a frowning, half-averted face, as if again suspecting a lie. When he's finished, she looks over at the big screen where more overblown men in super-hero costume feign combat. She says, "I really don't know what to tell you, Sevigne. I envy Larry de Vos. If only love were as easy to hand back as a book."

She gets up, turns and stalks towards the exit and then, her timing perfect, wheels around.

"Men don't just walk away from me. You'll call, or you'll write, or you'll come shuffling back to my door." Her face strains to back up the bold words. "I just don't know whether I'll answer."

She's gone. He sits shaken, holding on to the mug as if it were the corner post of a boxing ring—the one thing still supporting him. The taproom's attentive occupants should erupt in applause; all he hears is the sportscaster's faint exclamations and the crowd's muted clamour. He sips from the mug, gags, spits ashes.

"Sev! Hey, great, come on in! Did I forget an appointment or something?"

Sihouetted against the glass with the lake and city as daz-zling backdrop, Kim Moulton in a muscle shirt and long shorts skips lightly, deftly—foot to foot, side to side, whip-steps and double cross-overs—the full pro rep. Rap music thumps out of speakers by the big screen where a fresh pair of wrestlers hams it up. His face is shadowed by the backglare but a goateed grin is visible. Backwards baseball cap over an NBA buzzcut.

"Came on impulse," Sevigne mumbles, shielding his eyes with his damp hand. "God. It's like some modern minstrel show."

"What's that? Hey—bet you could show me a few moves with this thing!"

"Not at present."

Moulton trips, steps clear, drapes the rope over the back of his neck. "Guess I'll cut it a bit short today. Thanks for dropping by though. What's up, buddy?" He's watching Sevigne closely. "Everything all right? I mean with your last assignment? Which was . . . hmm . . ." Striding to his desk, he gestures at the padded chair. "Make yourself at home." He taps a key on his laptop computer, clearly relieved to have an excuse to look down. Some kind of tattoo now on his right shoulder.

"Slim," Sevigne says.

"Slim!" Moulton says. "Oh, that weight-control product, S.L.I.M.! So what have we come up with so far? Sit down."

"Nothing so far. I've barely cracked the folder. My life is going straight to hell."

Moulton's brows jerk up and his eyes, bloodshot with sweat, shift round as if in search of a security buzzer. "Wow. Well. I'm sorry to hear that, Sev."

"You realize Slim is what they call AIDS in Central Africa? Where millions of people are dying of it?"

"You're kidding!"

Sevigne shakes his head.

"Wow. I did not know that." He squints down—apparently straining to call something to mind—then levels a dead serious, rank-pulling stare. Voice suddenly lowered: "This product does predate the AIDS epidemic, however. I believe it dates from the early seventies. In fact"—pensive pause, glittering rictus—"I actually remember that first campaign! Which is why they're now in need of a, a, a facelift. A hip new image. A new *sound*. Anyway S.L.I.M. is just an acronym—Slimmer, Leaner, In, Minutes."

"What's in it, sulphuric acid?"

Moulton with a muscular frown scoops a bottle of water off the desk and cracks it open. His tattoo is of a snake twined around an anchor. "I really haven't a clue what the active in-gredient is, Sev. That's not our business anyway. Something to suppress the appetite, must be. 'Minutes' is just poetic licence."

"Slim," Sevigne says softly, looking outside. In the façades of mirrored towers appear the mirrored walls of facing towers, re-reflections winking back and forth in a ceaseless speed-of-light loop. "Slim, slim, slim."

"Look, are you all right?"

Astonished, he swings his eyes to Moulton. "No, I'm not all right! I can't do this stupid S.L.I.M. jingle, I'd hate myself if I did it. Hate myself more, I mean. It's just another goddamn package of lies, and they're cruel lies." *Sevigne Torrins, guardian of the fair sex.* "She's right, Una's right! I'm turning into a liar!"

"Look, Sev, I'm sorry if you're having problems these days at . . . Man I've been there, OK? I'm on my third marriage now. Relationships!" He throws up his hands. "We should go for a beer some time. I mean, if the assignments are problem-atic for you at present, I'm confident the firm can reassign you to a file you feel a bit less . . . a bit more . . . a bit less . . ."

Dragging his shadow home behind him like a kill he observes with a kind of horror green sprills of crocus and tulip bristling out of the small plots of concrete planters. From a hoarding laminated with posters a name, a face leaps out: Carmine LaStarza. His torso is now burly and hirsute, his face now clean-shaven, but the wolfish glower is the same. *Canadian LightHeavyweight Championship Bout.* The date is just a week ago; years and years ago. No sign of the lost child's poster. An image comes of a sobbing father in a long, earth-coloured coat ranging the city tearing down posters and stuffing them into crammed pockets.

Sevigne stops in at the Skull. Through the glass stanchions

of the bottles his mirrored eyes have a febrile and famished intensity. He drinks quickly, with grim resolve. The bartender has no idea who won the fight. Who is this LaStarza? Stock car races on the TV above him, and now Sevigne envies Ray out riding eye to eye with the westerlies, his city losses left behind, Ray playing that soul-clarifying, madly escapist game with the tractor-trailers. Sevigne's with him, Ray bunched down over the handlebars in the wake of a giant rig with winged-moose mudflaps, the sun of the high plains near Coeur d'Alene radiant in a sky of weightless purity and the grass of the plains still fallow brown and pinned flat in patches under hummocks of snow. On a straight between two towns with towering silos the second truck appears, gathering slowly in mirage-light off the blacktop. Now it looms to sudden hugeness as if accelerating. You open her up and you're shaken by the rapture of the engine as power thrills through it and gravity buckles you backwards hanging on, speeding up, the ruptured white line stuttering under your boots like tracer fire, and for a moment the face of the oncoming driver is framed high above you in the windshield, gawking. You're in the tunnel, in the howling penumbra, a portal of light and open highway ahead and as you rocket free everything's altered, it's summer with the sun on the summit of the sky and the grainfields in hot dry wind flexing under their emerald pelts, and the truckers' air-horns fading. . . .

On the TV, snarling stock cars hydroplane, jockey on the wet turns. Grown men in outsized go-karts. Reminds me of something. He rolls another. *You know too much, Sev, to buy shares in the Beat dream.* He can't seem to get drunk enough to go home. Finally he gives up. When he tries to pay he's two dollars shy, but the bartender's easy, I've seen you around, he says, you're Ike's partner, right? *Partner.* Mercantile, lawyerly sound to it.

Yeah, just pay next time you're in.

For Sevigne and Mikaela the next dozen hours in the apartment are like a bad acid trip or feverish delirium. At first she simply can't believe it. *You're telling me that you and that loud-mouth little bon-bon?* Then she's enveloped in a sadness that leaves her exhausted, short of breath, she's slurring her words, weeping along with him, her hands kneading his chest as if trying to reactivate his heart. Then comes the anger. She collars her hands around his throat as he sits on the bed bolt upright with arms limp at his sides and eyes that seem to implore her, Go ahead, I won't stop you! Under the pads of her thumbs she feels the throat's pumping, jugular heat, and can't squeeze. She draws her right hand back and slaps him, hard, across the face.

Just thought you'd put an old record on the stereo while I was out of the apartment, eh?

She was never in here, Mikaela, I swear on my soul!

For what that's worth.

She rips up the song-sheets for their collaborative song.

As if I'll ever record this now. Stick to baking soda from now on, you lying bastard.

But Ike—

I want you out of here.

What about the test, Ike? Tell me!

Sometimes I really wonder if there's a single solitary adult living in this whole part of the city. I mean, what's so bad about getting older? Everybody just wants to stay a fucking college student for the rest of their lives!

When he fell through the door with his peaked face and huge, hunted eyes, she said nothing about the test, she could see something bad was coming, something. Maybe he was going to confess flat out that he was scared of having a family and couldn't do it. Nice time to come clean. Then regret cut into her because she had known how he was feeling, oh, she'd *known* but couldn't bring herself to stop the process, had told herself his feelings would probably change—sure, that's the way, step lightly, say nothing, it'll all work out. Carry a rabbit's foot. Smart girl. But fuck it, it was *his* fault, he was an adult and she was no mind reader (except, true, when it came to him), *and mature adults have to be clear about what they really want.* (Nadine.) Finally (all these thoughts compressed into a few seconds) she swore to herself that whatever happened, whatever she felt, she would never stoop to make him stay on, never violate her own pride by playing on his sense of guilt and compassion.

Once she learns what he's done and decides she wants him out of her place and her life, it's easy to keep her word. Easier to give up dreams, she thinks, as you get older and learn that the losses don't destroy you, just slow you down. She lies that she never had the test. Says her period came this morning. Then we both lost our dream today, he says, and the words make her even madder, she thinks he's pretending the baby was his dream too, when actually he's relieved, she knows it. Then he explains about his book. He explains sheepishly, almost apologetically, as if the miscarriage of the novel is nothing compared to *her* loss, when she knows how much it must mean to him. You wanted it too badly, she tells him, on cruel impulse. Just stop wanting things and they'll happen overnight.

Till 3 a.m. they drink, talk, and are silent. She drinks lightly but she drinks, she has to. It's agreed that he'll leave in the morning. Drunkenly he throws himself down on the tiny sofa, legs flopping over the end, and she tells him not to be melodramatic, just come sleep in the bed. Eyes open they lie on their backs on opposite sides of the mattress. When sleep finally comes, it's shallow, broken by jarrings awake to the shock and bitterness of the betrayal and then snatches of heartsick dream. *What is the earth but a teardrop on the face of the sky?* A low clear voice is murmuring in her ear but when she opens her eyes, he's asleep on his back, lips rigidly closed. Later they wake together and embrace, kiss deeply, he wants to make love to her, his eyes are burning with love and desire and contrition, but she says no, hugs him hard, turns away. It's one of the toughest things she can remember doing. She's seized by the same valedictory desire—an aching throb between her legs, aching beat of her heart—but she can't do it, not after her own lie. He'd know. The staring marble-eyed baby in her arms shrivels to a white grub wriggling in her palm. Then Nadine is on stage in a cabaret full of leering soldiers gripping the leads of attack dogs with bared yellow fangs and lolloping tongues, straining to get loose and at the singer, claws clicking on the floor. Nadine in her black beret is singing so exquisitely—she who's tone-deaf—that Mikaela is moved to tears. She must wake and write the song down. Then she is awake. The dead hollow light of an overcast dawn is in the room and on the knotted, tortured sheets, and for some time she and Sevigne lie locked together weeping in each other's arms.

20

The Funeral of Valentino

"DON'T BEAT yourself up so much, Sev, shit happens. Hold still."

Eddy watches him struggle to sit up on the stool. Sevigne winces, clutching his side.

"And keep your face to the window, I just almost cut your ear off." Eddy grins wryly. Sevigne might be ready for a stunt like that now—send the lobe to Ike, by courier.

"But I can't even say how it all happened, Eddy. You'd think if you built the maze yourself, you'd know how you got in."

"You're going to look good this way," Eddy says by way of distraction. (Appeals to vanity are always a safe bet.) He stands back to admire his handiwork, puts down the scissors and grabs the electric shaver. "More women problems than ever."

"Not where I'm going."

Turning on the shaver Eddy rolls his eyes with pleasurable frustration. Sev is overreacting again, but there's no talking him out of it. He's going back up north. He's been passing out on Eddy's chesterfield for three nights now, running errands during the day, picking up last cheques, having late dinners back here. They talk and they argue and Sevigne drinks, though not so much, he says, as before. Since reaching his decision, he says, he's felt calmer. But after a few drinks he'll start in on himself. The fact that he cheated on Ike strikes him as a capital offence instead of what it is—just plain stupid, the woman's amazing—though Eddy can understand his reluctance to be a dad at their age. The fact that he hurt Ray and Una hangs on him too—as if it's possible, Eddy thinks, to get through a life without hurting anyone. The fact that, past the roots, hair is a dead thing on the body (this came up two nights ago when he was drunk) really bothers him and he wants it all off for his clean start.

Almost done. Sevigne will be leaving first thing in the morning, and to Eddy it's a bit of a relief. Deadlines breathing down his neck. Like a lover blowing in his ear. And he does still love it, all of it, *On*, his new columns, the exposés he's writing for *Shift* deconstructing cultural personae (the fad cats the sacred cons the CanCult gravy-trainers)—he's even had feelers from the big presses about a book of them (E & E, for one). But he's feeling tired, bone-tired, and for the first time. Refusing to run any more of a sleep deficit, his body is cutting off his credit line and calling in all debts. He feels like a high-powered sports coupe stalled, out of gas, on a rush-hour freeway.

The *Star* spread out on the floor is covered with dark coils of hair, flecked here and there with last night's blood, as if Eddy had just roughly sheared a ram. The headlines showing through are all about Waco, Texas. Actually Eddy is a bit worried for his friend—he seems just unstable and stubborn enough to go through with his plan and maybe land himself in deep shit. Which is maybe what he wants right now. Like last night, getting involved when he should have just kept walking.

With affected pizazz Eddy flashes a book-sized mirror in front of Sev's nose. "Ta da!" For Sevigne the budding tentacles of the maple outside are replaced by his own features—re-blackened eyes, an unstitched laceration across the forehead, his pallor heightened by the exposed gunmetal-grey scalp. With wonder and disgust he runs a hand over his head. Eddy has been insisting he can't just disappear, he's been the talk of the town since the E & E screw-up, everyone's going to be after the novel. And now with Lois back at her desk . . .

"So what do you think, Sev?"

On the island he'll have to take up where Eddy has left off, stripping everything down and away; seeing if what's at the heart of him is any more than Eddy's version of "the soul" as an opportunistically morphing core; stripping the novel equally bare and demanding of the slightest syllable—Is it true?

He says nothing.

At night and at dawn his losses weigh on his chest like fathoms of water. At least on Rye Island he can cause nobody else sorrow. And he has to go. Insularity is a cosmic law—atoms are tiny atolls awash in cellular oceans, cells are islets in the bloodstream pulsing through the body to the heart, the heart is a volcanic island under the sternum's skylike arch, each body is an island in a far-flung archigelago.

Last night weaving anonymous backstreets "home" to Eddy's chesterfield (he'd twined a rose to a bare bough of her apricot tree), he saw figures in shadow beside a Dumpster across the way. On some obscure instinct he crossed over. A rat-faced kid in a puffer jacket and court shoes was hunched in the angle formed by the Dumpster and the brick wall carefully pissing into something. A beer bottle. Behind him were two slouching boys and a skinny girl in leather jackets, combat pants and boots, reversed baseball caps, the shorter boy giving a cigarette and talking in low tones to the crumpled centrepiece of their tableau—an old bum wearing a woman's kerchief, wrapped in his coat on the pavement against the wall. The kid's tone was insincerely consoling, the bum muttering some unclear response.

For the old guy! the kid with the bottle said. His eyes were wide and very clear and ice-cold with cocaine or maybe speed and they showed no surprise or concern at Sevigne's approach. He needs a drink, the kid said. He turned away and knelt in front of the bum, blocking Sevigne's view. The shorter, stocky boy looked on with a predatory smirk; the tall one seemed twitchy. The girl watched Sevigne.

See, Dad, I promised we'd find you something.

What do you want? the girl said to Sevigne.

Iss warm! Hands shaking, the bum held the bottle close to his mouth, yearning to drink, but perplexed. Sevigne stepped forward, heart thumping.

Go ahead, Dad.

Don't drink it, Sevigne said. Just leave the guy alone.

None of your fucking business! the girl said.

The kneeling kid jerked his head around.

Yeah, fuck off, dude.

Let's get out of here, the tall kid said.

Yous leave me all the hell alone!

The kneeling kid stood and started pouring the bottle's contents over the bum's kerchiefed head. Sevigne moved in. Tyler! the girl cried, the kid swivelling his rat face with vacant bulgy eyes and Sevigne's right fist burying into his throat. Somewhere the bottle landed and smashed. Before the kid hit the pavement the other three were charging in, mobbing Sevigne, and after a brief struggle he was down, tucked fetal, boots slamming in from all sides and crashing into his forehead, his spine, his kidneys, the hands cupped over his testicles and face. With each blow a white-hot flash burst under his eyelids. Strange sounds were coming out of him. They were just finding their range and rhythm when one of the boys shouted, *Car, Car!* and the girl, out of breath, said, *Fuck it, man, let's go.*

The thuds of running boots shook through the pavement as fading aftershocks. On his eyelids came the heat of a car's headlights—sunrise on the face of a survivor washed up on a shore. He opened his eyes. Grotesquely lit by halogen high-beams, the bum loomed over him, wobbling, tussocks of white hair flaring from his ears and nose. Car doors opened nearby. Sevigne lay spattered with blood and urine. He smiled, winced, smiled up at the whiskery, dripping face.

3

Rye Island

May the day come, and perhaps soon, when I
can flee to the woods on a South Sea island,
and live there in ecstasy, peace and for
art . . . far from this European struggle for
money.

PAUL GAUGUIN, in a letter, 1890

I

No Other Place

WAKENED by the gale he lies in his down mummy bag on the floor of the light-chamber listening to breakers shudder in and withdraw down the slope of the cobble beach west of the tower. Through high windows the night sky hangs heavy with stars. In Ojibway the Milky Way is Tchibekana, the Road of Souls, a celestial path traversed by shades of the dead towards a heaven in the west.

His bedding occupies the centre of the circular concrete floor, not a dozen feet in diameter, where the lamp and its huge lens once sat. Exhaling vapour he wriggles out of the warm bag and stands up. A dozen miles east, the corona of the unrisen moon is swelling into the dark over the low mountains; the pond in the meadow at the island's heart gleams faintly with starlight, and beyond it woods of maple, birch and conifer taper west to a battered point where geysers of wavespray are shooting half as high as the tower. Farther out a chunk of ice like a small berg, strobe-lit red by the light-buoy, rides the heavy seas, far beacons replying from the mainland capes, the Canadian red, the American green.

Gusts rattle the panes in their lead sills, whine through the balusters of the catwalk, funnel into the mouth of a gargoyle whose high eerie wailing is like the lamentation of a musical saw. Outside, above the catwalk, the serpentine heads of eight gargoyles project from the tops of the mullions at the eight corners of the roof. Back when the powerful lamp still burned, condensation would drain off through the fanged mouths. Six of the mouths are now stuffed with wool socks, one serves as a vent for his heater's fluepipe, the other is left open for air.

He steps to the south panes and looks down the height of the tower and the cliff to a crescent of sand and the sheltered waters of the cove, a reassuring eye of stillness in the larger ferment. A few miles southwest runs the shipping lane. In daylight through binoculars he can sometimes make out the names of big ships remembered from years back; after dark, their stacks and bridges festooned with light, they glide grandly past like floating chateaux. The lane is empty. He is alone with the gale like Turner, his favourite painter, self-lashed to the bridge of a steamboat during a North Sea storm to encounter it eye to eye, no barriers. And now the rising moon is spotlighting the lake torn and plunging southeastward past the shores so that the freighter-shaped island itself seems in motion, Sevigne in the wheelhouse high above the granite decks, lonely, amazed and elated.

The dawn breaks windless, clear and mild. He pushes out through the low, rusted access door and walks the circuit of the catwalk to survey his domain. The blue spill of the distances and the air's freshness and tentative warmth draw from him a yip of joy. Then snatches of song. Scraps of poetry. It's all coming back to him. He is a muezzin in his concrete minaret but with different allegiances. Climbing onto the sill he banters with the gargoyles as he tugs socks like rootless blue tongues from the snarling mouths. He empties his Tupperware "chamber pot" over the railing on the cliff side, feeling a childish delight in the faint, delayed splat of liquid cracking the foil-thin ice over sand at the water-line.

He rolls a cigarette and draws smoke deep into his chest. The day, like the lake spreading uncontainably westward, fans open, all promise, before him. Mornings he loves feeling these first definite pangs of hunger, his body signalling its readiness to bite off and take in more of the world. For his last weeks in Toronto and his haunted stay in the Soo his appetite was truant; out of shape and gripped by a kind of existential dyspepsia, he couldn't imagine ever again eating with gusto. He has a last slow, luxurious puff (a subway-ad image of himself as the Lone Smoker briefly obtruding) and then ducks back inside. Leaving the door open he brews coffee on his camp stove and boils up a skilletful of oatmeal with raisins, dates, almonds, dried apricots, powdered milk and butter.

Six flights of concrete stairs zigzag down to ground level inside grey walls of increasing thickness. He comes out the door and crosses a large sheet of exposed granite that forms a kind of parade ground in front of the lighthouse and the keeper's house—its whitewash blistered and slate roof hammocked, but ground floor still habitable. In the belt of mixed pines between the granite sheet and the central meadow he passes the stillhouse, a narrow squared-log structure like a barracks or small covered bridge set into a rift in the woods under the biggest of the white pines. It seems to have lapsed further into the rift, the shingles of its sagging roof mossed and welted, tin chimney crumpled, windows caved in. Snow lies melting in the furrows between the rift's inner slopes and the walls. He forces the rusted tin door. In dank twilight the interior is like a disused shrine, empty but for the remains of the still—a squat dark shape hunkered idolwise in the centre of the floor. The half-frozen floorboards are black with rot and the chill air deadens his footfalls. Running his hands over the rough green copper pot of the still, where Papère Noel's hands must have passed, he dutifully tries to feel moved. All he feels is the irony; he has brought little liquor out here to Rye, only a careful, daily ration, as if travelling back in time to the source of the Torrins curse in order to end it.

Already missing the light above, he turns back to the door.

Past the stillhouse a needled path tramped clearer by the day curves on through stippled light into the meadow with its spring-fed pond. This open space has the damp, turfy odour of an alpine meadow at winter's end, mosses squelching underfoot, weeds and grasses beginning to spring back. Soon to leaf, frail birch and trembling aspen rim the meadow over lichened rocks, low alder and juniper like gorse; a melodious gurgling comes from the creek and unseen lesser rivulets draining the pond and the sodden half-acre around it. The lake lies a short way downhill along the creek, three blank crosses lapsing into the earth beside it, while offshore, like a hunk of coal in a pool of sparkling mercury, an islet sits blackened with the refuse of recent fire. Between Rye and that nameless rock—Nile Islet, he decides—runs the Canada–U.S. border.

He has walked every foot of the island several times over, sensing he will not be able to settle to any real work until he has mapped the place into his muscles and brain. Kneeling he drinks from the pond where it tapers and funnels into the creek. Little moulds of slushy ice drift under his eyes and the day-moon shivers on the stirred surface like a ghostly lily pad.

How sweet and cold the water is.

At school in a classics essay he argued that a main difference between Western and Eastern thought was embodied in the myths of Narcissus and Li Po—Narcissus pining away and dying over his own image in a pool, even trying to kiss it in the River Styx while being ferried to Hades; the drunk poet Li Po falling out of his rowboat and drowning while trying to kiss the mirrored moon. So the progeny of the humanist West were all liable to sink into themselves, into their own minds, that cranial house of mirrors. Here on the island he must emulate Li Po; at least in part. He has brought along no mirrors.

Forget yourself, he thinks, and you might write something great.

He leans farther out to sip the moon, his own face however eclipsing it.

A sleek raven croaks rustily from the tip of a young jack pine that quivers under its weight. At least Sevigne knows what this bird is; the woods are chittering with other, smaller birds whose names he can only guess at, or invent. Every few days the raven crosses from the Michigan side to scavenge the island's woods and shores. Caliban, he calls it. He croaks back at the stern-faced bird who drops off his perch with ratcheting sharp cries and great flaps of his black-fingered wings and makes for Sevigne as if to strafe him. His shadow sweeps over the pond and downhill along the creek out over the border straits and up the banks of Nile Islet from water-line to tonsured crown like a soul in rapid ascent.

On the first page of a blood-leather-bound diary purchased in the Soo, he inscribes in weighty majuscules:

CONFESSIONS OF AN ANACHRONIST

May 9—"red sky at night"—temp. 5°C—this a.m. mounted thermometer outside window in front of "desk"—deal table from keeper's house, drawers empty. Full hour wrestling it up here resting every step by end but worth it, captain's view SW over pond towards prow of island, sunset. Began by hand complete rewrite of Islands. S.B.: 'Ever tried. Ever failed. Never mind. Try again. Fail better.' No flab, no lies—vow underlined by horizon, essentialist landscape whittled to 4 billion yr old bone. Now avian twilight, high circonflexe of geese northbound for tundra, loons surfacing to cruise w/ black periscope heads. Gulls aspool above offshore rocks. Aerial Caliban flying in to scavenge.

If not for the miscarriage, their child might be coming into the world today, Sevigne's life on another path, in another place.

No lies.

Love, forgive me.

There is no other place, now.

2

Jude

AFTER GETTING OFF the Greyhound in the Soo he humped his duffel bag to the Ancient Mariner past an ageless string of glass-brick taverns, diners, candy-cane barber shops, grimy bowling alleys and pool halls, which down south would have figured as mentionably retro but here were simply the living, local culture. The busy cook told him that Amy and Wolf had just left town to visit friends in Winnipeg and would not be back for several weeks. After a mug of draft beer on the house he walked back the way he had come, and from the edge of town, in icy drizzle, thumbed a ride out along Base Line Road. It was dusk and midweek, the other camps deserted, the leafless dreary woods still pocketed with snow.

At some point over the past year, thieves had jimmied the lock and made off with the booze, the worthless TV, the eight-track stereo/radio and the shoebox-sized display case containing Torrins's boxing medals—probably just brass and tin, but still Sevigne reproached himself for having left them there where he'd felt they belonged. They'd missed what was hidden—his father's ample toolkit and fishing rod and rifle—and he spent the next week scrounging further supplies from the camp and trying to hitch rides into town to find more. Finally he succumbed to necessity and rented a car. Using an old RCMP pamphlet on Arctic survival he made long lists and carefully checked things off, striving against his nature to be practical and not impetuous, anxiously watching his funds shrink away. The ancient propane camp stove would have to be replaced. And the kerosene heater. But in the medicine chest he found a first-aid kit, a copious stash of painkillers, and a plastic vial of sulfa drugs with "Torrins" typed on the label.

The directed bustle of his days was a relief, at times almost a pleasure; evenings in the cabin were another matter. On his last evening he stood before his father's long-neglected book-shelves with a tumbler of rye and picked out his Desert Island Ten, most of them portly classics he had not yet read, though by writers he had: *Jude the Obscure*, *Middlemarch*, *Parade's End*, *The Brothers Karamazov*, *Ulysses*, *The Magic Mountain*, the *Iliad*, the Upanishads, a thick treasury called *Great Poems in English*, and (one of his mother's old unfinished books, the pressed-violet bookmark still faintly fragrant) *A la recherche du temps perdu*.

That night as he lay in his childhood bunk, the ache of lost time was like an icy wedge worked into a crack in his heart and waiting for the axe blow to finish the job.

Lester Trubb sat on the stern bench with squat legs splayed, the baggy crotch of his olive work pants sagging. His leathery left hand held a beer tin, his right tillered a deafening old Evinrude 50 as they thumped over the waters off Corbeil Point. From the dock the bay had seemed calm under seam-less, lowering cloud, but out here it was running a swell and at times as they slammed down into troughs, freezing spray would shower over them and the tarped cargo. In the bow Sevigne moved deeper into his father's hooded parka. Trubb in a light check flannel hunter's jacket seemed unruffled, somehow keeping his cigarette lit through the spray and now a spatter-ing of icy rain. He took the cigarette out of his mouth only to swig beer. The kerosene drums and propane canisters were stowed a few feet in front of him. "Don't sweat yourself!" he called, his eyes blurred behind big, green-tinted glasses set under the brim of an earflapped hunter's cap. He twitched a smile, tight-lipped, his cigarette optimistically lifting.

They rounded the point where an old skeleton-tower lighthouse decayed on rickety limbs over the lobed and cloven granite of the shore. Back of the tower, black spruce, tall aspen and jack pine formed an impenetrable palisade. Trubb with sudden animation explained loudly that one of the light-keepers had fallen to his death from that tower back in the forties. Or took a dive. Too much time to think, eh. Here on the open lake the swell was fuller. Rain blurred the Michigan shore, folding it into the larger greyness now eliding water and sky; their twenty-four-foot shell with little freeboard might have been bearing straight into the North Atlantic.

"How long to the island?" Sevigne yelled over the motor's labouring and the rhythmic, hollow drubbing of hull on water.

"What island's that?" Trubb yelled back.

Sevigne stared at him.

"See, there's plenty of islands. North Sandy is just a few miles south. Over there."

"Right."

"You mean Rye, I guess." Trubb crumpled the beer tin in his fist, tossed it over his shoulder into the frothing wake. "She's a ways yet, can't even see her. Least I can't." He tapped the rim of his glasses and grinned. "Straight off the bow should be, have a look!"

Ahead there was nothing but ranked grey waves—more and more of them capped with spume—advancing under a low ceiling of storm clouds coiled like entrails. And then, a hundred feet to starboard, an ice floe.

Sevigne turned around. Trubb had removed his camouflage cap and with a stolid air was sleeking back receding hair that flowed behind his ears in a ducktail. His sideburns were long and bushy and flared at the base. He had no neck. Pushing his lips out he nodded, palm raised as if taking an oath—*Going to be just fine, son, promise*—then lobbed Sevigne an Old Milwaukee over the cargo. Sevigne tore it open and sucked the welling foam into his mouth. Trubb's rates had been good, in fact he'd had to come up with a rate, he'd never taken anybody out as far as Rye; now Sevigne wished he had sprung for a guide with a bigger boat and better eyesight. So much of his savings had gone on equipment and food. He yelled a warning about ice, but when he looked ahead again they were abreast of the floes, past them, Trubb amiably cursing himself, didn't see a goddamn thing.

Trubb never had taken anybody out to Rye, he'd said, but as a boy he'd gone out that way across the ice with his old man, at least as far as it was safe to go in winter. Pretty exceptional ice fishing. One time he and the old man were on the snowmobile a bit before sunrise. Their headlight showed a fishing hut on the ice just east of Pancake Shoals. There was a pick-up parked there but no light from inside of the hut. The old man told him to sit tight while he went to have a look, but Trubb followed, found him glued to the spot in the doorway of the hut shining his flashlight in. Trubb looked around his elbow and saw in—two men sitting to either side of the froze-up hole, their lines coming out of the ice, still gripping the rods. Beards and faces frosted over. Almost empty quart of something beside the door. The old man figured they dozed off blind drunk and the heater cut out on them. Wouldn't have taken long, not at twenty below. Like with that old buck on Batchawana Island? Didn't see it myself, but my cousin Tim swears on the Good Book, he's that type, eh. He and his boy Josh found this poor old son of a bitch froze right into a pond standing up. Pond froze right up around his fetlocks in the time it took him drinking. Sometimes they take their time, eh? But here's the thing of it—*the insides of him were gone.* Gutted, boy, like by a butcher. Wolves got to him while he was still warm. Or maybe foxes. How's that for a story? You write that one down. I got others. I've had some occurrences to tell of. You write them down, start up a web site—"True Tales of a Northern Guide and Trapper" or something—city types eat that stuff up like candy.

In the city Sevigne had come to sense that everybody has one basic story they ceaselessly tell and retell and act and live out in all its various shades and mutations. His own seemed to have something to do with islands and towers; Trubb's clearly hung on the Gothic, italicized discovery of some creature who'd perished in wretched circumstances, in the snow, the bitter cold. The story constituted a tacit boast. It's a fight to survive up here, they didn't make it through, I'm still around though, see? All Trubb could remember hearing of the Rye moonshiners was how a couple of them had gone through the ice, their flatbed overloaded with crates of rye, and when the US Coast Guard had dredged them out later that year, they were still sitting in the cab *with the bones of the driver's hands holding the wheel.*

The white tower appeared first, disembodied from its island base so it seemed to emerge from the waves like a luminescent waterspout, or the whittled spire of an iceberg. As the bow of the shell bucked high over a whitecap, tree-lined cliffs appeared, then a grinning slash of sand—the fabled cove, their refuge. He was starting to feel seasick. He looked back at the stern. Trubb seeing nothing had propped the tiller in the crook of his elbow and was shielding match and cigarette with cupped hands. For a minute more Sevigne was alone with the island, which repeatedly sank and then rose up ever larger as they laboured towards it.

For years his father had spoken of this trip; momentarily his fear wheeled round into excitement. Then as the island's shoals began complicating the waves, a white-clawed cross-sea reared out of nowhere and slammed them to port, spray and spindrift geysering high above them and showering down. They shipped gallons. Jarred from his reverie Sevigne glanced back. Trubb now appeared wet and alert, frowning at his doused cigarette, tossing it overboard, sheering course a point starboard. They split three more big waves bow-on before thumping down into magically calmer seas in the lee of the island, the wind on Sevigne's damp face milder and scented with hints of spruce and cedar, moss and thawing soil.

Rounding a point of grey- and salmon-speckled granite they entered the cove. A squad of mallards, startled by the engine's echoing growl, burst up off the water. Pans of ice half the size of the boat thickened as they neared the beach, Sevigne leaning over the bow to watch them cleave and buckle, sink, shunt aside. Trubb cut the engine. A few feet from shore the keel scraped onto a ledge of thicker ice and Sevigne, anxious to plant his flag, vaulted out with the tieline clenched between his teeth. His right foot punched through a soft patch. Water of a shocking coldness flooded the boot. He knelt on the beach and tied off to a chunk of driftwood and for a moment he remained there, quietly retching. Trubb, hands on the port gunwale, cigarette in mouth, was clambering round the cargo and over the bow.

With axes they hacked away at the ice until they were able to drag the boat a few feet onto the beach and start unloading. Load after load the two men tumped up a steep path—a natural gravelly cleft in the rock face under the tower—Trubb wheezing and coughing around his cigarette but uncomplaining. They piled things at the base of the tower. Finally Trubb with a dubious shake of his head crowbarred open the door and they started up. Sevigne couldn't help rushing, bounding ahead up the dusty concrete stairs, so that on gaining the light chamber he was again briefly alone with his island. Quickly he lapped the circuit of the windows, joy like drunken song swelling in his chest.

"You really plan to set up in here?" Trubb was huffing his way up the last few steps, pulling a can of beer from the outer pocket of his jacket. "Pretty cramped."

"But look at the view!"

"Love to, kid, but these glasses." Trubb lowered his broad bottom onto the narrow sill, his back against the high windows. "Anyways the cold'd kill you. Be like living in a storm-lantern. You'd go through fuel like nobody's funeral. Like those two Yanks—the deer hunters, got stranded on Parisienne by the early freeze-up in '83? Stayed out in the open, on the shore, afraid of being missed. By the time we got out to them. . . ."

"But it's almost spring now," Sevigne said, "and you're bringing that second load in the fall."

Trubb took off his cap and raked back his hair, staring lev-elly through tinted glasses, eyes visible but unreadably dimmed. For the first time it seemed clear that he was playing a part, whether consciously or not—inventing himself, the Frontier Guide and Trapper. Even him. Even here. It made Sevigne anxious for him to go. "I'll be back," Trubb said, "you don't worry about that. Like you paid me. But you're going to want to come off by then. I'd bet the business on it. I've lived alone mostly my entire adult life and it's all right by me, no complaints whatsoever. I can see wanting to steer clear of the shit. But alone in a town where you've your dogs and your satellite dish and seeing folks out your window or in the store is different than alone out here."

Sevigne nodded and smiled absently. Time to embark on his new life of solitude and artistic discipline. Now the shade of some feeling—impatience? apprehension?—skimmed under the surface of Trubb's laconic face, like something unknown passing under a boat in deep waters. He swung his lensed eyes away and seemed to squint hard out the streaked, dusty windows.

"She's getting a bit rough, that much I can tell."

"I'll see you to the boat," Sevigne said.

They bailed with tin pots and laid a ballast of cliff-fall granite over the keel. Trubb gave Sevigne another can of beer and told him to sip her slowly some lonesome night—he'd be back with mail and supplies somewhere between the first and fifteenth of November, weather depending. Turned from the shore, right hand on the tiller as he chugged out through the bobbing floes, Trubb without a glance back raised his free hand and held it high.

3

The Savage

CLEAR DAYS the glare through the high windows onto his page is so dazzling he wears sunglasses, which along with his bristly hair and stubble-beard must make him resemble some *latte* dabbler in the Annex. He has never felt farther from that world. He wonders if his face is showing signs of change, of radical simplification to the clear-eyed, unflinching dignity he has seen in photos of Zen *bikkhus* and young Civil War privates, or Métis rebels in prairie rifle pits, their eyes full of fate, on the brink of death or some lesser encounter with the armies of logic, irony and progress.

He has no way of examining his face closely. At night when he works with candles or the kerosene storm-lantern on the table, his reflection in the panes is vague—the dim simu-lacrum that a shade might see of itself if there were mirrors in the afterworld. When a freighter passes after dark he wonders if the night-wheelsman can see a faint glow from the Rye lighthouse; Sevigne is an epigone of the stubborn Flaubert, whose burning midnight oil, night after night and year after year, became a beacon to bargemen passing in the dark Seine below his window.

Ce n'est pas une petite affaire que d'être simple.

Now there was a heroic life.

How good to find he still can be alone. He works long hours and when not writing he performs simple, bracing chores—hauling water into the light chamber, repairing the outhouse roof, sawing and chopping driftwood, fishing in the cove—and at times he hunkers in the Ojibway vision pit on the cobble beach staring northward over hypnotic waves, white-capped under a surf of scudding clouds, to the blue-grey groundswell of the mountains. Maybe the sacred in a secular age was just this—a shrinking of the ego into abeyance, so the world, as in childhood, could pervade you whole.

Evenings he walks downhill from the pond through dense brush to the island's western tip, Caliban the raven tracking him from tree to tree. As he nears the shore, chill flaws begin to penetrate the woods, the dwarf maples and mountain ash thin out and vanish and the conifers shrivel as if he were moving north a hundred miles with every stride. He emerges on a gale-swept Arctic shore, a few ancient spruce bent and twisted like gleaners and the copper-lit seas thundering in to explode cliff-high as the sun founders, a sinking fireship. The island comprehends such extremes—all landscapes, seasons, weathers, tempers. Come morning he'll fish in icy cove-shallows of a pellucid, Caribbean turquoise. No need to dream of elsewhere or return to his past, each day he's less apt to feud or fraternize with his spectres, though at some point every night his mind doubles back, in regret or desire, to Mikaela. Her shadow (and sometimes Una's) presides over rampant fantasies; and yet he does not really wish her here, not now.

June 8—revise Ch. 3. 'It is in order to shine sooner that authors refuse to rewrite. Despicable. Begin again.' A.C. Clear morning sky though w/ low fog on all shores, sundial shadow of lighthouse tapering over pond and woods to western point of Rye—13°C—gauze-green of new foliage in birches aspens maples. On Nile, magenta fireweed over charred ground makes islet a mound of banked embers. Yesterday aft. on warm covesand blowing harp, Midnight Rambler, sipping Trubb's gift of watery beer—dove in to bathe—leapt out steaming, hollering up at sky. Moon in her hammock. Sunbeams in forest like banisters of gold sloping down through radial upreaching branchwork. Still few flies. Meadow an addict's palette of weeds & wildflowers, dogbane like apple blossom, Devil's paintbrush, many other unknowns to find names for.

Some evenings after his sunset hike and a supper of rice and beans or fried whitefish (he flings the scraps off the catwalk, Caliban snatching them from the air far below) he props his feet on the deal table, pours a tot of rye from his small store and turns on the radio of his cassette player. He keeps hoping to hear Ike in Ruby Rick's "Top Forty Showdown," but so far nothing. The evening news is reliably bad. More slaughter in a Bosnian town with the aptly internecine name Goradze; more slaughter in Somalia. Sevigne is the kind of idealist easily disturbed by news from abroad, but now the reports—like local notice of layoffs at the mills and a bylaw aimed at the hardened jaywalker—seem part of an implausible fiction, the whole newscast a solemnly executed skit having no connection to reality. *Night swell opalescing under bruise-green thunderheads—lightning like a great insight leaping synapse between cloud and water——*

Dave Dawson's land and marine weather forecasts seem even more fanciful. The island's weather always differs from the Soo's and seldom even corresponds with Dawson's forecasts for Whitefish Bay, so Sevigne has come to ignore the guy—his suave drowsy voice, his cornball "Joke of the Day"— and to consider that he, Sevigne, is not just forty miles northwest of the city but set on a different plane, his radio a short-wave receiver that by some mysterious transmission conducts frequencies from other continents or dimensions.

In the sunfilled tower one day in July as he sweats over his page like an insect under a magnifying glass, the drone of an engine breaks through his mumbling. If it's Trubb it means an emergency. Maybe his mother—another earthquake in Cairo? He grabs the binoculars and runs through the open doorway onto the catwalk. The air is humid, calm. A white houseboat, like a trailer on pontoons and bristling with antennas, is puttering into the cove. On the front deck stands a bandy-legged man with a solid paunch slung off a thickset body—a slab of a man, a power athlete a few years gone in beer. He holds a bottle. He wears only a pair of baggy shorts, sunglasses and a bandana. Two women in bikinis—the brunette bronzed, the redhead burnt—issue from the doorway behind him to crowd the tiny deck. Binoculars to his eyes Sevigne squats down, as if the balustrade of the catwalk could hide him.

They drop anchor midcove. In a pontoon launch that seems perilously small for the big man they come ashore; he ferries first the women one by one and then a second man, long and scrawny and hairy as a spider, his perfect foil, a cinema sidekick. On the beach the invaders deploy towels and sunchairs, a plastic cooler, a large cassette player, a beach hibachi.

These first faces seen in months register as prognathous and snouty, asymmetrical, as if distorted by the binoculars' old lenses: on the giant's hog-bristled face, a grotesque rictus of laughter. Sevigne in his tower gazes down on the proceedings as on the preparatory rites of a cannibal tribe. A blaring rock

classics station and conversation, ever louder with beer, rever-
berate up from the cove. So the big man is the owner of a fit-
ness centre in the Soo, his sidekick an employee of some kind,
the sinewy brunette an aerobics instructor and the redhead a
waitress, quiet and clearly bored by the shop talk and the gossip—gossip of a torpefying banality yet with an anthropologi-
cal interest that keeps Sevigne alert at his keyhole. He doesn't
feel smug so much as bewildered. The group's interest in the
island seems to end at the beach; the mainland's concerns and
antagonisms are surreal.

In the limpid depths of the bowl-shaped cove the houseboat's shadow rests, an unmoving square, on the agate cobbles
of the bottom.

At three p.m. the big man, Willy, lights a cigar and the hibachi. The good aromas of charcoal briquettes and leaf tobacco
loft up to the catwalk. Then smells of cooking meat. Caliban
flies past the tower's base out over the clifftop, reconnoitres,
returns to perch on a ledge. Willy's rising voice booms off the
rock face as he sings along with Nazareth, "Love Hurts." Jake
on a "suds run" is buzzing out to the houseboat. Side by side in
the shallows the women sit, bottles in hand, their soft chatter
now and then ruptured by the brunette's snorty, explosive
laughs.

Others have come in past summers. On the sand and cobble beaches he has found rusted beer tins, broken glass, plastic
wrap, condoms, rotting toilet paper, shotgun and rifle shells
and, in the forest's sombre depths, the rusting question mark
of a tent peg. In the outhouse, a faded '85 issue of *Soldier of Fortune* bears the teasers *New Ops in Africa!* and *Pistol Whipping
Today*, the articles themselves missing and presumed used.
At eye level on the north face of the tower there's a cursive
graffito in green: *Andrew + Tanya August 10 '76 Lovers Forever*

Sevigne ducks back inside, squats at the camp stove beside
his table/desk and opens a tin of refried beans. When they're

done he sprinkles on cayenne pepper and Parmesan cheese and dicings of the pungent chives that grow wild around the keeper's house—last but flourishing descendants of a vanished garden. Afterwards fresh raspberries in condensed milk. He makes a pot of green tea, stuffs dampened wads of toilet paper into his ears and gets back to work.

In early evening, as shadows of the cliffs and the trees overlay the beach and then the cove, the party returns to the houseboat. Willy wheels a barbecue onto the front deck and lights it and goes back inside. Blue glimmerings through the window make Sevigne think of undersea documentaries he saw as a child, though the faint soundtrack is of manic dialogue and every few seconds canned laughter ripples over the water, resounds off the cliffs. Through the binoculars he sees Willy come out and turn on the deck light, prong slabs of something onto the barbecue, swagger back inside. The moon rises in twilight. A night or two off full, it's reflected like a buoy bobbing in the cove's lapis shallows. An evening so balmy and aromatic begs to be shared, and he thinks of Mikaela; he'll have to make do with a dram of rye. Caliban lights on the deck rail as Willy emerges again. Startled, then angry, the man rushes the bird, his hands flailing. "Scram! Scram, you black fucker!" Caliban flaps clear and disappears behind the boat—Sevigne squinting through the binoculars trying to find him—then reappears on a tine of the antenna. He drops onto the roof, hops across to the front edge and perches by the deck light, peering down at Willy's back.

Sevigne grins, toasts the bird, throws shadow-jabs. That's it, Cal, get in there. Get inside him. Demand our tithe. As Willy starts back through the doorway, Caliban swoops on the grill and the man, as if expecting this, pivots and lunges wildly with the meat prong, a clumsy, desperate fencer. Calmly Caliban flaps up out of reach, something small in his beak. Willy seizes the can of fire-starter and spritzes upward and the bird with sharp rapid croaks lifts on a thermal of fear, banks away, glides low over the cove and sets his prize—a hot dog? a strip of fat?—on the beach. Ruffling fastidiously he enters the shallows and dunks his head like a loon several times. When he finally flies out of sight—into the forest or back over the lake to Michigan—Sevigne returns to his desk, lights the lamp at its lowest setting and tries to read. More Hardy.

Some time later he looks up from the page. Willy is laughing again, the sound louder, drunker and charged with a new undertone that stands the hackles on Sevigne's nape. Jake is tittering nervously. And a woman—the redhead?—is crying, "Oh man, you're an asshole! I mean, I can't believe it—what an asshole!" Sevigne leaps up and out the open door onto the catwalk where the air is dreamy and warm. Out of the night like a projectile launched from the houseboat flies an incendiary ball, screeching, veering and dipping, a black nucleus haloed in flame and beating the air with fiery wings, passing close by the catwalk in a gust of heat. Its throttled cries freeze the blood and stop the throat. Sevigne runs inside and bounds down the stairs two at a time. He bursts out the door, looks up and around: a slow comet is pulsing just over the treetops in the direction of the meadow—the meadow which for weeks has felt no rain and will go up like stubble and ignite the forest. The moon lights his path as he runs barefoot through the pines. He emerges into the open just as Caliban flounders down, wings thrashing, amid the low alder and juniper across the pond. Small blue flames still flicker on the body, an acrid gassy stink fills the air. Sevigne stamps sparks from a juniper bough—the gin-smell of its berries rising to him—and kneels beside the bird. Its quivering beak is gaped open, soundless. He pulls off his T-shirt and dabs out the last flames. The shrivelled body, featherless, pink and puckered, twitches, the claws contract and relax, eyes like bubbles of hot tar bulge from the singed head. Tears in his own eyes Sevigne hefts a broad flat stone with both hands and smashes it down.

Bare but for his shorts he runs back through the moonlit colonnade of the pines and across the granite sheet and up the lighthouse stairs, filling the stairwell with stertorous echoes of his breathing, swearing. He pulls the rifle from behind his desk and slips the safety catch. Stomps out onto the catwalk. Its rear window a screen of flickery light, the square boat like a floating television chugs out through the narrows of the cove. "Fucking bastards!" Sevigne screams, "Come back!" Maybe they saw him, lit up by their victim as it passed the tower like a flying torch. They want to avoid trouble. And they'd have had it. He slams the butt three times against the railing, which shudders and hums eerily, and he looks down at the rifle, half surprised. *A storm. May a storm come up and take you.* He fires a round into the sky as if to seed the clouds. *Or lightning.* Ejects the shell. No sign they've heard his voice or the shot. He fires again, into their receding wake.

I'm never going back there. Never.

4

Detours

RYE ISLAND seems to lie at the heart of some meteorological singularity; the summer goes on freakishly hot, day after day the mercury reading five degrees higher than reported for the Soo. Is it a sign of global warming, that fever afflicting the planet as it sickens? Poisoned. But all that seems improbable here. Here time seems to be moving backwards, if it ever has moved; in late afternoon towering banks of cumulus mass over Superior and thunder rolls out of the west like rumblings of the Lost Herds in a late stampede. One day as he sits working, peripheral vision or some inscrutable instinct draws his attention outward. What looks like his father's vessel is passing a few miles south on a bearing for the Soo. He hurries onto the catwalk. Through binoculars the magical name *Algonordic* appears on a hull mottled with smuts of rust and blistering paint; despite the air's warmth the deck rail and coaming aisles are deserted and the glare of sunlight off the wheelhouse panes hides the occupants. He follows his father's crewless ship until it's lost to sight, a ghost ship like those medieval ones whose sailors succumbed to the Black Death and then drifted on unmanned for years, sometimes finding unlucky ports.

One night he wakes to a sound like sleet or freezing rain tapping at the windows. He opens his eyes and sits up. The grey floor like the parchment wall of a vespiary swirls with tiny shadows cast by moonlight while outside the stars seem to reel and spill and revolve as if the earth were plummeting through space. He leaps up and goes for the access door, left open for air. The water-blisters are swarming out of the northwest; the door faces southward but a few have gotten in. Stunned or dying, they rest on the bright floor of the light chamber, curled green tails twitching. He pulls the door shut and stands by his desk as they stream towards him thick as a blizzard or some biblical curse. You'd think they were flying straight out of the moon. In their millions they clip the windows and bounce off and hit again or veer around the tower or plunge out of sight. He sags into his chair and watches, mouth slack. He loses all sense of time. Then the blizzard thins out, abruptly ceases; the night world reappears; the catwalk is squirming with tiny shapes and the woods and calm lake are left seethingly active, larval in the moonlight.

Dubious of his father's reports of fantastic evanescence, he tells himself he will explore in the morning, the insects will still be there. He wakes to a cool front scudding in from the west and finds the catwalk swept clean and the forest and the choppy waters purged, nothing left but a few papery husks on the light-chamber floor and on the shores a fading odour like rotten seaweed.

By August the turquoise waters of the cove are almost tepid. Sevigne has taken to crossing the cove—racing his shadow as it skims over the logs and cobbles twenty feet down—then pushing out through the narrows a dozen strokes into the usually unswimmable lake. One hot afternoon impulse and risk tempt him onward. He has an urge to cross the floating border like his father, and stand on US soil amid the fireweed and few skeletal trees of Nile. His body these days feels so strong and he so fully within it—an owner and not a tenant—he half believes he could swim to the Soo, and at first the cold of the open lake is exciting, and the extremes: when he breathes, the heat of the sun on his face and the rainbow shatter of light in his wet lashes, when he looks down, icy blackness pierced by auroral streamers receding into the depths. He is swimming through space above the northern lights—over Chagall's Vitebsk! *Stars at elbow and foot.* He's soaring. How could he have hoped for such elevation in the city? The disembodied city! When all joy, he feels now, even mental joy, is founded in the body.

In the channel between Rye and Nile, starting to feel deeply chilled, he enters a vein of water so cold that the first breath he draws there is broken and brings no air. It's water churned up from depths below the thermocline or blown in from mid-lake by the winds. He cranes his head up, looks around. Nile is farther out than he thought. He should turn back, but it isn't like him—as if somebody were waiting ahead on the shore, on every goddamned shore, stopwatch in hand, *Wimp, come on*, and he pushes on, striving to generate warmth, but the cold palsies his limbs and truncates his stroke and the winds funnelled through the strait churn up waves against him.

Soon he would gladly turn back but now Nile is closer than Rye and he'll take the closest shore. An eerie abatis of blackened timber rises from the depths to the islet's banks. He puts on a burst of speed and soon drags himself onto a slick, liver-like slab of rock marbled with streaks like dirty fat and lies there prone and gasping. He would stay there embracing the warm stone, letting the sun bake winter out of him, but the winds are chilling him further and his teeth won't stop chattering. Arms crossed over his chest he runs along the shore to the lee side. It's no good, even out of the wind his body is cooling. His throat is parched and a bitter paste of fear coats his tongue. Momentarily he has the wild notion of signalling a distant freighter for help, or of swimming out to the light-buoy pulsing red and to cling there like a limpet as if it could warm him, as if you could not possibly die in the embrace of such an artefact of human order. Like that hitch-hiker (Trubb again) on the Trans-Canada last winter. *OPP found her clinging to a road sign—Sault Ste Marie 100 klicks—had to chip her off inch by inch.*

He grits his teeth and with a running start dives in. A dozen strokes out, the full shock of it hits him. It's too cold to draw proper breath. He makes for the place on the south shore where the creek plunges a few feet over a ledge and an exposed pine thrusts from a granite cleft. The west wind has made a harsh example of the tree. Gaunt limbs swept downwind, it seems to gesture with tragic defiance, a hunched old man de-claiming a soliloquy to the wilderness.

Sevigne looks up for his mark. He has drifted off course, slapped east by the waves. Face swivelling upwind for breath he inhales mouthfuls of water; the big lake is aggressively alive. A strange, sly numbness begins creeping upward from his toes and down from the tips of his fingers, so in minutes his feet and hands are all but impervious to the water's bite. Then his ankles, wrists. A cold gangrene is bleeding inward to his vitals. He tries to cup fingers hard for a proper draw and flutter-kick with his feet but he can't feel them and he's slowing though he's working harder, millwheeling arms like a panicked novice. His forearms and calves are gone and now the anaesthesia reaches into his thighs; he can't be sure if his feet are still kicking. He fights on, buffeted by waves, eyes straining into the depths for any sign of shore. They say it's painless. When the numbness touches the heart, he thinks, and peers up: the contorted pine is close but his legs are sinking, only his arms working on, clutching and pulling at the water as if on a line tossed from the bank. Some-thing unbalances him and he rises as if shoved from below. He tries to stand, sags back in, onto all fours. The shallows by the creekfall are cloudy and warm. He's spitting through chattering teeth, weakly laughing, groping his way in to shore.

With the arthritic choppy steps of an old man he runs up-hill along the creek within sight of the crosses at the meadow's edge and through the pine woods to the tower. In the light chamber he turns the heater to full, buries himself in his sleeping bag and blankets and lies shivering until dark, eating trail mix and sipping rye in hot sweetened milk.

The day the monarchs appear it's as if a low streak of wind-blown cirrus orange with sunset is approaching from the north under puffs of high cumulus, noon-white and becalmed. In the smoky warmth of Indian summer Sevigne, working with a plane on the warped front door of the house and thinking of Torrins, stops, the tool loose in his hand. This morning Dave Dawson reported the butterflies would be winging it south for Mexico over the Trans-Canada and Whitefish Bay, so drivers and boaters ought to keep their eyes peeled. Then, while an interviewer with a heavy cold snuffled in the background, a naturalist explained how in crossing the lake the monarchs would make a wide detour, each generation turning at exactly the same point. It was thought that perhaps they were retracing the flyway of prehistoric ancestors who'd had to steer around a mountain or a giant glacier.

As the monarchs pass overhead he can see they're not flying in the solid formation Torrins once described; from far off their numbers only make it seem that way. In fact they're gradually dispersing, like long-distance runners spreading out over a course. A few stragglers loop low over the woods, wind-whirled autumn leaves, while others alight on Nile Islet as if fooled by the goldenrod flickering there like kin. Now it seems to Sevigne he understands their trajectory, that phantom detour, the obstacle once encountered, which—like an old flame or parent fought with and seemingly transcended—goes on exerting influence, nudging you towards the paths you believe you choose.

5

The Interview

ON A DAY of sun and big winds with the shadows of clouds crossing the water and the crests and hollows of the mountains tigered with autumn hues, he's fiddling with the radio dial when Una's voice leaps out at him. His fingers freeze. She's being interviewed. The interviewer's voice—pitched low and slow but continually picking up speed, hitting higher notes, being reined back in—is somehow familiar. Sevigne grins. Eddy must be pressing his chin to his chest to get a deeper, mellower tone, the voice of a small-hours FM DJ—but his manic enthusiasm keeps poking through the persona, like a bushy tail out of sheep's clothing. Such wily misbehaviour—Eddy and Una pretending they're only acquainted professionally, if at all! Sevigne laughs out loud and is startled by the sound, the first laughter he has heard in days.

"Now, I think it's fair to remark that the new piece you just read from features a number of uhh . . . walk-on appearances by characters that insiders, at least here in Toronto, will have no trouble identifying. Is that a fair assessment?"

"But Michael, as a writer yourself you must know that literature doesn't—"

"In fact if I'm not very much mistaken"—Eddy is clearly enjoying this, the cordial scandaleering, the brash energy of the exchange—"one of the characters bears some resemblance to me. Or so my um, my 'colleagues' inform me."

"Misinform. Miss the boat!"

"But then I get off lightly. Some of your other prototypes aren't nearly as fortunate."

Sevigne reaches for the bottle of Golden Wedding. Last of the six he brought, an ounce a day. But not today.

"For example, there's that pompous grey-bearded critic . . ."

Una is chuckling. Sevigne drains his glass. Towards him over the lake the shadows of clouds advance like a dark armada.

"And an intense, self-absorbed young poet named Niall."

"But Michael, you know fiction doesn't work that way! Of course it's true that on some level it all comes out of your life, and if we were being honest we would have to admit we write out of hate as often as love. But at the same time compassion is of the essence, or you'll just turn them all into . . . just caricatures. Now maybe we should talk about the actual *writing*."

"Hate and love at the same time!" Sevigne cries at the radio. "And what about imagination?"

"'Turn *them*?' Who's 'them'? So we are talking about real people!"

"Oh, Michael!" Una's laughter is losing its typically unselfconscious zest, beginning to sound edgy, forced. Eddy must sense as much. Or she's kicked him under the table. In a lower, more sober tone he says, "Well, your portrait of the doomed biker/novelist Aaron is certainly compassionate—especially that final highway scene which I won't give away here for the sake of readers who'll want to catch the full piece when it appears in *On* 6, due out at Christmas. By which time your next book of poems will also be out, isn't that right?"

They riff awhile on the vicissitudes of poetry publishing while Sevigne tenses over his paper-strewn desk, clasping the radio/tape-player by its ears. He wants to shake Eddy by the lapels for betraying him—though perhaps to him it's no betrayal, just gossip and healthy for Sevigne's career?—and at the same time compel him to say more about Ray. It sounds bad, though—Ray's story. Aaron's story.

"Afraid we're all out of time, Una, though I'm sure we could go on all day."

"Well, I know you could, Michael Korkola!"

He lifts the machine in both hands as he gets to his feet, up-ending the chair backwards onto the bedding. He strides to the access door and kicks it open. As if with an instinct of self-preservation, the radio appeasingly spouts music—a zippy ragtime piano number marking the transition between shows. Out on the catwalk a bitter west wind slaps his cheeks; the rocks offshore are seething, shuddering with a mantle of grub-white gulls whose shrill, tinny cries cut into him. He sags to his haunches and covers his face, the box in his lap tinkling merrily.

6

Winter Hero

TRUBB is due any day. Sevigne has been looking forward to his arrival, but not any more. The world has already found its way back to him. He's uneasy about the mail Trubb will bring, further news to shatter the peace of his refuge. Confirmation about Ray? Maybe a letter from Mikaela bristling with anger, words he will never be able to forget, or respond to. He lies awake in the freezing light chamber while the insomniac sea paces back and forth below him with slow, crashing strides. For two days the island has been mauled by a nor'wester ripping the last leaves from the trees and driving before it great boulders of dark cloud that roll down the sky towards the tower. With the stronger gusts, the unstoppered gargoyle keens like a fury and the flue-pipe of the heater shudders and moans. Should have moved down into the keeper's house weeks ago; he's hoping to stick it out until after Trubb comes, simply to show the man that he can, but his kerosene is running low and there's no break in the weather, Dave Dawson's drowsy prognostications for once seeming to hold: "The marine forecast is calling for ahh continuing northwest winds gusting up to around fifty knots, and waves in Whitefish Bay ranging from eight to ahh ten feet. There is a small-craft warning in effect."

On the fourth of November the winds die down but the groundswell and cross-seas leave the lake in turmoil. Sevigne sits at his desk in a hooded parka and fingerless wool gloves trying to work on his novel and push a nagging unease beyond the pale of consciousness. His supply of staples is down to two or three weeks; the storm is supposed to resume tomorrow. What if the weather doesn't relent and Trubb is unable to get out to him? He'll notify the Coast Guard eventually, surely, and Sevigne will be all right. *So get on with it.* But whenever an aching of cold in his feet or fingers impinges on his concentration, the fears return. The cold is doing that—monopolizing his thoughts like any active threat. It's the cold itself he's afraid of. He has been downcast since the radio episode and more and more he finds himself replying aloud to mental voices— Ray's, Una's, Eddy's, Ike's. The wind's maddening, obsessive monologue.

He wants to leave. It hits him now. Not to go back there, but to leave here.

Just before noon he becomes aware of a buzzing sound growing over the roar of waves on the cobble beach. He leaps up. Trubb and his scrappy vessel are pitching over the heavy swell near the entrance to the cove. For a moment they actually vanish in a trough between waves. Sevigne takes the stairs two at a time and runs outside and scrambles, half sliding, down the scree cleft in the rock face, Trubb now ploughing across the cove, the thrum of his engine echoing off the rocks.

Throwing over the tie line Trubb grins, but his lips are blue in a deadly pale, drenched face. "I tell ya," he says in a frail, quavery voice, "that was some fucking crossing. You don't pay me enough."

"Jesus, Lester, I'm sorry, I never expected you today!"

"Never's the whole point of it. It was now or never. Weather's going to go to hell from here." As Trubb struggles over the bow Sevigne offers a steadying hand. To his surprise Trubb takes it. The hand is clammy, shaky, the face deeply lined, creased between the eyes like a mourner's face at a funeral. He removes his glasses and dries them on his jacket. It takes him three matches to light a cigarette. After a long drag he smiles, lips tightly compressed.

"Guess now I'm supposed to kneel and kiss the sand."

"I was wondering if you'd even make it out here!"

Trubb turns bloodshot eyes on him. "A deal's a deal, at least when I make one. I said I'd be here."

"No, no, I meant because of the . . ."

"Just tell me you don't mean to overwinter."

Sevigne rubs his beard, looks down at his boots. He's bursting with things to say and to ask, but his social voice is like a foreign body stuck fast in his throat. With a sort of numb compulsion he walks past Trubb, climbs over the bow and sets about unhooking bungee cords and peeling the puddled tarp off the cargo. Icy water sloshes around his boots. Trubb digs a can of beer from inside his jacket and opens it, takes a long swig, sighs deeply. "Well, you look all right. Better than I expected. You look well. But there's no need to serve out the full twelve months. Leave that stuff alone till I can help you."

Sevigne is grunting as he wrestles a ten-gallon fuel drum over the gunwale. Forcing a grin, he starts rolling it up the beach, the jolly buccaneer with his rum keg. How fast the habit of faking it comes back! In a bluff, robust tone he says, "You seem as if you could use something hot, Lester. Why don't we carry a load up top and I'll brew you some coffee? We can deal with the rest after."

Trubb looks uncomfortable. "How I was thinking," he says, "is we just leave the drums right here on the sand to buy us some freeboard and head home, right now. You and me."

"But, you do know I was planning to stay. And you just made the trip out, with all these supplies . . ."

"Less two drums. Had to toss the fuckers. I was shipping the head off every third wave. Had to lock the tiller and tip 'em over the stern."

"Shit," Sevigne says, straightening up, sitting down on the fuel drum. "Shit, shit, shit."

"Well, they were extras. On me. You still have what you paid for. But you could have used those extras. If you'd stayed."

"But I still have enough, right?—as much as you thought I'd need?" Sevigne seems to want two opposite answers. Trubb frowns and flicks his cigarette butt into a small hole he's dug in the sand with the toe of his boot.

"OK. Let me level with you. I figured you'd be dying to come off by now. Begging me to take you off. You've been out here six months! I almost came out here last month—I figured you'd be ready then. Those extras, they were just in case you really felt like playing winter hero. I frankly wasn't expecting to leave alone."

"I was planning on staying," Sevigne says. Then hears himself add, firmly, "I'm going to stay."

Trubb spits into the sand. "Right. Just like that hippie kid in the seventies tried to winter on Michipicoten."

"But I'm ready!"

"Let's just take up one load for now," Trubb says. "Have that coffee."

In the drafty light chamber they huddle beside the heater and at Trubb's request Sevigne spikes his coffee with rye from the cargo. While Trubb warms up, Sevigne with a queasy stomach tears into his mail; he has already prepared letters to Ike, Eddy, his mother, Lois, Bryon, and Ray (c/o Eddy), leaving space at the end of each for a response to whatever messages Trubb might bring. There's nothing from Ike, Ray, Lois, or Bryon. Suppressing the various implications of their silences, he begins with his mother. A birthday card—a cartoon showing two pith-helmeted explorers with giant butterfly nets encountering a Bedouin in the desert. One of the helmets is saying, "We hear there's a good man living somewhere in

these parts. We were hoping to catch and stuff him for the
British Museum." As Sevigne opens the card a cheque for a
thousand dollars flutters into his lap. He shuffles it under the
envelope and glances up: Trubb, sipping spiked coffee, is pretending not to have seen, but twitches of amusement show at
the bristly corners of his mouth. Sevigne rakes a hand through
his own hair, hard. Here the cheque is useless for all purposes
save to undermine his pretence of self-sufficiency. The card
contains birthday wishes and a reminder that on *her* twenty-
sixth birthday Martine was nursing him, only a few weeks old,
while Bryon played on the floor of the screened porch in Sault
Ste Marie. *My dear boy, how the years fly!*

Voler, to fly. Yes, and to steal.

Heart jackhammering he tears open Eddy's letter, written
last month. Just after the Harbourfront ambush. It's word-
processed and laser-printed on *On* letterhead. Sevigne scans
the letter with eager, fearful eyes. Breezy good wishes, excited
updates about *On*—nothing about Ray on the first page, nothing about mugging the Sevman on national radio. Lois well
and back at 'em. Sends kisses and regards. Your poems to be
out on the shelves by next fall.

Page two and still no Ray. Christ, could he be forgetting to
mention a friend's death? Or is he hoping to spare Sevigne
further pain?

Or perhaps Una does write fiction after all.

I'd better mention too . . . so begins the last paragraph. That
word, "better," is always coming up just when things are about
to get worse. I'd better go. You'd better go. I'd better tell you
straight.

> *Nobody's seen Ike for awhile, she isn't playing her old gigs. Her*
> *CD has really taken off and they say she's writing her next one.*
> *Sev, it's also rumoured that she's pregnant. I'm telling you be-*
> *cause you felt so bad when you left. So you can lighten up now,*

put your RC slash Romantic slash Desert Hermit guilt on the back burner pending your next relationship, she's having her baby after all. Don't know when, don't know who. There are rumours, but you know how I feel about spreading rumours (!). All music types. Just hope to God it's not Bruce Cockburn. Shit, sorry, you like Cockburn, I forgot.

I do miss you, Sev. You are missed in general. Take care of your bad self and come back to us safe and sane.

Sevigne gets up heavily and sits at the table to scribble his postscripts. To Ike he adds nothing about the rumours. For a moment he wonders if the child could possibly be his, but then decides, No, impossible. Sure didn't take her long to find somebody else though. Rereading the letter he sees that it's sullied with platitudes and pieties—*I wasn't worth it anyway*—and he crumples the whole thing into a ball and tosses it on the floor. Trubb glances over. To Eddy he repeats his request for news of Ray. Trubb is rising stiffly, stepping to the northwest panes, tilting his mug back to drain it. The restless static of sea-light on his lenses is like a projection of his anxiety and impatience. Panic sweeps over Sevigne. He doesn't want Trubb to go.

"You really mean to overwinter," Trubb says.

"Well," Sevigne says, "it's always been my plan." He seals the last of the envelopes. Numbly he gets to his feet and he hands the lot to Trubb. "Look, Lester, the weather's no good, why don't you just stay the night? Please. I can fix you a hot meal and we can take our time unloading. Have a few drinks. You can leave in the morning, or in a day or two. It's bound to clear up."

"Dave Dawson says not. Supposed to get worse. Anyways I've got to be back for tomorrow day, taking some doctors from Saginaw up into the hills for deer. You really mean to stay, we better unload her now." He puts his earflapped hat back on, frowning while he adjusts it, then whips it off and slaps it against his knee. "God *damn* it, kid, I'm not going to mince words with you. You got to come off this island with me, and we're going right now. You could die out here—why, dying out here would be the easiest thing in the world to do! You're all right, kid, but I know your . . . I seen kids like you before. Holy Joes—that's what we call yous, all right? College kids the lot of you—city kids. Big dreamers. I've guided some like you back into the woods to hole up and play Indian, eat your rock tripe and your blueberries, fine, it's your business, you pay me, the country's yours and I won't be meddling. But you got to understand you'll be on your own out here. It's not like when I was a kid—the weather's changed, ice is one big question mark now. All pressure ridges, soft spots, open leads. Snowmobiles go through every winter and nobody ever came out this far anyways. I'm not about to risk my neck trying. God damn it, kid, I won't even know you're in trouble!"

Foreboding sweeps through Sevigne, a bitter draft inside the body. Trubb's uncharacteristic ardour is convincing. If only he could let himself be convinced. He would like nothing better now. Pride holds him silent—that and the shadow of his father. If only Trubb would stay a day or two, so Sevigne could pack up and make an orderly, honourable retreat, not flee in panic, and over terrifying waters, leaving behind him a welter of abandoned effects—another pathetic story for Trubb to tell his corporate hunters.

Fighting in vain to keep his voice slow and deep, Sevigne says, "Maybe you should let the Mounties know I'm here."

"I talk to the Mounties or the Coast Guard and they'll have you off of here within a day. Which'd be just fine by me."

Behind the green lenses he finds Trubb's narrowed eyes, which to him convey not so much an appeal as a kind of existential challenge. Finally he has to look away, down at his mummy bag on the air mattress.

"Don't tell them," he says.

From the beach he watches Trubb, tiller in fist, ply out across the cove, his frail doughty craft lifting its bow and spreading wide silver wings of wake. Dark seas beyond the narrows rear up and rumble and spit, as if waiting for prey. Sevigne shudders in his parka. With the departure of human company the mercury seems to be taking a sudden, irreversible dive. It's the fourth of November 1993. Winter.

7

In a Field of Wreckage

14 Nov -4° C no hint of wind—ice seaming together on cove, spring keeps pond & creek clear so far—stripped, sallow earth in meadow lies like corpse waiting for shroud. With Trubb all life gone save for few grouse in cedars, last gulls on rocks, field mice and spiders here in house—captive audience. At sundown bone birches/bare maples superimposed on flayed red sky. Have been working outside boarding windows fixing woodshed door cutting & laying in stovewood. Snowsmell richens the air. End of day radio & finger of rye then can write by lamplight, but odd—days past said I wd bargain w/ whatever power to lose all need for sleep & have 6 hrs extra per & finally time enough—now nothing but time unbroken time & cant work

This week faint gunfire from north shore—Trubb? As cold deepens terrific craving for meat. Took Dad's rifle this aft. into woods for grouse—saw only snakeskins draped over boughs like sphagnum moss, berry-clusters of mountain ash, poison anyhow, scarlet & steel-hard as bloody shot.

Snow is falling on Spirit Island, fine flakes sifting gravely out of a windless sky and then thickening till the treeline forty feet away is hardly visible. Boots up on the deal table he is lounging with a drink, looking out the only window he has left unboarded. He has set up in the front parlour of the keeper's house. An ancient mattress, half gutted by mice and with springs sticking out, blocks the doorway to the back room; the pine stairway seems to climb directly into the ceiling, Sevigne having improvised a barrier of scrap boards to seal off the upper floor.

Two of the six panes of his window are scrap plywood fixed in place with putty. Two of the remaining panes are cracked. He misses his panoramic light-chamber, but this parlour, heated for now by the rusty cast-iron stove, is warm. He misses Trubb as if he were an old pal, and he misses Caliban, buried by the sea in a child's cairn of lichened cobbles. With a fevered longing he misses the world—the smoky taste of Ike's kisses, her throaty voice, aimless lazy evenings in the apartment. The city. Parties, their glib chatter and gossip and hypocrisy— wonderful, human! And Una, even now, her majestic fleshi- ness a challenge to Bay Street's anorexic soul.

He is listening to the radio—he has been more and more— and his cassettes, Ike's albums and the mixed tapes she made him a lifetime back. The early dark and increasing confine- ment make him prodigal with his batteries. He's prodigal with his liquor, too, but no matter, Papère has made him an early Xmas gift. Yesterday morning, crouched in the shallow crawl space under the house with flashlight and hammer, prying apart old crates, he found one at the back that wouldn't budge, as if it contained pig-iron or was frozen to the rock. With both hands he tugged hard; it scraped slowly towards him. As with the other, empty crates, the top came off easily, the nails weak with rust. He shone the flashlight in: sixteen clear bottles scurfed with sawdust, corks brittle and darkly stained. The inner sides of the crate were padded with balls of yellow newspaper. He pulled out a bottle—a forty-ouncer— and blew off the dust. The liquid was clear, though with a faint amber tinge towards the bottom where a fine sediment swirled like soiled flakes in a snow-globe. The cork was crusted fast. He twisted firmly, eased it out: vapour shot back through his sinuses like a whiff of ringside smelling salts. He sipped and it scorched his tongue, dispensing fire from the back of his mouth to the pit of his stomach. Boiling sap with an aftertaste of rust. Sugared ammonia. Wincing he uncrumpled a ball of newspaper, which fell to pieces in his hands. He puzzled together a story from the Toronto *Telegram*, October 12, 1930: *Canada's Pickford to Step Back in Time for New Silent Picture.*

His discovery of the cache seems a blessing, now. Drink not only evokes memory, it also lends it substance, so his lost and his dead seem almost there in the room—tacit company while the first truly Arctic night frosts over his window, sealing him in. He and Meeka and Bryon on the sandbar in the middle of the bay where you could sit wigwam-style with your face clear of the water and sing camp-songs and lose count of the stars; the autumn day his father took him shooting in the brilliant hills back of the cabin and they came upon the remains of a deer—a few flies orbiting inside the carcass—and Sevigne, fascinated and repelled, asked, Do you believe in a life after death? And his father said, You're mine.

He has long since given up hope of hearing any of Ike's songs, so when she comes on the air with a new one he almost drops his glass. He's disoriented; the tune is familiar, the words not. Then it hits him—*Under my skin like fire.* It's the song they were composing together, she has ripped his lyrics out from between the staves and substituted her own. Or maybe her new lover's? No. Her own. And delivered with such hoarse, quavery passion: *But this isn't enough, you should have hurt me more . . . I want to remember you better, you should have hurt me more. What's wrong with a scar? What's wrong with a real good scar?*

Face scalded he leans over the deal table and fiddles with the tuner, but it's as clear as it's going to get. Clear as crystal, clear as day. He knows it takes years for statutes of limitation to take effect, but doesn't distance count for anything? He's not even in the world any more, not as she knows it. *You call this a hurt? You call this breaking my heart? You should have broken it better and scattered the parts—Yeah, so I wouldn't have to put it all back, wouldn't be able. . . . Oh, what's wrong with a scar? What's wrong with a real good scar?*

"And that was Ike, Ike with her hot new hit single 'Scar,' last week clocking in at number nine on Ruby Rick's top-forty face-off. Now be sure and check in here tomorrow at eight sharp and find out where Ike's sitting pretty this week here on your music main squeeze CROK 1030 with Ruby Rick Mason rockin' what ails you from now until midnight tonight with the hottest songs of yesterday, today and . . ."

He hefts the squawking radio overhead and hurls it at the wall between the window and the front door. With a dull crunch it hits and falls to the floor, aerial snapping, Ruby Rick cut off in mid-phrase. Sobered, he kneels and lifts the damaged radio into his lap, a driver with a stray run down on the highway, then tries the tuner and the volume knob. The red plastic backing has come off. Parts rattle within, the batteries jammed into their slot so that he needs his penknife to pry them out. He makes space for them, replaces them, inserts a cassette, his signed copy of *Against All Odds*—"Love Forever, M." Still no life signs. Peering into those entrails of red and green wire and alien, cracked gadgetry, he knows Trubb might be able to save the thing, but for him it's hopeless.

He is watching a freighter split apart in wild seas, in sleety darkness, then understands it to be the *Daniel J. Morrell*, which foundered near here in November '66, around the time (his dreaming mind computes) of his conception. From a lifeboat the huddled survivors—Sevigne now among them— watch the bow-end slide under the waves while the stern forges on into the dark, its running lights still aglow; like a headless body walking. This is in fact how it happened. *Now the Morell of this story*, intones a deep, documentary-style voice ... and he begins to laugh and wakes himself up. By flashlight he records the dream in his journal, adding to the straight description, *Searchers later reported sailing through "a vast field of wreckage."*

There are many such entries for the last few weeks. He has been spending more and more time in the mummy bag, awake, asleep, or, increasingly, in the surreal limbo between, conserving body heat and fuel while trying to read, by the hypnogogic light of his moonshine, *The Brothers Karamazov. . . . Dream of myself as Alyosha wandering through museum of opened torsos preserved in brine—grey curdled viscera, wizened genitals, hearts like slimy cobbles black & still.* Evil dreams but O the anodyne that fuels them: the liquor makes a fuse of his tongue and esophagus, burning downward to ignite a merry Yule fire in the belly. Sweet Agni. On the first morning of December the thermometer mounted outside reads -16° c; for the next two days the lower atmosphere lies static while overhead a solid mass of slate-grey cloud billows eastward.

The island in its cladding of snow and mist floats like a squat berg in polar doldrums. The cove, the pond, the creek are all thoroughly frozen and for water he has to crouch on the steep Precambrian shore and dip buckets in the lake. Around him, bitter pines misted with powder, the lake liquid ash, the sun through scudding cloud so pale it might be the moon. The spectrum is reduced to this narrow band: variations on grey, which is no real colour but the ghost of all colours. The light-buoy throbbing red like a floating heart is the lone exception, though lifeless.

The storm begins in the night. He wakes to the sound of wind sobbing through the crevice in the roof upstairs and rattling the door latch, breakers battering the windward shores.

A gale this time, a hurricane. Gyring drunk, he remains in his bag by the woodstove trying to return to sleep. Then something smacks into the window. Holding the flashlight he lurches to his feet. The previously undamaged panes are intact, but the outside thermometer is skewed away from him, torn off its axis. He fumbles into his boots and parka and unlatches the west-facing door, which flies in on him, almost knocking him down. With a ravening howl, wind drives snow into the house. Papers whirl up off the table. He leans out through the door and pulls it shut behind and staggers along the wall, hand braced on the concrete to keep from being blown into it, eyes needled with frozen spray skimmed off the distant waves.

Under the window lies an arm-sized chunk of bough ripped from the red maple nearest the house. The pines beyond have been swept clear of snow and are flailing, moaning, as if in agonies of supplication. He shines his flashlight on the thermometer: smashed and empty. Through the panes his beam like a diver's arc-light illuminates a section of the table, its doused lantern and strewn papers. He picks up the bough to dry by the stove and hobbles back to the door.

By the second night, effectively sealed in by the verglas coating every surface of the island, ineffectively sedated with rye, he's aching to sleep but still unable because of the storm's cataclysmic sound effects and his fear that the house will collapse or his barricaded door blow in. Iced branches in the forest shatter constantly. The louder cracks may be of whole trunks. One jolts him from a half-sleep with a microdream of the island being shelled by a destroyer off the coast———

His fear of anything but the storm itself is absurd, but this elemental siege is pounding his reason numb. His mind roams chimerically. So much is conceivable in a storm-swept house on an island with three visible graves and (so he has heard) many unmarked ones, dating from centuries when the island was sacred to the Ojibway. But the recent ghosts are the ones that unhinge him. According to Trubb—that trusty curator of horrors—the light-keeper who hanged himself in the forties did it the end of November, just before the tender-ship came to take him off. Used his belt. In the pine woods. Yet in the house some nights Sevigne starts awake, drenched and trembling, positive that something hangs above him in the dark. In his stupor he has heard rhythmic creaking, as of a heavy bag swaying from a girder in a dark gym, and felt the chill, intimate drafts made by boots dangling above his face. He lies staring upward with gaping eyes—too afraid to reach up—till finally the pine beams and the surrounding room define themselves out of the night.

Perhaps it's the moonshine, wildly overproof. He tries to cut himself dry at five shots but often at four his resolve collapses and he pushes on, like the severed *Morrell*, with journal entries and unsendable letters, frenetic blues harp, ballads sung at beerhall volume, poems by anon. reeled off to crowd his hovel with the voices of others, any others, alive or dead:

Half through, half through
To the port of the Soo
'Tis ninety fathoms deep—
And there lies the crew
Bound through for the Soo
Where the black weeds willow and sweep.

Snuff the lantern, polish a lens in the featherfrost of the panes to look up at a circle of night sky shrouded with stars—God, so lonely! Those levies sealed into tunnels in the pyramids gazing up narrow airshafts a hundred feet long, their world reduced to a wafer of desert sky where circumpolar stars would briefly appear: Altais, Alderamin in Cepheus, the Dragon's tail. . . .

He's back in the mummy bag, adrift. In a forgotten memory he and Bryon and three Egyptian boys, brothers, are climbing into the bare Muqqatam Hills for the 26 July flyover. The other boys are sons of one of Everson's colleagues at the embassy; they've done the hike before and deftly lead Bryon and Sevigne up a switchbacked goat trail, dusty and dung-cobbled, the oldest brother in new Levi's while the rest of them, younger, wear shorts. They reach the summit just before noon. The city below them to the west and the flat empty plains eastward span away in astonishing recession—on one side so many millions living, on the other side not a soul—and the boys scramble to find higher or fatter boulders, vying for the true summit and the best view. Then, as if it were suddenly dusk, the panorama begins to fade, the sun dulling as winds spin up and fling fistfuls of dirt into their eyes. The Egyptian boys (now, fifteen years later, he can't recall their names) firmly usher him and Bryon a short way along the ridge to a windowless hut of stone, an old goatherd's hut, they say, where they take shelter while the storm whistles around them. They drink Orange Crush and eat Mars bars and dates and flatbread and soft cheese amid odours of dried goat dung and urine. Time passes—maybe an hour. They hear nothing of the MIG fighters that were to fly over at noon. The pilots too must be waiting out the winds.

The winds die down and the boys venture out and stake out new high points, squinting into the east. Their vista regains clarity as if a mist were melting away in strong sunlight. The smallest Egyptian boy leaps up, proudly pointing: a formation of gleaming MIGs is soaring towards them, their wingtips so close they could almost be one long machine with seven cockpits, flying at sub-radar level straight for the flank of the hills. A chevron-shaped shadow scuds under them over the desert floor. Steeply they climb towards the crest and thunder overhead as the boys crane their necks and pivot on their perches:

the MIGS are swooping away, down the other slope to barn-storm the watching city, seven contrails like parallel streamers braided behind. Over the perimeter of Cairo (which seems silent under their roaring, as if holding its breath) they per-form three circuits and then beyond Giza, near the pyramids, shoot straight up and trace a mile-high Ferris-wheel loop before levelling and starting back east. Once again they climb towards the boys and with a sonic boom they flash overhead and back out across the empty flats to recede and diminish—glints of light flying at the speed of light—and it's then, out of view of the city and with no one watching but the boys, or so it feels, that the head MIG at some slight wing kiss or malfunction tilts, swerves, spins spastically away. Glittering downward it corkscrews faster and faster and meets its shadow on the desert floor. In pathetic silence the broken formation flies on; from the wreckage a black contrail rises. As Sevigne scans the sky for a parachute, the younger Egyptian boys turn wide-eyed to their brother, who buries his face in his hands.

8

Alone on a Wide, Wide Sea

12 Dec 8 p.m.—temp ?? but cold as a bailiff's bed—wind in love w/ sound of its own voice. Tender-ship must have come in night, buoy gone this a.m. when went for water—like finding Pole star Venus or Moon scraped from sky—underfoot everywhere icy but have been in forest collecting stormfall. Again at work on book am warmed by description of Desert AND by shine which is summer's heat distilled— Sun to grain to malt to mash to spirits   Let the friars guzzle their stars, give me bottled August—& a white sail in the eyefar

One night as he lies in his musty bedding sipping from the bottle, the lake freezes over. The sound of it, like the head on a fresh-poured beer hissing, crackling softly as it dissolves, draws him out of the bag and into his boots and parka and outdoors, bottle in hand. He sits swilling on the edge of the vision pit on the cobble beach as a crystal membrane feels its way out from shore (so slowly one could never detect it sober!) towards the gull-reefs and open waters beyond. The sound is seemingly answered from the sky by faint cracklings of the northern lights—prismatic filaments rippling in the solar winds like blue-green currents under ice.

Tonight there is nowhere in the world to be but here. "My library was dukedom large enough," he bellows and laughs and awards himself points, somebody has to, as he walks the full perimeter babbling, "You must always be drunk—on poetry, wine, or virtue as you choose!" and "While you live, drink!—for, once dead, you never shall return"—warming the atmosphere with his breathing, lying on the rocks of Rye's End to feast on the cold-honed stars, great winter constellations. *Rubáiyát. Kumbayah.* Some time later, incandescently drunk, he stands and lobs the empty bottle far out over the ice. *"Absinthe . . . makes the heart . . . founder."* With a soft hollow thunk it breaks through, bobs up.

Mornings he hides his face in the mummy bag to shield his parched crusty eyes from the rarefied light seeping in through the window. The light seems to come expressly, aggressively for him, like closing-time house lights in a bar—you grimace and lower your face—marking the end of squalid ecstasy and the renewal of obligation. Worse though is the revival of personality. He sets about outwitting the light with a curtain (a black sweater nailed over the panes) and some hair of the dog, the black dog. *My New Found Land!*

While supplies last, dude.

He is thinking aloud all the time.

Then a day he wakes chilled and fearful from a long nap full of voices, and among them *the Winddigger.* Evil djinn from the bottle. Watching his step (the mice here are all scorpions in disguise) he trudges outside for wood. In the dusk the trunks of the red pines are swarming pointillistic columns, boughs drooping under the load of caterpillars coating each tree like a living paste or a sheath of pure energy. He edges towards them holding out a stick, as in those summer infestations in the Soo,

one time Bryon firing a BB gun over and over at a poplar convulsed with squirming shapes and Sevigne trying to stop him
and Bryon snapping, You're an idiot, Sevigne, we have to kill
them or they'll kill all the trees! He was right. Sevigne probes
gingerly at a trunk to assure himself they can't be real. The instant he makes contact, a clot of them breaks off from the mass
and scurries up the stick towards his hand like a single hideous
organism, and he screams and pitches the stick away. The vision dissolves. For three days he drinks only tea and water.

At dusk on the shortest day of the year he shoots a grouse,
maybe the last on the island, and in the woodshed he guts
and plucks it for his evening meal. The bolus of snow he eased
into the bird's beak after killing it remains there unmelting,
the severed head lying amid gory sawdust on the stone floor.
After stoking the fire he comes back outside, climbs down to
the beach and laces skates and pushes out across the cove in
sapphire twilight to where the windscoured ice of the lake
runs sleek and black and fast. He's soaring now, hands behind
his back and stooped forward like Hans Brinker, jolting over
corrugated patches and milky upwellings, his heart in his
throat every time a crack zips under him and the surface shifts
and booms with cavernous echoes. He can see how thick it is
along the fault lines but still each crack gives him a rush.
    A half-mile out he finds an oasis of perfect ice, black
sheeny mica so smooth and solid his blades can hardly bite in
for stops and he keeps falling and sliding, leaping up, joyously
skating circuits of the oval until it's looped and herringboned
with tracks. He stops to catch his breath and looks back at the
island. A sinew of woodsmoke rises straight from the chimney
and at treetop level sheers towards him, diffusing. He gets a
whiff of burning cedar, sweet and sharp. Where a short time

ago his eyes strained to find the night's first star, now untold thousands make a mist on the sky—the Road of Souls a ridge of conifers dusted with snow. He returns to the warm house to roast the bird, singing as he opens tins of potatoes and peas and corn and sips moonshine, face glowing with exertion and the heat of the fire.

Hunting the grouse and then tying his skates he got frostbite on his trigger finger and the pinkie of his right hand. The trigger finger, constantly active with pen or manual tasks, soon recovers, but the pinkie grows worse and by New Year's Eve is swollen and studded with pus-filled blisters. The corner of the palm below the finger is also affected. With his penknife he lances the blisters—they give off a rank, sour odour as they break—then applies more antibiotic cream and takes aspirins and vitamins before bed. By morning the hand is tender and hot. The infection is edging up into the middle fingers and a faint red line, like an advance column, extends down from the puffy redness at the hand's base into the blue-whiteness of the wrist. He's been holding off on the sulfa drugs, reserving them for something "more serious"; now he finds that the vial contains not the full prescription of thirty capsules but eighteen, as if Torrins—who never did have much use for doctors or medicine—had started on the drugs, then just forgot them.

He may be feverish or simply feeling the cumulative effects of the drinking. He is trying to drink little, but without moonshine the pain is far worse, the ghost-colloquium in his brain goes back into session and he feels half-mad, or possessed. He never realized how much the winking light-buoy and passing freighters dulled the edge of his solitude. Now with the buoy removed and the shipping lanes frozen over he is so alone that the human sphere beyond his island seems barely real, his life there a bizarre, episodic late movie seen once while half-asleep, or high.

By the fourth of January he is definitely feverish. The drugs have rolled back the infection into the top of the palm, the pinkie, and the adjoining finger, but the pinkie itself looks worse. And the drugs are running out. Holding a pen or his heavy paperback *Ulysses* is a test; in the course of vital chores like chopping wood and keeping his water-hole open the slightest pressure on the inflamed finger sparks agonizing pain. When he removes his mitten the smell is fetid. Oh Christ, he thinks out loud, this is really bad. A gangrenous pinkie. Of all the pathetic ways to go.

By the fifth, the pain makes it impossible for him to chop kindling and he is reduced to collecting pine-cones in the woods. On the evening of the sixth—dizzy, faint, unwarmed by his poorly stoked fire—he swallows the last capsule and examines his blackening finger, nose wrinkled in disgust. He decides to wait twenty-four hours to see if the drugs will have some kind of after-effect and further localize the infection, now largely contained above the lower knuckle. By sunset of the next day the infection is rebounding, swelling back to-wards the border between his finger and palm. He begins drinking hard, with dire purpose. For some time the required state eludes him, even with the overproof rye; then suddenly the job is done, fear gone, in its place a fatalistic keenness and morbid fascination. Stripped to the waist he kneels before the open door of the woodstove, slides the whetted blade of Torrins's horngrip hunting knife into the coals. After a few minutes he removes it and dips it steaming in a tin cup of moonshine. Particles of ash diffuse through the moonshine. Now, he says. Now. He takes a long drink, the liquor smoky and warm from the blade, then lays his right hand palm-up on the split-log chopping block and curls his fingers away from the obscenely fat pinkie. With his thumb he holds the fingers clear. He sets the blade at the very base of the pinkie and begins to cut, feels searing heat, yells and bears down with everything he has. As if watching a televised operation he sees the blade slide, crunch through skin and meat and sheeny white cartilage and dark bone and now the blood and yellow pus oozing. There is little pain. He staunches the wound with gauze soaked in liquor and iodine. The antiseptic sting is dull, a muffled scream, weak signals from inebriate nerves. Like a rotten blood-sausage—nothing remotely human—the pinkie lies on the log.

The hand is infected, whether from his amputation or because the bacteria had already made a return beach-head on the palm he can't say. But his fever is worse and the wound remains raw and pustulant. His body sweats and shivers, his own sighs wake him from weightless geometrical dreams, he stretches his aching legs full out in the bag but seems to need them stretched farther, farther, as on a rack. Now would be the time to do it, if do it he must—trek back across the lake to safety. But forty-foot trips to the outhouse have become an ordeal and Batchawana Bay is almost twenty miles off. And there may be open water. Maybe on skates, he thinks, or says, or thinks himself saying. *Many make claims for lush numbness of hypothermia.* In Arabic a mirage is *bar al shaitan*, lake of Satan—like that mythic frozen lake in hell from which his leviathan head rears like an island of basalt. *I however tend to favour fire.* In Italian the words for Hell and Winter look, to his eyes, similar. They open wide in darkness and he shudders: the Winddigger. *How plump the children are!* They close. A baby born with the cord around its neck, the cord metamorphosed into a writhing worm and the baby's sealed eyes hatching open. Then stars piercing down through the ceiling like stalactites in their cold, pure canticles. *Some say in ice.* Or a lid of nails. A white foal grazing in a blazing pasture.

Gusting wind behind him he skates out from the island and racing the moon's image over ice makes astonishing time. A widening channel intervenes, the full moon awash there, blanched and bloated memento....He turns back, the dream shifting. Still in his sweaty bag. In the giant gymnasium of his last exam he fixates on elaborating the letters of his name with fussy serifs and arabesques and other pseudomonastic illuminations, the execution of which proves increasingly difficult owing to extreme digital palpitation. Still he doodles on and in the fullness of time is content with the dyslexic palimpsest. Next he applies himself to the name of the course, The Philosophy of Reason 222, and the name of the teacher, Dr Goodwit, but soon he recurs to his own name which now reveals itself as gravid with sinister cues and anagrams. *Sevigne* clearly contains the portentous number SEVEN—and are there not seven letters in that very name? And in Torrins. And in Goodwit! And the seventh letter of each name: E-S-T. Is. Is what? Just *is*, the miracle of pure being? Sevigne thinks not—NOT—once more a word he embodies by name. Likewise never. IS NEVER. ENGINE. TORN. The engine is ever revving. VINES. GIVE. ROT. SON. Vines never rot, Rev. SOREN—the very man he is to expound on today! Kierkegaard will mean guardian of the church, gravedigger, sexton. ROT IS EVER. SIN IS THE ENGINE. The cranial voices begin to gibber and gabble with a dreadful autonomy. Wary of disobliging them he turns amanuensis, though the pages of dictation he receives turn out in the main illegible. SOREN'S SORES INVERTING. STRIVE ON, SINGER! Illegible with haste. Institutional goons will soon arrive, rivet-eyed proctors stalking the desk-lined aisles of the gymnasium. Echoes and shadows roost in the rafters. In loafers and corduroys they are gentle, one at either arm leading him up the aisle, and one by one like lamps coming on along a dark river the faces of his peers turn towards him.

He lies on his back in the bag, his throbbing hand pushed out into the soothing cold beside his face. He is using the kerosene heater but even on full it radiates less than half the heat of the stove. Outside there is sun, but in the house only twilight, three anemic, dusty beams slanting down through the panes. Now and then he sips from the bottle. The fever and the effect of the moonshine have become indistinguishable. Cutting off his hand would be the logical next step; he starts giggling weakly. Like the knight in that film, losing limb after limb. It's only a flesh wound. Eddy loved to do that routine at Bawating. A biplane is flying out of the sun to strafe the lame knight and his massed, bannered legions. Archers loose a shower of arrows at the plane and they deflect off the metal with a faint concentrated rattling. The plane comes on, engine ever louder. Dizzily Sevigne sits up, thrashes free of the bag, gropes for his parka and in stocking feet lurches outdoors into the powder snow and the stupefying sunlight. Polar winds are driving in off the lake. He shields his eyes and turns in a full circle. Out of the clear skies to the south comes a single-engine airplane fitted with skis and flying low. It buzzes Nile Islet and then, shadow rapidly preceding it over the ice, it makes straight for Sevigne. He raises his good hand and waves with joy, grinning and laughing helplessly. A bay opens in the plane's gleaming underbelly and something like a crammed canvas rucksack tumbles down into the pines by the tower. The airplane roars overhead. Sevigne wheels around. The invisible pilot is climbing away from him, banking east towards

Batchawana Bay, waggling silver wings in acknowledgement
of Sevigne's wave. "Don't go!" he cries. "Come back!" A dull
thud echoes out of the woods behind him. He sags to his
knees. You waved with one hand, he thinks aloud, incredulous—with one fucking hand! He covers his eyes with his
good hand, sobs shuddering out of him. When he looks again
the plane is a satellite gleaming small and high over that desert
of blinding ice furrowed with low, dune-like sastrugi.

Trubb must have sent somebody. Trubb sent an airplane
and he waved with one hand, *all's well*, instead of both,
send help.

By the time they come again, if they do, there may only be
one hand to wave.

The rucksack from Trubb contains unbelievable treasures—
fresh butter and cheese, white bread, chocolate, steaks in waxed
paper, an apple and orange, a dozen potatoes, tinned milk,
crackers, coffee, tobacco, a dented can of beer, toilet paper,
candles and matches, tins of Sterno, a Hudson Bay blanket,
batteries, flares, aspirin, a first-aid kit—although no antibi-
otics. The brief, carefully printed note reads: *Well your almost
halfway through. Am sending Jens over in the Cessna to check if
your alright and drop you some extra things. You deserve them for
going through this. Actually you deserve a kick in the ass but that
will have to wait til spring. P.S. Your mother sent the money for the
stuff so you dont owe me any extra. Stay warm and keep eating.
L. TRUBB.*

Under Trubb's note is a chirpy Christmas card from Martine, who seems to think he gets regular mail delivery, somehow. *Promise you'll spend next Christmas here with us!* The words
set off another seizure of sobs. Now the smallest thing can
make him weep. Trubb's laconic message makes him weep

with every reading. *But that will have to wait til spring. Stay warm. You dont owe me any extra.*

Spring.

He devours the bruised apple and the orange and swallows two aspirin and sets up the propane stove by the door, his defunct appetite reviving. The world knows he is here and is pulling for him. Maybe giving Jens the thumbs up inadvertently was the right thing to do. Dreading the humiliation of a full-scale rescue—helicopters, headlines, maybe followed by an arrest and unpayable bills—he resolves to wait a day on the flares, then decide. With his left hand he makes his first entry in two weeks: *Jan 17—day of manna—deus ex machina—Trubb Trubb Trubb.* The cheese and butter and fried meat (venison, or moose) are delicious and revitalizing but too fatty for his shrivelled stomach and he lies awake for hours tossing and moaning in his struggle to hold them down.

In the morning he eats more prudently and by afternoon—heartened by the infection's failure to advance and sick of the kerosene's stink and fickle heat—he decides to build a fire. After draining the palm and numbing it in a bucket of snow, then re-dressing the wound, he goes out to the woodshed to cut kindling and split logs from his meagre supply, meaning to do a proper creosote burn. All his recent fires have been shoddy jobs. He knows he's running a risk, but fatigue has made a fatalist of him.

Kneeling before the stove in his parka he feeds birchbark, twigs, dry slats, and poorly cut kindling through the iron door. It's like reaching his hand into a freezer. The birchbark will only smoulder, damp, so after four matches, though irritably aware of the danger, he crumples the wrapping paper from Trubb's package and shoves balls of it in. The paper flares and the slats and kindling start to catch. He lays a split log on the kindling and sets a bucket of snow on the stovetop to melt.

Sitting at his desk, forcing himself to use the damaged

hand, he carefully writes "Jan 18" in his journal. Pain and faintness preclude further inspiration; after a few minutes he returns to the stove, squats down and cranks open the door. Dense smoke erupts into the parlour. He leaps up, kicks the door shut, stands coughing in the haze, then leans his good hand and face towards the flue. A kind of liquid crackling can be heard and heat is pulsing off the steel. He takes the bucket and holding his breath he yanks open the stove door and dumps in the snow and kneels and rakes it around.

Now the flue is giving off a muffled roar. The inside will be a solid pillar of flame. He tries to remember what his father told him about creosote fires, how to combat them. It takes water—wet blankets wrapped around the flue, soaked newspapers in the firebox. He has kept another bucket by the stove with water for emergencies but the contents have long since gone for cooking and tea. A fire engine—it takes a fucking fire engine. All weakness deferred he runs outside and in the falling snow refills the buckets while thick smoke pumps from the chimney top.

Indoors the roar is mounting like the howl of a fighter jet revving for takeoff. The black steel of the flue is starting to glow orange from just above the firebox to where it bends into the concrete chimney below the ceiling. He tosses a handful of snow at the flue. It sticks there, greys to slush, spits off as droplets, vapour, all in a second. He begins packing balls of grainy snow and throwing them at the flue with his four-fingered hand. *Just like you, boy. Never cared about things and how they work. Forever in your books and your head.* Back off, old man. *It's the truth! You and your generation—you can all cogitate and keep tidy desks but you can't actually* do *anything. Make anything. You can plan but you can't endure.* Fuck off, Sevigne says, breathless, you can all fuck off! and he heaves a snowball at the glowing face of the flue with such power it shudders.

Now on every trip outside for more snow he carries or

hauls something with him—his manuscript, books, kerosene
heater and disconnected pipe, camp-stove, moonshine, food
bags, bedding and air-mattress, toolkit, table, gun, Ike's cassette—and beaches them on the snowy granite. He rolls the
fuel drums out of the woodshed clear of the house and ducks
back through the door to fight the roaring dragon of the
chimney with the arsenal of a child.

Outside, a column of oily smoke dense with snapping
sparks and live fragments debouches from the chimney and is
lost in blowing snow. Nothing of this will be seen from shore.
From upstairs a muffled explosion, a hunk of concrete flying
out the window in a shower of glass. Minutes later when he
emerges for more snow, a veil of smoke is sliding from under
the rotten eaves and fangs of fire appear between the shingles
round the chimney where the snow is melted, steaming. With
a low *whump* an ellipse of flame leaps from the chimney, then
another that clings to the tip and makes a torch of it.

Indoors the heat is infernal and the pipe's rising howl
seems to presage detonation. Above the flue's white-hot, nearly
translucent elbow, the dried-out pine of the ceiling is on fire,
ignited by the heat. With expiring hope and strength he goes
on throwing snow. Minutes later as he kneels outside with the
buckets, the house hits flashpoint, flames fork from the broken
upper window and scurry like fusefire down the line of the
eaves. Fire appears through the door as a burning slat tumbles
downstairs; a chunk of the chimney blows off, leaving the flue-
top exposed like bone. For a while he stands in the falling snow
among his effects, his shouting drowned out by the uproar as
he dodges spitting cinders and hurls snowballs into the fire.

In the snow-muffled silence of the stillhouse, he lies in the corner farthest from the door. He is feverish, at times delirious,

and beyond exhausted. After giving up on the house he shovelled down into the forest depression where snow hid most of
the stillhouse door. He unburied its rusted top half and kicked
it in, then brought all his things through but for the fuel
drums and the table. By flashlight he curtained off a back corner with two Hudson's Bay blankets nailed and draped from
beams under the low rafters.

Beside him on a sheet of tinfoil on the floor, a large beeswax
candle burns for warmth and light. For now he will not be able
to use the lantern, or the camp-stove, or the heater; in his condition cutting a hole for the pipe through the snowed-in log
wall is impossible. There will be an opening in the roof peak
above the remains of the still, but it's too high for his pipe to
reach and must be blocked, no trickle of cold air descending.
Air leaks in only over the top of the door. Still, the building, half
underground and insulated by tons of snow, is habitable, the
last habitable spot; and the darkest, its one broken window
sealed by a snow-wall like the tongue of an advancing glacier.

Down here night and day are indistinguishable. When
finally, reluctantly, he blows out his candle, the darkness is
total, unlike anything he has experienced. From sunlit tower
to twilit house to this bunker, this foundered ark; now to
see light he has to shut his eyes and conjure it on the inside of
his lids. The only sounds are of his own asthmatic breaths, fitful convulsions of dry coughing that leave him drained and
gasping, and sometimes a faint gnawing, scraping, as of unseen mice.

Trubb had it right. The descent here is easy. Dying here
would be the easiest thing in the world.

He wakes one day at noon, chews soda crackers, warms a small
tin of condensed milk over a candle and drinks it. As always

when awake he studies and sniffs and palpates the hand, looking for any sign of improvement. Then he sleeps again, till the chattering of his teeth wakes him. PM 7:25:14 JAN 19, it will be dark outside, though not so dark as in here. Weak and achy he gets dressed and crosses the building whose modest length stretches ahead like an endless corridor in a febrile dream. He crawls out over the drifts, emerges from the pines onto the granite sheet where his table and chair sit dusted with snow beside the blackened hulk of the house. He has never seen northern lights like this before. Blood-red, they drip down the face of the sky in great rills and streamers, an apocalyptic manifestation tinting the snow and the tower and the frozen lake pink and seeming to emit a faint sound as of ice crystals blowing over the lake. He aims the flare gun at the heart of the display. Please, Trubb, be watching. The haloed pink orb squibs skyward and then slows, loops downward, fizzles out. He sends up another and follows it until vertigo overcomes him, the aurora like a red galaxy spiralling away as he topples back into the snow. Peace steals over him. Robed phantoms stammer their Hail Marys on the rosary of Orion. The shores are equidistant and the one is life and the other annihilation; the lights on either side are few and faint and he wonders who will possibly see.

With three candles lit for warmth he gnaws a raw potato, eats snow from the bucket, sleeps again, wakes unsure of where he is. PM 2:16:52 JAN 25—but what day did he come underground? The candles are dead, beeswax puddled hard on the tinfoil. *Plus de feu. Pour l'amour.* His mother's wistful soprano would shepherd him into sleep every night that autumn the *Fitzgerald* went down and they so afraid for his father. *Ma chandelle est morte. Je n'ai plus de feu. Ouvre-moi ta porte. Pour*

l'amour de Dieu. Too weak to rummage for food, and recalling
something that he and Bryon would do as boys, he picks chips
of beeswax off the tinfoil and lets them soften in his mouth.
They convey the faintest suspicion of fresh clover honey the
colour of morning sunlight, summer breakfasts on screened
porches in another life.

His hacking cough wakes him. The stink of himself and of
his winter bag sour with fevered sweats makes him long for
the remission of further sleep. Somehow hibernate and spring
might come, the life-force return. He sips from his last bottle
of moonshine and cooks oatmeal over a tin of Sterno, fatalistic
about the fumes. He must have something hot to eat. But the
slimy gruel disgusts him. He might find respite from this mor-
tal apathy in his letters, but he has so few to reread. He knows
that once in that other world he was "loved," and he himself
"loved," but the thought of it is like the memory of a memory,
the dream of a dream. In memory again he's going through
the motions with Mikaela, and Una, and Molly, and Meeka,
but his torpid flesh absents itself from the recollections, turns
away as if in shame or boredom, makes no cellular acknowledgement. *Do there embrace.* And what was the aim of all that
gymnastic frenzy and heartache? More of the same—new
generations, new cycles of pain inflicted and incurred, more
personal hells to be poeticized. Genitalia had always seemed
to him floral and beautiful but now seem ugly, the penis a burrowing blind-eyed thing like a naked mole-rat, the vagina its
soil-burrow; semen spouting into the woman like gouts of
blood from the neck of a guillotined man. Months later, after
hours of excruciating travail, a squalling purple mass is voided
into the world. *You see at last, my Brooke* (the Winddigger back
at his ear) *the Romantic is a cynic in chrysalis   the saint a serial
killer manqué   In the long run I always find your type my most*
Go to hell!

He wakes to a ferocious griping in the bowels and snatches

his parka, fumbles for the flashlight, can't find it. There isn't time. He stumbles through absolute blackness towards where the door should be. No razor transom of daylight. He feels for the loose knob and finds it, pulls inward and the door creaks open—shrieks open, the first sound in days—on a black wall too solid for darkness: snow. He gropes for the shovel, knocks it over, bends with hands scrabbling and then realizes it's too late. Shoving down his layers he squats to the side of the door and lets the awful flux slobber out of him spasm by spasm, his temples vised between shaking knees, scalding waves of tears squeezing into his eyes. In his degradation the voices heap scorn on him. Having failed to live in a big way, he's now failing even at death—failing to go quick and clean. The dead man rising and throwing off his grave-clothes to soil his own tomb.

In the cabin he is helping his father into bed one night when Torrins says, Sev . . . want to tell you something.

What? he says, exasperated—the words pulling him by the ear back into a moment he is trying to forget even as it occurs.

Sum total of all I've gleaned. In one pithy summation.

What is it?

Entrusted to you, on the house.

He glares at his father, waiting. After a silence intended as dramatic—or is it simply a lapse, time's cunning slippage in drink?—Torrins forms a sardonic grin, tugs him close, says with casual finality, It all gets beaten out of you.

He keeps trying to stand and return to digging out the door. He seems to remember having worked on it once, maybe

twice in the recent past; his sense of time has vanished with his
will. He is breathless, dizzy, confused, his "sleeps" ruptured by
dreams where impersonal fingers tighten around his throat
and wake him, choking. Hard to imagine oxygen running
out in a space this size but it would of course in time it must.
And the fumes, the paraffin. Still, in the bag, in the shelter of
his crude bed-curtains, he is warm. He is floating over the
Western Desert palm-lined with ginger-coloured wadis and
canyons, his eyes even his pores insatiably drinking in the fluid
of the sun's light like a luminous elixir . . . then again pulled
down by corporeal gravity, the eternal Porlock Knock in the
form of racking coughs, bed sores, whiffs of a frozen latrine,
sheer animal fury at his nose, which is constantly running.
Now much of the time he doesn't know if he is awake or sleeping, and then he doubts his very substance and if he is actually
doing a thing—lying in the dark sternly speaking to his hand
as he massages it—or recalling the act years later, from another place, or life. Saying his goodbyes face by face, his
mother weeping, Ray repeating *When I go I want a real death—*
none of this slow dribbling away in a nursing home or on some fuck-
ing machine. Then placing the muzzle of a gun between his
lips. The brassy tang startles him with a fleeting, incandes-
cent memory of Ike, making her come. The sight fits neatly in
the gap between his teeth. *You see my boy you two were made for*
each other   Now if I might as it were cite you "temptation solely a
phenomenon of the city"
     Well I won't do it then to spite you I won't
     Oh but that's only to spite your face   and nose now somewhat
frostbitten
     He reverses the rifle and fires it through his blanket-wall
towards the hunkered bulk of the still. The muzzle flash is
blinding, the report rendingly loud. But then silence, no
voices. His hand on the grip suffers no painful aftershocks
from the recoil, and yet it feels, is feeling the cold for the first

time in weeks. He probes the palm with his good hand—still feverish and tender but the swelling has definitely gone down.

He lights candles, forces himself to chew more saltines, with a spoon eats off the floor a mixture of snow and molasses and powdered milk and the contents of a vitamin C capsule. Flashlight in hand he gets up and shuffles to the blocked window to scoop more snow into the bucket, but a minute's effort leaves him so queasy and exhausted he has to return to the bag.

He starts once at a sound of footsteps slowly crossing the creaky floor. The steps stop just beyond the hanging blankets. He feels for the rifle, can't find it, clutches the neck of the empty bottle by his head. With the other hand he casts the flashlight beam over the blankets, through the bullet hole hemmed with powder burn.

What is it? Who are you?

He's viewing himself from the rafters. Out of a bearded, concave face the figure in the sleeping bag peers up with enormous eyes—the unblinking eyes of a fighter stunned by a hard blow but still conscious. Get up, he whispers. Get up! And feels the lush lethargy of the injured man, punch-drunk, tempted to let eyes just close for the opium kaleidoscope swirling under his lids while the count goes on. *Five. Six.* Back in his body he struggles to rise, slumps over, head lolling over the flashlit side of the air mattress, eyes inches from the tucked-in plug. For some time he stares vaguely. *Umbilical.* The plug comes sharply into focus. *Nine.* He reaches, pulls feebly and finally it extrudes and pops open and he gulps in the rich, rubbery air pressed from the hole by the weight of his body. It seems to be inflating him—head, throat, chest, his shrivelled, stagnant limbs. Soon he has enough strength to grope upright and stand wobbling on the funhouse floor, where he sucks more air from the mattress, replugs it, drags it behind him as he parts the blankets and staggers towards the door.

When the shovel blade finally breaks through and his head and shoulders lurch after it into the icy air—air as bracing and intoxicating as pure oxygen—he thinks for a moment it must be day, the light on the snowy pines and forest floor is so intense, the shadows so defined, the full moon a beaming sun after the total darkness beneath him, behind him.

With cobbles uncovered and hacked free from the icy beach he builds a shelter in the corner of the stillhouse nearest the door—two low stone walls extending at right angles from the building's log sides, closing off the north-west corner. The stone walls do not quite meet; he crawls through that gap to enter his shelter. He chinks the walls with shredded sphagnum moss and uncovered leaves, drapes blankets over the inner sides and the entrance, roofs his kennel with a Hudson's Bay blanket held in place with stones. His body heat and a candle keep it habitable. He removes the lyric sheet of *Against All Odds* from the plastic case and puts the signed photo of M., "Love Forever," on a ledge beside his pillow.

Between the shelter and the stillhouse door he sets up the kerosene heater (having chopped and shaped a pipe-hole through the logs) and he cooks beside it with the camp stove on the deal table, door open for air. His hunger is obsessional—a violent, constant outcry in his flesh and very marrow as much as in his belly—and he makes three heavy meals a day, his supplies of staples like oats, beans, noodles, dried fruit and powdered cheese plentiful after a month of near fasting. So far only his vitamins, overused in illness, are running low. On the advice of his Lands and Surveys pamphlet he collects frozen rock tripe from the walls of the cliffs and boils it into a bitter, gelatinous gruel he chokes down with molasses.

He has cleaned and swept the Augean floor of the still-house and shovelled out the doorway, aired his bedding in the winds and sunlight of the meadow, built from crates a shelf for his books and a small "desk"—like a tray for breakfast in bed in that other world—so he can work inside the shelter. Above the table he has set up burnt-wood shelves for his food and his pots and utensils, arraying everything with immense care in a sacrosanct pattern. Nails in the wall for his clothes. Racks for the rifle, shovel, broom, and axe. All paths around the island shovelled clear.

Filling Trubb's tumpsack with snow and hanging it from a white pine, he makes a heavy bag for exercise. In his new rage for order he adheres to a strict daily regime—cooking breakfast; cleaning up; writing letters; walking the paths and scouring the forest floor of branches and pinecones like a Prussian forester; working again on his novel (two hundred words a day); cooking lunch; reading Proust in French; exercising; bathing by the heater with a rag and a pail of snow; making repairs, shovelling, chopping and stacking wood as if he had a stove to burn it in; cooking dinner; cleaning up; reading aloud from the Upanishads; minutely recording the day's doings in his journal, as if keeping some neurotic ledger.

What can be said about a people, he wrote in the same journal just months ago, *with a dozen words for different kinds of schedules and only one for all the forms of love?* He came here in part to transcend an era, re-open negotiations with the dark gods; he maintains his hold on hope and sanity with a routine obsessively secular, rational, systematic.

Luc was still weak and dazed from his brother's blow and now the propwash of the huge rotor seemed to be forcing him to the tarmac. His brother's face squinting upward had an unforgiving hardness, but he shot an anxious glance towards Luc, then seemed to look away relieved. The camouflaged helicopter lifted higher, its dragonfly tail swivelled round and the blunt head lowered and butted north into brilliant skies over the river. . . .

Coming to on the beach minutes before, still immobilized, Luc had heard the helicopter nearing. It had roared close above him, green-bellied and slow, and with a piercing emptiness he'd foreseen everything—his father gone with no goodbye, his brother more estranged than ever, and Mera, in another hemisphere, drifting further from him. And she was *drifting—as he lay on the sand by the river stunned into clarity he could at last admit it. He heard the chopper touching down. Like a fallen boxer trying to beat the count, he rolled onto his stomach and tried to rise. He was on his knees now, blood thudding in his temples as the dark wet beach reeled under him. He feared it was too late to reach any of them, but he did not stop trying to rise.*

On the last day of March he is in the forest working out on the bag, feeling strong and sane and grateful for the birdsong, the spokes of sunlight glowing down through the pines, when over the sound of his blows and his grunting comes the heavy bass throb of a big engine. He runs through the trees into the snowy meadow and with a whoop he slides over the pond's wet ice, runs back into the forest along his shovelled path, emerges out of breath among the boulders and crouched conifers of the point. Beyond the grainy rind of shore-ice the lake as far as the horizon is spattered with ice floes riding the low swell down from the northwest, and there among them, a few hundred yards south, shines a ship, an icebreaker fresh-painted red and white, her aft-deck outfitted with two squat, powerful cranes. Men are silhouetted head and shoulders in the wheelhouse, while on deck there are men shouting, grappling a hook onto what looks like a lantern on a small radio tower on a podium of black steel. He has to fight the impulse to rush out to where the ice ends and holler and wave. The crane chugs as it hoists the light-buoy over the gunwale trailing long loops of chain, the lantern starting to flash red as the hollow podium settles on the water; the other crane is hefting a concrete cylinder which it drops from deck-height to punch cleanly through a floe and vanish. Brilliant links of chain clank after it over the scuppers. Sevigne stands on the shore and beams, clenched fists uplifted, shaking.

Epilogue

A Song For Fighters

It is not down in any map;
true places never are.

MELVILLE, *Moby Dick*

*T*HE LAKE *is not a lake but a landlocked sea, bigger than the Aegean Sea, or the Gulf of Sidra, or Lake Victoria the source of the Nile, and if at the shallower sounding where the* Fitzgerald *went down the Great Pyramid of Cheops could be placed, its capstone would barely break surface, like the upcrop of some uncharted reef or a remote, subsiding island . . .*

With the child beside him he is driving west along Superior an hour out of the Soo where Highway 17 hugs that ragged, mountainous shoreline, its solemn promontories and misty river mouths, cliffs and beaches, cobbled, wreck-ribbed coves. It's a cloudless, sparkling autumn morning shot through with torrential light. Three and a half years have passed since his departure from the island and now, looking back, he's struck again by time's dual nature—how it gives a general feeling of skimming past, yet on close reflection every year is cargoed with many years of experience.

You are what you've lost, as much as what you've gained or hung on to. No, more, far more. Mikaela is still lost to him. On the cliffs north of Batchawana Bay where years ago thumbing west he asked a driver to stop for him, he pulls onto the gravel shoulder so that he and Nina can get out and search the lake for Rye Island. She's excited by the idea. So many things about this journey excite her, though the best so far has been the camp in the Soo where they stayed three days watching the freighters pass, wading, canoeing in the river, exhuming the brothers' forlorn toys from the bunkroom and taking them out on the screened porch in Indian summer sunlight. There Nina would play while Sevigne sat reading or watching the sun trace its lowering arc over the river. The last white lilies were gone. He slept in his father's old bed, she in the bunkroom. Mornings they would drive into town for the Shipboard Special at the Ancient Mariner, Amy squeezing onto the banquette to shoot the breeze with Nina, then touring her through the kitchen while Sevigne sipped black coffee and read the papers.

Now—as on that other day, years back—the sky is clear, stretched taut enough to fracture and glacial blue like the bed of a crevasse, the sea a deeper blue with sunlight quavering over it in myriad scales and the low mournful capes and mountains of the coast like slagfires of sulphur and ruby. He loves his new polarized sunglasses, they show him the insides of the clouds, but his eyes are no longer good at a distance; he blames his long year of work by candlelight and lantern. Nina sees something though. She says she does. She's squinting with her mother's heavy lids set over his own dark eyes, making a brim of her small hand in guileless burlesque of him squatting beside her. He sights down her arm into that blinding, familiar expanse, seeing nothing. He'd be inclined to doubt her, or to think that what she sees is a figment of her wish to collaborate in the making of myths and frontiers, were she not describing "a small shiny white thing, it's different to the light on the water." He tells her he sees it too; then shivers, a crow lighting on his grave.

"Will you take me out there, Papa?"

"I'll take you some day."

They're travelling west across the continent from Toronto to Vancouver, where six nights from now Ike will play the final show of her current tour. Nina isn't missing her yet, but then she's used to her departures (sometimes now to Europe, often to the States) and she's comfortable spending time in other houses, with other adults.

He learned about her on his passage back from the island with Lester Trubb, who'd brought him a number of letters—who on first seeing him on the beach had broken rank with his own watching shadows and embraced him roughly, clearly relieved, though maybe a bit chastened as well; Sevigne's survival, albeit less a finger and a house, had played havoc with his most cherished assumptions. Heart thudding, Sevigne had folded the letters into his shirt pocket and buttoned it closed and helped Trubb haul his effects down out of the tower onto the beach. Trying to tell his winter stories he heard himself stuttering with impatience, confusion, his words like shards of ice in a river at breakup all trying to jam through a choked channel. Finally he fell silent. They pushed off, the motor's metallic gargling a nerve-shattering novelty. Behind them the island shrank away and then mirage-like detached itself from the horizon to hover over the glassy lake, and in that full-fathomed limbo between unrealities he dug out his mail.

Eddy couldn't tell him anything about Ray—no one had heard from or about him since he'd disappeared. *Let's just hope he's down in Mexico or somewhere warm.* Ike had recently had her baby, he wrote, but he said nothing more, leaving Sevigne to make vague, anxious calculations. *And we're all dying to see you, Sev. In fact I almost did see you, back in the winter.* It seemed Eddy now had his own literary talk show on TVO, and the producers, hearing from him about this "unplugged young eccentric" quilling novels in a lighthouse up north, had seriously considered profiling him along with a woman poet holed up in a cabin near Temagami. They meant to call the episode *The Unwired Wave*, but hadn't managed to find the third local case required for a wave, and after inquiries had baulked at the cost of renting a chopper to airlift Eddy and the crew in before the year's shooting wrapped in March. *Sorry, Sev. I know it would have been great—for you and for the novel. You probably could have used the company too.*

Laughing up tears he folded and refolded the letter till it was the size of a business card and tucked it back into his shirt. Then opened the next. Lois Shapiro with her old prickly vigour protested that she was now well, pledged autumn publication of his poetry, and continued interest in his novel. His mother sent love and another cheque and asked if he had received the extra food she had paid the tour guide for. From Istanbul came a formal invitation to Bryon and Tralee's perennial wedding—now set for Cairo in the fall—along with a brief, welcome message from Bryon, who really hoped Sevigne was all right and could make it.

Then the letter saved until last, the one he'd yearned for and prayed against, here in his hand. With Trubb whistling behind him he skimmed his eyes down a page framed by churning water, at several points backing up to reread. He was a father now. Mikaela felt things had turned out for the best and she really preferred he didn't start thinking of responsibilities to her or the child, not now. In some ways she regretted her lie at the time, but she'd felt that he'd forfeited his rights in the matter—she still did—and she'd needed him gone, a clean break. No more long messy ones for her. But now with Nina two months old and looking so much like him, it was only right to tell him about her, let him see her when he returned. If he wanted that. *If I'd been two years younger & you were a few years older, further along with your career, maybe things would have been different. I mean more natural, more relaxed. Everything got so sped up there, I know. And maybe I pushed you harder than I should have, without really knowing it. Maybe I should find it more difficult to remain angry at someone who's always working so hard at being alive (what I still love you for, Sevigne), but I do remain angry. You really have to see Nina though. Call us when you get back.*

So he'd left his place of exile single, a stammering recluse, and set foot back on the mainland a father. Under his breath

he said I knew it, after all, and Trubb, setting a greasy, nico-
tined hand on his shoulder: "How's that? Oh, still talking to
yourself, eh. Going to take a while to break that one." And
then the hamlet of Batchawana Bay closed around them,
beeping and raucous, thronged, it seemed to him, like some
bustling county seat, and that evening the Soo was a major city
convulsed with strange crowds gaping and jostling, crude of
voice and manner, then balmy Toronto for a brief, stupefying
spell seemed every metropolis in the world.

When he overcame the shock of being around people
again, he wanted to be around them all the time. He got over
it. But by spring of the next year his daughter, Nina, both
pearl and burden, was saddled on his shoulders Saturdays
steering him by the ears through Little Portugal, Little Can-
ton, Kensington Market where he had a tiny walk-up; and as
Mikaela's trust and the child's love grew, long weekends when
she had to travel and perform. Nina had a regular "caregiver"
too, now Mikaela could easily afford one. To Sevigne she
looked more beautiful than ever. Her musical and maternal
fortunes had been rejuvenating.

In October of that first year Sevigne flew to Cairo for his
brother's wedding, a small but extravagant affair on Gezirah in
the Nile, culminating in dinner atop the occasionally revolving island tower. On Rye—Gezirah's negative pole, isolated
and freezing—he'd reconceived a hunger for blood connec-
tions. There Nature had broken him, had all but killed him,
forever reducing and complicating his romanticism; his and
Bryon's visions of life had hardly converged, but they got
along now, spinning their differences into dry collaborative
jokes, tolerant in the way of family growing resigned to each
other's contradictions. The writing of his novel seemed to
have exorcised other demons. For him the pretty, flighty
Tralee aroused no illicit fevers, while Everson Milne had all
but lost his aura of garlic and capitalism. Cairo itself in the

unflinching light of North African October seemed purged
of former shadows and in the crypt-cafés of the Cities of the
Dead Sevigne sat at peace, or something like it, drinking
thimble-cups of sweet thick coffee and delighting the locals
with his mangled Arabic.

At dinner he sat beside the regally opinionated Yasmine
Salloum. On the other side of him Martine, holding his four-
fingered hand, overheard them discussing the special need for
form, for barriers, in passionate writing like *carpe diem* poems.
That's what tightened her face into that rueful smile. Because
when you "seized the day", it still turned into evening on you.

Her affair had been all but over since the night at the oasis
but somehow it had kept limping along, on again, off again,
until two weeks ago. Superstitious as ever, she'd been worried
about the effect of her infidelities on her son's new marriage;
meeting Nadir within a day or two of the ceremony seemed a
poor way to confer luck on what already promised to be a troubled union. For some time it had been evident that Nadir was
conducting other affairs, likely with other foreign women, but
in moderation he still excited her, and she had been unwilling
to give him up altogether. Then one day in the academy he had
asked to use the telephone in the office. From where she sat
awaiting him, on an exercise mat beside the wall mirrors, she
could hear his voice through the old vents that ran between the
rooms. Her Arabic was weak, but his hushed, husky intona-
tions made precise translation unnecessary. She looked at her
own face in the mirror. It seemed to shame and embolden her.
He was reconfirming a date for later in the day, she supposed,
or for tonight—something of that nature. When he swept
back into the room as if with the intention of briskly transact-
ing some minor piece of business, she informed him it was
over. By rapid turns he behaved hurt, then affronted, then
openly disdainful, assuring her it had been over in his heart of
hearts for months, he had been wishing to stop it but had been

afraid of disappointing an aging woman. Disappointing, she said and laughed harshly, You've been disappointing for a long time. And she told him to get out.

(And how virtuous she'd felt afterwards, for days, as if having acted expressly to preserve the sanctity of her marriage, for the sake of Everson—who knew nothing, or pretended to. No, past a certain age nothing surprised you, and nothing fooled you either, least of all yourself.)

Martine could read people's characters in the way they danced the way a fortune-teller read futures in a palm; dancing with Sevigne towards the end of the night, she felt in him both his old lightness and a new solidity. He was drinking little. He was more sure of himself, a man and a father, arrived, it seemed, in one of life's extended summers (she'd known several) where with any luck he might sojourn for a year or two, or five. Yet he kept single, a choice she found it difficult to understand. Bryon with his rocky engagement, Sévi with his island retreats and bachelor flats . . . she could only wish both well, with love and a helpless shrug. As your energy waned, your circle of concern contracted; some time ago her heart had thrown up its hands. She passed him on to Tralee and finished the waltz in the arms of her husband, recalling another husband, father to her sons, and missing him for the first time since his death.

Six months later, in April '95, a hundred people crowded into Eddy's Annex apartment, where the ghosts of Lois's favourite artists shared the stereo—Paul Robeson, Caruso, Louis Armstrong, the Gershwins. Like Torrins, like that whole functional productive generation, she'd been a minimizer of complaints, a discounter of dangers. She hadn't admitted she was simply in remission from cancer, had broadcast the doctors' assurance of "a clean slate"—a suspect phrase, since even gestation and birth stamp tokens of struggle into the flesh, so no body after conception is a *tabula rasa*.

Her body wasn't here tonight; she'd been privately buried.

Guests at the wake were discussing the last time they'd seen or spoken to her. It was a mixed crowd, though mainly young. To Sevigne it seemed some invisible MC must be edging up the party volume while dimming the lights. Actually no lights were on, the dimness was of falling dusk, and nobody moved to turn one on and snap the spell. In that warm envelope of twilit chatter, where "Lois" was still the word most spoken, you could almost believe she must be there in the crowd.

Hours passed, lamps came on. Lois's name was no longer the password. Two guests on their way out were exchanging cards, not furtively but with aimful, unabashed bonhomie, while Eddy remained busy at the book table. Through Sevigne's mind rang Dickinson's cadence about Trade encroaching upon Sacrament—but he was no longer a purist, this was a benign opportunism Lois would have endorsed and had probably asked Eddy to arrange, her titles on display at her last party, the work of words going on.

A few copies of Sevigne's first book *Sad Vicinities* were part of the display. After returning from the island and seeing the proofs and finding the poetry far too young, too naive, as if written by somebody else, he'd begged Lois to delay or cancel the thing. She'd chided him to leave it alone. It was a first book, a *youthful* book, she said, and writers really ought to write young when they were young. . . .

Sevigne pushed out onto the balcony, which seemed dangerously overcrowded—the only part of the apartment that still was. The night was windless, mild, laced with tobacco and grass smoke and a laughter that guests were much freer with outside. He recognized the loudest laugh. Under cherry-red patio lanterns he and Una embraced. Crisply she kissed the air an inch from his cheek.

"I'd like to apologize in advance," she said, "for my next book."

"No need for that, Una, I've been browsing in the magazines." He smiled, wryly. "You're looking really well. God, how long has it been?"

"Over two years. What are you *doing* these days, Sevigne Torrins, still hiding out? Nobody ever sees you! Are you working on something? I liked sections of your book . . ."

He told her he'd been writing reviews for Eddy, articles, waiting on tables, sparring a bit at the gym. Helping part-time at a winter shelter downtown—he had to, after his experience up north. He saw his daughter as often as he could. He was hoping to get up to the camp more often, summers.

"But you're writing?"

"Every day. Same novel. I can't seem to finish it, I'm learning so much now and it all wants in. You've started something new?"

"It's how I deal with things." Her Adam's apple moved slightly. "I've been seeing someone. Tony Hannon? He says he met you once—at that premature celebration Eddy gave you."

"He seemed like a good guy."

"Gooder than some." Her smile was tight.

"I guess most celebrations," he said, "are a bit premature."

After a silence they talked about Lois, the last time they'd seen her, and of that pivotal afternoon when they'd visited her at home. A spent vortex of feelings revived and briefly whirled around him. How was it that both "illusion" and its opposite, "disillusion," could mean negative things? To drop illusions should be a good thing, yet when push came to shove you never gave them up happily—each one had to be frayed through struggle and blunder to a painful thinness, then stripped away with violence, a scale of still-living cells. For a while in his eyes Una had embodied all the promise of the city, of every big city in the world, those towering repositories of

accessible fame and quick fulfilment, enduring beauty, unde-
manding love. . . . He'd set her up, he saw now. In the end,
they'd set each other up. Yet his body had loved her after all.

She left at midnight. Others trickled away after. By two in
the morning only Eddy and Sevigne remained. They put on
coffee and a Tom Waits CD and set about collecting glasses
and bottles, wrapping or eating the unfinished food, washing
dishes. *I made a golden promise . . . that we would never part.*
Everything was done by three-thirty. They were both flagging
but they resolved to stay up; the point of a wake (Sevigne urged
and Eddy agreed) was to accompany the ashes or the body or
the memory of the dead through to dawn. To witness on her
behalf the sun's return. And Sevigne began telling of his father's
wake, of how he and Amy and Dr Pacini and Leo Hogeboom
had stumbled down to the dock at sunrise, breathing gusts of
vapour and shivering with fatigue, spinning stories about the
man, their giddy laughter muted as if the river's huge silence
were a stern reproof. First ship of the morning was a Scottish
freighter upbound for Superior, its grey bow like an axe-blade
cutting through mists over the floating border midstream.

"Of course the body *would* be absent here too," Eddy said,
his tone authoritatively low and measured, weary eyelids pink
but undrooping. These days, master of his own show, he managed himself as if a miked camera were constantly trained on
him: "Postmodern wake. No body. Everyone leaves early. Back
to their busy lives. Have a Scotch."

"Just beer."

"Whatever."

They sprawled on the eroding chesterfield, heels on the
bay window-sill, Eddy pouring steaming coffee from the pot
into his own mug of Scotch as they waited for the sun.

She is driving a rented car west over the low mountains of Vancouver Island towards Tofino and Long Beach. Years ago she and her bandmates drove out this way in a borrowed vw van to body-surf in the freezing waves, play guitars on the beach, pick up sunbleached boys in wetsuits. Now, her tour over, she's alone, hankering for a day and night all to herself before she returns to meet Nina and Sevigne in Vancouver.

They'll be on the road today too, driving west out of the Cypress Hills where they camped last night. They'd called her from a diner payphone. She was at a fussy nouvelle cuisine place in Gastown having dinner with the show organizers when her cellphone burbled. Nina, stuttering with excitement, reported having flapjacks and maple syrup for supper and said she couldn't wait to sleep in her green mummy bag in the orange tent. Hearing her so full of the trip and not obsessed with arriving—with seeing her mother again— brought relief, and absolution, and a short, hard pang of jealous hurt. Sevigne was warm, but quiet and reserved, as he always is now. He must know that she knows what he wants— how he's pledged himself to win her back, like some courtly lover out of a Leonard Cohen song. So in some ways he hasn't changed. He won't stop trying. She's no longer sure she wants him to. And now it's like some movie caper, a transcontinental car chase with Sevigne and the child pursuing her, narrowing the gap, she with only an hour or two of mountain highway left before the coast.

She'll have to tell him about the latest sighting. As the vanished Ray turns into a kind of legend, like an ODed rock artist, visions of him grow ever more common. Sevigne says people are finally reading him, every month another ex-best friend publishes a tribute or re-evaluation, reports keeps coming in of him zooming past here and there on highways from Alaska to Mexico. You never meet the actual witness. She always has hated the way fans and people in her business love rubbing up against self-destruction (as long as it asks for no concrete help, as long as it can be bought and sold, sold, sold), but now she wonders if she might have seen him too, a few miles this side of Duncan, blurring past in the opposite direction while she was only half aware.

At the time, she was singing into the small silver mike of a portable tape recorder. Phrases towards a new song. Now with the tour over, her need to write songs is edging back, like sexual desire in the months after childbirth. Tonight she'll take her twelve-string and pad of paper down to the beach with a bottle of white wine. Sevigne gave her an idea, when they called. In the cabin, in an old paperback, he'd been reading about a man named Sonny Liston, heavyweight champion of the world around the time Sevigne's father was trying to make the Olympic team. Sevigne described him, Liston, as a tragic figure, hated by white society and disowned by his own people, called a thug and a gorilla—a man who as ex-champion had died broke, drunk, and discarded—but like many boxers he'd possessed an untutored eloquence and had come up with these lines Sevigne loved.

"Go ahead," she'd said into the cellphone, giving the eavesdropping flirts at her table a sweeping scowl. "We're all listening."

Like a man risking a proposition, at first shyly, then sensing its absolute rightness and taking heart, he began, "Someday. . ." and paused. Cleared his throat and took it from the top: "Someday they're going to write a blues song just for fighters. It'll be for slow guitar, soft trumpet, and a bell."

In her mind already she could hear how it would start.

Acknowledgments

For help of one kind or another I owe thanks to many, and especially, as always, to Mary Huggard. My Canadian publisher Louise Dennys and my British publisher Frances Coady have been greatly helpful, both as publishers and as editors, and I thank them again here. People whose advice and encouragement have been especially important over the last four years are John Metcalf (again), Mark Sinnett, Julian Scala, Michael Holmes, David Staines, and Mary Cameron. Doris Cowan's final edit was thoughtful and meticulous. Susan Huggard's help was again invaluable.

Others to whom I'm grateful—whether for advice on certain technical matters or for various sorts of inspiration—include Judith Adamson, Ken Babstock, Sarah and Jeremy, Brian Brett, Stephen Cain, Eliza Clark, Judith Cowan, Lynn Crosbie, Joe Curzon, Tamas Dobozy, Pamela Donoghue, Peter Fallon, Eric Folsom, Wayne Grady, Neil Graham, Michael Harris, John, Lambie and Pelly Heighton, Maggie Helwig, Stephen Henighan, Paul Hodgson, Helen Humphreys, Bill James, Amanda Jernigan, Tara Kainer, Janice Kirk, Christine Klein–Lataud, Ken Kucharic, Wendy Lesser, Edward Lobb, Ellen McKeough, Andrew McLachlan, Colin and Ken McPhail, Peter McPhee, Chris Miner, Kent Nussey, Peter Oliva, David O'Meara, Jason Ouimet, Toni Pickard, Al and Eurithe Purdy, Nancy Roberts–Moneir, Ray Robertson, Alec "Nemo" Ross, Jay Ruzesky, Stephanie Saunders, Martha

Sharpe, Merilyn Simonds, Russell Smith, Kate Sterns, Mary Tilberg, Chris White, Stephen Williams, and Michael "The Ice Man" Winter.

In Portsmouth Village, Annette Willis, Sabina Singh, and Mr. Kelly Snow were a community of (welcome) distraction.

Many at Knopf Canada have been helpful and patient, especially Noelle Zitzer, Nikki Barrett, Michael Mouland, Sharon Klein, David Schimpky, Deirdre Molina, and Susan Roxborough.

Finally I want to acknowledge with gratitude the support of the Wurlitzer Foundation—which gave me two months of solitude to work on the book—and the Canada Council and the Ontario Arts Council, from both of which I received a grant during the course of the writing and rewriting.

Permissions